THE
GOLDEN
CALF

Also by Helene Tursten

Detective Inspector Huss
Night Rounds
The Torso
The Glass Devil
The Fire Dance

THE
GOLDEN
CALF

HELENE

TURSTEN

Translation by Laura A. Wideburg

Originally published in Sweden, as *Guldkalven*, in 2003

Copyright © 2003 by Helene Tursten

Published in agreement with H. Samuelsson-Tursten AB, Sunne, and
Leonhardt & Høier Literary Agency, Copenhagen

English translation copyright © 2013 by Laura A. Wideburg

First English translation published in 2013 by
Soho Press
853 Broadway
New York, NY 10003

Library of Congress Cataloging-in-Publication Data
Tursten, Helene.
[*Guldkalven*. English]
The Golden Calf / by Helene Tursten; Translated by Laura A. Wideburg.
p cm
Translated for the original Swedish to English.
HC ISBN 978-1-61695-008-8
PB ISBN 978-1-61695-298-3
eISBN 978-1-61695-009-5
I. Wideburg, Laura A., translator. II. Title.
PT9876.3.U55G8513 2013
839.73'8—dc23
2012041039

Printed in the United States of America

10 9 8 7 6 5 4 3 2 1

To my sister Pia

THE
GOLDEN
CALF

Prologue

FUZZY IMAGES FROM the bank's security cameras flickered across the TV screen. Three masked men were aiming weapons at customers and employees inside the building. The robbers wore dark overalls, black ski masks, and black gloves. Only their eyes were visible. Behind the counter, one of the men threw a large nylon bag at a cashier. A customer lay prone on the floor in the middle of the room while the second robber aimed a rifle directly at his head. The third armed man was posted near the entrance, his back to the camera. He kept glancing nervously in all directions. Then, in the upper corner of the picture, the glass door opened, emitting two spindly legs in calf-high leather boots. The robber at the entrance stepped forward and pulled an elderly woman into the frame. He spun her around by her arm, and she lost her balance and fell.

The movements of all three robbers were jerky, since the camera recorded footage in short sections in order to save film. Nevertheless, it was obvious that the robbers were becoming increasingly nervous. The man behind the counter was making threatening gestures at the cashier, who filled the bag with bills as fast as she could with shaking hands. The masked man seemed to become irritated as something shifted near him, and he hit the cashier across the mouth with the rifle barrel. She fell to the floor, out of sight.

• • •

". . . THESE BRUTAL PICTURES from inside the bank building." The female newscaster's well-modulated voice issued from the speakers of the wide-screen television. "A fourth man was waiting outside in a getaway car, a red Saab 9000, according to one witness. A similar car was reported stolen in Arvika a few hours earlier, which the police suspect was the same vehicle. A nationwide alert has been issued. The elderly woman seen in the video suffered a broken hip, and the cashier lost several teeth; both women have been admitted to the hospital. The hostage and remaining bank staff have received help from a crisis team. It is believed that the robbers got away with more than a million kroner. This is the fourth-largest bank robbery in northern Värmland this year, and so far there have been no arrests. The low police presence in the area may be why the criminals targeted this bank. Often, the only police car in the area may be more than twenty miles away, which delays response time."

"SUCH ANIMALS," THE man sitting on the sofa growled as he clicked off the television. There was a moment of silence after the picture faded.

"How horrible!" The man's young female companion laughed nervously. "Can you believe he was pointing that rifle right at her head? She must have been terrified!" She paused as the man filled her wine glass, then she continued, "But honestly, Philip, one million kroner. That's not bad at all. It's probably the easiest way to get hold of a lot of money fast." She giggled as she sipped.

"Too dangerous. You could be shot and killed."

The man lifted his glass to his nose and inhaled slowly, enjoying the aroma.

"Mmm. Sun-ripened blackberries with a hint of vanilla. Hope they catch those guys and throw them in the slammer. And let them rot there, I say," said the man who had embezzled a hundred million dollars.

Chapter 1

DETECTIVE INSPECTORS IRENE Huss and Tommy Persson parked on the street between a blue-and-white patrol car and the anonymous car of the forensic technicians. The garage entrance had been blocked off by a sloppily parked silver Mercedes Cabriolet, its top raised.

The detectives hunched their shoulders against the harsh sea wind as they walked toward the front door. The house was brand new, but the surrounding grounds were nothing but clay and mud. One step off the stone pathway and a shoe would be sucked off by the muck. Despite the lack of landscaping, Irene saw that the location of the house was fantastic, high on a hill with a magnificent, wide-open view of Askim Bay. How could anyone afford property like this? The villa itself was all terracotta brick and huge panes of glass. Obviously the architect had spared no expense.

Tommy stopped to take a good look at the Cabriolet. He gave a silent whistle and sent Irene a meaningful glance. They continued to the front door and rang the bell. A female officer opened the door immediately. She looked young and serious.

"Hi. I'm Tommy Persson, and this is Irene Huss from Violent Crime."

"I'm Stina Lindberg," the uniformed woman replied. "The technicians have just arrived."

A baby was crying inside the house. Stina glanced nervously in that direction. "It's the baby," she explained. "Their baby. . . . His wife found him . . . her husband . . . when she got home." Stina's cheeks were pale, and she was obviously struggling to control her discomfort. A murder would rattle anyone, but everything was much worse when children were part of the picture.

A tall policeman in complete protective gear appeared in the spacious hallway. Both Irene and Tommy knew Criminal Inspector Magnus Larsson well and were happy to see him. As Irene and Tommy pulled on their own protective overalls, hats, plastic gloves, and booties, Magnus gave them the rundown.

"A woman called 112 and said she'd found her husband shot. We arrived within fifteen minutes of the alarm. She was calm at first, but she broke down after a few minutes. She had her mother's telephone number programmed into her cell phone, so I've called her. Someone has to take care of the child. Her mother is on the way, but she was in Borås when I reached her."

"Who lives here?" asked Irene.

"Sanna Kaegler-Ceder and Kjell B:son* Ceder."

The names felt vaguely familiar to Irene, but she couldn't place them. She noticed that Tommy also reacted to the names, but before Irene could ask, loud shrieks from an unhappy baby echoed through the house. All three police officers hurried toward the noise.

The living room was large, with a huge glass wall facing the sea. Irene had been right—the view was fantastic. A young woman sat hunched in a round swivel chair covered in leather the color of eggshells. Eight identical chairs ringed an elliptical glass table, which sat on a matching shag carpet, which popped against the dark terra-cotta tile floor. Oversized modern oil paintings stood out against almost-pure-white walls.

---

*The colon here indicates an abbreviation of a longer name. In this case, for example, B:son could stand for something like Bergson or Borjeson.

Irene and Tommy nodded at two uniformed officers standing beside the woman, before taking a closer look at the unmoving figure curled in the chair. Irene realized she had seen the woman's face before. Again, she had no idea where or when.

Sanna Kaegler-Ceder stared into space with empty eyes. Her pale complexion and stiff expression made her face seem mask-like. At her feet was an infant in a blue corduroy baby bouncer. Irene guessed the baby was, at most, six months old. He was screaming, his face bright red from the exertion.

The glass wall continued to another doorway leading to an octagonal room enclosed in glass. In the center was a spiral steel staircase to the second floor. Sanna Kaegler-Ceder's husband lay on his back at the foot of the stairs. The two technicians near him were setting up their camera equipment. They nodded to Irene and Tommy.

"We need fifteen minutes," the older of the two said.

"That's fine," Tommy replied.

Irene walked to Sanna and lightly touched her shoulder. Sanna didn't appear to notice.

"Hello," Irene said softly. "My name is Irene Huss. Do you think your baby might want something to eat?"

The woman's only reaction was a slight flutter of her eyelashes.

Irene sighed and picked up the wailing bundle of a baby. A noticeable odor cried out for a diaper change.

"Come on, Tommy. Help me find the changing table and some baby food," Irene said with determination.

"What? Me?"

"It hasn't been that long since you changed your own baby's diapers."

"You're right. OK, off to find a dry diaper." Tommy made a raspberry sound and tickled the baby's tummy. The baby interrupted his crying to peer up at him.

After a few minutes of opening and shutting doors, they found a large bathroom with rose marble walls. There was an enormous changing table, complete with every possible item for baby care. The baby wore a soft denim romper suit and a light blue sweater with MADE IN NEW YORK written in flashy silver across the chest. As Irene lifted him from the table, his bottom dry, he began to fuss again. His hunger was making itself known.

Tommy had already gone to find the kitchen. When Irene, carrying the baby in her arms, followed, Tommy held up a bottle he'd found in the refrigerator in triumph.

"Hey, buddy! Now you'll get some grub!" Tommy said as he began to heat the bottle in the microwave.

On the counter was a plastic bottle top, which Tommy screwed in place with a practiced motion. He instinctively checked the milk's temperature against the inside of his wrist, then handed the bottle to Irene. Even though it had been years since his youngest child's last bottle, the preparation routine came back quickly.

Irene looked down at the baby, who was greedily sucking down the milk. The ultra-modern kitchen glistened in glass and brushed steel. Irene looked for somewhere to sit down, but there were only tall stools next to a bar counter. Irene leaned against one of the stools as the little boy noisily slurped the last drops. Then she lifted him to her shoulder and patted him on his diapered bottom. A huge burp was her reward.

"Huss, now your jacket will look like a seagull pooped on it." Tommy grinned. He found a roll of paper towels on a steel cylinder and helped Irene rub off the milk stain.

As they walked back to the living room, the baby fell asleep. Irene set him back into the baby bouncer and spread a soft, yellow blanket from a nearby chair over him.

Sanna hadn't moved. She appeared catatonic. She wore light-brown pants and a cobalt-blue top with a deep décolletage.

Between her breasts glittered a large cross with closely set white and blue gemstones. Their crystal clear sparkle could hardly have come from anything other than authentic sapphires and diamonds. *Sanna Kaegler-Ceder walks around with a fortune around her neck*, thought Irene. *And her reserve capital is on her left ring finger.*

One of the force's crime scene technicians, Åhlén, stuck his bald head through the doorway to the octagonal room. He motioned to the officers, and Irene and Tommy walked over. As was his habit, Åhlén pushed his thick bottle-bottom glasses up his stubby nose with his left forefinger before he spoke.

"I've already secured the wife's prints and taken her jacket. No apparent spatter, but we'll have to wait for analysis. This is the scene of the crime. We haven't found the murder weapon yet."

"Are you absolutely sure this is the crime scene?" asked Irene.

"No doubt about it. See for yourself," replied Åhlén, gesturing toward where the body lay stretched out.

Kjell B:son Ceder was well-dressed in a dark suit. Two bullet holes marked his forehead, and his head lay in a pool of blood. A broken glass lay on the floor nearby, and the unmistakable scent of whiskey hovered.

"He's been dead for hours. Rigor mortis has set in completely," the technician continued.

"Looks like an execution. Two shots right into the brain," Tommy stated.

Irene was surprised at how much older than his wife Kjell B:son Ceder was. Even in death he was a good-looking man. His hair, though thickly matted with blood, was steel gray and full. All of a sudden, Irene realized where she'd seen him before: for the past few years, he had been the restaurant king of Göteborg. Irene's husband was a head chef at a competing restaurant, so she'd often heard Ceder's name. Krister worked at Glady's Corner, one of the finest restaurants in Göteborg, with a star in the international restaurant guide. The other two starred restaurants in Göteborg were owned by Kjell B:son Ceder. One was located in the twenty-eight story Hotel Göteborg, one of Göteborg's tallest buildings, which Ceder also owned. Whenever Irene was in her boss's office, she would see the mighty silhouette of the hotel rising above the rest of the city from Superintendent Sven Andersson's window. Slightly to the southwest, she could see the two Gothia Towers next to Svenska Mässan, the Swedish Conference Center. Gothia Towers also had a hotel and restaurant and was the main competitor of Hotel Göteborg.

"Stridner has promised to show up in all her imperial majesty," Åhlén said. "If I'm not mistaken, here she is now."

Irene and Tommy had also heard the energetic clack of high heels hitting the stone floor. No other person burst into a crime scene with quite the same tempo as Professor of Forensic Medicine Yvonne Stridner.

She swept through the entrance of the octagonal room, placed her bag on the floor, and took in the crime scene in one glance. Without greeting any of the officers, she got right to the point:

"Is this actually a murder?"

Irene, Tommy, and Åhlén all started in surprise. The professor rarely asked questions. Usually, she imparted certainties and issued commands.

"He's been shot. Two shots," said Åhlén dryly.

Without further commentary, the professor put on her protective gown, gloves, and plastic booties. Just like her not to bother with protective clothing before entering a crime scene, thought Irene.

Stridner tossed her cape over a chair with a black oxidized steel frame and white leather cushions. Perhaps it was more comfortable than it appeared. There were five more chairs like it in the room as well as a matching table and chandelier.

Stridner walked over to the body and began her

investigation. Tommy nudged Irene with his elbow. "Let's go and try to talk to Sanna Kaegler-Ceder again."

Irene nodded. They could do nothing here until the body was removed, not even go up the spiral staircase to check the second floor.

Sanna Kaegler-Ceder was in the same chair, but she'd swiveled it toward the rain-streaked glass and was staring into the rapidly gathering twilight. The baby was fast asleep in his baby bouncer, blissfully unaware that he'd just become fatherless.

"Please forgive us for disturbing you at this sad time. My name is Tommy Persson, and I'm a detective. Are you able to answer a few questions?"

The woman did not move, just kept staring out at the autumn weather. When they were about to give up hope of response, she ducked her head slightly. Tommy interpreted this as a slight nod and asked a question quickly before she changed her mind.

"What time did you arrive home and find your husband's body?"

The woman swallowed a few times, then managed an answer. "I called . . . right away."

"The alarm came at four twenty-three P.M.," Magnus Larsson interjected.

"And the first patrol car arrived no more than fifteen minutes later?" asked Tommy.

"Correct," said the other detective.

Tommy turned back to Sanna and continued in a gentle voice, "Did you go to your husband before the police arrived?"

She shook her head slowly. "I saw that he was dead. All the blood. . . ."

"Where were you standing when you saw him?"

"At the entrance. . . ." Her voice failed her, and she swallowed hard.

"So you were standing at the entrance to this room?"

"Yes," she whispered.

It didn't seem possible, but the woman became even paler. Her lips turned blue-gray, and Irene saw that she was about to faint.

"Come, let's have you lie down on the rug," Irene said as she helped Sanna to the floor. She lifted Sanna's lower legs a few centimeters, and the color slowly began to return to the woman's face. After a few minutes, Sanna said, "I'd like to sit up again." Irene helped her back into the chair. The young woman was still so pale that her face appeared to blend into the white leather. There was no question that she'd received a shock, though there was always the possibility she was reacting to committing a murder.

"When did you leave the house today?" asked Tommy.

"I didn't leave it today. The last time was yesterday afternoon."

"At what time?"

"Around four. We went to my sister's place to spend the night."

"Did you take your son with you?"

"Yes."

"So you spent the night with your sister?"

"Her husband was on call. We were both going to be alone that night anyway."

"Do you know who your husband planned to meet yesterday evening?"

"No idea." Her voice seemed tired and uninterested.

"When was the last time you spoke to your husband?"

"Yesterday at nine in the morning."

"Did he say that he had to meet someone that evening?"

"Not that I remember."

"Had you already made arrangements to spend the night at your sister's, or did you just decide to yesterday?"

"I called her yesterday around lunch. We'd been talking

about doing this—having a nice evening with some good food and wine. She's also on maternity leave."

"Did you call up your husband and let him know that you were going to your sister's?"

"No."

"Why didn't you?"

"I'd told him that I might go when I talked to him on the phone that morning."

"So you didn't try to call him today?"

"No. He knew that Ludwig and I were at Tove's and not at home."

"Tove is your sister's name?"

"Yes. Tove Fenton. Her husband is a doctor. He was on call. . . ." Her voice sank to a whisper, and she didn't finish her sentence. Before any of the other police officers could ask another question, a young policewoman came in. Up until then, she hadn't moved from her post at the door. Irene remembered her first name was Stina, but she'd already forgotten her last name.

"The mother is here. That is, her mother." Stina motioned toward Sanna. They could hear an agitated female voice at the outer door.

"I have to know what's going on . . . my daughter! And Ludwig. . . ."

There was jostling at the doorway to the living room. Sanna's mother was trying to push inside, but two officers were holding her back. She was not as tall as her daughter, but she had the same pale coloring. Sanna shakily got up and walked toward her mother on unsteady feet.

"My dearest Sanna! What has been going on? The police called. . . ." Sanna's mother stopped talking the moment she saw the expression on her daughter's face. She stopped trying to force her way past the police. "Is it . . . Ludwig?" she asked in despair.

"Why are you wearing that ugly jacket?" asked Sanna—then she fainted.

Chapter 2

"HE WAS SHOT at point-blank range," Professor Stridner said. "The shots entered through the forehead, and I can't see any exit wounds, so presumably the bullets are still inside the skull. This suggests a small-caliber weapon."

"When did he die?" asked Tommy.

"Rigor mortis has started to subside. He has been lying on a warm floor equipped with heating coils . . . let's say eighteen to twenty-four hours. I can't be more precise than that." Stridner was a consummate professional, and she continued in her matter-of-fact manner. "I knew Kjell when we were children. He was one year younger than I was, but we lived nearby growing up. We played together a lot."

Irene was surprised by Stridner's revelation. The victim was a childhood friend of the professor's! They'd played together? Had Stridner ever played like other children? Not just dissected dead frogs and small birds?

They stood now in the middle of the living room floor. Kjell B:son Ceder's body had been removed to the pathology department's morgue. Sanna, Ludwig, and Ludwig's grandmother had gone to the Ceder family's apartment in Vasastan. Apparently, they had kept the apartment even though they'd lived in this house for a while.

"Do you still see each other socially?" Tommy asked when he had recovered from his surprise.

"Now and then. My husband and I were invited to the hotel

opening. Very elegant, I have to say. We also attended his wedding when he married Sanna. My husband and Kjell also know . . . knew . . . each other via Rotary. Small world."

"Do you know if Ceder had been married before?" asked Irene.

"He had."

"Did he have any children in that marriage?"

Stridner shook her head, and her red curls bobbed. "No. She died tragically in a sailing accident. They'd been married only two or three years."

"Was that a long time ago?"

The Professor looked at Irene with irritation. "At least fifteen years ago. And why would this be important?"

"This means that Sanna and her son will inherit everything."

Stridner gave Irene a long, thoughtful look. "Kjell is . . . was . . . always a lady's man. He had many love affairs over the years. We never thought he'd ever marry again. He surprised everyone who knew him when he suddenly married Sanna Kaegler. His first wife was extremely wealthy, and he'd been living the playboy life for years. He didn't just have the money she left him. He was quite successful in the hospitality business."

"When did he and Sanna marry?"

"One year ago exactly. The end of September. There was a big party at the restaurant Le Ciel at Hotel Göteborg."

"One year ago. Ludwig is six months old. Sanna must have been pregnant when they got married."

"Yes, although it didn't show. She was stunningly beautiful. But Kjell's friends were more than wary about the whole thing. There were rumors about her questionable business affairs."

"According to the media, she used to have enormous amounts of money," said Tommy. "Do you know if she still has any left?"

"I have no idea. If she'd gone through it all, I imagine that would be a good reason to marry Kjell," Stridner said. She glanced at her wristwatch. "I'll try to take a look at him this evening, and tomorrow I'll perform the autopsy. You'll hear from me." She tossed her last sentence over her shoulder on her way out. The sound of her voice died away in the hall, accompanied by the staccato of her heels.

Irene and Tommy climbed up the spiral staircase to the second floor above the octagonal room. Even up here, glass panels enclosed the entire space, which rose above the roof of the rest of the house. The architect had succeeded in evoking the airy feeling of being in a lighthouse.

"What a view! Imagine sitting here in the evening and watching the sun set into the sea," Irene said as she looked out into the darkening evening.

"I'm glad I don't have that view."

"Why not?"

"Too expensive. And look at all the booze you'd need." Tommy grimaced.

He was probably right. The first thing they'd seen when they reached the top of the stairs was a well-stocked bar cart. A generously sized wicker sofa with puffy red cushions dominated the room. Two wicker chairs, in the shape of half-shells, hung from the ceiling. Irene was reminded of birds' nests as she watched them sway in the breeze from the open door. Tommy went outside to take in the view from the small balcony that ran around the outer walls. He returned and closed the door behind him. The breeze died quickly.

"So, do you think Sanna did it?" Irene asked him.

"Statistically speaking, yep."

"Åhlén didn't see any spots on her jacket sleeves."

"No, but maybe there were spots yesterday afternoon, if that's when she shot him. If she shot him."

Irene thought this over. "So, you think she shot Ceder, went over to her sister's, spent the night there, and then returned the next day to 'discover' him."

"Something like that."

"We'll have to talk to the sister and find out which clothes Sanna wore yesterday when she came over. And we have to check if anyone was in contact with Kjell after four o'clock yesterday afternoon."

Tommy nodded. "Might as well get started," he said.

"I'll call Sven. He can ask Birgitta or someone else to get in touch with Ceder's office and question his employees. You and I can certainly find that sister of hers. I'm sure there aren't too many doctors by the name of Fenton."

SANNA KAEGLER-CEDER'S SISTER lived only a few kilometers south, just across the city limits into Hovås proper. Irene and Tommy turned into the small cul-de-sac ringed by single-family houses with big yards. The houses were a bit older, built in the fifties or sixties. The Fenton's house was at the bottom of the street, and Irene guessed that it, too, had a view of the sea. Not that they saw anything of the water in the darkness and rain, but they could hear how the wind drove the waves and flung them crashing onto the shore. A clear scent of salt and seaweed hit Irene's nostrils, and she took a few deep breaths. Her own townhouse was just two kilometers from the ocean, but the distinct aroma of sea air never made it all the way past the other neighborhoods between her place and the water.

The house was large and built in a bungalow style using dark-brown wood and white Mexican tiles. As Irene pressed the doorbell, she could hear children screaming happily inside the house. After Irene rang the doorbell a second time, a woman opened the door. For a confused moment, Irene thought she was looking at Sanna, but this woman had more crow's feet around her eyes, revealing her as the older sister.

"Hello. I'm Detective Irene Huss. May my colleague, Tommy Persson, and I come inside for a moment?" Irene held out her hand to greet the woman.

"Just tell me what happened! My mother called. . . . " Tove Fenton's voice was shaking, and it was obvious she'd been crying, but she didn't step aside to let them in.

"We're here to tell you, but we'd prefer to come inside first," Irene said calmly.

The woman reluctantly stepped out of the doorway. They could see a little girl with golden curls, about three-or-four years-old, scampering naked through the hallway. She squealed happily, pulling a heart-shaped Winnie the Pooh balloon by a string. When the girl saw Tommy and Irene, she stopped and stared.

"Hello," Tommy and Irene said in unison. They smiled and waved.

"Felicia! You're supposed to be taking a bath! Get right back in the tub this minute!" Tove shrieked at the little girl, who looked at her mother in fright. "Are you listening?"

The mother stopped her frantic yelling abruptly when she saw a pool of urine forming at the girl's feet. Tile floors are certainly practical, Irene thought. No one spoke and everyone heard the trickling sound get interrupted by the click of a key going into the front door lock. The door opened to reveal a man Irene assumed to be Dr. Fenton coming home.

He was a large man of about fifty, balding and somewhat portly. As soon as he saw the police officers, he held out his hand to greet them, something his wife had not yet done. His smile was wide and friendly, and his tan face looked pleasant and good-natured.

"Morgan Fenton," he said with a British accent.

Irene and Tommy introduced themselves. From the corner of her eye, Irene could see Mrs. Fenton carrying away the crying child.

"My wife called me at the office, and I came as soon as I could. What happened to Kjell?"

The doctor had trouble pronouncing the name Kjell, but otherwise his Swedish was very good.

"I'd like to speak with you together once your wife is able to join us," Irene said.

"Sure, sure. Go ahead and hang up your coats," he said as he pointed to the hangers in the hallway.

He escorted them into a large living room. Here, too, an enormous glass window highlighted the magnificent ocean view, and Irene could just make out a generous terrace outside in the darkness. The room had Chesterfield sofas and a table and cupboards in dark, polished wood, and its focal point was a large, open fireplace. Combined with the paintings and textiles, the furnishings gave a distinctive English feel. The contrast between the two sisters' living rooms was striking. Dr. Fenton must have actively taken part in the interior decoration. It was classically English and a bit old-fashioned.

Irene and Tommy sat down in leather armchairs as Tove came into the living room, a red flush spreading from her neckup to her cheeks.

"Tell me right now what's going on!" she demanded.

"We must ask you a few questions before we can go into detail," Irene said mildly.

Tove Fenton struggled with her impatience as she looked at Irene expectantly.

"Could you tell me what time your sister arrived here yesterday?" Irene began.

"Right after four in the afternoon," Tove replied promptly.

"What was she wearing?"

"Wearing? Her brown mocha outfit."

"What does it look like?"

"Pants and a short jacket in light-brown mocha. Why do you need to know?"

"Routine. How did she seem?"

"What do you mean?" Tove was tense, and her face revealed her irritation. In the background, children were screaming with increasing volume, which seemed to unsettle her even more.

Dr. Fenton stood up. "My dear, let me take care of them."

Tove sat down in the space her husband had vacated. She crossed her arms tightly across her chest as if she were trying to hold on to the last bit of warmth her body had.

"Was she upset? Worried? What was her mood?"

"No, she was just like normal."

"Did she surprise you, or were you already planning for her and the baby to come over?"

"We'd talked about having a nice evening together on one of Morgan's on-call nights. Yesterday, Sanna called me up, and we decided it was a good night."

"According to your sister, you enjoyed some good food and wine."

"That's right."

"So it was just the two of you?"

"And the children, of course."

"The children are still quite young."

"Well, Ludwig, Felicia, and Robin are still small, but Stoffe . . . Christopher . . . was also here."

"Who is Christopher?"

"Morgan's son. He's fifteen."

"Does he also live in this house?"

"Every other week. This week he's here."

Irene made a mental note that she'd also have to question Christopher to check on timing. "Is he home right now?"

"No, but he'll be here any time. He has hockey practice."

"Did Sanna call her husband on the phone at any time while she was here?"

Tove appeared to think this through carefully, but finally she just shook her head.

Dr. Fenton returned to the living room with a wide-awake baby in his arms. The baby was a few months older than Ludwig, and Irene realized this must be Robin. He looked tired as he leaned his fuzzy head against his father's chest and sucked hard at his bottle. The smacking sound rang through the room.

Irene explained what had happened to Kjell. Tove threw her hands up over her face and began to wail. Her husband turned white.

"Good Lord! Murdered!" he exclaimed.

Tommy asked, "Have either of you heard anything about Ceder being threatened?"

"No, never, although there are some tough characters in the restaurant business," Dr. Fenton replied.

Tove let her hands fall away from her face. She glared accusingly at Tommy.

"That's why you were asking about Sanna! You believe she did it!" Her voice rose hysterically. "She most definitely did not! She couldn't have—she was with me!"

Her husband laid a protective arm around her shoulders while simultaneously trying to calm his tiny son, who had responded to his mother's cries with his own.

From the corner of her eye, Irene caught the flash of a disappearing face near the entrance to the living room. She rose quickly and followed the shadow. On the other side of the kitchen, a door was being carefully and quietly shut. She strode to the door and knocked. Then, without waiting for an answer, she walked in.

Christopher Fenton was almost as tall as she was and bulky despite his age. He was going to be a good-looking man once his acne cleared up. Irene hoped he'd change his style in clothing from baggy pants and Fubu T-shirts to something more fitting by then.

"Hello. My name is Irene Huss, and I'm a police detective. My colleague and I are investigating a serious crime."

The boy didn't move, just glared at her. Since Irene was used to teenagers, both her own and others', she wasn't thrown off. "We've just begun our investigation, and we need to find a few witnesses to fine-tune the timeline. We have to check some alibis and that kind of thing. Totally routine. You'd be a real help to us if you let us ask you a few questions."

Irene saw his attitude soften out of pure curiosity. She was always amazed that a few words of police jargon had the power to provoke curiosity in all kinds of people, no matter their age.

Irene took a quick look around the messy room. The bed hadn't been made, and on the overloaded desk, there was a computer surrounded by a scattered heap of empty potato chip bags. It was hard to walk without stepping on clothing, comic books, CDs, or just plain garbage. There were a number of posters on the walls: hockey stars and hip-hop groups as well as a few of Britney Spears in various stages of undress. The room smelled of a teenager at the peak of puberty.

Mostly for effect, Irene took out her little notebook and a pencil with a broken point. That didn't matter, since she didn't expect to write anything down. In her most official tone, she asked, "When did you arrive home last night?"

The teenager shrugged. "Don't know."

"Your best guess?"

"Maybe, like, four thirty?"

"Was Sanna Kaegler-Ceder here when you arrived?"

"Yeah. Her car is sick!" For a second, he forgot to be cool.

"It's an unusual automobile." Irene was non-committal.

"You can't buy CLK-class in Sweden! You got to, like, import it from the US," Christopher said.

"Really? She must be really rich."

"Her old man has got it made."

Irene pretended to write that down in her notebook. Then she asked, "So, were you home the rest of the evening? In this house?"

"Yeah."

"Were you with Tove and Sanna?"

Irene realized that she'd implied something she hadn't meant to. The boy stared at her. "What the fuck! I'm not with either of them!"

"No, of course not. I just wanted to know if you knew where they were the rest of the day. Did they leave the house that afternoon or evening?"

"No, don't think they did. I heard them, like, laughing and shit."

"You weren't with them when they had dinner in the kitchen?"

"No, I ate in here. I was on the computer."

Irene looked toward the desk and noticed it was by the room's only window. "Would you have noticed if the Mercedes drove away during the evening?"

"Yeah, of course. It was right there, like, where your car is." He nodded toward the window. She could see their police car beneath the circle of light from a streetlamp.

"So what happened? Why is Tove crying?" Christopher asked abruptly.

"Sanna's husband Kjell is dead. He was shot—murdered."

Christopher stared at her for a long time. The gangly teenager showed no fear or sorrow, but rather curious interest, as if the murdered man had been a character from a television show and not a person he knew.

"What did you think about Kjell B:son Ceder?"

Christopher shrugged again. "Hardly knew him. I saw him, like, two or three times."

Perhaps this explained why the boy didn't seem perturbed by the news.

"Can you remember what Sanna was wearing last night?"

He thought for a moment. "Some kind of brown pants and a blue T-shirt."

"No jacket?"

"Nah."

"Was it the blue blouse cut low in front?"

"Yeah." The boy blushed. Irene realized that Sanna certainly could not have left the house without Christopher knowing about it. Irene couldn't think of any more questions, so she thanked Christopher for his helpfulness.

Back in the living room, Tommy stood by the doors to the deck talking to Dr. Fenton. Tove was on the sofa with her baby on her lap. Both of them had calmed down, and the baby was nearly asleep. Tove looked up at Irene.

"So I see you talked to Christopher," she stated flatly.

"That's right. He confirmed that Sanna was here from four thirty in the afternoon and on through the rest of the evening."

"That's exactly right," Tove said, content. She stood up and perched her baby on her hip. "I'm just going to give Robin another bottle and put him down for the night. Then I'm going to my mother's to be with her and Sanna."

IN THE CAR, Tommy rehashed his conversation with Morgan Fenton.

"Fenton told me that he'd known Ceder for quite a few years. He also told me that Sanna knew Ceder for a long time before they became a couple and decided to get married. They met while Sanna worked in the finance industry. If I understood him correctly, Fenton has a brother who worked for a London bank that had invested in Sanna's high-tech business. Ceder also knew this brother, and the two were partners when Hotel Göteborg was built. It was all a little muddled, but I think I got the gist of it."

"Hmm. So there were a number of connections before Sanna and Ceder had their unexpected wedding—a bank in London where Fenton's brother is employed, and the friendship between Morgan Fenton and Sanna's soon-to-be husband, Kjell."

"So it appears."

"I bet Fenton put his sister-in-law in contact with his brother at the London bank." Irene was thinking out loud.

"That's pretty obvious. But Fenton said he was surprised that Ceder had been shot at his home in Askim and not his apartment in the city. It sounds like Ceder was seldom at the house."

"Why not?"

"According to Fenton, Ceder didn't much care for the house. It was mostly Sanna's creation. She wanted a more child-friendly place to raise her son."

"So Ceder had the house built for Sanna and her baby?"

"That's what I got from Morgan."

"Strange. That place is practically a mansion. It must have cost—" Irene stopped in the middle of a sentence as a thought hit her. "Do you think that they might have been thinking of a divorce?"

"It's possible."

"Sanna would have been better off as the widow of a rich man than as a divorced single mother."

"Again, it's possible."

"You said yourself that statistically she's the most likely suspect. In that case, she must have shot him before she headed over to her sister's place. Christopher had a good view of the car because it was parked right outside his window. And he said he heard the sisters laughing and chatting all evening."

"So where's the weapon?"

"No idea. We'll have to search along the road between the two sisters."

"We still don't know the exact time he was killed."

"No, we don't, but I put my money on four o'clock yesterday afternoon."

Chapter 3

"STRIDNER CALLED YESTERDAY before I left. She told me that Ceder was shot sometime between five and nine at night. She is going to follow up with a more exact time of death once she's done with the autopsy. Beyond that, we have to wait for test results—and we sure as hell know how long that takes."

Superintendent Sven Andersson stared over the top of his reading glasses. Four of his detectives were present for this "morning prayer," as they liked to call their daily meeting. The others had been called to a double homicide in Långedrag. So far there were no details on that case. All they knew was that two men had been found shot to death in a single-family house.

Irene, Tommy, and Birgitta Moberg-Rauhala were sitting around the table. Kajsa Birgersdotter was filling in for Birgitta's husband Hannu, who was away on paternity leave. Kajsa worked General Investigations, just as Hannu had many years before. She'd been with Irene's team for almost two months now. In the superintendent's opinion, she wasn't a real asset to the team. He thought two women were already more than enough, though he admitted that these two were pretty decent, for women cops. But Kajsa reminded him of his former Sunday school teacher—flat chested and colorless. Of course, most young women were like that nowadays. No curves and nothing for a real man to hold onto.

Tommy and Irene exchanged looks. Hearing that the death had occurred at a later time undercut their theory. It would be hard to break Sanna's alibi. Nor did things improve when Birgitta spoke.

"I called Kjell B:son Ceder's secretary yesterday. Ceder left his office at six thirty. The attendant in the parking garage confirmed the time. I've also had a chat with their head of security, Michael Fuller. The garage has a video surveillance, and at 6:29 exactly, the security camera recorded Ceder getting into his Jaguar and driving away."

"Did he tell his secretary where he planned to go?" asked Tommy.

"I asked her, but she didn't know. He didn't mention anything to her."

"Sanna said that Ceder hadn't told her anything, either. We'll have to press her again to see if she remembers anything more today," Irene said.

"OK, you and Tommy can revisit the recently widowed, while Birgitta and Kajsa go chat with the restaurant and hotel employees," said Andersson. "Touch base with their head of security again and see if we can't get a copy of the video. I've already assigned two of our men to knock on doors in Askim. Perhaps they can give us a time frame for when Ceder arrived at the house."

"That's possible," Irene said. "It seems he drove the Jaguar into the garage. I didn't see it, but Åhlén mentioned it when I ran into him in the hallway this morning. He'd taken a peek into the garage before he left the house yesterday."

"Åhlén likes cars," Tommy said. "Did you guys know that he has an antique MG?"

"An MG? How does he fit a wife and seven kids into an MG?" asked Birgitta. She rolled her beautiful brown eyes— eyes that had managed to melt her husband, Hannu, the man of ice from the northern wilds of Finland.

"I believe he can't, and that seems to be the whole point." Tommy grinned.

"They must have another larger car," Birgitta decided. She had become so much more practical since she'd become a mother. Over the past two months, Irene had not heard one word from her about scuba diving, skiing, or wild parties. Their conversations now revolved around homemade versus commercial baby food, the recently built house in Alingsås, and the shamefully high price of diapers. Come summer, Irene's own daughters would be leaving the nest, each with a high school diploma in hand. Katarina had been talking about going to Australia to work for a year before going to college—with no idea what she wanted to study or do in the future. Jenny was focusing her efforts on her pop band, Polo, which had seen some success in the Göteborg area.

"There's one more thing Åhlén told me," Irene said. "The alarm system at the house wasn't activated. According to him, they hadn't finished installing it yet."

"You can't finish everything at once," said Tommy.

"Jonny and Fredrik will be back after lunch to report on the double homicide in Långedrag. We don't know much right now," said the superintendent.

"Haven't they been identified yet?" asked Birgitta.

"No, not yet."

Irene downed the last of her cold coffee. She needed another. She definitely had not had enough coffee for this kind of morning. She needed all her focus for this case.

"There are too many guns in this city," she muttered as she headed toward the nearest coffee pot.

WHEN IRENE TRIED calling the Vasastan apartment, she could only get Sanna's mother, who apologized and told Irene that their doctor had prescribed Sanna some sleeping pills for the night and she was still asleep. It wouldn't be possible to talk to her until later that afternoon. She and Irene agreed that the detectives would come over at around two o'clock.

"So, what do we do now?" asked Tommy. He was busy cleaning his ears with a cotton swab, an unnerving habit. Irene kept pointing out that it was a dangerous one, telling him her doctor said you shouldn't put anything smaller than your elbow in your ear. Tommy would agree, and then he'd turn the cotton swab around to work on the other ear. We're just like an old married couple, Irene thought, though she never said so out loud. They had been students together at the Police Academy in Stockholm, where they'd been the only ones in their class from Göteborg, and had been good friends ever since.

Tommy got up, the cotton swab still in his ear. "I wonder about the first Mrs. Ceder, the one who died in the sailing accident. Maybe we should look into that."

"What's the connection? By the way, have you figured out what B:son stands for?"

"It's an abbreviation for Bengtsson. I checked it out yesterday. Now, back to the accident. No, I don't really think that they're related, but it's odd they both died unnatural deaths. What are the chances that both partners of a marriage suffer violent deaths? Even fifteen years apart?"

Irene thought about that. "You may be right. According to Stridner, Ceder inherited a lot of money from his wife. It's never without cause that my police instincts go on alert."

"Always follow your instincts."

"Go ahead and investigate yours, too," said Irene. "Meanwhile, I'm going to poke around Askim and see what I can find."

THE KAEGLER-CEDER FAMILY house sat upon a hill at the end of a long driveway. A path of flagstones led to the front door, but beyond that, the rest of the property was a dreary clay field: not a single bush or tree to obscure unwanted and dangerous visitors. An ideal situation for Irene and Tommy; someone must have seen something.

But no one had seen a thing. The house was far from the closest neighbors, who were away on vacation to the Mediterranean. They were retired, according to a second, talkative neighbor, and weren't expected home until the end of the month. The chatty informer had been gone herself the evening in question, attending an investment club meeting—"Mostly just to meet with friends, since the stock market isn't doing much these days"—and didn't arrive home until just before midnight. Her husband had been in Brussels on a business trip since Sunday evening.

The third neighbor was not as pleasant or helpful. He was late-middle-aged, overweight, and bald. Irene had to ring the doorbell several times before he came to open the door. When he finally did, he wore a light-blue, plush bathrobe that, once upon a time, might have been elegant, but now wasn't much more than a rag. It was hard to tell what stank more, the bathrobe or its owner, but the stench of stale alcohol probably emanated from the man's very pores. He'd stuffed his bare feet into a pair of worn-out leather slippers. He hadn't seen or heard a thing last night.

"I don't understand what you want from me. I was watching television all night. I didn't see nothing."

"I'm sorry to bother you, sir, but we have to ask a few more routine questions. Do you live alone?"

"Yes," he grunted.

"Any cars come by and head up the hill?"

"Not that I know," he said, irritated. "So what happened?"

"A man living in the new house has been murdered."

"Well, I hope they tear down the place—it's ruining my view."

He shut the door in Irene's face.

A family of five lived at the last house. The girls ranged in age from eight to fifteen. They'd all left home at quarter to six yesterday evening. The mother had dropped off the eight-year-old at ballet lessons downtown and then gone directly with the eleven-year-old to figure skating. The fifteen-year-old had been at riding lessons and had to be picked up on the way home, since there were no buses after eight. They hadn't gotten home until nine. Their father had been at a business dinner with an important client and didn't get back until eleven.

Strange, Irene thought. *All these people live in some of the most expensive houses in Göteborg, but they're never home to enjoy their luxurious surroundings. Most of the time, these houses are empty.* Irene noticed shield signs in front of all the houses that warned presumptive thieves of top-grade security systems. *Probably a good investment.*

LATER, IRENE RETURNED to the Ceder house. The police officer on guard duty let her in, and her steps echoed desolately as she walked over the tile floors toward the bedrooms.

Ludwig's room had a surprisingly pleasant color scheme. The walls were painted a warm, light yellow with a sky-blue border, along which various painted boats floated. There was a silky-soft, wall-to-wall carpet in the same beautiful sky blue. Shelves and tables were covered with a riot of stuffed animals in various sizes, and over the crib dangled mobiles in bright colors. On the wall next to the bed, a photograph of Sanna smiled down, holding newborn Ludwig in her arms. A small, bright red car stood in the middle of the floor—a toy that the little boy wouldn't be able to use for another three years, until his feet could reach the pedals. But the boy's room was not why Irene had come back.

Sanna's bedroom next door was large and bright, with sliding glass doors and a view of the ocean. A colossal round bed stood in the middle of the floor. On one side of the bed was a small panel with buttons. Irene pushed one at random, and heavy black curtains slid over the glass doors. The room was completely dark. With another button, the curtains slid back open, and the pale light shone through the outside rain again. Another button made a huge television screen on the wall spring into life. Irene sighed. She wasn't here to admire interior decoration, and as luxurious and trendy as the room was, it all seemed too impersonal and cold.

Irene experimented with the button panel until the mirrored glass closet doors opened. She had never seen so much clothing in her entire life—at least not meant for one person. She scanned the closet and confirmed what she suspected— only women's clothes were stored there. The single article of clothing meant for a man was a brand new, white velvet robe. Most likely the unused Scholl sandals in size twelve were also not Sanna's, but everything else was. Irene read the labels on the items: Versace, Kenzo, Prada. There were other brands she didn't recognize but she could tell they were of exquisite design and excellent quality.

Slowly and methodically, she walked through all the rooms in the house. In Sanna's bedroom and the hallway, there were pictures of mother and son, but Ceder didn't appear in any of them. In fact, there was hardly a trace of him anywhere. However, Irene did find an unopened spray bottle of shaving cream and a package of disposable razors in the bathroom.

Ceder may not have visited the house regularly, but male visitors were obviously still welcome.

THE ONLY POTENTIAL witness was a man who lived near the villa. He explained he'd been outside walking his dog, despite the bad weather. Before he'd gotten all the way to the Ceder place, he'd seen the back of a jogger running away down a jogging path that ran along the coast to Billdal. However, the witness had been a hundred meters away and had seen the jogger only from the back. The man had been wearing a dark jogging outfit and a knitted wool cap. He was slightly above-average height and must have been in good shape, since he was running rather swiftly. That's all the description the police could get.

The neighbor had walked his dog to the driveway of the Ceder house and turned around. Although the road was narrow and hardly saw much traffic, the city had put in street lights all the way to where the path turned off to the bike trail. The witness thought he'd reached the Ceder driveway at 7:15 P.M. He could say with certainty that there hadn't been a car parked in the driveway, and he was fairly sure there were no lights on inside the house, although the outdoor lights above the garage door and the front door had been lit.

"And even this description doesn't tell us much," Irene said later. "The Jaguar was inside the garage. Or perhaps Ceder hadn't arrived home yet. The outdoor lights could be the kind that turn on automatically as soon as it gets dark. Or maybe they leave the lights on twenty-four-seven. It's a popular jogging route, although it was terrible weather for jogging."

"We'll have to find out who was out jogging in that weather," Tommy said. "We can't eliminate the jogger until we know who he is."

Tommy and Irene kept their voices low. They were at a restaurant on their lunch break, and there were a number of other diners around them. Tommy had suggested a sushi restaurant, much to Irene's surprise. Apparently, he wanted something healthy. Perhaps he has put on a few kilos, Irene thought, but he doesn't look that fat. Irene was fond of sushi, which was something of a rare treat for her, so she had agreed to meet him at The Nippon in the Vasastan district.

Their waitress arrived with bottles of mineral water and chopsticks. She was a pleasant, plump Asian woman who wore a staid white shirt and black skirt. Though it was hard to tell, she seemed around fifty. An older man, perhaps her husband, was busy preparing sushi as fast as he could behind a glass counter in a corner of the restaurant. Behind him, Irene could see another chef preparing the hot dishes. The décor was pure Japanese, without any unnecessary details.

A second, younger waitress brought their sushi dishes. Tommy poured a generous amount of soy sauce into a small porcelain bowl and began to dip pieces of sushi into it. Thin slices of raw fish were draped artfully over balls of rice on plates of red and black lacquered wood. Two pieces were topped by large, flayed shrimp. The sushi rolls were filled with rice, vegetables, and shrimp. The meal was delicious, and soon Tommy and Irene were comfortably full. The only drawback was being forced to eat with chopsticks, especially whenever the rolls fell to pieces.

"I've talked to the technicians," Irene said. "They're still going through the house and property with a fine-toothed comb. At first I thought this case was cut and dry, but now it seems that we don't have a single viable lead. No one has seen or heard a thing." She sighed.

Tommy didn't appear too worried. "We'll have to ask the newspapers to put out a public notice. 'If anyone has seen anything around the time of the crime, blah, blah, blah. . . .'"

"Probably," Irene replied. "But first we have to figure out the exact time of death. And it's very important to find this jogger—damn!" Irene swore as her last sushi roll fell apart. She fished the piece of shrimp out of her bowl of soy sauce.

"On another topic, I've found out more about the sailing accident," Tommy said. "I've looked at the investigation report and newspaper clippings. Kjell B:son Ceder married Marie Lagerfeld, the only daughter of the shipping magnate Carl Lagerfeld and his wife Alice, in 1985. Marie was a late child; her parents were both over forty. Her mother died when she was a teenager, and her father died two years before she married Ceder when they were both thirty-five. Neither of them had been married before and neither had children. The Göteborg high society was speculating about an heir. In the summer of '88, they'd been married for three years. They decided to sail to England on a large sailboat with two other couples. All six people on board were experienced sailors wise to the dangers of the open ocean. This was in the middle of August, and the weather was calm when they left Göteborg. Once out on the North Sea, the wind picked up. It was raining, and the seas were high. It was very dark. Three of them were sailing the boat while the other three tried to rest. During the storm, the sheet came loose, and Marie and Kjell went on deck to fix it. For some reason, neither of them was wearing a life vest, which seems crazy because the weather was so bad. The report mentioned that there had been some heavy drinking earlier, which would explain their carelessness. Kjell came rushing into the wheelhouse and yelled that they had to turn around because Marie had fallen overboard. They circled for hours and tried to find her, but in vain. Her body was found three months later by the crew of a fishing boat. The body had gotten tangled in their nets, and by then, it had decomposed."

"How horrible!" Irene shivered.

Tommy leaned forward and said in an even lower voice, "The thing that bothers me is that Kjell and Marie were alone on the deck when she fell. No one else saw a thing. According to Kjell, it all happened so fast. He'd already wrapped the sheet around the winch and was sheeting it home when he suddenly realized that Marie was no longer beside him. As he looked around the deck, he saw it was empty. He began to yell and scanned the water but couldn't see anything. He even checked the cabin, in case she'd gone below without him noticing. But she wasn't on the boat. She'd disappeared into the sea."

"So you think she might have been pushed?"

Tommy nodded.

"He was suspected of it even back then. She was worth several million, and as her husband, he was her only heir. However, there wasn't a shred of evidence that things had happened any other way than Ceder had described. Still, I think his explanation of what went on was pretty weak. He should have noticed if she were washed overboard." Tommy thought a moment and then said, "He didn't marry again until sixteen years later, and that was to Sanna Kaegler, who was pregnant before the wedding."

"Maybe he wanted to make sure she could bear a child," Irene said. "Men also have their biological clocks, don't they? Maybe he just wanted to have an heir—better late than never. His first wife hadn't had a child after three years of marriage."

"Technically correct," Tommy said. "The first Mrs. Ceder was three months pregnant at the time of her death."

"A double tragedy, in that case."

"I found out as much as I could about Ceder while I was at it. He was already running a restaurant that had earned a Michelin star when he met Marie Lagerfeld. After she died, he bought another restaurant, and in the mid-nineties, he started building Hotel Göteborg. When the hotel was finished, he moved his newest acquisition, Le Ciel, to the top floor."

"Did he use any of the inheritance to build the hotel?"

"Perhaps some of it. The hotel was a really massive project. I don't remember how much it cost to build, but I doubt that he paid for it in cash. There must have been banks involved as well."

"Probably. But he still had enough money left over to build that house in Askim."

"Yep. It'll be interesting to take a look at his apartment."

"We should head over there now." Irene waved for their waitress. "Can we have our bill, please?"

• • •

WITH A GENTLE hiss, a state-of-the-art elevator lifted Tommy and Irene to Kjell B:son Ceder's apartment, which took up the entire top floor of the building. The elevator was the only modern touch in an atmosphere that otherwise seemed caught a hundred years in the past. Everything else in the magnificent stairwell breathed fin de siècle.

Sanna Kaegler Ceder's mother warily opened the outer door. When she recognized Tommy and Irene, she immediately let them in, chattering, "You wouldn't believe the nerve of those journalists! They have no respect!"

She stopped speaking when Sanna came into the hallway. Mother and daughter shared a resemblance, though the mother was shorter and plumper. Both daughters, Tove and Sanna, had inherited their mother's pale Scandinavian beauty, though she had now faded to colorlessness. It came to Irene's mind that she didn't even know the mother's name.

"I'm Detective Inspector Irene Huss. We weren't properly introduced yesterday," she said with a smile.

A cold and clammy hand was limply placed into Irene's. She had to hold on firmly so that it wouldn't slip off. It felt like a wet rag.

"I'm Elsy. Elsy Kaegler."

Elsy also greeted Tommy, who put on his most charming smile. He was especially skilled in dealing with middle-aged and elderly women and was always the one to interview anyone in that category. By now, Irene and Tommy had worked together so long that they didn't even need to discuss who would do what. It came automatically.

The light from the hallway lamp shone unkindly over Sanna's face. She looked tired and wasn't wearing any makeup. The skin around her eyes was swollen. Her blonde hair was pulled tightly into a ponytail high on her head, held in place with a black velvet band. She wore a black leather jacket, a white silk blouse and black linen pants. The diamond cross still glittered from her deep décolletage. Even in her grief, she was elegant and fashionable. She gave Irene and Tommy a slight, rather royal nod, as if deigning to acknowledge their presence, before she slipped past them in her narrow stilettos.

Irene felt overly conscious of her worn deck shoes. She had no intention of removing them, not with a hole in her right sock, which her big toe poked through.

Irene and Tommy hung up their coats in the hallway and were steered by the nervously chattering Elsy Kaegler into a large room with a high ceiling. The plaster stucco around the base of the heavy crystal chandelier was molded in an elegant rococo style. Three of the walls had bookshelves from floor to ceiling. Clearly this was the library. The last wall was dominated by a large, open fireplace. On the mantle was a black urn flanked by two golden candelabras.

Irene was sure of one thing: Sanna had never lived in this apartment. There was not a trace of glass, modern art, or brushed steel. This place was decorated with expensive antiques and genuine carpets.

". . . and what difficulty we had bringing all of Ludwig's and Sanna's things here," Elsy was saying.

Sanna was already in the library. Irene took a chance and said in a light tone, "Why did your husband stay here? You and Ludwig had already been living in the house for months."

Sanna seemed prepared for that question. She gave Irene a chilly look and said calmly, "We have never lived together."

"Not even after you were married?"

"Never."

"Why not?"

"We chose to live apart," Sanna said stiffly. "Neither one of us wanted to live with anyone else over a long period of time. These days, living apart is no longer unusual."

That may be true, Irene thought, but only when the partners have to live a long distance apart, or when people feel they're too old to adjust to someone else's habits.

As if she were reading Irene's thoughts, Sanna threw back her head defiantly and said, "We entertain a great deal, and we each had very full lives, which we didn't want to give up when we married. I kept my own apartment and stayed there until the house was ready for me and Ludwig."

"When was the house finished?"

"At the beginning of July."

"So you no longer have your apartment?"

"No, I sold it. Otherwise we wouldn't be here now." Sanna waved her arm as if to indicate the entire huge apartment.

"So did you spend time with your husband? Go to parties and events together and things like that?"

"Of course we did. And we have Ludwig."

As if he had heard his name, there was the sudden sound of a child's cry.

"Oh, now he's awake," Elsy said. "I'll go. . . ."

"Yesterday you said that you'd spoken by phone with Kjell the day before. Around nine in the morning. Is that correct?" Irene continued.

"Yes."

"Was he at the house or was he here?"

"He was here."

"So you didn't see him at all on Tuesday?"

"No."

"When did you last see him?"

"Last Saturday. We had lunch together at Le Ciel. Ludwig was with us, but he slept the whole time."

Irene wondered how she should continue. She saw out of the corner of her eye that Tommy was following Elsy Kaegler to talk to her out of her daughter's hearing. Such a strange arrangement, Irene thought. People living separate lives even though they're married and have a child together. Irene decided to go a bit deeper into the matter.

"Didn't Kjell want to live with you and Ludwig?" she asked cautiously.

"No. He didn't like children."

"But even so—"

"That's how it was!" Sanna snapped.

Why would a young woman marry an older man who didn't like children and then have a child with him? Simply because he was rich? Irene realized she couldn't ask that question, even though it would be interesting to hear the reply. Instead, she headed into another line of questioning.

"Do you know who Kjell was supposed to meet yesterday evening?"

"I have no idea."

"Perhaps you have a guess?" Irene continued stubbornly.

Sanna appeared to waver for a minute, and then said firmly, "No."

"Do you know why Kjell wanted to meet this person at the house and not here at his apartment?"

Sanna turned beet red from her décolletage to her cheeks. One of Irene's questions had finally touched a nerve.

"I have no idea! I will never forgive him for that! My house . . . my house . . . he's ruined it! I'll have to clean. . . ." She stopped in the middle of a sentence when she heard laughter in the hallway. Tommy came marching into the library carrying Ludwig in his arms. Elsy Kaegler was following him with a worried look on her face. She rubbed her hands together, making small, scared sounds as if Tommy were about to drop Ludwig on the floor.

"Here you are," Tommy said. "All fresh and clean and ready to go! He's hungry now, though." He smiled at Sanna as he handed Ludwig over to her.

Sanna nodded but gave no hint of a smile nor thanks as she took her son and placed him on her hip.

"You'll have to excuse me," she said. "I can't answer any more questions now. I have to take care of Ludde." She left the room without even a glance back.

Neither Tommy nor Irene had a chance to stop her. The snub had been quick and effective. Elsy started to wring her hands and mumble again while Tommy and Irene headed back into the hallway in turn. Although they couldn't get any more information today, Irene was absolutely sure that they'd be back. Sanna probably realized this as well.

"SANNA'S PARENTS HAVE been divorced for twenty years," Tommy informed Irene once they were back in the car. "Elsy is an elementary school teacher, and her ex-husband is a principal at a high school here in town. Apparently, he remarried rather quickly, and there are two sons from the second marriage. According to Elsy, he hasn't paid any attention to his daughters since he remarried."

"Do you think that Sanna married Kjell B:son Ceder as a father substitute?"

"I don't know. Apparently, lots of young women think that older men are more attractive: as a lover, as a partner—all sorts of ways!"

Wow, what's eating him? Irene glanced at Tommy, who had turned away and was glaring out the passenger side window. The tightness of his neck muscles told her he was furious. What's going on with him? Maybe a belated midlife crisis? Irene didn't know how she should handle the situation. They sat in silence for the rest of the way to the station.

SUPERINTENDENT ANDERSSON WAS in his office, waiting for their return. Irene realized at once that something big had happened because Andersson had dug out his coffee maker and was brewing a huge pot. He rarely made his own these days, since there was the vending machine just down the hall.

Irene did a double take when she saw that the normally colorless Kajsa Birgersdotter had dyed her hair a deep-reddish chestnut. The new color actually looked good on her. Kajsa's dove blue T-shirt reflected her eye color in a flattering way. Has she gone and gotten herself color analyzed? Irene's thoughts were interrupted when Andersson finally began to speak.

"Stridner just gave me a call. The Ceder autopsy is done. He died from two bullets to the brain. The shots were fired at close range. It's a small-caliber weapon—a shitty little ladies' gun. But Stridner also discovered something else. . . ."

Andersson paused dramatically, a conspiratorial smile spreading across his face. "Ceder had an operation—what are they called again? So he couldn't have kids. He was castrated!"

"Castrated?" exclaimed Birgitta.

Andersson nodded, content with his declaration.

"You mean he had a vasectomy?" Tommy said quietly.

"Yeah, yeah, that's what it's called," the superintendent said.

"So he wasn't castrated, just sterilized," Tommy clarified. "The sperm ducts were severed so that semen wouldn't exit the body, but everything else is intact and functional, sexually speaking."

"How do you know all this stuff?" Andersson said sourly. He hated to be caught up short in front of his subordinates.

"I've actually had one," Tommy said, unperturbed. "I thought three children were enough."

Kajsa Birgersdotter said something under her breath, as she got up quickly from her chair and left. Tommy appeared just as surprised as the others in the room. Irene watched his surprise fade and be replaced by the stiff, angry expression he'd had earlier in the car.

"What the hell's gotten into her?" Andersson asked. He was irritated that he no longer had control of the room. He took off his glasses and let them drop loudly on the table before he continued. "Let's not worry about her for now. We have to discuss what's next in this investigation. Perhaps we should find out who the real father of the baby might be?"

"Could Ceder have had the operation after Ludwig was born?" asked Irene.

"Stridner said that the procedure looked at least five years old," Andersson replied with triumph in his voice.

This was sensational news, although, as Irene thought about it further, the information would not make their investigation any easier—rather, this was an unexpected complication.

"So who the hell is the father of the boy?" the superintendent asked again.

All three detectives appeared to be deep in thought. Finally Irene said, "Well, we can always run a DNA analysis just to exclude Ceder. We have Ceder at the pathologist's, and I'll be able to get a sample from Ludwig."

"Sanna Kaegler will never agree to that!" Birgitta said with certainty.

"Who says we need to ask Sanna for permission?" Irene said, and smiled.

Chapter 4

IRENE HATED EARLY mornings. The earlier she had to wake up, the more she hated it. It was just "not her thing," as the twins would say. In her next life, she'd be a nightclub star. Those working hours would fit her better.

The early start was necessary today. She didn't want to leave any chance that Sanna would get to the Askim house before she did. Sanna would probably hire a cleaning service, but Irene didn't want to run the risk that Sanna would decide to clean the house herself.

Neither Krister nor the girls had gotten up yet. After three cups of coffee and two cheese sandwiches, Irene felt up to driving. Should she take Sammie out for his morning walk first? A glance at the clock told her it was much too early. Her dog was the most sluggish member of the entire family. He was snoring along with Krister in the warm spot Irene had left in the bed.

THE OUTDOOR LIGHTS were still on above the garage at the crime scene in Askim. Although the skies were clear and there was a hint of dawn in the east, the house loomed in shadows. Irene told herself this was just her imagination, knowing what had taken place inside its brick walls.

She unlocked the door and stepped into the hallway. She took out a large plastic bag, put on plastic gloves she pulled from her pocket, and headed straight to the garbage can underneath the kitchen sink. She reached in and fished out a big wad of paper towels. They were the paper towels Tommy had used to wipe away the baby food Ludwig had burped onto her shoulder. Irene stuffed the wad into a small plastic bag and then put the whole thing into the larger bag.

Her footsteps rang through the empty house as she walked to the bathroom where she'd changed Ludwig's diapers. Irene noticed that the bottles and jars above the changing table had been disturbed, probably when Elsy was hastily packing what the boy would need for a few days.

Irene stepped on the pedal that lifted the lid of the diaper pail. She took care of the used diaper the same way she had with the wad of paper towels: first popping it into a smaller plastic bag and then that into the bigger one. *There we go. Now the lab has enough to work with.* Honestly, she wasn't really sure if the stuff in the diaper would yield any useful DNA, but she hoped so.

Impulsively, she went into the glass-enclosed conservatory, not because she wanted to see the murder scene a second time but because she wanted to watch the sunrise. She climbed the spiral staircase and stood to look east. There wasn't a cloud in the sky, just the trail of a jet plane, which the first rays of the sun picked out in a golden shimmer. For a moment, the silhouette of the forest appeared to go up in flames, spreading rapidly across the tops of the trees. The sky changed gradually from lemon yellow to turquoise blue. Only a few minutes later, the color show was over, and Irene watched a normal sunrise that promised a fine day. She turned to look over the leaden sea heaving in great swells; the vista was like a lighthouse's. *I wonder if Sanna came up with this or whether it was the architect's idea.*

As she headed down the winding steel staircase, she started to think about the money again. *Who had paid for this house, Sanna or Kjell B:son Ceder? Even if Ceder wasn't Ludwig's biological father, he'd acknowledged paternity since he hadn't officially denied it. Did Sanna inherit the whole lot, or was there a prenup? How much money were we talking about here?* Irene realized that it wouldn't be easy to find answers to these questions. Maybe they weren't even relevant to the investigation. Sanna had an alibi. There was nothing to connect her to the murder of her husband.

ÅHLÉN ARRIVED AT the station the same time as Irene, both slightly late to the "morning prayer." She took the opportunity to hand him back the key to Sanna Kaegler-Ceder's house, which she'd borrowed from him the evening before. Åhlén held the door open for her.

Superintendent Andersson was already standing in front of his team and was showing slides on a screen. The screen rolled down from the ceiling, but something had gone wrong with the mechanism that kept it all the way down, and it kept unlocking and sending the screen straight back up. Andersson was characteristically frustrated.

As usual, Irene looked for a seat next to Tommy, but changed her mind when she saw him sitting between the newly red-haired Kajsa and Birgitta Moberg-Rauhala. Instead, she slid onto a chair next to Fredrik Stridh. Fredrik was so absorbed in what he was seeing on the screen that he did not notice when she sat down.

". . . both bodies were in the kitchen. They were fully clothed. There are no signs that they'd been tortured or abused in any way before they were shot. As you can see in this picture—"

The superintendent stopped mid-sentence as his pointer hit the cement wall instead of the soft screen.

"That damned thing. Can we get someone in to fix this piece of crap?"

"I'll take care of it as soon as you've finished your run-through," Tommy promised.

"Why don't you do it now?" growled Andersson. He tried to take several deep breaths to bring down his blood pressure. Andersson was supposed to retire this coming summer. He'd turned sixty, and he'd already had a one-year extension. Irene was always worrying about his health, since she knew he had asthma and high blood pressure. The fact that he was extremely overweight contributed to the severity of the conditions he already had.

"I'll need a ladder, and it'll take some time for me to find one," Tommy said patiently.

"Fuck the screen and just show the slides on the wall," Jonny Blom said.

For once, Irene agreed with Jonny. It didn't happen that often. They'd had a frosty relationship ever since they'd worked on the packing murder case that had taken them from Göteborg to Copenhagen. In recent months, though, their relationship had begun to thaw. There were signs that Jonny was actively trying to get his drinking under control. Rumor had it that Jonny's long-suffering wife had made an ultimatum: the family or the bottle. It seemed there was something to the rumor. While nobody discussed it openly at work, Jonny was actually showing up on Fridays and Mondays, and he didn't come to work hung over or reeking of alcohol as often as he used to. He had a lot to lose. With four children, he had the biggest family in the department. Only Åhlén beat him when it came to children, but he was a technician and not an investigator.

Muttering to himself, Andersson tried to focus the slideshow images on the wall. The picture showed two men lying on a polished wooden floor. They could see a glimpse of a fireplace in one corner of the photo and the bases of some kitchen cabinets. One of the men was on his back. He had two shots in his forehead right above his nose, and he stared unseeingly into the camera. The other man was on his stomach. It looked like he'd fallen flat on his face. Blood had run onto his shirt collar and the floor. Both men looked fairly young. Andersson turned to Blom and said, "Why don't you take over? You were at the crime scene."

"Sure." Jonny stood up and took the pointer from the superintendent. "The bodies are lying two meters from each other. The man lying on his back owns the house. His name is Joachim Rothstaahl. We have not yet identified the second man."

"When were they shot?" asked Tommy.

"Monday evening. Sometime between six and ten P.M. At least, that's what forensics can say so far. They'd been lying there for over a day and a half by the time they were found."

"Who found them?" asked Tommy.

"Rothstaahl's father."

"What do you know about the owner?" asked the superintendent.

"Joachim Rothstaahl is thirty-two-years-old, and he's some kind of finance guy. He calls himself a consultant. The father informed us that Joachim had taken over his grandfather's summer house. He was supposed to move into it with his girl-friend this weekend. She lives in Vänersborg. She was working during the day, and on Monday and Tuesday evening, she was at home packing for the move. Rothstaahl had already told her that he had an important meeting on Monday, and he wouldn't be at home, so she didn't call him that night. But when she couldn't reach him on Tuesday, she began to worry. She called a number of people, and finally she reached his father, who went out on Wednesday and found them both. There are no signs of a break-in at the crime scene. As I said, the bodies are two meters apart. We believe that Rothstaahl was shot first. The other guy was trying to run out the door between the kitchen and the bedroom when he was shot in the back of the head."

"Have you found the bullets?" asked Irene.

"No. There were no exit holes, so they're probably still in the bodies. Fired from a girly gun." Jonny grinned.

Irene studied the photograph of the two men. Jonny's last comment raised the hair on the back of her neck. Could it be possible?

"How many shots did each man receive?" she asked quickly.

"Don't you have your own case to work on? Why do you always interrupt—"

"—because our case is connected to yours," Irene said.

"Your case? How?"

"Just tell me how many shots were fired."

"Two. Two apiece, that is," Jonny said sullenly.

"Irene's right," Tommy said. "It does resemble the Askim murder."

"Stop right there!" said Andersson. "What makes you think the murders in Askim and Långedrag are related?"

Irene hesitated. It was mostly a gut feeling. Before she could figure out how to put it into words, Tommy spoke.

"Here's how they are alike. There's no sign of a break-in. All three men were shot at point-blank range with a small-caliber weapon. The murders happened within a twenty-hour time period, and neither of the two men we identified was ever involved in a crime. Both took place in areas of Göteborg that otherwise have low rates for murder and violent crimes."

"So who's the third guy? Do we have any reports of missing persons that might match the body?" asked Birgitta.

Jonny shook his head. "No one who looks like him has been reported missing. We turned him over and took his photo before he was taken to the morgue."

Jonny clicked for the next slide. The man in this photo was younger than the other one. He was blond with fairly long hair. Despite having been dead for some time, one could tell that he'd been rather good looking.

Kajsa Berggren leapt out of her chair. She didn't run out of the room this time, but pointed at the picture and waved her arms around excitedly. "I know him! I know who he is!" she yelled.

"Who?" asked Andersson, confused by her excitement.

"That guy is Philip Bergman!"

"Who?" the superintendent asked again. Andersson did not like Kajsa's strange outbursts. Usually she was so quiet and well mannered that he forgot she existed. And then, all of a sudden, she'd have an outburst and do something erratic.

"Kajsa's right," Tommy said. "That really is Philip Bergman. Bergman-Kaegler. And that brings us back to Sanna."

This was too much for old Andersson. He slammed his palm on the table and roared so loudly that his voice echoed through the room, "What the hell is behind all this?"

Irene could sympathize with her boss. There was something familiar about that combination of names: Bergman-Kaegler. Unlike her boss, she decided to wait and see how this would play out.

Kajsa Birgersdotter made a valiant attempt to explain. "Sanna Kaegler and I are the same age. Maybe that's why I follow her in the news. . . . Philip Bergman and Sanna Kaegler were old friends who started an IT company together. It became one of the largest in the industry. They all got really rich! The tabloids always wrote tons about them and their fancy apartments in London and New York and how successful their company was. And then the tech bubble burst, and their company went bust. And then that guy Bonetti went missing, too."

Andersson groaned loudly, but Irene was all ears. She and Tommy had been involved peripherally in the search for Thomas Bonetti.

Witnesses had seen Thomas Bonetti in his Storebro Royal Cruiser 420 leave from the outermost dock at Långedrag one drizzling evening in September 2000, at about eight. Although there weren't many people at the harbor at that time, the ones who were there couldn't miss seeing the luxury motor yacht back out of its mooring. The ship was not built to be overlooked. That was three years ago, almost to the day, and it was the last time anyone had ever seen Bonetti alive.

Bonetti had told his parents that he was heading over to the family's summer cabin on Styrsö. He told them he had a few things he had to think through in peace and quiet.

Neither Bonetti nor the boat had ever been found.

Bonetti's passport was still at his parents' house, along with the clothes and personal belongings he'd brought with him. Since he also had an apartment in London, his parents thought he might have gone there to wait for the worst of the uproar around the bankruptcy to die down. However, they could not explain how he could have gotten to London without a passport. Only when an eviction notice for non-payment of rent arrived did his parents realize that something was wrong. The apartment was in central London and extremely expensive. Thomas had been extraordinarily proud when he'd managed to snag it and never would have willingly risked losing it. Apparently, only then was his father, a celebrated lawyer, convinced that this was not one of his son's usual episodes of minor mischief. The parents filed a missing person's report, but by then, Interpol had already issued a warrant for his arrest on suspicion of serious white-collar criminal activity.

Irene and Tommy had taken the ferry to Styrsö Island during a cold and windy day in December. Although it had been barely a few degrees below freezing, they felt frozen the minute they left the warm ferry. The biting, cold wind blew through their clothing, and snow whipped them in the face with small, hard pellets. It felt like they were fighting their way through polar regions—only the wolves nipping at their heels were missing. Irene had a wrinkled sheet of paper with the directions Thomas Bonetti's mother had written.

Head south past the bridge to Dansö Island. Go past Solvik Inlet. Continue to a yellow house with a glass veranda. The path divides; take the left. Follow the path along the shore, about 100 meters. Big dock with a boat house. Stone stairs to the right. There's a low, red house with a sign saying Västerro, and that's the one. The mother's handwriting was elegant and clear. A key to the house was taped to the paper. When Bonetti's mother had handed it to them, she explained that no one had been to the cabin since Thomas had gone missing, not even Thomas's older sister.

By the time Irene and Tommy finally reached the house, they were numb with cold. It wasn't much warmer inside, since the place wasn't heated, but at least there was no wind. The cabin had low ceilings but was fairly spread out. It had been built high on a hill, nestled among rocks, and even on a day like this, the view was astonishing. The wind whipped the black water of the sea to froth as it hit rocks and reefs. They could get a glimpse through the driving snow of the other islands in the archipelago to the south and southeast.

They had gone through the entire house meticulously, and there had been no sign that Thomas Bonetti had even been there, whether alone or with someone else. There were no signs of violence, and everything was in good order.

They locked the door behind them and begrudgingly headed back out into the cold. The ferry home left from Styrsö Bratten, which meant that they had to walk even farther, this time against the wind. Coffee had never tasted as good as the cup they had when they finally reached the ferry café. Irene would have gladly ordered a barrel of it—not to drink, but to use as a warm bath for her feet.

"Bonetti!" Andersson growled. "We checked up on him

years ago, and he's still missing! How could he be involved in these murders?"

"Sanna Kaegler, Philip Bergman, and Thomas Bonetti were the founders of ph.com. They lost an incredible amount of money when the bubble burst. You remember the headlines," Tommy said.

So that was the connection. The light bulb lit, and Irene remembered the story of Bergman-Kaegler. They'd been a household name. When she and Tommy were taking a few days to investigate Thomas Bonetti's disappearance, ph.com had been merely a background issue. The Internet bubble had burst in the spring of 2000. In September, by the time Bonetti disappeared, it was already history. Bonetti had been involved in a number of suspicious business affairs, and any one of them could have provided a good reason for him to lie low. That is, if he was lying low voluntarily. As time went by, and there'd been no sign of life from him, rumors began to circulate: he'd had plastic surgery and was seen by some tourists in Miami; he'd been glimpsed snorkeling in Egypt; he'd been on a luxury Mediterranean cruise, or seen at a sex club in Paris. One tipster said he'd seen him in Copenhagen pushing a twin stroller. None of the tips proved to be true. Thomas Bonetti's description made it hard for him to hide, even if he'd undergone plastic surgery. He was thirty-one-years old and 155 centimeters tall. He weighed about 100 kilos. He had a pinkish tinge to his skin color. His hairline was receding, and he only had a few tufts of hair where bangs were supposed to be. His hair had natural red highlights, and his eyes were a watery light blue. He had thick round glasses in all the photographs that had been published. The rumor that he'd changed his appearance by wearing tinted contacts had been eliminated when his parents informed the police that Thomas couldn't wear contacts of any kind. They also did not believe he was hiding in countries that were hot and sunny. Thomas couldn't stand heat, and his skin couldn't tolerate the sun.

His bank accounts in both London and Sweden revealed that he'd taken all his money out the day after he disappeared. A sum of five million Swedish kroner had gone via Luxembourg to the Cayman Islands. There, all traces ended.

Five million kroner would last a long time, but it costs money to stay in hiding. If Bonetti had continued to burn through money at the rate he'd done during his heyday, he should have gone broke by now.

"At least a billion kroner went up in smoke in the bankruptcy," Tommy pointed out.

"They were in good company. A huge number of Internet companies went bust. At the turn of the millennium, the burst of the dot-com bubble affected the economy of the entire world," Birgitta said.

"That's right. They weren't paying any attention to their finances, and the money just went up in smoke. Bonetti wasn't the only one who took money out of the company right before it went bankrupt. That must have been the money he had in his various bank accounts. However, we still have a lead via the bank account in Sweden, which holds the money he inherited. The day he touches that money, we got him," Tommy said.

"Who set up the account?" Birgitta asked.

"His father set it up when Thomas inherited money from his paternal grandparents. According to his father, it's a long-term savings account that doesn't have a card attached, so if he wants to get the money, he has to contact the bank personally. At that moment, he'd leave a clue as to where he was, and then we'd get him."

"Or at the very least, we'd have proof he's still alive," Irene said.

Tommy nodded.

Birgitta pointed at the picture on the wall and asked, "How are Philip Bergman and Joachim Rothstaahl connected?"

"According to Rothstaahl's father, the two of them had been pals for a long time," Jonny replied. "That's all we know right now."

"It appears that the death rate around Sanna Kaegler's closest friends and relatives is particularly high," Irene commented drily.

"Yep. We need to figure out what really happened with the company. Who else was involved? And we have to check whether can connect Thomas Bonetti and Joachim Rothstaahl."

"Just a second, let's back off a bit," Andersson said, looking around the room. He took a deep breath before he continued. "Let's go back to the case in question. Two crime scenes and three murders. So far we have nothing concrete to connect the two crime scenes, and we don't actually know whether all three of them were killed by the same weapon. And what would connect Kjell B:son Kaegler to some damned Internet business?"

"So far we have no connection," Tommy replied calmly. "However, he was married to one of the founders. One other founder has been killed, and the third disappeared without a trace three years ago. The only thing all three victims have in common is Sanna Kaegler."

Andersson kept breathing heavily as he thought about all these unexpected complications. There was a whistling noise coming from his windpipe, which made Irene nervous. She thought he might have an asthma attack. Finally, Andersson made up his mind.

"We're going to sit tight until Philip Bergman's identity has been confirmed. Once it has, I want Irene and Tommy to head out and have a chat with that prima donna Kaegler. And don't press too hard until we're sure that Ceder is not the father of her son. Anything new from the lab?" The last question was directed to Åhlén who seemed to be dozing. Irene gave him a sharp poke in the ribs with her elbow, and he jerked upright. He got up, walked over to Andersson, pushed his glasses up on his nose, and faced the room. As usual, he looked like a mole coming up to the surface.

"Sanna Kaegler's hands had no trace of powder or soot residue. On the other hand, there was a considerable amount on the victim around the entrance wound and the face, which indicates he was shot at close range. We have estimated the distance at half a meter. There are no signs of forced entry to the house, but we found some muddy footprints with clay residue inside by the door at the rear of the house. There's a lot of clay outside the doorway, and on the inside doormat, there are blurred footprints of size forty-four jogging shoes. There are also signs of dried moisture beneath a clothes hanger. The theory is that the murderer could have entered through the back door, hung up his wet coat, and changed to dry shoes. Neither the outer nor inner back doors have any sign of forced entry. Either the murderer had a key to the house or else the door had been left open."

"There are no other footprints on the floor?" asked Tommy.

"No, only the ones on the mat. He could have also put on plastic foot coverings over his muddy shoes."

"He could hardly have gone unnoticed by Ceder in that case," Irene said. "Those plastic coverings make a lot of noise when you're walking in them. Not only that, they're slippery on tile floors."

Tommy nodded in agreement. "True. I believe he was already inside the house and waiting for Ceder."

Irene reflected on the smell of whiskey in the house. She quickly put together a possible scenario.

"Ceder was up in his lighthouse room, drinking a glass of whiskey. He was carrying the glass in his hand as he walked down the stairs. The killer was at the foot of the stairs waiting for him."

"Maybe he was hiding below the spiral staircase," Åhlén said, unperturbed by the interruption. "That's where we found this." He pulled out a plastic bag from the pocked of his lab coat. "This is an elastic reflective band a lot of joggers use. They put it on their right upper arm when they're jogging at night along roads with vehicle traffic. We have found half of a thumb print on it."

"Wonderful! Now we just have to find a guy with half a thumb!" Jonny laughed at his own joke.

No one else in the room was laughing. They were all used to his lame jokes by now and didn't bother reacting. Åhlén had given them a good clue. If they were able to find a suspect, there was a chance they could tie him to the crime scene by the thumbprint. It would be much easier to prove the case.

"As far as Långedrag goes, Malm says that the preliminary report will be available this afternoon at three," Åhlén said.

"You haven't told us anything about the bullets!" protested Andersson.

"No, because there's not much to say. A .25-caliber pistol. Not mantled. Massively deformed after ricocheting around the brain. Ballistic examination will be difficult." Unaffected by Andersson's critical tone, Åhlén stuffed the bag back into his pocket and drifted out of the room.

There was silence after he left. Finally, Andersson took a deep breath and said, with the whistling sound coming out at the same time as his voice, "Jonny and Fredrik are to continue searching for possible witnesses to the Långedrag case. Question Rothstaahl's father and girlfriend to see if they can try to remember if he mentioned a specific person he was planning to meet. Birgitta will contact the relatives of that Bergman guy to get a positive identification. Once that's done, Irene and Tommy will question Sanna Kaegler. Be tough on that woman. I can smell the shit stinking from here, as far as she's concerned."

Good thing that Sanna Kaegler isn't around to hear that, Irene thought. *She'd be more offended by being accused of stinking of shit than being connected to a murder.*

"And what's my job?" asked Kajsa.

At first, he looked shocked that she'd spoken to him that way, but after an awkward pause, he said, "You're going to have a special assignment. Since you're already interested in those clowns who built up a company that was worth a billion before bankruptcy, I think you should dig up all the facts you can on them. Find every single piece of info that's out there."

Kajsa turned momentarily pale and then brightened up. "Okay, I'll dig."

Chapter 5

TOMMY DECIDED TO deepen his knowledge of Kjell B:son Ceder. The circumstances concerning the death of Ceder's first wife were especially interesting.

"As Andersson likes to say, this smells like shit!" Tommy said to Irene, smiling.

"You think?"

"Yep. I'm going to follow my investigator instincts."

"Then I'll follow mine and dig up what I can on Thomas Bonetti. Remember when we were poking our noses into that case? By the way, lunch at twelve?"

"Sounds good. Then I think we should hear what Svante Malm has to say at three o'clock regarding the results from Långedrag. I agree with you that these murders are connected."

"Your investigator instinct again?"

"Nope. Common sense and pure logic."

WHEN TOMMY AND Irene had gone to Styrsö that cold December day three years ago, neither of them had any idea what industry Thomas Bonetti worked in. They'd thought of him as a rich techie who'd gone missing with a lot of money. As they had headed back on the ferry, Tommy had theorized that Bonetti was lying on a beach in the Bahamas, holding a drink with an umbrella in one hand and a buxom blonde in the other, while poor police officers froze to the bone searching for him.

By lunchtime, Irene had a much better understanding of Bonetti's past. She didn't like him, but that was the fate of most of the people Irene learned about from the crime register.

At the time of his disappearance, Bonetti was thirty-one-years-old, but he looked more like forty in the photographs. He was the only son of the famous lawyer Antonio Bonetti. His father, who had emigrated from Italy, had fair skin and red hair. Nothing in Thomas's appearance suggested his Italian heritage. Thomas had a sister who was two years older. He went to a private school during his elementary and high school years and then began to study at Göteborg's business school. While at university, he was arrested twice for possession of narcotics. Both times cocaine was the drug of choice, but the amount was so small that he'd gotten off with light punishments. He had never been in the military

After working at a Swedish bank for a few years, Bonetti moved to London. He decided to start an investment bank with another Swede whom he'd known since his university days. They met a Norwegian man their age, who was already working in the finance sector and wasn't happy with his income. He wanted to start something of his own, so he joined his new Swedish friends with the intention of making some fast cash.

Bonetti's Swedish business partner was named Joachim Rothstaahl. Irene felt her pulse race as she read the name. Positive confirmation that Bonetti and Rothstaahl were connected! One missing without a trace and the other killed along with another of Bonetti's later partners. Her head started to spin. She had to make sure she knew exactly how all these people fit together, but the most important fact was established. Seven years earlier, they were already in business together. Perhaps there wasn't a connection to the three murders, but this fact could be important.

The Norwegian man was named Erik Dahl. The name

didn't ring a bell, but she wrote it down for further research. The three business partners, using the right contacts and many elegant meetings at one of London's finest restaurants, managed to convince numerous businesses and people from Scandinavia to invest money in their management fund, which they named Poundfix. They made sure to have famous English politicians and a lord or two at all their functions so that they would have a cover of respectability.

In practice, the fund was nothing more than a pyramid scheme. The new money coming into Poundfix was used to pay the high dividends and to redeem the investments when people wanted out. It worked for a while, but the bubble burst when their largest customer, a Norwegian company, demanded an audit. There was no money to audit, since the three partners had already made off with it. Thomas Bonetti had seen the end coming and managed to pull his money out before the ceiling fell in. He had a couple million kroner in his pocket by then.

Joachim Rothstaahl came through the experience with no more punishment than a good scare. Since he was a Swedish citizen living in England, he couldn't be forced to face a Norwegian court. Erik Dahl, on the other hand, was the one who had to face the music in Oslo. He was sentenced to seven years in jail for major embezzlement.

Irene stopped. Could Erik Dahl have been released from prison? Was he now looking for revenge on his former partners? He wouldn't have been out of prison at the time of Thomas Bonetti's disappearance, but maybe now? She made a note in her notebook to follow up, when she realized that there was a problem—what was the connection between Erik Dahl and Kjell B:son Ceder? She glanced at the clock and saw it was time for lunch. It had been a fruitful morning.

THE OBLIGATORY THURSDAY pea soup with pancakes was always a favorite. Perhaps a little more thyme in the soup would have been nice, but there was no need to be petty. Tommy probably didn't even notice that the soup was lacking as far as herbs were concerned. He was gesturing wildly with his soup spoon to emphasize his points. Irene noticed a drop of mustard fly off the spoon and land on the paper tablecloth. Tommy didn't see it, or perhaps didn't care. He was totally caught up in his morning's research.

"There's no way to get a clearer picture of what actually happened on deck that night. Only Kjell B:son Ceder and his wife Marie were there. Perhaps the man who steered the boat might have seen something. Guess who he was?" Tommy grinned, and Irene frowned when he didn't continue.

"I have no idea," she said sourly.

"Edward Fenton!"

Irene stared at him. "Fenton? You mean Doctor Fenton? Morgan Fenton?"

"No, Edward! Morgan Fenton's younger brother! Don't you remember that Morgan Fenton mentioned a brother who was employed by a London bank? Both Edward and his girlfriend were on the boat as well as Morgan and his late wife! She was pregnant! It must have been that kid you talked to yesterday."

Irene nodded. Christopher Fenton was fifteen-years-old. He'd also been on that fateful trip, although just a baby in his mother's womb. She tried to pull together what she already knew.

"So both Morgan and Edward Fenton were friends with Ceder sixteen years ago. They also knew his first wife Marie. Morgan Fenton divorced and married Tove Kaegler, and a few years later, Kjell B:son Ceder married her sister Sanna. You said yesterday that Sanna had business connections with Edward Fenton and was also mixed up in that Internet business. This means that Edward also knew Thomas Bonetti and Philip Bergman. Interesting—but complicated."

"Exactly! So I sniffed around the Fenton brothers, but I didn't find much. Morgan is an orthopedic doctor here in

Göteborg, and Edward .
ment bank named HP J
pean office in London. T
Swedish woman, who died a
father was an Englishman. He is still
in Spain for the past few years."

"He has to be really old."

"Well over eighty."

"How old are the Fenton brothers?"

"Morgan is fifty-one, and Edward is forty-two."

"So Edward's our age," Irene pointed out.

"Yep. Their parents divorced at the end of the seventies, and their mother moved here with Edward. A few years later, Morgan also came to Göteborg and started studying medicine. He decided to stay, and he got married here."

"So that's why Morgan speaks Swedish so well. He's been living here for more than twenty-five years."

"That's right. He stayed here, and his brother Edward returned to England. He studied economics at Cambridge and shot straight up in the financial world. He also made a good marriage, though he didn't marry the woman who was on board the sailboat when Ceder's wife drowned. Edward's wife is an American, and they've been married for ten years. They have two children."

"Wow, you found out an incredible amount on Edward Fenton. How'd you do it?"

"Online. There's lots of stuff on him. He's an important man in banking circles, or so I understand. And he's also in the American tabloid press. His wife seems to be from an influential family. Her father is Sergio Santini, and her name is Janice. Her father is one of those self-made men that the Americans love so much. He was poor but worked hard to get an education. His career took off, and now he has a business empire and is as wealthy as Midas."

ed into the financial world as well?"

...d that he doesn't work for his father-in-law."

"He already had a good position when he met his wife. Perhaps he didn't want his father-in-law or his brother-in-law to be his boss."

Irene told Tommy what she'd found out concerning Thomas Bonetti and his earlier escapades on the London financial market. As she expected, Tommy was excited when she revealed the connection between Bonetti and Joachim Rothstaahl.

"It's like we had a sixth sense about it. The murders are connected!" he exclaimed.

Irene asked him to keep it down. Others were beginning to pay attention to their conversation. Even if it wasn't uncommon to hear police talk in the cafeteria, there's nothing like the word *murder* to make people prick up their ears.

Tommy lowered his voice. "It's clear that everyone involved knew everyone else for some time. We have to find out how exactly each and every person knew each and every other."

"We have to dig into the past. As usual." Irene sighed.

Tommy was interrupted by his cell phone vibrating in the pocket of his denim jacket. "Hi, Birgitta," he said.

Tommy listened for a while and then turned to Irene. He gave her the thumbs-up, and Irene knew what Birgitta must have found: the third victim was indeed Philip Bergman.

TOMMY AND IRENE arrived at the apartment, but only Elsy Kaegler was there. She was watching Ludwig while her daughter ran errands. Sanna had a lot of things to do, Elsy informed Irene. She had to contact the funeral home, which would be taking care of her husband's burial, for starters. Elsy didn't believe that Sanna would be back until later that afternoon. Irene asked Elsy to tell Sanna that she should expect a visit from the police later, at four thirty P.M.

• • •

SVANTE MALM, THE technician, had acquired at least a thousand new freckles during his vacation in Greece. Irene thought of her fair-haired husband Krister's freckles after their vacation in Crete a month earlier. He could have given Svante a run for his money. In her opinion, pinkish people shouldn't go tanning. They just ended up looking like boiled tomatoes. After some time, their skin peeled off, and they were just as pale as before. Irene had been telling her husband this for at least twenty years now, but it didn't change a thing. Krister burned every year. Svante, on the other hand, looked rested and rejuvenated, and he waved happily to Irene and Tommy when they slipped into the room and took a seat in the back. From the front row, Kajsa turned and smiled at them, but Irene didn't smile back. She knew Kajsa's smile wasn't meant for her.

Andersson cleared his throat. "I just want to say a few words before Svante takes over. The two victims have been identified as Joachim Rothstaahl, thirty-two, and Philip Bergman, thirty. Bergman's parents identified him earlier today. His father last saw him when he was heading off on Monday evening to meet with Rothstaahl. He also pointed out that his son was missing a brand new jacket and a briefcase. The jacket is made of light-colored leather. Bergman's car is also missing. He'd borrowed his father's car, a black Saab 93 Aero. Bergman doesn't live in Sweden any longer. According to his parents, he's been living in Paris. Honestly, why do all these guys have to live abroad? Can't they swindle people while living at home?"

There were widespread chuckles among his listeners. Svante Malm's horse-like face lit up in a smile. "Did you lose a lot of money when these so-called 'fund managers' speculated with your stocks?" he teased.

"Never had stocks and never going to get them, either," replied Andersson.

"Smart of you, but hindsight is twenty-twenty. It's tougher for those of us who are young enough to be in the new pension system. We had no choice in the matter, and that was our pension money that disappeared in tech and communications stocks. Not to mention that a great deal of the old pension system's stocks were transferred there as well. My brothers and sisters, our golden years are going to be rough."

"So you're going into politics?" Jonny asked sarcastically.

"Oh, no, but believe me, our pensions are blown."

"Stop bitching about your pension and start working for your wages instead," Jonny said.

Andersson looked irritated, but nodded in agreement.

"All right," Svante said. "So we have the double murder in Långedrag. I have some pictures to show you of the house and the surrounding area."

Svante turned on the projector and turned to face the photographs. As the screen still hadn't been fixed, he was projecting them directly onto the wall.

"The property is pretty remote, though not far from Käringberg Hill. The house is a summer cabin, which has been remodeled into a year-round, eighty-five-square-meter residence with three bedrooms. The car port was added later."

The house was built of wood and had been recently painted light blue with dark blue trim. It didn't seem all that large or special, but once Svante showed more photographs, Irene changed her mind. The property spanned an enormous natural area on a rocky hill, complete with an expansive ocean view.

"It had been raining hard beginning Monday night until Wednesday afternoon," Svante continued. "By the time the bodies were found on Wednesday, most potential clues had already been washed away. We've haven't been able to find any trace of a third car. Only two cars left tracks on the gravel driveway in front of the house."

Tommy raised his hand. "Were there any traces of the car Rothstaahl's father drove there?"

"No, because he rode there on his bike. His parents live only a kilometer away. Joachim inherited the house from his grandfather a few years ago. He repaired it and, according to his father, was planning an addition once he moved back to Sweden."

"So where was he living?"

"Paris," said Jonny.

Both Tommy and Irene reacted to this, but Irene was quickest. "So both Joachim Rothstaahl and Philip Bergman are . . . were living in Paris," she said.

"That's right."

"So why did they have to meet in Göteborg?"

Jonny had no answer and shrugged.

Svante changed to a close-up picture of a door handle. "This is the outer door, which was unlocked when Rothstaahl's father arrived on Wednesday. There is no sign that the lock had been broken. The patio door was locked by a bolt that could only be opened from the inside."

A series of photographs from the inside of the house followed. Svante flipped through them until he came to the kitchen.

"There was a bag with three bottles of red wine, one bag of French rolls, and two loaves of *pain riche* on the table. A packet of roast beef and a large bowl of potato salad were found in the refrigerator, as well as recently purchased brie and a package of margarine. In addition, there were four half-liter bottles of strong beer, one unopened liter of milk, and a small carton of eggs."

"Sounds like a romantic evening for two," Jonny said. "Were they lovers?"

Svante shrugged.

"That Rothstaahl guy was about to move in with his

girlfriend, so he couldn't have been . . . you know . . . that type," Andersson barked.

"You don't say!" Irene said so softly that only Tommy could hear her.

"Of course, we collected as much as we could as far as hair and fibers are concerned, but I'm pessimistic regarding those, since the house was really filthy. Right now, we can't say we have anything that is of the slightest use. Not even anything like the reflective ribbon out in Askim. We're working through the fingerprints now. The bullets are still in the bodies, so we don't have to look for them. On the other hand, I have a theory regarding how the killer did his work. I am assuming the murderer is a single person."

Svante turned off the projector and turned on the overhead. He placed a sketch of the house, which he'd drawn in red and black ink.

"When you enter the house, the kitchen is immediately to the right. If you go to the left, you come to the living room. Straight ahead in the hallway are two doors. One is to the bathroom, and the other is to the closet. I believe the killer was hiding in the closet. Alternatively, he could have entered through the house's outer door after Rothstaahl and Bergman had arrived, if they left the door unlocked. Though if that were the case, I believe the guys would have seen the killer through the kitchen window, and one of them would have gone into the hallway to meet the visitor."

Svante showed the next picture, which was taken from above and revealed the mess on the floor of the hall closet. In addition to the jumble of shoes, cushions for outdoor furniture, and exercise outfits, there was a dark blue terry-cloth belt that looked like it had been thrown on the floor, with half of it landing on the threshold.

"I noticed that the door was half open. It couldn't be shut because the belt was there. This could be because someone didn't *want* the door shut. Like if someone were standing inside the closet looking out. From here, it's only three steps to the kitchen where the victims were standing. The suspect probably surprised them. Rothstaahl probably didn't even have time to realize what was happening. I believe that Bergman turned around and tried to escape into the bedroom. He had just enough time to realize what was going on."

Svante's scenario was believable but also unpleasant. The two men didn't stand a chance. Although Andersson and Jonny joked about a "lady's gun," this killer knew exactly what he was doing.

The question was still *why*.

Svante Malm thanked them for their attention and left the room, saying he'd let them know if anything else turned up.

"I was talking to one of Rothstaahl's uncles this morning. He lives at the beginning of the turnoff to the house. It appears that Grandfather Rothstaahl bought a great deal of property out in the countryside in the early fifties. Wish my grandpa had done that," Jonny said, making a face.

"So what did Grandpa do? I mean his, not yours," Tommy asked.

"They were in the clothing business. Joachim's father and uncle took over the company, and they still sell clothing. Joachim didn't want to go into the family business. Anyway, the uncle says he saw Philip Bergman's car turn up the road at seven thirty, but then the car drove off a few minutes before eight, with Bergman at the wheel. He recognized the tan leather jacket."

The superintendent appeared to be thinking. "Maybe Bergman drove off to buy something they'd forgotten, and then he drove back. They were shot after. . . ."

One look from Jonny made Andersson fall silent. Jonny shook his head. "No. The uncle and his wife were sitting beside a huge picture window from seven thirty until ten that night.

They had a fire going in the fireplace and were listening to music. Bergman didn't return. They saw no other car between seven thirty and ten."

"Are there any other houses along that road?" asked Irene.

"No, just the uncle's at the head of the road and Joachim's at the end."

"So it's a cul-de-sac?"

"Right."

"What's the distance between the two houses?"

"About one hundred meters."

"Did they hear anything sounding like gunshots?"

"No."

Irene paused. "Just a thought . . . if they were sitting in front of the fireplace, perhaps they weren't able to see the entire road? And if they like to look at the ocean view, I doubt they were doing so last Monday night because it was raining."

"I was in their house this morning. The fireplace and their armchairs are in a glass-enclosed addition of the living room, so there are windows on three sides. The fireplace is in one corner and their armchairs face the ocean. The road runs fifteen meters below the house. If nothing else, they can hear whenever a car is coming. Though the uncle and his wife are both in their sixties, neither are deaf," Jonny said.

"But Philip Bergman couldn't have driven the car away, since it obviously didn't return. Philip was definitely murdered in his cabin, and the car is still gone," Tommy said.

"Philip wasn't the one driving the car away since it's gone," Irene said. "It must have been the suspect who leisurely drove away from the scene of the crime. He didn't just take the car. He got Philip's jacket, too. In the rain and darkness, Rothstaahl's uncle must have assumed that the person behind the wheel wearing the tan jacket was Philip."

"Highly probable," said Tommy.

"At any rate, we're closer to pinpointing the time of the

murder: sometime between seven thirty and eight P.M." Irene's colleagues were nodding.

Jonny's forehead furrowed. "But then why didn't the uncle and his wife hear the shots? There were four. Could they have been playing music so loudly that they wouldn't have heard them?"

"The suspect used a silencer," Tommy said.

"Why do you think so?" asked Andersson.

"No one heard the shots in Askim either. Why risk someone hearing shots? A silencer on a fine-caliber pistol using unjacketed bullets, which were seriously deformed. Accurate shots for fatal results. We've got a guy who's a professional," Tommy said.

Irene was inclined to agree with him. "A high-caliber weapon is heavy and needs a holster to keep hidden. People often still notice it because of unusual bulges in clothing. A fine-caliber weapon is easier to conceal beneath clothing."

"So what did Philip Bergman have in his briefcase that the suspect wanted?" asked Kajsa.

This was an important question that they all had lost track of. Jonny glared at Kajsa, mostly because he didn't have a good answer. "No idea," he finally said.

"And Irene brought up a good question," Kajsa went on. "Why did they have to meet in Göteborg when both of them were living in Paris?"

"We should figure that out," Tommy said.

"How has your research on that dot-com company been going?" Andersson asked Kajsa encouragingly.

"It's moving right along, thanks," she said. "I'm meeting a journalist tomorrow who is writing a book about the dot-com crash. He's written a chapter on ph.com, and I'm hoping he can give me some good information."

IRENE SAW HER opportunity to jump in and share the results of her investigative efforts with Tommy. "Bonetti and

Rothstaahl ran shady business deals together in London," she began. "There's another dark horse, namely the Norwegian Erik Dahl. We'll have to follow up. Philip Bergman, Sanna Kaegler, and Thomas Bonetti founded ph.com, and ran it until it went bankrupt. The Fenton brothers and their old pal Kjell B:son Ceder were all on the sailboat when Ceder's first wife died. One year ago, Ceder married Sanna Kaegler in a surprise wedding. And now it appears that Philip Bergman and Joachim Rothstaahl were planning a new scheme. Where in this spider web of relationships do these three murders fit?" Irene asked her colleagues.

"Perhaps four murders," Tommy said.

"What? Four?" the superintendent exclaimed.

"Don't forget Bonetti. There hasn't been a sign of life from him for three years. Perhaps he's been killed."

Birgitta, usually silent, now asked for the floor. "Maybe we ought to investigate Bergman and Rothstaahl's apartment. The one in Paris."

"Paris! That's out of the question," Andersson said.

"How else will we find out what they've been up to?" asked Birgitta.

"We should send a request to the authorities. . . ." Andersson said half-heartedly.

"Perhaps, but it would be a long time before we'd get an answer. From what we've heard about these gentlemen already, I hardly believe the authorities have any idea what they're up against. If our friends had just begun to plan their project, there should be information on their computers. Have you already looked at them?" Birgitta aimed her question at Jonny, but Fredrik Stridh replied.

"No—since there weren't any computers in the house. There was a printer with a bunch of cables on the desk in the bedroom, but there wasn't a single computer."

"These aren't the kind of guys to have desktop computers.

They'd have laptops, so they could work from hotel rooms and airplanes," Birgitta said.

"I believe we have the answer as to what was in the briefcase that the killer took with him," Irene said. "Bergman and Rothstaahl's laptops."

"Perhaps there's something backed up in their Paris apartment," Birgitta said.

"Can you stop going on and on about Paris already?" Andersson growled. "Keep talking to Bergman's parents. Perhaps they know what our guys were up to. Find out how much money they stashed in various places. That goes for everyone involved—check finances. Irene and Tommy, I want you to go have another chat with Sanna Kaegler-Ceder. See how she reacts to the deaths of Bergman and Rothstaahl. Jonny and Fredrik, keep following up with Rothstaahl's parents, neighbors, other relatives. . . ." Andersson fell silent for a moment and then exclaimed, "I knew I was forgetting someone! Kajsa, keep finding out whatever you can on that computer company where all that money disappeared."

"Internet company. It's called ph.com." Kajsa sighed.

Andersson pretended he hadn't heard her correction.

SANNA KAEGLER-CEDER HAD put on discreet makeup and appeared much more energetic than the day before. Her freshly washed blonde hair flowed over her shoulders and shone in the light of the art nouveau ceiling lamp. She let in the detectives and led them into the library. The scent of citrus and jasmine followed in her wake. Irene noticed Sanna's black leather suit with its mid-length jacket cut, and her diamond cross necklace hanging in its familiar place.

The evening sun filtered through the dirty windows and lit up the dancing dust particles floating in the air. It made Irene think of a generous fairy shaking magic dust from the tip of her wand and watching it drift down to settle on the polished side table. She didn't know if it was an old memory of the *Sleeping Beauty* film or the heavy odor of old books that reminded her of fairy tales.

Sanna would definitely be the princess in a modern success story. She was young, beautiful, and rich. Her prince, however, didn't fit the part. Kjell B:son Ceder was rich enough, but he certainly wasn't young, and he certainly was not the father of crown prince Ludwig.

Following Sanna's invitation, the detectives sat down on the sofa while she sat in one of the armchairs. Her hair, backlit by the window, glimmered like a halo, but her face was in shadows, hiding her expressions and giving her the upper hand. Irene suspected that was why she offered the sofa to them. Sanna sat quietly, waiting for their questions.

"When will you be moving back to the house in Askim?" Tommy began.

"On Saturday. The house will be cleaned tomorrow, and the alarm system should be functional by then."

"Our technicians mentioned that the alarm system was not on the evening your husband was murdered."

"No, Mike—that is, Michael Fuller, the head of security at Hotel Göteborg—is going to help me with the alarm system. That's his specialty."

Tommy nodded and continued in his same relaxed tone. "I would like to know if you've heard from your former partner Thomas Bonetti since his disappearance."

Sanna stiffened. She hadn't been expecting that question. Her voice was tense after she took a moment before answering.

"No. He just . . . disappeared. Why do you want to know?"

"Do you have any idea why he disappeared?"

This answer came more quickly. "No idea. We haven't been in contact at all since ph.com went bankrupt in April 2000."

"Why not?"

"We . . . didn't part friends. Philip and I were trying to talk to him. He didn't agree with our goal of finishing the website and arranging all local offices to work for the company's IPO. We were working like slaves twenty-four-seven! Thomas was in charge of our finances, but he never understood you have to risk it all to win it all. We were aiming to be a global company. His goal was to get ph.com listed on the stock market and grab as much money as possible before getting out."

Her voice was filled with hate by the time she finished. It was obvious she didn't think highly of her former partner.

"So he took out a lot of money before the bankruptcy?"

"That's right."

"How much?"

Sanna shrugged her shoulders. "I really don't know for sure. We bought him out for five million, but we also know that he moved money from ph.com to a bank account he'd set up somewhere. We reported it to the police later. I really don't know exactly how much money it was."

"Do you have any kind of estimate?"

"Perhaps five or six million."

This meant that Bonetti had had at least 10 million kroner at his disposal when he disappeared, not 5 million as the police had estimated. Was Sanna correct? That was a lot more money.

"Is it possible that he may have taken even more?" asked Irene.

"Yes, we suspected he took more. Maybe as much as 2 million American dollars."

"Did you and Philip Bergman get together after the company went bankrupt?"

"Yes, but not so often. He was still living in London, and now he's moved to Paris."

"When was the last time you saw each other?" asked Irene.

"Actually, it was in London two years ago."

"Have you kept in touch some other way?"

"By email. He sent a card when we got married and when Ludwig was born."

"Do you know what Philip was doing in Paris?"

"Doing?" Sanna repeated.

"What he was working on."

"Business. He was a very good businessman."

"Do you know what kind of business?"

"He was the manager of mutual funds."

"Which firm was he working for?"

"He had a company with another guy," said Sanna.

"Do you know what its name was?"

"I've probably heard it mentioned . . . Euro Finance or something like that."

A bell went off in Irene's brain. "What was the other guy's name?"

"Joachim Rothstaahl."

"Do you know Joachim Rothstaahl?"

"Not so well. We met a few times in London."

Although Irene was expecting this, she felt it difficult to control her emotions. It certainly must have shown in her face.

Joachim Rothstaahl had run a fund management company with Thomas Bonetti, and now it appeared that Bonetti's former and new partners had gotten together to start their own similar company. Was this new company also a pyramid scheme? Were things getting too hot for Bergman and Rothstaahl in London? Was that why they had to move to Paris?

It seemed as if Sanna were reading her thoughts when she asked sharply, "Why are you asking all this about Thomas and Philip?"

Instead of answering Sanna's question, Tommy asked a new one. "So, besides email and a few cards, you haven't heard anything else from Philip Bergman?"

"No, not more than that."

"Did you know he was planning to return home to Göteborg last weekend?"

"No. Did he?" The surprise in her voice seemed genuine.

"I'm afraid you must prepare yourself for some bad news," Tommy said in a calm manner.

Her princess face hardened, but Sanna did not say a word.

"Both Philip Bergman and Joachim Rothstaahl have been found dead. They were shot—murdered. I am very sorry for the loss of your friends," Tommy said with true compassion.

Sanna did not move at all. Irene heard a soft, gurgling sound and realized that Sanna was trying to say something. Slowly, she stood up while gripping the armrests of her chair. A despairing whimper came from her throat and rose to a heart-rending wail. "Noooo! Not Philip! Not Phil. . . ."

This time Irene was able to catch her before Sanna fell to the floor.

"SO SHE FAINTED again," Andersson said.

Tommy nodded. "Yep. It seems she does whenever her emotions are too strong. At least, that's what her mother says. Her blood pressure is too low. Though I think the reverse should be true."

Irene shuddered as she remembered the tumult. Elsy hadn't made things better by running in circles, wringing her hands. Finally, she decided to call the doctor who'd prescribed the tranquilizers before. The doctor had his private practice a few doors down and arrived within ten minutes. It felt freeing to hand over all responsibility to him. Sanna had shown signs of coming to but would surely faint again if she tried to stand up.

"She fainted in Askim as well," Irene said. "But I have the feeling that it was due to the fact that Kjell B:son Ceder was in *her* house."

Tommy nodded. "I remember her saying that the house was sullied."

"But she had a real shock when she heard that Rothstaahl and Bergman were dead," said Irene.

"I believe it was mostly Bergman's death that affected her. She didn't know Rothstaahl all that well."

"We have to take everything that lady says with a grain of salt," Irene said. "And I believe we should have a DNA test run on the two gentlemen in the morgue. Perhaps little Ludwig truly is fatherless."

"Do you think that either of them could be the boy's father?" asked Tommy.

"Who knows? At the moment only Sanna knows who the father is. Perhaps the father knows as well, but that might not be the case. Everyone assumed that Ceder was the father."

"But both Sanna and Ceder knew he wasn't. So why did Ceder decide to take on some other guy's kid?" asked Andersson stubbornly.

"We'll have to ask Sanna when the time is right," Tommy said.

"There's a lot of questions that woman has to answer." Andersson stood up and rubbed the bags under his eyes. He looked old and worn out. *Why does he stay on the force?* Irene asked herself and then answered her own question. *Because the force is his life.*

"Well, I think it's time to call it a day," Andersson said. "See you at morning prayer tomorrow."

Andersson walked over to the door and took his threadbare coat from the hook.

Chapter 6

"BERGMAN'S CAR WAS found in Saltholmen," Andersson said when they gathered the next day for morning prayer. "It was found parked in a meadow that is used as overflow area for long-term parking during the summer months. The technicians are looking it over now." Andersson paused. "There wasn't any leather jacket or briefcase in the car."

"Saltholmen is where the ferry boats to the archipelago leave. Also the ferries to Styrsö Island," Irene pointed out.

"You thinking about that Bonetti guy?" Andersson asked.

"Yes, I am," Irene said.

"So you think there's something fishy about the Bonetti case."

"Absolutely. There are connections between our murders and Bonetti's disappearance. We weren't able to get anywhere the first time we investigated. I'd like to take a second look at the material we collected in that case. We know more now, and maybe I'll see something that didn't seem important at the time. And, with what happened to Bergman and Rothstaahl, I believe we can view the Bonetti case as a homicide and not a case of a missing person. At least unofficially for the time being."

"Let's not jump to any conclusions here. Damn it all, we already have three official cases of homicide on our hands! Bonetti was wanted for financial crimes, and you yourself said he had sticky fingers, so the guy certainly had enough reasons to disappear."

Andersson's face was turning red, and he was drumming his fingers on the table in irritation. He knew he had to let her follow her instincts, though; they'd proven right in more than one past investigation. A true homicide detective had experience, intuition, and stubbornness, and Irene had all three.

"All right. You can spend the day on the Bonetti case," he said glumly.

Irene nodded without showing an ounce of triumph. She knew very well that she could be heading down a dead end and a whole day's worth of work would have been wasted. On the other hand, there was nothing unusual in digging into a related cold case. Often something that seemed unimportant at the time would show its absolute importance after further facts had been brought to bear.

"Tommy, you've been questioning Sanna Kaegler-Ceder," continued Andersson. "I want you to lean on her a bit. She must know a great deal more than she's willing to admit. She knew all of the victims to some degree. And, like I mentioned yesterday, check the Kaegler-Ceder's finances. Money is always a strong motive for murder."

The superintendent looked over his team. Kajsa was missing. She had already left for her meeting with the online journalist, but she'd said she'd be back by the afternoon meeting. Birgitta was also absent, since Philip Bergman's parents had requested that she come over at eight A.M. They wanted to leave town and travel to their summer cabin to avoid the stream of reporters. Last night's headlines had been huge. TWO WELL-KNOWN FINANCIERS KILLED! and GOLDEN CALF MURDERED!

Kajsa had mentioned to Irene that the press often called Philip Bergman "the Golden Calf." His name came from his phenomenal ability to attract investors without needing to lift a finger. Everyone had fought to have the chance to dance around the Golden Calf.

Andersson stood up. "OK, gang, let's get going." He turned in the doorway, "I'm in some stupid meeting this morning, but you can reach me after lunch."

Andersson did not look particularly pleased as he made this announcement. He despised meetings. No matter what the proposed topic of the meeting was, they all boiled down to the same thing: trimming expenses and ruining a well-functioning organization. He'd been a policeman now for more than forty years and everything had been better before, if you asked him.

Irene started by skimming through the witness reports from Långedrag's small harbor one more time. Three men and two teenagers had seen the same thing at eight P.M.: Thomas Bonetti speeding into the parking lot in his BMW. He'd parked and taken two duffel bags out of the trunk. One of the men remembered that Bonetti had been speaking on his cell phone as he'd gotten out of the car. The police were not able to trace the call. Grumbling loudly, Bonetti had lugged the bags to his boat. All of the witnesses had the impression that the larger bag had been extremely heavy. Once he'd lifted the duffel bags onto the boat, he got on board, started the motor, and cast off. The five witnesses had watched the boat until it disappeared out to sea.

Nothing in the five witness reports gave Irene anything more to go on. Too bad they hadn't been able to trace the cell call.

The interviews with Bonetti's parents hadn't given them much, either. He'd only told them that he needed some peace and quiet to think things over. Neither of them had any idea what it was that Bonetti had to think over. At one point, Irene felt Antonio Bonetti was using an imperial tone when he'd said, "Thomas is involved with global business. In that realm, you can't talk about what you're working on. All great businessmen learn this fairly quickly. You only leak the information that you deliberately want to come out, and you make it seem as if it was given in extreme confidence. Since he didn't tell us what he was up to, there was certainly something important going on."

Well, getting ready to disappear off the face of the earth could certainly be classified as important, Irene thought sarcastically. *And a great businessman?* As far as she was concerned, he was a swindler. She stopped her train of thought. *Didn't Sanna also say that Philip Bergman was a great businessman? Did they actually take themselves for serious men of business?*

There was one last witness. The same day that the police had made the disappearance known to the public, a woman had dialed 112 and reported that she wanted to speak to someone involved in the investigation. She had talked to an investigator Irene only knew by name. At the end of his report, he'd written his own comment: "The witness is slurring her words and is obviously intoxicated. Promised to contact her if we believe it will help the investigation."

Nowhere in the material was any indication that the woman's report had been followed up on.

Her name was Annika Hermansson. She was the nearest neighbor of the Bonetti summer cabin and recognized the boat as well as the sound of its motor. According to her report, the boat had passed her house at eight thirty P.M. and was tied up at the Bonetti dock. Ten minutes later, it started again, which surprised her and made her curious, so she decided to take a closer look using her telescope. The boat had gone behind Branteskär, and he must have tied it up there, because she didn't see him come out the other side. According to her report, she'd waited for hours to see him come out. When nothing happened, she got bored and went to bed. When she woke up later, she saw that Nisse's Cairn, a cairn of stones nearby, had been moved. According to her, the police really must investigate why the cairn had been shifted. It could be a sea hazard.

The detective had written in his report, "Branteskär is marked on the sea chart and is 2.5 kilometers from the witness's residence on Styresö Island. Considering the late hour, the distance, and the darkness, there is no possibility that the witness could have seen anything through a telescope."

Irene agreed with her colleague, but at the same time, this was the only report from a witness that had not been checked. She picked up the phone and dialed the number that Annika Hermansson had left three years earlier.

THERE WERE ABOUT thirty passengers on the lunchtime ferry to the islands in the southern archipelago. Most of them were mothers of young children and retirees who'd been shopping in town. The sun was shining through sparse clouds, and the tops of the waves glittered. Seagulls hovered near the boat's hull, perhaps in hopes that it was a fishing boat. After a pleasant half-hour journey, Irene could see the settlement of Styresö Bratten.

The contrast from her earlier visit was remarkable. A light breeze drifted through the crowns of the birch trees, giving off the scent of summer despite the fact that one or two golden leaves had already appeared. Irene looked at the ferry thermometer and unbuttoned her coat. It was almost twenty-one degrees Celcius, which was quite nice for the middle of September.

Irene walked the same way she'd gone with Tommy on that windy, cold December day more than three years ago. The address she'd gotten from Annika Hermansson led her to the house with the lovely glass veranda that she remembered from her first visit. The glass was mullioned with small, colored windowpanes in red and green. The large, wooden house resembled many of the other houses on the island; it had presumably been built at the turn of the previous century as a summer home for a wealthy Göteborg family. As Irene came closer, she saw that the old house was beginning to look dilapidated. The yellow paint was coming off the walls in strips, and the paint around the windows was almost gone. The beautiful downspouts with dragonheads were nearly rusted through, and the grass of the tiny lawn was almost knee-high. A swath of honeysuckle from the overgrown garden wrapped itself around one of the downspouts.

Irene knocked on the cracked door. After a moment, she heard a husky voice yell, "Come on in, the door's open!"

Irene entered the house and was immediately struck by the odor of the dirty house: cigarette smoke, old wine, and rancid cat food.

"Hello!" Irene called out.

"Hello there! I'm in the kitchen!" a raspy female voice replied.

Irene stepped over the junk that littered the narrow hallway and aimed her feet in the direction of the voice.

The kitchen was large and light. The sun shone through the southern window. It would never be too sunny, though, because it would have to first make its way through a thick layer of salt and dirt. *External blinds, how practical*, Irene thought. The kitchen décor was from the seventies: all pine paneling, the stove and the refrigerator an avocado green. The smell in the kitchen was nauseating, and Irene was thankful she hadn't stopped for lunch before this visit.

The woman was sitting at the table, scratching behind the ear of the black cat on her lap. It was purring so loudly the sound filled the kitchen. Both the cat and the mistress looked up when Irene entered the room.

"Hi, I'm Irene Huss. I'm the detective who called you earlier this morning. Are you Annika Hermansson?"

The woman nodded.

"I'd like to speak to you about the disappearance of Thomas Bonetti. You had called—"

"It's about time! I called over and over again, but nobody cared. Apparently it takes years for the police to come out and take a look unless people are telling lies about you. Then you come right. . . ."

The woman stopped and mumbled something to herself. There was a wine glass on the table, half full, and she took a long drink. "You want anything?" she asked, gesturing at the wine box placed on the kitchen counter.

"No, thank you, I'm on duty," Irene replied as she forced herself to smile.

Nothing about Annika Hermansson made Irene want to smile any wider. The woman's hair was dyed black, and a few inches of gray had already grown back in. Her face was slack and doughy and showed obvious signs of long-term alcoholism. Her stomach beneath her dirty T-shirt was a big, round ball, but she had the thin arms and legs of an anorexic. She reminded Irene of a spider. It was difficult to tell how old Annika Hermansson was, but Irene guessed about fifty.

"Well, well, that's all right. There's not much left in the box. Billy will be here soon with a new one," Annika muttered.

"Who's Billy?" Irene asked the drunken woman, mostly so she could start a conversation.

"My son."

Irene lifted old newspapers and other scraps from a stool so she could sit down. Angry with the disturbance, the cat hissed at her and jumped to the floor.

With great difficulty, the spider woman got up and walked over to fill her glass from the wine box. As she shuffled back to her place, she spilled some wine on the floor but didn't bother wiping it up. Breathing heavily, she groaned as she made herself comfortable again.

"What happened that September evening three years ago?" Irene asked.

"I heard that monster of a speed boat coming and thought

it was odd so late at night and at that time of the year. Those Bonettis never come after September. The boat was their son's. I've never liked that guy. Always boasting and lying. He's five years older than Billy, but none of the other kids ever wanted to play with him. Not even Billy, for that matter."

She fell silent long enough to drink a disturbing amount of wine in a single swallow. To help keep track of the conversation, Irene said slowly, "So he wasn't popular in his circle of friends."

"Friends? Ha! That boy had no friends."

Annika's laugh was raw. Irene glimpsed teeth that were in desperate need of a dentist, if they could be saved at all. They reminded Irene of the blackened remains of a garden shed she'd seen burned down years ago.

"How long have the Bonettis owned their summer cabin?" asked Irene.

"A long time. Long before Thomas was born. His sister was a baby when they moved here. I wanted to babysit her, but they wouldn't let me. I was just eight-years-old, but I still knew how to take care of an infant. I had two little brothers."

Irene felt liked she'd been dunked in cold water. Thomas Bonetti's sister was thirty-five, which meant that Annika had to be just a year or two older than Irene herself. Since Billy was around twenty-eight, Annika had to have been sixteen when she'd had her son.

"Do you have any other children besides Billy?"

"Nah, he's the only one. He was enough for me." Again Annika broke into her hoarse laugh. She dug through the clutter on her table, and with a triumphant cry she pulled out a wrinkled cigarette pack. With shaking fingers, she pulled out a long though rather crumpled stub and stuck it between her chapped lips with a sigh of contentment. Her red-rimmed eyes met Irene's. "Do you have a light?"

Irene shook her head. After another round of digging, Annika found a box of matches. She managed to light the cigarette butt after a few attempts and inhaled deeply before releasing the smoke through her nose.

"I never told anyone who Billy's father was. Nobody needs to know. But his father has paid up all this time. Even now. Just so I never tell. . . ."

She broke off in the middle of her sentence, and glared at Irene malevolently through the smoke, causing the doughy bags under her eyes to tighten.

Time to return to the subject at hand. "So that evening when Thomas disappeared, you heard his boat going past outside?"

"Yes, as I said, it was odd because—"

"What time was it?"

"Sometime between eight and eight thirty in the evening. Don't really remember."

"How can you be so certain of the time?"

Annika pointed at the opposite wall. Irene turned and saw a large kitchen clock made of pine.

"Billy made it in woodshop. It runs on a battery," Annika explained with obvious pride.

"Tell me everything that happened. You heard the boat going past and. . . ."

Irene nodded encouragingly so that the woman on the other side of the table would continue.

"He killed the motor and tied up at their dock. Nothing strange about that, but then he started up the motor again and sped off."

"How long did he stay before he took off again?"

"Fifteen minutes at the most. More likely ten minutes."

"So you heard him start the motor again, but you couldn't see it?"

"Nah, their dock is on the other side of the spit. But I saw the boat again once it headed back to sea."

"What did you do then?"

"Went up to my telescope."

"So you went up to get your telescope. . . ."

"Didn't you hear me? I went up to my telescope! I didn't *get* anything!"

Irene paused, unsure of how to continue. Annika sounded aggressive, and she was already drunk enough to become enraged. If that happened, there would be no chance to get a suitable testimony from her.

"Do you have a special kind of telescope?" Irene asked, making a tentative effort.

"A special telescope? You bet your ass I do!" A coarse laugh crossed the table along with the smell of sour wine.

"How could you see anything? It was dark."

Annika rose to her unsteady feet. "Let me show you."

She wobbled across the kitchen floor, through the cluttered hallway, and toward the foot of the stairs leading to the second floor. With a solid grip on the handrail, Annika managed to heave herself up the creaking stairs.

The stairwell opened into a large room. Directly ahead there was a balcony window facing the ocean. On the balcony was an enormous telescope.

"A Swarovski with fluorite lenses," Annika said proudly.

Irene didn't know much about telescopes, but she knew enough to recognize that this was an advanced model. An eyepiece was placed above the tube at a forty-five-degree angle. She took off the lens cap and aimed the telescope at a small motorboat that was puffing along on the water. The passengers were just red and blue pricks. When Irene looked through the telescope, she was taken aback.

The man had a mustache and glasses. The woman was wearing a red jacket and handkerchief, and a few wisps of her gray hair fluttered in the breeze. The couple seemed to be in their seventies. They were talking to each other, and the woman handed a steel thermos to the man.

When Irene looked back out to sea without the telescope, all she could see was a tiny boat and two spots of color.

"Good heavens, this is some telescope," she said.

"Yes, indeed! The twilight factor is sixteen point zero at twenty times magnification," Annika clucked contentedly. This meant that as long as there was any bit of twilight left, you could see anything you wanted from this telescope. And out here in the archipelago, twilight lasted longer than in the city.

Irene stepped aside. "Would you please focus this on Branteskär?" she asked.

Annika bent down and adjusted her telescope. "There. I've focused it on Nisse's Cairn."

"Thanks."

Irene could see a tiny island with steep sides heading straight down to the water. Farthest out on one edge of the island, she could see the top of a pile of stones.

"Are those stones on the other side of the island from our perspective?" Irene asked.

"That's right."

"Why is it called Nisse's Cairn?"

"Because Nisse was the guy who made it. He'd run his boat right onto the rocks between Branteskär and Ärskär. So he built the cairn so that the rocks would be easier to avoid. Now the cairn has been moved. I've told you guys at the police station over and over that it's been moved, but would you listen?"

"When did you notice that the cairn had been moved?"

"Right then! When Thomas disappeared. I noticed it just a day or two later. I didn't think much about it at the time, but when . . . they said he'd gone missing . . . then I remembered that someone had moved the cairn." Annika wavered and then sat down in a worn out sofa. She burped loudly and yawned. She slowly lifted her legs onto the sofa so she could lie down. Less than a minute later, she started to snore.

• • •

"I'LL BE DAMNED!" Andersson said.

He looked at Irene with respect. Not bad to find a new piece of evidence after three years.

"So, have you thought about how you will proceed now that you have this drunk's testimony?" he asked.

"I believe we should take a closer look at Nisse's Cairn. According to Annika Hermansson, it was moved around the time of Thomas Bonetti's disappearance. And, according to her, she saw his boat go behind Branteskär, but she didn't see him leave the island again," Irene said.

"So you think his boat is buried beneath the rocks?" Jonny Blom said, grinning.

"No, but I believe Thomas is," Irene said.

There was a moment of silence.

"That's what you believe," Andersson said at last.

"It's clearly possible. I believe Annika about the cairn having been moved. Even though her entire house is a pile of garbage, she has that telescope, which must have cost a pretty penny. Åhlén believes it must have been at least fifteen thousand kroner. My guess is she hardly ever leaves her house, and the telescope is her only contact to the outside world. I am positive she knows each and every contour of the islands she can see through her telescope," Irene said.

"So," Andersson said with a sigh, "you want us to check beneath the cairn."

"That's right."

Andersson's forehead wrinkled. "All right, then. It'll be done. I'll give the boys at the sea police a call and tell them to bring some technicians with them to that island."

"It's called Branteskär," Irene said.

The superintendent pretended not to hear her. Instead, he turned toward Tommy. "What has Her Highness Lady Ceder said today?"

"Nothing."

"Nothing at all?"

"Nope. She moved back into her Askim house today. She's gotten a doctor's order that she is supposed to rest for the next few days. Her mother says she's refusing to talk to anyone resembling a journalist, but she can hardly refuse to talk to us—she's just delaying the inevitable by getting that doctor's order. I'll be able to have a chat with her on Tuesday at the latest," Tommy said.

"That damned woman! We ought to bring her in and grill her," grumbled Andersson.

"She's a smart one, but perhaps not as smart as she thinks she is. I've gone through the Kaegler-Ceder finances. Sanna's millions have disappeared at a rapid rate. Last year her taxed income in Sweden was fifty-two thousand kroner, and her savings are two hundred and nineteen thousand. Unfortunately, I haven't been able to tell if she has money in other countries, but at least here in Sweden, her fortune is running out."

"Did she use it up by building the Askim house?" Birgitta asked.

"Not likely. I called the state property assessment office, and the property in Askim has been owned by Kjell B:son Ceder for years. He'd inherited it from his first wife. He'd kept it as the value rose over the years."

"And then he let Sanna have it," Birgitta said.

"Right, though Ceder's company built the house. His restaurant and hotel are also owned by his company, which is called K B:son Ceder AB. One interesting point: his company's tax declaration also shows that the company is on the brink."

"On the brink?" echoed Andersson.

"It's lost an incredible amount of money. From what I understand, it's lost so much money that it's about to go bankrupt."

"And yet Sanna has been able to decorate her home in her

expensive taste without anyone complaining about the cost. Isn't that interesting?" Irene said.

"Well, maybe that's what Ceder did: complain. We know that they met on the Saturday before he was shot. Perhaps they discussed house expenses as well as the company's bankruptcy," suggested Tommy.

"According to the restaurant employees, they weren't arguing," Birgitta said.

"Maybe not, but remember, the employees work for Ceder. Perhaps they're worried about losing their jobs. Who will be inheriting the company now that Ceder is dead? Sanna, of course."

Birgitta shook her head. "I was the one who talked to the employees. The head of security, Michael Fuller, saw the Kaegler-Ceders in the dining room, and he insists that they weren't arguing. Also, the maître d' and the waitress at their table, as well as another server, have given similar testimony. I would have noticed if there was something wrong about their statements."

"This doesn't mean that they weren't talking about her house and the bad financial situation the company was in. Perhaps they'd already stopped arguing about the fact that the money wasn't there. Perhaps they were trying to figure out what they could still save."

"Stop speculating and go talk to Her Highness," Andersson barked. "Ask her a direct question. Damn it all, it's time that woman started giving us some real information!"

"She's a tough nut to crack," Tommy said. He looked defeated.

"So? You've been talking to her. Don't give up. She knows much more than she's letting on." Andersson turned to Birgitta. "So, what have you found out about Philip Bergman?"

"I've talked to his parents. They're completely overcome with grief. It was not easy to talk to them. Philip was their only child. I learned that Philip had been living abroad for years. First in London and then two years in Paris. I asked them why he'd moved to Paris, but they didn't have an answer. All they could say was 'business' and 'bank consulting.' They're impressed by his cleverness and very proud of his success as a businessman."

"Businessman!" Andersson snorted. "He just used other people's money and made it disappear."

"You have a point. I was thinking about why he decided to go into business with Joachim Rothstaahl. My instincts tell me they were up to something shady."

"Did you find anything at the Bergman house?"

"No. His boyhood bedroom hadn't been changed since he'd left home. I was allowed to search through his room, but there wasn't much there to begin with. His father told me that Philip had packed a large duffle bag and told them he wouldn't be home that night. He'd asked to borrow his father's car. All he said was that he was going to Joachim's place, but he did not mention meeting a third person. There was no computer in the room, nor any papers. Not a single lead. According to his parents, he'd booked a flight back to Paris for Wednesday. So anything of interest is going to be in Paris."

"Paris!" Andersson muttered.

Birgitta ignored him and continued, "Philip had almost no resources in Sweden. He was still a Swedish citizen. I found an old complaint from bankruptcy court. He hadn't bothered to pay off a car loan. That was right before he moved to London."

"What do his parents do?" asked Irene.

"His father is an optician, and his mother is a nurse. They live in a townhouse in Tuve. Philip grew up there."

"Sorry for interrupting," Kajsa said, "but Sanna's mother moved to Tuve after her divorce. Philip and Sanna met each other in secondary school."

Andersson looked at Kajsa in surprise before he

remembered he'd given her special duties. "You can tell us more about those two crazies after we're done with Rothstaahl," he said.

Kajsa nodded politely.

The superintendent turned to Birgitta. "Anything else?"

"No. He probably took everything that would be of interest to us in that duffle bag, including his laptop. I still think that we should go to Paris as soon as possible to secure any papers or discs. Perhaps he even had a computer in his Paris apartment."

Fredrik Stridh spoke up. "I agree with Birgitta. We haven't found a thing that would give us any insight into what Joachim Rothstaahl was up to. There isn't a single clue in his house. Probably the killer took everything with him. Maybe the killer is headed for Paris, too. Joachim lived at—" Fredrik looked down and began to spell out an address from his notebook— "Boulevard R-a-s-p-a-i-l."

Birgitta gave a shout. "Bergman has the same address! He's at 207."

"Bingo! So is Rothstaahl," Fredrik said.

Both Birgitta and Fredrik turned toward Andersson. His glum face had acquired more worry lines.

"No," he said. "It costs too much to go to Paris just to look at an apartment. We can ask our French colleagues for help."

"We can?" said Birgitta. "We have two Swedish citizens who were killed on Swedish soil. It just so happens that they both live in Paris, but I hardly believe our French colleagues are interested in getting tied up in this investigation."

Andersson glared at her. She turned away from him pointedly and looked at Fredrik before she asked, "What else do you have on Rothstaahl?"

"The first thing I found out was that the rumor that Rothstaahl was going to move in with his girlfriend is wrong. The woman in question is an old friend from Vänersborg who has a new job in Göteborg. She was going to sublet his house for at least a year. She was planning to get the keys from him and sign the lease on Tuesday because she knew he was returning to Paris on Wednesday," Fredrik said.

"So he was returning on the same day that Philip was," Birgitta said. "Why did they have to meet in Göteborg? They're neighbors in Paris!"

"Exactly. Did Bergman's parents give a reason for his homecoming?" asked Tommy.

"Just that he'd come home to see them and to meet some old friends."

"Which he didn't. He met the friend he sees daily in Paris," Irene stated.

Fredrik nodded. "And Joachim Rothstaahl came home to get his house ready to rent. Both Bergman and Rothstaahl arrived on the same plane Friday night. On Saturday, Rothstaahl was at his house but ate dinner with his parents that evening. On Sunday, the entire Rothstaahl family met at Rothstaahl's aunt and uncle's place. According to his parents, he went right home to his house once they left. That was the last time they saw him. His mother had a short phone call with him on Monday during lunchtime. He seemed fine. The family is in shock and has no idea why anyone would want to murder Joachim. They own a number of clothing boutiques all over the country, but Joachim was not involved in the family business."

Irene took a closer look at the enlarged photograph of Joachim Rothstaahl, which had been pinned to the bulletin board. It was his most recent passport picture. Joachim had a narrow face dominated by dark brown eyes. There was a friendly glint to them. There was also a vague smile on his thin lips. His thick brown hair had been combed back from his high forehead. The living, sympathetic young man looked down at Irene from the wall. Next to it was the photo from the crime scene. It was almost impossible to recognize Joachim Roth-staahl in that photo.

"They own the Zazza and Escada boutiques," Birgitta said.

"Oh my, they must be very wealthy. Those are big chains," Irene said. She had bought a couple pieces of clothing from Escada. Zazza's clothes were more in line with her daughters' taste.

"I've been going through Rothstaahl's background and finances as well," said Jonny. He waited until everyone was ready to pay attention. "Joachim returned to Sweden after the crash in London. He was unemployed for six months until he found a job at a bank here in the city. Going back through his finances, they appear ordinary. He lived in his house without needing to pay rent. Two years ago, he got a job at a foreign bank and moved to Paris."

"A French bank?" asked Irene.

"No, an American one. It's called HP Johnson. And—what's the matter now?" Jonny stopped when he saw Irene's face.

"HP Johnson is the bank where Edward Fenton is the European Head!"

"So?" Jonny's expression didn't change.

"HP Johnson is an investment bank. Kjell B:son Ceder, Sanna Kaegler, Philip Bergman, and now Joachim Rothstaahl have all been connected to this bank. Perhaps Thomas Bonetti was, too, when he was in London. That should be easy enough to find out," Irene said enthusiastically.

"What is the difference between an investment bank and a normal bank?" asked the superintendent.

Kajsa cleared her throat nervously. "An investment bank holds risky capital and places it in investments where they believe the highest return can be found. It can be enormously profitable. I can tell you that in 1990, risk capital investment banks in the United States were holding $3.5 billion. By the turn of the millennium, they had $104 billion."

"And what is risky capital?" Andersson asked with irritation.

Kajsa thought a moment before she said, "It's like money you have versus money you need. You're able to play with it. You can take big risks. Easy come, easy go."

Andersson nodded. "So what else have you found out about Rothstaahl?"

Jonny replied, "Not much. Of course, he's been living in Paris the past two years, just like his pal Bergman. Perhaps there could be something if we went. . . ."

"So we're back to that, are we?" growled Andersson. His face turned deep red, and Irene was able to hear the sound of air whistling through his lung pipe again. Andersson sat still, drumming his fingers on the table. No one else wanted to break the silence. Glaring angrily at Birgitta, he said, "And if we did . . . is there anyone here who can speak French?"

Only Kajsa Birgersdotter raised her hand.

"I see. Well, that's that," Andersson said.

"But the French can speak English!" protested Birgitta.

"Not many of them," growled Andersson.

Irene was convinced that Andersson had never set foot in France.

"All right, Kajsa, it's your turn. So what have you found out about that computer company and Bergman and Kaegler?"

Kajsa stood up and turned toward her colleagues. Without lifting her gaze from the paper in her hand, she began to read aloud, "Sanna and Philip were classmates during secondary school. They were inseparable for many years. People assumed they were a couple, but no one was really sure. They both studied economics in college, but they both seemed bored. They borrowed money from a bank and bought into a clothing company. Both Philip and Sanna were extremely aware of fashion. They were able to increase the store's sales within a year or two. This company was called—" She stopped in surprise before she continued, "Zazza Boutiques."

"So, there's an early connection between Bergman, Roth-staahl, and Kaegler. It's totally obvious, but I can't get the pattern," said Irene. She sighed.

Kajsa nodded and looked back down at her sheet of paper.

"After a few successful years, Sanna and Philip sold their Zazza shares to the Rothstaahl family, who then became sole owners of the chain. Rumor has it that there were issues between Bergman and Kaegler and the older generation of Rothstaahls, which is why Sanna and Philip sold out. But they got a lot of money from the sale. They met Thomas Bonetti after that. Thomas Bonetti was incredibly rich after his time in London. They decided to invest in the new business of Internet shopping. According to Philip, Internet shopping was the future. In a few years, everyone would be doing their shopping on the Internet, and Bergman, Kaegler, and Rothstaahl wanted to get ahead of the curve. So in 1998, they founded ph.com."

Kajsa stopped to take a breath. Before she had the chance to start reading again, Andersson said, "So you're telling me that Bergman and Kaegler had already been in business with Rothstaahl before they even started their computer company?"

"Their dot-com company," Kajsa corrected. "Yes, they'd been in business together before. At any rate, we know for sure that Rothstaahl's uncles owned shares in Zazza. They've retired now, and Joachim's two cousins are running the chain."

The superintendent looked glumly at Irene. "And now it appears that Bergman and Rothstaahl were putting together something new. Irene, you and Kajsa better go to Paris as soon as possible. I'll talk to the higher-ups. If we're ever going to solve this case, we have to know what these two gentlemen were plotting to do."

Both Irene and Kajsa jerked to attention as if struck by lightning.

Chapter 7

DELICIOUS SCENTS MET Irene when she opened the door to her townhouse. Krister had called her earlier that afternoon and asked what she wanted for dinner. She knew exactly what she craved. "Your fish soup. With plenty of garlic and saffron, please. And afterward, a little chocolate mousse would be perfect." Bouillabaisse à la Glady's was one of the prime attractions at the restaurant where Krister was the head chef. They couldn't take it off the menu, just like their famous chocolate mousse. The recipe for the mousse was a closely guarded secret, but Irene knew that Krister had a little trick that involved a dash of good cognac.

This was one of their sacred Third Weekends. Every third weekend, Irene and Krister were off work at the same time on both Friday and Saturday. That's when they would try to gather the whole family and enjoy a good dinner. The twins were happy to join the meal if they didn't have other plans, but they often disappeared after dinner. Krister used to look displeased, saying, "Why does everything start at the time we used to go home for the evening?"

Krister had given Irene the product codes for a white and a red wine that he wanted to serve this weekend. He never bothered to give her the names for any wine because he knew she couldn't pronounce them. The recently introduced self-service option in the state-run liquor stores were perfect for her.

As usual, Sammie was the first to welcome her home. His

tail wagged like the rotor blade of a helicopter, and he was skipping around her eagerly. Although he was the ripe old age of ten, he was still happy and healthy. His sight and hearing had declined noticeably in recent years, but Irene suspected that he had started doing what all older people do: he heard only what he wanted to hear.

"Hi, sweetheart," Krister called over the exhaust fan. "Did you find the wine?"

"Yes, I did. Two bottles of each," said Irene.

She broke away from Sammie and carried the green plastic bags into the kitchen. The bottles clanked as she set the bags on the table. Without taking off her jacket, she walked up to Krister, grabbed his shoulders, swung him into a tango position, placed him on one of her bent knees, and gave him a kiss on the lips.

When she released him, he ended up laughing on the floor. "You're crazy. But that's what happens when you marry a former jujitsu world champion. I have only myself to blame."

Before Irene got away, he pulled her to him and enveloped her in a bear hug. His kiss sent hot waves through her body.

"What are you doing?"

Irene and Krister stopped and looked toward the kitchen door. Their daughters looked back at them, aghast.

"We're wrestling," said Krister. Chuckling, they parted. Irene went out into the hall to hang up her jacket. Krister scrambled to his feet and headed back to the stove.

"What did you make for me?" asked Jenny.

She had been a vegan for several years. At the moment, her hair was jet black with purple highlights, and she was all dressed in black. As a singer in one of Göteborg's most famous pop bands, she had major investments in hair and fashion. Next week her hairstyle could be a blaze of neon pink, accompanied by a second-hand outfit inspired by '70s flower power.

"You get vegan moussaka. Made of oat milk. Still in the oven," said Krister.

He had become quite fond of vegetarian cooking. Jenny's vegan diet was still sometimes a challenge.

"Great! Did you make dessert?"

"Yes, but unfortunately for you, it's chocolate mousse. You may make yourself a fruit salad. Add a dash of port wine and. . . ."

Jenny interrupted him with a loud sigh. "Pappa! You know I don't drink alcohol."

"Well, a tiny splash won't hurt. Enhances the flavor. Think of it as a spice," suggested her father.

"I'll take the port, and you get the fruit salad," Katarina offered generously. She smiled at her sister, who did not look as amused.

"Are you staying home tonight?" asked Irene as Jenny danced out into the hall and up the stairs. "Yes," said Katarina, following her sister's exit with her eyes. "But not overnight."

"Is it still . . . what's the name of that new guy again?" teased Krister.

"What do you mean *new*? John and I have been together for six months. Or almost, in any case," said his daughter. She picked up the wine bottles from the plastic bags and scrutinized them. "Christobal Verdelho. White, so it's for the fish soup," she noted. She read the label of one of the red bottles. "Hécula. Spanish. What's for dinner tomorrow?"

"Pork stew with mushrooms and lingonberries. Mashed potatoes on the side."

"Sounds good, but I won't be home. We're planning to sail to Anholt early tomorrow morning. Sleeping on the boat and getting home on Sunday."

Katarina's boyfriend occasionally borrowed his parents' sailboat. Neither Irene nor Krister had any sailing skills, but they trusted John. He had sailed since he was in diapers and knew the archipelago like the back of his hand.

"Just the two of you on board?" asked Krister.

"Just us."

"I hope you're bringing life jackets? I mean, if you fall in. . . ."

"We always wear our life jackets when we go into open water," Katarina assured him.

I wish other experienced sailors would do the same, thought Irene. Why had Kjell B:son Ceder and his wife Marie not worn their life jackets when they went out on deck that stormy night sixteen years ago? The boat had been in the middle of the North Sea, and it was practically a gale. Tommy was right: there was something fishy about that accident. Could the incident have any connection with the murders that they were investigating now? It seemed unlikely, but. . . .

"Hello! Earth to Irene!" said Krister. He smiled at her.

"What? Sorry," said Irene.

"I asked you where the corkscrew is, and Pappa asked if you would like some sherry before dinner," said Katarina.

"No, thanks. Whiskey. In the top drawer by the stove," said Irene, still lost in thought.

Krister and Katarina exchanged glances.

"Go ahead and sit down on the couch, Mamma. Pappa will get you your whiskey while I open the bottle of wine. And don't worry about Sammie. I'll take him on his walk after dinner."

There was a scrabbling of paws on the parquet floor in the hall. Sammie had clearly heard his name and the word "walk." There probably wasn't much of a problem with his hearing after all.

"Go lie down. You'll have to wait," said Katarina.

"Wait" was not the word Sammie wanted to hear. When he

realized his walk had been postponed, he lowered his tail and padded up to Jenny upstairs.

Irene followed her daughter's instructions and went into the living room. She sank down on the couch and pulled her legs underneath her body. Only now did she realize how tired she was. Her head felt full of wool and her muscles like jelly. Could it be age? No way. As long as she managed to get to the dojo on Sunday to train with her jiujitsu group, her energy would return. Afterward, she and Krister would go vote in the EU elections. She was still unsure how she'd vote. In the morning, she planned to jog five miles, though her right knee was starting to give her trouble. She always had to wear an elastic brace around it when she went running. It was an old injury from her years as a handball player. Maybe she should have surgery soon, instead of waiting. Gloomily, Irene felt that her bodily decline had begun.

"Sweetheart, there's just a bit of the whiskey left. Do you want to drink it up or have something else?" Krister's voice came from the kitchen.

"Go ahead and pour it for me. I'll buy a new duty-free bottle when I go to Paris," said Irene absently.

There was silence from the kitchen area. Irene heard Krister and Katarina rush toward the living room. They stared at her. Irene made a dismissive gesture.

"All right, I'll tell you all about it. Just hand me my little bit of whiskey first," she said.

ANDERSSON CALLED AT nine o'clock that evening and confirmed Irene and Kajsa would go to Paris. Birgitta had obtained a key to the Paris apartment from Joachim Rothstaahl's parents. They'd seemed reluctant at first to give it to her, and it took all of Birgitta's patience to coax it from them. She'd also found out that Joachim Rothstaahl and Philip Bergman lived in the same apartment. None of their parents had mentioned it during the initial interrogation. Birgitta had called Philip's mother and asked whether it was true that her son shared an apartment with Joachim. His mother had said it was, but she hastened to add that it was only temporary. Philip had been looking for a place to live, but it was both difficult and expensive to find anything in central Paris.

"You can stop by the police station tomorrow. The key is at the reception desk. You are booked for the eight-twenty A.M. flight Monday morning from Landvetter, and you'll return on the flight that leaves at eight P.M. from Paris," said Andersson.

Irene felt slightly dazed. "I'll make sure to pick it up. And thanks for all the trouble of booking and—"

"Don't thank me. Birgitta did all the work," the superintendent said.

Irene realized that this made more sense.

"By the way, there's a stack of papers I'm leaving for you, too. Kajsa found them. You'll have something to read on the plane."

"Stack of papers?" echoed Irene. By the time Andersson called, the small shot of whiskey had been joined by two glasses of wine, so Irene was not as clear-headed as she wished. Especially when her fatigue was added to the equation.

"Kajsa was sent the chapter from that journalist's book. Apparently, he writes about all these computer companies and the money that disappeared after the crash. And he gave her the section that dealt with the Bergman, Kaegler, and Bonetti company," said Andersson.

"Ph.com," Irene said.

"Right. This investigation is so extensive I can't keep all the details clear. But it's probably good if you and Kajsa know the background behind those three and their past cons."

Irene knew her boss was not interested in anything having to do with computers. Or any white-collar crime, actually, because that often required good computer skills. It was with ill-concealed relief that he left the high-tech and financial questions to her and Kajsa.

Irene wondered about that journalist's chapter.

Chapter 8

IT WAS AS if a surge of electricity swept through the nightclub as the young man entered. The guests might have noticed the two people following right behind, but all eyes were on him. He walked down the stairs with practiced elegance, well aware of the impression he was making.

At the bar he ordered three vodka martinis. His friends laughed at something he said, obviously no longer sober. With nonchalance, he handed the bartender his Visa card, which stayed there the rest of the evening. It took just a few minutes before the first beautiful young woman came up to him, soon joined by many more. He knew many of them from his previous visits. He invited all of them to a round of champagne. Naturally, it was the most expensive brand in the house.

All of the women were younger than twenty-five.

The woman who had entered the bar with him was beautiful in the classically Nordic way. She had light blue eyes and platinum blonde hair swept up on the top of her head. She used very little makeup, but her clothes signaled direct purchase from London's top designers. Although she was tipsy, it was clear she was bored. After only a few sips of her martini, she stood up abruptly and gave the young blond man a light kiss on the cheek. She spun around on her stilettos and disappeared up the stairs. The blond man did not notice.

The lighting by the bar was stronger than other parts of the room, and it made the young man's hair shimmer. He wore it slightly longer than was fashionable, but his features were attractive—high *cheekbones and a strong chin. He frequently fired off a blazing smile. He was in good shape and wore elegant clothes of the best brands. His appearance embodied success.*

His male friend was his opposite: short and fat. He looked forty-years-old, but had just turned thirty. His reddish-blond hair had already begun to thin, and he sweated profusely. His suit, obviously not tailor made, stretched over his portly body. He couldn't care less. He had enough money to buy a new one—in fact, he had enough money to buy anything he wanted.

The party lasted until the early hours of the morning. The two men and the young girls were the only ones left at the bar, which wouldn't close until its wealthy guests decided to leave. The employees knew they'd receive generous tips for their trouble, which included ignoring the white powder the young man snorted from a line off the counter. Or when the fat man brought one of the young girls into the men's restroom, forced her to lean over the sink, and then raped her. One of the security guards peeked in, but hastily drew back. Keeping silent about what he'd seen would certainly be worth a bill with a high number on it.

These employees were used to this particular gang coming in to party. This evening's escapades were not out of the ordinary. A typical after-work evening for the owners of ph.com. The facts behind the above are true. The girl reported the rape to the police, but then decided to retract it.

The bar is Zodiac, and I've been there myself to interview the employees, many of whom saw the owners of ph.com often, as this was the favorite haunt of the famous threesome whenever they were in Göteborg. The bosses of this company were certainly good at one thing—partying all night.

Ph.com is an example of the many dot-com companies that grew like mushrooms toward the end of the nineties. I won't address their finances in this chapter; greater detail can be found in Chapter Six: The Advisors—Investment Banks and Bankers. Instead, I would like to paint a complete picture of what happened and why. The incredible saga of ph.com's success and fall began in 1998 when Philip Bergman and Sanna Kaegler met Thomas Bonetti at a party in Göteborg. They've told the tale of how they decided to become an Internet company in various interviews.

All three of these young people believed strongly in the new trade that had started to take off on the Internet. In the United States, there were already successful Internet companies such as Netscape and Amazon (see Chapter Four: The First Internet Companies in the United States), in addition to others like Intel, Apple, Computer, and Compaq. The quick returns tempted institutional investors to place investment capital into these kinds of companies—even those not yet on the stock market. American retirement fund managers were very particular about investing in the new high-tech companies. According to an American journalist, during the nineties, up to 40 percent of venture capital firms' money came from retirement funds.

Between the summer of 1998 and 1999, Internet stocks rose by 400 percent. Interest in the new companies was enormous, and it seemed the stream of money would never end. New Internet companies of this era rarely lacked investors.

In hindsight, it is shocking how careless investors were. The new Internet companies weren't making profits and, in fact, many of them were racking up huge losses. The value of stock was based on popular opinion that the Internet revolution was going to change everything. No one wanted to miss a thing. During that party in 1998, the trio came up with their grand plan: create an international Internet company and get it listed on the stock market as soon as possible. There weren't any discussions on what they wanted to sell, just that it would be sold via the Internet. They wanted to become one of the leading Internet companies worldwide.

Philip Bergman and Sanna Kaegler had just sold their shares of the clothing boutique Zazza. Rumor has it that they were forced out by the other owners, the brothers Gillis and Walther Rothstaahl, because of difficulties working together. Bergman and Kaegler *insisted that they'd tired of Zazza and were looking for something more trendy. "We took Zazza from the backwaters to the absolute top, and now it's time to move on," said Philip Bergman to a Göteborg Post financial reporter. Zazza bought them out at seven million kroner apiece, a good return since they'd only brought one million to the table.*

Philip was a visionary and had the gift of gab. He was incredibly charming and charismatic. To put it bluntly, he had everything he needed to become a successful Internet entrepreneur.

Sanna was highly aware of the latest trends and had a nose for the future of fashion. She'd been successful as PR and Marketing Manager for Zazza. Although she could also be quite charming, she was more introverted than Philip. She never opposed any of Philip's ideas. They complemented each other and were each other's best defense whenever things got rough.

Thomas Bonetti stood out in their company. He was definitely not 'one of the beautiful people,' and he never would be. He wasn't interested in fashion at all and knew nothing about the industry. However, he had worked internationally and had contacts within the large banks from his year spent working in London.

The three of them should have been a winning combination. They planned to create the first European Internet company, so they could have the "advantage of being the first big player," as Thomas Bonetti would tell his new business partners.

In March, they'd decided to sell expensive clothes paired with matching accessories. If a customer bought an Armani suit, he or she could also choose appropriate shoes, tie, shirt, and cuff links to match. Even the right socks and aftershave.

"We'll be able to give the customer everything he needs in a single minute. It's perfect for the time-stressed modern man," Philip touted at the first (and only) meeting for the company's initial employees.

At the end of April 1998, the trio traveled to London and checked into the exclusive London Hilton. Though Sanna expressed worry at the expense, both Thomas and Philip believed they needed to set the right tone. All three of them were certain of the company's global success. They wanted to attract the kind of risk capital indicative of a world-class financial center. Their London trip needed to foster the right connections to give their project legitimacy. Before they even arrived, they'd already scheduled meetings with the most influential law firms and accounting firms in the city. If they had partners with good reputations, it would be easier to contact financial advisors who could introduce them to the big investment firms.

The trio realized fairly quickly that they should find an American investment bank. The United States was still the biggest market in the world. In order to create the right impression for the biggest fashion houses, they wanted to prove that they had good advisors with contacts on Wall Street. So, not surprisingly, they went directly to HP Johnson. Representatives from the American bank's European office were soon victims of the Swedes' charm. Philip boldly asked for a $100 million investment right off the bat.

The HP Johnson bankers would receive a return of 7 percent, which meant seven million dollars right to the bank. HP Johnson was definitely interested.

Since HP Johnson was an old investment bank with a good reputation, ph.com would be their first step into the world of the Internet. Many of their competitors had already entered the market, and the bank's managers thought it was high time to get involved. By the fall of 1998, HP Johnson gave the green light for ph.com and became their official financial advisors.

There is nothing to indicate that the bank ever checked into the background of the three Swedes. We can only speculate why they were remiss.

By then, ph.com was in full swing. They'd hired one of the world's most famous law firms, Andersen, Andersen & Schoultze, as their legal advisors. Until then, ph.com had been financed by the Bergman-Kaegler-Bonetti trio, but now they brought in outside *investment capital. An investment memorandum stated that each one had contributed $150,000 in start-up costs, and invoices recorded another half a million—a total of $950,000.*

The three of them began to prepare for a tour of Europe and the United States to continue contacting merchants and procuring capital. After the round of financing which ended in February 1999, ph.com had raised $40 million in starting capital. It—

"SOMETHING TO DRINK?"

The flight attendant's voice interrupted Irene's reading. She glanced at the drinks on the cart and asked for Ramlösa mineral water. They'd get coffee a few minutes later.

Irene nudged Kajsa, who was sitting beside her, snoring with her mouth open. She started as she woke up.

"Coffee . . . or Fanta . . . with milk," Kajsa mumbled.

"She also wants a Ramlösa," said Irene.

They were given the bottles of mineral water. A flight steward arrived a few minutes later with a cart of sandwiches and plastic coffee mugs.

"Were you able to read through all of that?" Kajsa nodded toward the bundle of paper on Irene's lap.

"No. It's not all that easy, since I don't understand all the concepts. I did manage to get that they made it to the top of the financial world—not because they had something to sell but because they were good at charming old bankers. It's unbelievable."

"Yes, it is, isn't it?" Kajsa said through a mouthful of ham sandwich.

Irene had a feeling they weren't talking about the same thing, but she let it go. She hurried through her breakfast so that she could continue reading. She skimmed through the next few pages, which detailed who invested how much when, and picked up the story further on.

• • •

IN DECEMBER, PHILIP found a large office complex near Charing Cross Road. He hired Swedish architects to renovate the building to have more of a 'cool attitude,' as he put it. The renovation was scheduled to finish in January. Before the last carpenter picked up his toolbox to leave, ph.com was already hiring employees. They had no trouble finding competent young people eager for a job. They used England's most famous recruiting agency to find a hundred employees, with an average age of twenty-five, for the London office. Many came directly from consulting and their own connections to influential managers. Ph.com began its global expansion in the spring of 1999. They opened a large office in New York with another hundred employees. More offices followed in Stockholm, Frankfurt, Paris, and Amsterdam.

Philip Bergman's vision included a ph.com launch in both Europe and the United States. The website, to be designed by Electroz, would be in six languages. Country-specific prices, customs fees, and taxes would be automatically included and converted into the appropriate currencies. All the clothes would be available in several colors to be combined with many different accessories. The format of the website would revolutionize the market and amaze customers with its fresh take.

A few advisors recommended a smaller launch, since constructing such a website would be complicated. Both Philip and Sanna were adamant, and Thomas Bonetti supported them. Bonetti's financial experience meant he knew what it would take to create a high value on the stock market: many hits for the website, quick growth, and numerous employees. They could not show any doubt about their company's success.

Other advisors were against the idea of 'selling a lifestyle.' They believed fashion houses wouldn't agree with the concept and would demand that ph.com buy an entire collection before the season opened. This would mean enormous warehousing costs and the risk of buying the wrong things. Sanna was enraged. "I've worked in fashion and design for years, and you don't know what you're *talking about!" After that, the critics were silent. It's unwise to bite the hand that feeds you.*

No one was allowed to question the work ethic of the company, either. It was part of the culture of the workplace to come early, leave late, and work weekends. If an employee protested, his or her job was gone. Employees had no right to a family life. They were surrounded by other ph.com employees at all times, and before too long, an inner circle developed around the management trio. Everyone in the company believed in the future of ph.com.

Worldwide media began to pay attention to Philip Bergman and Sanna Kaegler. The two of them loved the spotlight and often gave tours of their trendy London apartments to writers from glossy interior design magazines. Thomas Bonetti also lived in a fine home, but he refused to give tours. Their rents were paid by ph.com. Their salary was $150,000 a year. They were on the cover of Fortune magazine. Their mantra was that their website would reshape Internet retailing.

Then the problems began. Bergman and Kaegler kept vetoing any of the website designs that Electroz proposed. Electroz gave up after February 1999, and ph.com was left without a technical partner. For the first time, Philip Bergman was nervous. He had promised investors that the site would be up and running by April, and the trio was supposed to conclude another round of investments in March. No one wanted to derail these plans by officially delaying the launch.

Around the same time, Thomas Bonetti pointed out that the company's financial procedures and checks were either lacking or being ignored. Departments were placing orders without informing the accounting office, which was his area of responsibility. No one was writing their monthly reports, so it was impossible to find out the true state of the company's finances. Thomas's worries were consistently rebuffed, and Bergman and Kaegler began to work against him. Before too long, employees noticed a division in the top management. Perhaps Thomas Bonetti had already decided it was time to take care of himself. During one particularly drunken party, he revealed to other employees that he planned to leave the company as soon as it was introduced on the stock market and he could sell his shares. The second round of financing was spectacular. Ph.com also found a new technical partner, Watsis. However, Watsis had doubts about the short timeframe. Completing an entire website by the first of June was impossible. In spite of this, Philip Bergman made the launch date official. He had to keep his investors happy. The trio kept web designers in New York, while administration and logistics offices stayed in Stockholm and Berlin. Because of the extreme deadline, their expenses were higher than normal.

One team of consultants declared that the earliest date for a successful launch would have to be the first of November. Though Philip Bergman and Sanna Kaegler protested mightily, they finally acquiesced. If they were determined to have the trendiest and most advanced website in the world, they had to wait until it was actually functional.

They kept up appearances to those outside the company, and positive reviews in the financial press kept things humming for ph.com. The demand for Internet stocks was still enormous. The second round of investment had finished, and people were already in line to be part of the third. The financial advisors at HP Johnson were rubbing their hands together with glee. It wouldn't be long until the stock's initial public offering (IPO).

The third financing round's success went above expectations. The value of ph.com had reached $150 million.

During this period of initial success, the relationship between the Bergman-Kaegler duo and Thomas Bonetti became increasingly strained. By the fall of 1999, the split was obvious. Bergman-Kaegler wanted to get rid of Bonetti, because he "wasn't moving in the same direction."

At the same time, it was clear the website would still not meet its extended deadline. It failed during test runs; the pages taking too long to load. The launch was delayed by another month.

The glassy offices in Sweden, Germany, England, France, Holland, and the United States were filled with young employees who traveled all over the world and stayed at the best hotels. They pulled in huge salaries even though they had no actual work duties until the website was functional. No one in the company knew what they were supposed to be doing in the meantime. The young employees had fancy titles, and the company was filled to the brim with vice presidents. The new launch date was close, and everyone's expectations kept rising.

Soon there were problems with the merchants, too. Many famous brands pulled out. They would not agree to filling purchase orders for clothes only after they'd been ordered by consumers via ph.com. An employee at ph.com (who was never identified) went ahead and ordered complete collections from houses such as Prada and Kenzo. Suddenly and unexpectedly, ph.com had enormous amounts of clothes that needed to be warehoused immediately. They were forced to rent and staff a warehouse in London's harbor—an expense no one had planned for. The company was rapidly burning through its money, and no one was keeping tabs on expenditures.

At this point, an anonymous investor appeared who wanted to put $15 million into ph.com, which Bergman decided would take care of the entire fourth round of financing. By now, the company was valued at $350 million without having brought in a single penny in profit.

The financial advisors at HP Johnson were content. Their investment had been converted into shares, and they now had ownership interest in the success of ph.com.

At a board meeting, the web launch was finally set for March 2000 at the latest. Sanna and her designers had placed huge demands on the website. Moreover, she declared most of the webpage suggestions "ugly, banal, or unfashionable." As a result, work kept being delayed, and the website became so over-designed that it was difficult to find the right button to click. Because of the pressing deadlines and changes in technical support, the platform was a mish-mash of overlapping source codes, making the website slow and buggy. In test runs, it could take up to forty-five minutes to make a purchase.

Panic rose as the date for the launch approached. The website was not working as promised. But they could not keep the investors waiting any longer—they were beginning to lose patience.

On the morning of December first, Philip Bergman popped a bottle of champagne to share with his exhausted employees. Finally ph.com was on the Net! Bergman had high hopes for the Christmas rush, hopes which did not materialize. Many visitors to the site left because it was too difficult to make a purchase. Interest began to wane. By January 2000, even Philip Bergman had to admit that ph.com was a major catastrophe. They had not even reached 10 percent of projections. However, top management kept up a positive façade and didn't bother warning investors of potential trouble—a practice that is illegal. In hindsight, it's easy to understand why they did this; they wanted the company to have an IPO so that they could all get rich quick.

The flood of money streaming out of the company, however, was beginning to affect the business. The trio decided to hold a fifth investment round. They needed at least $45 million. At a board meeting in January, they decided to hold off on an IPO until the following quarter.

Another major expense was the advertising budget. Sanna Kaegler had run an expensive ad campaign prior to the website launch. The campaign was paid for by a $9 million line of credit, but now ph.com needed to pay back the money. Sanna didn't seem bothered by this in the least.

The debts were piling up. They had too many expensive employees, too many expensive foreign offices, too many high-priced consultants, and too many outrageous warehouse costs. The six-month delay of the website launch had cost the company a fortune. Sales were catastrophically low. The company was bleeding out.

By Christmas, the trio had already tried to stem the tide by *cutting expenses, but they refused to close any of the offices or fire employees, fearing it would send the wrong signal to investors. The only concrete savings plan they ended up with was to cut long-distance phone bills and travel costs.*

The entire ph.com project was built on one major miscalculation. Their concept was to lure exclusive customers who wanted to purchase designer clothes via the Internet. Like Bergman had said, "We're going to bring a new kind of customer to the Internet! Our customers know what they want, and they have good taste and a great deal of money—but what they don't have is time! By offering a time-saving shopping experience, we'll generate profits with our large customer base!"

On the other hand, the fashion houses did not want to give ph.com any rebates. By then, it was clear that people shopped on the Internet to get good discounts. Obviously, ph.com didn't fit the bill, so sales didn't increase. Sales remained at 10 percent of projections.

During the first few months of the new millennium, articles critical of ph.com appeared in the press. Was there anything behind the cool, trendy exterior of the website? Bergman and Kaegler kept an optimistic face to the world, but they were hurt by the negative reviews.

Bergman and Kaegler were relieved when Thomas Bonetti came to them and said he was leaving ph.com for "other, new projects of his own." Bonetti wanted to leave the company immediately at the end of January. He refused a half-hearted offer to stay on board and was gone for good on February first.

The dot-com bubble burst in March 2000. Intel had given a projection lower than expected. All the tech stocks on the NASDAQ began to fall. By April, they were down by 25 percent. It took a few more months for the markets to realize what was going on. The European markets were even slower. Dot-com companies continued to go bust as the year 2000 progressed. Thousands of bankruptcies caused hundreds of thousands of cases of unemployment in the tech industry. In Sweden, the term 'dot-com death' was coined.

With its bad finances, ph.com could not hang on for much longer. There never was a fifth round of investment. By April 2000, bankruptcy was a fact. HP Johnson tried to save what it could. People were still talking up an IPO, but by April 15, the end had come. The company was swallowed by debt.

Sanna Kaegler was reportedly close to tears as she and Philip Bergman broke the news to their London employees. Philip said, "It's the fault of the investors. They've jerked the rug out from under us." They did not mention that investors had pumped more than $100 million into ph.com and would not see a penny from it.

Since there was hardly any accounting done within the company, it was difficult to tell where all the money had gone. Advertising and marketing had taken at least $39 million. No one really knew who had been paid what when. All in all, the employees of ph.com had burned through $109 million in less than a year. According to the exchange rate at the time, this was equivalent to one billion Swedish kroner. It's astonishing how all that money went up in smoke.

A few months after the bankruptcy, Sanna Kaegler and Philip Bergman claimed that their former partner Thomas Bonetti had embezzled millions of dollars. Bonetti refuted the allegations and accused the two of them of running through money like water and then placing the blame on him. There was never a criminal indictment, because Thomas Bonetti went missing in September 2000.

IRENE FINISHED READING just as the loudspeaker announced that the plane was beginning its descent. Passengers were requested to fasten their seatbelts for landing. Although Irene wasn't clear about every detail in the chapter she'd just read, she did know one thing for sure: the amount of money lost in the ph.com crash was absolutely unbelievable!

Chapter 9

IRENE AND KAJSA had both brought backpacks as their carry-ons, since they didn't need any luggage for such a short trip. How nice it was to avoid the crowd waiting next to the baggage carousels. Charles de Gaulle Airport was a dreary colossus of gray concrete, and they were happy they could get out of there quickly. They boarded the airport bus to the center of Paris.

"This bus is going into the city along the Boulevard Raspail," Kajsa said. "The question is, where do we get off? It's a darned long street."

She was studying the map she'd picked up at the information booth in the airport. After a while, she folded it up and said, "We'll get off right before Place Denfert Rochereau and walk along the boulevard until we reach number 207."

Irene took the map and tried to orient herself. She finally found Boulevard Raspail and saw that Kajsa was right—the street was amazingly long. Nonetheless, she wouldn't mind a brisk walk in the gorgeous weather, which reminded her of a Swedish summer day.

The bus neared the center of Paris. Traffic flowed smoothly along the wide boulevards. There were many tall trees and resplendent gardens between the stone buildings. In spite of all the asphalt and stone, Paris gave the impression of a garden city. The driver called out the stop they wanted, and they got off, breathing in the exhaust-filled air.

"I'm hungry," Kajsa said. "Can we have lunch before we go to the apartment?"

"That's a good idea."

They started to walk toward a wide boulevard marked on the map as Montparnasse. Right before they reached it, they found number 207, the apartment building where Philip Bergman and Joachim Rothstaahl had lived. The building was a bit shorter than the other nine-story buildings nearby and looked older, but it was well cared for and had light gray plaster with balcony railings painted black.

"We're here," Irene said.

"Yes, we are," said Kajsa. She pointed across the street filled with lively traffic. "And over there I see a promising restaurant."

There were in fact many different kinds of restaurants located at the large intersection. Two of them appeared to be fine-dining seafood places, while the others were small pubs and cafés. Kajsa wanted to sit outside so they could enjoy the sunshine.

One place had a large sign over the entrance, La Rotonde, and they decided to head there. Once they managed to cross the street, which was a tangle of crosswalks and traffic lights, they sank into wicker chairs around a small brass table.

With Kajsa's help, Irene was able to order a beer, a bottle of water, and chicken in Noilly-Prat sauce on a bed of mixed greens. Kajsa kept reassuring her that *poulet* did, in fact, mean chicken.

After lunch, they both ordered a café au lait and sat back in the creaking wicker chairs. Irene was grateful that she'd followed her instinct last night to throw in a pair of sunglasses. Hidden behind them, she could watch all sorts of people stream past their table. Even after they paid the bill, they remained in their chairs a few more minutes enjoying the warm sunshine.

"This city has a wonderful feel to it," said Irene.

"All day and all night," said Kajsa. "This city never sleeps."

"Have you been here before?" asked Irene.

Kajsa smiled broadly. "I lived here for five months, working as an au pair, but then I went back home. I didn't like caring for small children. The family lived far from the center and . . . the idea of becoming a policewoman sounded more exciting."

"Well, not surprising that your French is so good," Irene said.

"Although it's been ten years, I guess something stuck with me."

"You don't speak with a Göteborg accent, but your accent isn't a Stockholm one, either. Where are you from?"

"Eskilstuna."

"I see. So how did you end up in Göteborg?" Irene realized that her questions sounded like an interrogation, but even so, this relaxed moment was a good chance to find out more about her colleague.

Kajsa was silent for a long time before she said shortly, "The usual. A guy."

Irene sensed an interesting story behind this, so she asked another question.

"I see. Are you still together?"

"No."

"Did you find someone else after that?"

"No."

Kajsa did not try to hide her irritation at Irene's questions, but Irene was not going to give up so easily. She'd gotten Kajsa in the place she wanted her. Quietly she said, "Think about it before you rebound too quickly to a new guy. A married man, especially, always means trouble. Trouble not only for you, but also for him, his wife, and his children. The more children, the more trouble. Children must come first, since they suffer the most during a divorce. If you're a factor in the breakup, you'll find yourself at the back of the line in any relationship after that. Because all the blame will fall on you."

Kajsa's entire face went white, but she couldn't gather words quickly enough for a reply before Irene stood up.

"I believe it's time for us to get back to work." She used a cheerful tone. "According to Philip's mother, the apartment is not that big. We'll have enough time to go through it thoroughly before the flight home. Our bus to the airport leaves, I believe, at six o'clock."

Without waiting for her colleague to say anything, Irene headed off toward the nearest crosswalk.

Kajsa kept quiet as they walked toward the building they planned to enter. She wasn't an idiot. She probably understood Irene's message to keep away from Tommy. Irene also intended to have a little chat with him at a convenient moment. *There must be something wrong between him and Agneta. Or is there? Maybe he's just been hit by the proverbial male midlife crisis?* The thought had entered her mind before, and it could be that simple explanation. Although she always called Tommy her best friend, what did she really know about him? Not much. They never discussed their love lives or their sex lives, which wasn't all that strange. They'd both been married for quite a while, and they had kids. Their two families had spent time together, and Irene considered Tommy's wife her best female friend. Any fallout from an affair or a divorce between Tommy and Agneta would affect Irene personally.

They came to a halt in front of the entrance and read the elegant nameplates, in shining brass, which showed that J. Rothstaahl lived on the sixth floor. Irene pulled out keys from an inner pocket in her backpack, stuck one in the lock, and the heavy door opened on its iron hinges with a loud creak.

The entryway was cool and whitewashed, clean and pleasant. There was a vague odor of cleaning products.

"No elevator," Irene stated as she began to climb the stairs.

Kajsa followed her, still silent. Behind some of the closed doors, they could hear music or talking, but most of them were completely silent.

On the top floor, there were three doors. On one was the name J. ROTHSTAAHL. There was no sign for a resident named P. Bergman. She opened the door with the apartment key. There was a large scattering of mail on the floor inside, mostly advertisements. The hallway was very narrow, only one antique mirror on the wall with a matching table below. Irene noticed that the apartment did not smell musty, which was unusual since no one had been there for a week and a half. Maybe the old building was drafty.

"Let's split up," Irene said.

Kajsa nodded and went toward the kitchen past one of the open doors. Irene opened the closed door next to her to a small bathroom with a toilet and shower. She could smell men's cologne. A small black kit lay on the shelf beneath the mirror. She didn't see anything else. Irene went back to the hallway and opened the next door, which revealed an airy bedroom dominated by an extra-wide, queen-size bed with a beautiful white and blue bedcover. The high windows had long curtains made from matching fabric. The wood floor had been carefully restored. She could also smell men's cologne in this room. *Odd that the odor was so strong. . . .* She opened another door; as she suspected, it was a walk-in closet.

The push on her back was so unexpected that she was completely surprised. It was so powerful that her feet actually left the floor as she was shoved into the closet, and she would have hit the back wall head-first if not for her many hours of physical training. She managed to raise one arm to take the blow while hearing the door behind her close and lock. All she could see was darkness.

A sharp, paralyzing pain ran up from her right elbow. She tried to move her hand, but it didn't react. She groaned as she staggered to her feet, but she paused when she heard a sudden noise. Kajsa's voice came clearly through the thick wooden door.

"Wha—Nooo!"

Irene heard two dull thuds and then complete silence fell. Irene listened hard for any sound from the other side of the door, but all she could hear was blood pounding in her ears. Something had happened to Kajsa. Was their attacker still in the apartment? As if in answer to her question, she heard steps walking quickly across the floor. When the front door slammed, Irene realized she'd been holding her breath.

Whoever had attacked them was gone. She thought the attacker must have been a man—she'd had the impression she'd been hockey blocked from behind by a tall and rather hefty male. No woman had that kind of strength. Irene was 180 centimeters tall, weighed almost 70 kilos, and was in great shape.

With her working left hand, she began to search around the doorframe hoping for a light switch. An eternity seemed to pass before she found it, and to her great relief, the light bulb came on. She immediately concentrated on the lock. It was a well-built, old-fashioned lock, and when she peered through the keyhole, she saw that the key had been left in.

Sometimes, Irene joked that most things could be solved by violence, but there was an element of truth behind her statement. She took one step back and kicked the area around the lock as hard as she could. Her third kick broke the door open, and she stumbled out.

Irene found Kajsa in the doorway between the living room and the hallway. She was on her back and a pool of blood was forming beneath her head from an open wound on her temple. Irene fumbled around in her backpack and found her extra T-shirt, which she wadded up and applied to the wound. To Irene's great relief, Kajsa began to moan weakly and tried to shake her head, but instinctively stopped in the middle of the movement. She fell unconscious again.

Irene thought as quickly as she could. Her right arm was still as good as useless. She'd have to loosen her pressure on Kajsa's wound, but that couldn't be helped. Once she decided what to do, she moved quickly. She dug out her cell phone from the front pocket of her backpack and hurriedly scrolled through her contacts. She was grateful she'd left the country code in her phone after an investigation in Copenhagen a few years earlier. Sighing with relief, she pressed the button and prayed that someone would answer right away. Her heart leapt for joy when she heard a familiar voice say, "Inspector Birgitta Moberg-Rauhala."

"Hi, Birgitta, it's Irene. Do you have an emergency number to call for a French ambulance?"

Chapter 10

Inspector Verdier had cold, gray-blue eyes set close together beside his narrow nose. His thin, salt-and-pepper hair suffered from an unfortunate part. He wore a light beige trench coat over an impeccable gray suit, and he showed no sign of sweat even though it was a hot day. Irene thought that he looked like a character in the Ture Sventon detective series from her childhood. The difference between the story and reality was that the policeman looked like the criminal, Ville Vessla, and not the hero, Ture Sventon. Verdier had appeared at the hospital while Irene and Kajsa were still being examined. He had waited patiently while Irene was taken for an X-ray and as her badly sprained arm was fitted with a suitable sling. Irene was greatly relieved to hear that her arm wasn't broken. The doctor, a black man with tired eyes, wrote something illegible on a prescription pad, and in halting English, encouraged her to take two pills three times a day. Irene nodded and tried to look obedient. She asked how her colleague, Kajsa Birgersdotter, was doing, but the doctor shrugged and said, "Not my patient."

Inspector Verdier followed the doctor out the door, only to return a few moments later.

"Your colleague has a concussion," he said in good, but heavily accented, English. "She has to stay here overnight for observation."

There was no sympathy in his voice, only dry observation.

Irene thought he must have been assigned this case simply because of his English; he certainly wouldn't win any points for his bedside manner or social skills.

"I would like you to accompany me to the station and explain what happened," Verdier said.

He showed no curiosity in his expression, just chilly politeness. Before Irene was able to answer, the majestic notes of the French national anthem burst into the tiny examination room. Irene managed to fish her cell phone out of the backpack pocket to answer it.

"How are you two doing?" asked Birgitta.

"Fine. . . . Not so fine, actually. Kajsa has a concussion and has to stay overnight for observation. My elbow isn't broken, but—hey, can I call you back later?"

Inspector Verdier was staring her down and tapping a sign on the wall. It showed the red slashed circle around a picture of a cell phone.

Irene quickly gathered up her things. She slung her backpack over her left shoulder and draped her jacket over her arm. Verdier did not make any move to help, but at least he held the door for her as they left the room.

He led her through the crowded emergency room and out the door by the ambulances. A nurse was about to protest but fell silent when he flashed his identification. Irene realized that it must be forbidden for patients or relatives to leave through this door because they risked being hit by an ambulance coming in at high speed. Obviously, this rule only applied to regular people, not Inspector Verdier. With his trench coat fluttering behind him, Verdier strode toward the parking lot without even glancing behind him to see if Irene was able to keep up. He unlocked the doors to a dark gray Renault Megane. He held open a door for her again, and Irene was not surprised he was offering her the back seat. Her French colleague obviously did not want to chat on the way to the station. As Verdier drove through the afternoon traffic, Irene decided to call Birgitta. She answered at once.

"Why'd you hang up?"

"Not allowed to talk on the cell phone at the hospital. Now I'm in the back seat of a police car on the way to be interrogated."

"Interrogated?"

"Third degree, for sure. My French colleague is giving me the shivers."

She met Verdier's expressionless eyes in the rearview mirror and forced herself to give a small smile. Birgitta giggled on her end.

"Look on the bright side. At least you can avoid Sven right now."

Irene needed to hear that just then. She had no illusions that the superintendent had handled the news of what happened in Paris calmly. She heaved a great sigh and ignored Verdier's eyes staring at her from the mirror.

"Birgitta, would you be so kind as to contact the travel agency to rebook our flight for tomorrow afternoon instead? And could you please ask them to find a hotel close to the Rothstaahl apartment while you're at it? I don't have a car here. By the look of it, I hardly believe our French colleague will offer to be my chauffeur. As long as I'm here, I really should find out as much as I can about Bergman and Rothstaahl."

"That's great! At least Andersson can't complain that your trip was a complete waste. I'll call you when I've handled the travel agency. And by the way, I called HP Johnson's Parisian office this morning, and they told me that they never had an employee named Joachim Rothstaahl. Our young friend made up that story for his parents. Now we have to find out what those two guys really were up to."

As soon as Irene ended the call, she suddenly felt

abandoned. Her contact with her native country was gone, and she was on her own in a foreign capital city where she couldn't even speak the language. Not to mention that the only native she had contact with now was as friendly as a cold fish.

RIGHT BEFORE THE car swung in through the tall gates of the police station, Irene caught a glimpse of a building she actually recognized. The spires and towers covered with dragons and gargoyles could be nothing else but the famous Notre Dame cathedral. She'd recognized it from the Disney film *The Hunchback of Notre Dame* she'd seen with her daughters several years ago.

They walked through an imposing wooden door with massive iron mounting. It was covered with marks that, to Irene, looked like they were made by French Revolution battering rams and storming mobs. Now the gate was guarded by a uniformed policeman in a glass booth. He saluted smartly as they walked by, and Verdier waved a casual salute back.

They stepped into an ancient, rickety elevator. Verdier pushed a button marked "PJ." Next to the button, the words POLICE JUDICIARE were engraved on a brass sign. The elevator carried them up a few floors, and after that they walked along a dark corridor. Tiny, dirty windows along one side let in the least amount of light possible. Irene felt as if she'd traveled several centuries back in time. Only the dull sound of traffic and the sirens of emergency vehicles gave her any sense of the present.

After a long walk down the dim corridor, the inspector stopped at a closed door and unlocked it.

"Please enter," he said, as he held the door open.

They stepped into his office. A worn desk, two chairs, and a simple, wall-mounted bookshelf with a few binders were the only furnishings in the room. An old computer sat enthroned at the center of the desk. The room was chilly. Irene struggled into her jacket before she sat down on the chair Verdier pointed to.

Before Irene was able to launch her long tale, her cell phone rang the Marseilles again. Birgitta informed Irene that she'd booked a room at the Hotel Montparnasse Raspail. According to the woman at the travel agency, the hotel should be close to the Rothstaahl apartment. She'd also rebooked their flight.

As Irene stammered out the entire Göteborg murder investigation in stumbling English, Verdier sat quietly and watched her. There were no pictures or flowers on the windowsill, so Irene was forced to look back at Verdier. Irene had never imagined that a person could stare that long without blinking. It was effective. For a second, Irene felt ready to confess to hitting Kajsa on the head and locking herself into the closet just to escape his chilly gaze. She controlled her emotions as she did her best to describe the case's chain of events. If he could sit there cold as ice, well then, so could she.

When she finished, there was a long period of silence.

Finally, Verdier asked, "Why did your superintendent send two women here?"

Irene was not surprised by this question, but she was starting to feel fed up with the attitude. "He sent his two best detectives because this killer is especially dangerous," she said.

For a fraction of a second, a sparkle flashed in the French Inspector's eyes, but Irene couldn't determine why before it disappeared again.

He fixed her in his gaze for quite some time. Defiantly, she stared back, and to her great satisfaction, he was the first to look away. He tried to disguise it by getting up from his chair.

"Would you like a ride somewhere, *madame?*" he asked.

His voice was as coolly polite as ever, but Irene could tell by the emphasis he put on *madame* that she was supposed to notice he refused to use her title.

"Yes, please," she replied without hesitation. "You can drive me to my hotel on Boulevard Raspail."

She knew that she wasn't pronouncing its name properly, but she no longer cared. She just wanted to get out of this depressing room and away from the even more depressing Verdier. He handed her his card and said, "I would like your cell phone number, in case something turns up. Or I have to reach you." He managed to make it sound like a threat.

A YOUNG UNIFORMED policeman drove Irene back to Montparnasse in an unmarked car. This time, Irene decided herself to sit in the back seat in order to avoid a stumbling conversation in broken English. As soon as she sat down, exhaustion overcame her. Spending time in the company of Inspector Verdier had taken more out of her than she'd realized. Not to mention the attack at the apartment and the time spent in the emergency room. And she'd had no chance to look in on Kajsa.

The doctor had said she could visit Kajsa once she had been moved out of Emergency later that evening. Irene checked the time and saw it was only six P.M. She had enough time to search the apartment once more before she had to return to the hospital. Before then, however, she needed at least several cups of coffee and a sandwich. Her elbow was starting to throb, so it would be a good idea to get her pain prescription too.

She pulled out her cell phone and called Krister, who had just arrived home. He was alarmed when he heard about the attack, and once Irene reassured him that she was relatively OK, he promised to hold down the fort at home. Krister was Irene's anchor, and without him, Irene knew she could never have combined family and police work so well. Many of her married male colleagues with children had reached a similar balance at home. Like them, Irene rarely thought about it.

The car stopped directly in front of the entrance to Hotel

Montparnasse Raspail. She thanked her uniformed driver as she slung her backpack clumsily over her left shoulder. The hotel's glass doors swished open automatically when she approached. The recently painted terra-cotta lobby was relatively small.

The young woman behind the reception desk was impeccably attired in a dark blue dress. She was unusually tall and thin. She had dreadlocks that she wore wrapped around the top of her head until they hung down her back, and she had added glass pearls to many of them, so that they clicked gently as she stood up from her chair. She smiled warmly, and her teeth sparkled in contrast to her dark skin. *What is this woman doing behind a hotel reception desk?* Irene wondered. *She could be earning big bucks on designer catwalks. This is Paris, after all.*

Irene gave her name, and the receptionist, who wore a nametag that read LUCY, typed it into the computer. She gave a friendly nod. "Welcome, *Madame* Huss. I hope you will feel welcome here."

Her English was much better than Irene's. "Thank you."

Irene's eyes found a small bar at the corner of the lobby. "Excuse me, but would it be possible to have some coffee and a sandwich?" She wasn't able to hide the exhaustion in her voice.

Again, Lucy nodded. "Certainly, *madame*. I'll arrange it, but it will take a while." She leaned over the reception counter. "Forgive me for asking, but do you need some assistance?"

She was staring at Irene's shoulder.

"No," Irene said in confusion. "Just coffee and a sandwich, please."

"I mean, *madame*, you have blood on your sweater."

One glance at the mirror behind Lucy showed obvious bloodstains across Irene's left shoulder, ruining her light blue top.

"Oh, no!" Irene exclaimed. "And I've already used my extra

T-shirt to stop the bleeding! This is not my blood—it's my colleague's. She was the victim of—an unfortunate incident."

Before Irene had even consciously made the decision, she began to relate a somewhat censored version of the day's events. Lucy listened, enthralled.

"So, you are a police officer? And you did not intend to stay in Paris?" Lucy said, after taking a moment to reflect on Irene's tale of woe. "I know! One of my friends can help you! You need a change of clothes, right?"

"Right. I mean, thank you. And I also have a prescription. . . ." Irene said, her thoughts tumbling. She managed to find the doctor's piece of paper from her backpack. "Where's the nearest pharmacy?"

"*Madame* Huss, please give me your prescription. Go upstairs and relax in your room for a while. I'll come by with your medicine, your coffee, and some clothes. Your room number is 602. Please have a good rest."

Overwhelmed, Irene took the plastic card key and headed for the small elevator. It felt wonderful to let someone else worry for once, even though she'd always considered doing so a dangerous weakness. She'd never caved in to this temptation before. Maybe now was the time. Lucy's heartfelt sympathy had dissolved the lump of rage she felt at Inspector Verdier's ice-cold eyes and dismissive attitude.

The room was small, but it was clean and attractive. Actually, it looked as though the entire hotel had been renovated recently. A clean, inviting bed—what more could a person ask for?

IRENE WOKE UP at the knock at the door. The clock showed she'd slept for forty-five minutes. She didn't even remember lying down on the bed. She'd probably fallen asleep before her head hit the pillow—she was still fully dressed and on top of the bedcovers.

Lucy was waiting when Irene opened the door. She carried in a tray, and from her wrist dangled a large wax paper shopping bag in dazzling colors.

"Here you go, *madame*," she said with her shining smile. "My friend would like thirty-eight euros and the prescription cost eighteen."

Irene had only fifty euros in her wallet, but was relieved to see she had even that much. "Take this for now," she said. "I'll go and get more money. Thank you very much." Irene really did feel incredibly grateful.

"Don't rush. There's an ATM around the corner on the way to Montparnasse. Hardly more than a hundred meters from here."

On the bag, the words GALERIES LAFAYETTE were written in an elegant script. There was an attractive pale lilac cotton top and a few pairs of cotton underwear. At the bottom of the bag was a clear plastic makeup bag with small testers of cleansers and skin cream. There was even a mini mascara wand.

FINDING THE ATM was not a problem. Irene took out one hundred euros and went directly back to the hotel, where she paid her debt to Lucy.

Rothstaahl's apartment was almost directly across the street from Hotel Montparnasse Raspail. Feeling like she was taking her life in her hands, Irene jaywalked through the heavy traffic. When she got to the other side in one piece, she swore to herself she'd keep to the lights and crosswalks on the way back.

Irene put the key into the apartment's front door, then hesitated before she turned it. What if the man who'd attacked her and Kajsa had returned? She decided it was unlikely, but as she opened the door, she still had a knot of worry in her stomach and all her senses on high.

There was no scent of men's cologne. If only she'd

understood what that strong scent had meant before! She opened the bathroom door to notice that the grooming kit was gone. Had the attacker remembered to take his toiletries with him or had the French police come to investigate and taken it for technical examination? She walked back into the hallway and surveyed the scene. The large bloodstain in the doorway was still there. She took a quick look into the kitchen, bedroom, and living room, and her suspicions were confirmed—there was no sign that the French police had been on the scene. She had locked the apartment door as the ambulance was leaving, and Inspector Verdier had not requested the key—which she wouldn't have given him anyway. Perhaps he realized that.

The kitchen was tiny and a window opened to the interior courtyard. This side of the apartment building was not as well kept as the street-side façade. Plaster was missing. Obviously the most important thing was the public appearance on the side of the boulevard.

In one cupboard, Irene found simple white place settings, wine glasses, normal drinking glasses, utensils, and a few serving plates. The pantry held instant coffee and a few dry goods. Three pots and one frying pan were the only cookware she could find. Obviously the current resident didn't cook much. As Irene took a closer look at the furniture, she realized that the apartment must have come furnished. Nothing had a personal touch. No trendy design here—just run-of-the-mill stuff. This didn't fit with Irene's impression of Philip Bergman's ph.com glory days. This apartment would not be featured in a glossy interior decoration magazine. On the other hand, it was Joachim Rothstaahl's apartment. Perhaps he had different taste.

The bedroom had not changed since she'd left it a few hours before. An involuntary shudder went through her as she looked at the shattered closet door. Overcoming her hesitation, she entered the room and turned on the light.

Apparently, Philip Bergman and Joachim Rothstaahl shared the closet. Since Philip had been much taller and more athletic than Joachim, his clothes were larger as well. They were hanging neatly on clothes hangers. There were shoe racks beneath the clothes, and Irene couldn't help counting the pairs. Philip had forty-seven while Joachim had only twenty-two. Irene made a quick mental count and realized that she owned just nine pairs of shoes, if she included her rubber boots and the pair of boat shoes she was wearing at the moment.

The bedroom dressers were not as orderly as the closet: underwear, T-shirts, and socks were tossed in random piles.

Next, the bed. If her attacker had stayed in the apartment for at least a night, there could be traces of him left behind. Irene turned on one of the halogen bedside lamps and aimed it at the bed cover. She inspected the surface carefully, and she felt a shiver of excitement when she saw a few strands of hair on a bolster. Irene walked into the kitchen and found a roll of white plastic bags under the sink. She took the whole roll back into the bedroom. Since she had forgotten to bring gloves, she slipped a bag over her left hand. She didn't dare use the right one yet; every time she moved a finger on that hand, a wave of pain shot to her elbow. She was clumsy with her left hand, and it was difficult to try to pick up the strands of hair and put them into a second bag, but it worked. When she succeeded, she felt elated, but she knew there was still a lot to do. She carefully pulled back the bedcover and repeated the procedure with the two main pillows. There was a lot of hair. She put every strand into another bag. Malm and Åhlén's job would be to sort through them. It wouldn't be too difficult. Joachim's and Philip's hair could be eliminated immediately. Perhaps the third person's hair would be detected. And maybe some from the intruder, although there was also the possibility that some could have come from an innocent bed partner. Irene didn't expect that. She carefully knotted the bags and put them in her backpack.

In one corner of the room, there was a plain desk with a laser printer and a number of electrical cords, but no computer. Irene pulled open the desk drawers but found nothing of interest. On the wall above the desk there was a bookshelf with some binders. One was marked APARTMENT. Irene pulled down that one and began to flip through it. She found the rental contract, signed by Joachim Rothstaahl on April 1, 2001. He'd rented the fully furnished apartment for fifteen hundred euros a month. Irene calculated the exchange rate in her head; fourteen thousand Swedish kroner for an apartment that was only seven hundred square feet. Perhaps that was another incentive to find a roommate.

The next binder to catch her interest was titled Euro Fund in gold lettering on the spine. It contained a number of fat brochures printed on expensive paper. There were graphs and diagrams to give an impression of financial responsibility as well as a number of beautiful photographs of Paris. From the Swedish version of the text, Irene understood that the brochure was meant for investors for a mutual fund with a high rate of return. "Guaranteed to be the best fund with the highest return rates on the market today!" Irene stuffed the entire binder into her backpack.

The only expensive item in the entire room was a widescreen television that looked brand new. Irene noticed a shelf of videos, mostly American action and horror films. She recognized some of the titles: *Silence of the Lambs* and *Se7en*. As she shifted the video player, she saw a few films hidden behind it. She took them out and read titles like *Lover Boy* and *Beach Boy Sex*. The covers showed handsome, muscular men in provocative positions. She wasn't surprised, thinking back to her colleagues' hypothesis.

The apartment gave the impression that its residents had

been in a long-lasting, stable relationship. There was no indication that one of them was there only on a temporary basis. She felt pretty certain that their relationship was sexual.

In the article that she'd read on the plane on the way over, Philip was described as a magnet for young women, but that didn't mean he was drawn to them. *Perhaps the young women were a cover, especially if he wanted to keep his homosexuality hidden? Or maybe he was bisexual? Perhaps there was a motive for murder in a personal relationship among the people involved?* People's sex lives were always of interest in a murder investigation, but from experience Irene knew that it was difficult to get to the heart of the matter in such cases. People tried hard to hide the truth when they felt threatened by exposure.

A thought crossed her mind: *the shower. Perhaps there were hairs from the intruder caught in the drain.* She picked up the roll of bags and headed back into the hallway. She opened the door to the small bathroom. In the weak light from the lamp above the sink, she bent down to take a closer look inside the shower. She was disappointed when she saw no hair at all. Her bad knee creaked as she stood back up, but not loud enough to cover the sound of a key turning in the front door lock.

Chapter 11

"MERCI, MADAME LAUENSTEIN," said a male voice Irene immediately recognized. Relief and irritation swept through her as her fear dissipated. If this had been her attacker, she'd have had a difficult time defending herself with no weapon and an injured arm.

A woman's voice started speaking a stream of French until it was cut short by "*Oui, merci.*"

Irene heard the front door close. She knew her visitor would see the light from the bathroom door, which was slightly ajar. She was ready when he opened the door, and the light glinted on the barrel of his gun.

"*Bonjour, Monsieur Verdier,*" Irene said.

At least she'd manage to learn one phrase during her day in Paris.

Inspector Verdier pulled the door open all the way but did not lower his gun. "What are you doing here?" he snapped.

"I'd like to ask you the same question," she replied.

They glared at each other for a few moments. Irene was ready for his ice-cold stare, and she countered it with her own small, tight smile. He looked away. He was obviously used to people melting before his glare.

"Who let you in?" asked Irene, taking control of the situation.

"*Madame la concierge* . . . the woman in charge of the building. I wanted to see the scene of the crime." A muscle spasmed beneath one of his ears as he clenched his teeth. He lowered the pistol and put it back in its holster beneath his jacket.

"Why did you want to look around?" Irene asked.

Verdier took his time to reply. "The attack on you and your colleague is just one component of an even greater crime," he finally said.

"That's not exactly news to me. It's connected to the two murders in Sweden. Two Swedish citizens were killed, and the victims happened to be living in Paris—"

"Not that crime," Verdier interrupted. "A different one."

Another crime? Have the French police also found financial wizards with a bullet in the brain?

"Come," Verdier said. "Let's sit down."

They sat down in the living room, each in their own plush, beige armchair. The Frenchman moved his to sit directly opposite Irene. Perhaps he did this to avoid straining his neck during the conversation, but Irene suspected it was an old habit. He wanted to look his suspects in the eye. Irene, for her part, no longer felt like one.

Verdier spoke first. "You informed me about two murdered men active in the Parisian financial world, so I contacted a colleague in our department of economic crimes. He called me an hour ago to say that Joachim Rothstaahl was on his list. The owner of a Norwegian company had warned us about an offer to invest money in a mutual fund here in France. He'd had a good friend who'd lost a great deal through Rothstaahl and his friends' deception. He recognized the name and the brochure. They're using the same pattern they used in London. England sent us confirmation that Rothstaahl had been part of that fraud, although he wasn't convicted there. For some reason, the court case was handled in Norway."

Irene already knew the reason behind that, but she was surprised, partially by how quickly the French police had found information on the pyramid scheme Poundfix and partially by the fact that Verdier had spoken freely, and apparently truthfully.

At last she could comprehend a little of what Joachim Rothstaahl was really up to in Paris. He wasn't employed by HP Johnson's Paris office, as he'd told his parents. He'd just continued his London schemes with a new partner.

"Did your colleague know anything about Philip Bergman?" asked Irene.

"No, but he recognized Bergman's name. He had no idea that Bergman had come to Paris and was involved with Rothstaahl. Do you have any idea why he was here?"

Irene experienced a short internal battle. Finally she decided to put her cards on the table. She bent to pull the Euro Fund binder from her backpack and gave Verdier one of the brochures.

"Here you go. Say hi to your colleague and tell him thanks for the information. The text is in French. Speaking of French. . . ." Irene fell silent. She watched Verdier flip through the brochure before she got the courage to continue. "Would you be so kind as to call the hospital for me to see how my partner is doing? I can't speak French, and things are very difficult to understand on the phone."

"Certainly," Verdier said. "I'll call for you."

Irene quickly wrote Kajsa's name and birth date on one of the brochures. Verdier took his cell phone from one of his inner jacket pockets. Irene caught a glimpse of his gun and holster. A long phone conversation followed. From the multiple silences, Irene understood that he was being put on hold and transferred several times. Finally he finished the call and shut his phone.

"Your colleague is doing well, but she will be under observation all night," he told her. "If her condition does not change, she will be discharged at noon tomorrow. The nurse thought there was no reason for you to visit tonight. She said that Kajsa sends her greetings."

"Thank you very much," Irene said, meaning it with all her heart.

This meant that she was free to go back to her hotel room, take two pain pills, and hit the sack. Her elbow was throbbing. Dragging herself back to the hotel seemed like an insurmountable task.

Verdier stood and took a quick look around the apartment while Irene stayed in the armchair. When he returned to the living room, he cleared his throat and asked, "These two men. Were they . . . together?"

Obviously, he'd reached the same conclusion as Irene. She nodded as she stood up. "I believe so."

Verdier thought for a while. Irene was too tired to help him think things through.

"Tomorrow, after you pick up your partner from the hospital, I would like to meet with the two of you. I need her testimony about the attack for my report. When does your flight leave?"

"Five in the evening."

"Where could we meet?"

Definitely not in your depressing office, Irene wanted to say, but refrained. "We can meet here," she suggested. "If Kajsa needs to rest, she can lie down on the bed, and the bus to the airport leaves just a hundred meters from the door."

"Good. I will pick you up at your hotel at eleven thirty. We can get your partner and drive back here," Verdier said.

Irene had the feeling that he was making sure that they weren't going to sneak away to Sweden without having a talk with him. She was probably being unfair. Maybe he was just trying to be nice and helpful.

"Being here might help her remember exactly what happened and give us a better description of the attacker," Verdier said. Expressionless, he added, "Could you recognize who attacked you?"

Irene sighed out loud. *This man isn't at all kind or friendly, just unbelievably suspicious.* "I'm tired, and I need to take some pills for the pain," she said, indicating her sling.

Right now she just wanted to get rid of the Frenchman because there was still something she wanted to look for. But she didn't want Verdier watching. To her great relief, he just shrugged.

"Not much more to see here," he said.

They walked out the front door, and Irene locked it. They walked down the stairs in silence. Verdier held the heavy door open politely, and they stepped into the warm evening air. A weak breeze blew along the boulevard and carried with it the aromas from all the nearby restaurants. The building next door housed an elegant seafood restaurant. Along the outside wall of the building, the restaurant had set up stainless steel shelves heaped with ice to display all kinds of shellfish. Two men in rubber overalls were shucking oysters. The waiters ran back and forth collecting lobsters, shrimp, and oysters, which they then arranged on large serving trays. Irene was suddenly extremely hungry, although the last thing she wanted to eat was oysters. She'd eaten them once, and that was enough for the rest of her life. She'd been reminded of smelly snot when they slithered down her throat. No, indeed, oysters were the last thing she'd want to eat, and certainly not with Verdier for company.

"Good night, and thank you for coming and picking me up tomorrow morning. I appreciate the friendly gesture," she said, forcing a small smile.

"*Bonne nuit, madame.*"

For the first time since they'd met, Irene felt she could detect the hint of a smile on the Inspector's narrow face . . . but she could have been wrong.

They each went their own way, and Irene could see from the corner of her eye that Verdier was heading for the gray Mégane. She walked to the crosswalk. Beyond the wide intersection of boulevards, she spied a sign for Pizza Hut. After she crossed the street in an entirely legal way, she reached the restaurant and ordered a huge slice of pizza with a Coca-Cola and a salad. The place was packed with young people, but she managed to find a seat by the window. The pizza tasted fantastic, and she was momentarily able to forget the pain in her elbow. Light and movement pulsed outside the window, as people and cars sped past in a never-ending stream.

When her watch read nine thirty P.M., she decided enough time had passed. She walked back to 207 Raspail Boulevard, keeping an eye open for anyone else. It wouldn't have surprised her if Verdier jumped out of nowhere.

No Verdier appeared by the time she put the key into the door. She carefully pushed it open. Everything was quiet. Silently, she closed the door behind her. She found the switch to the ceiling lamp and flipped it on.

Maybe she'd gotten used to the smell of Rothstaahl's apartment, because it took her a second or two to realize that the scent of a man's cologne was stronger than it had been just an hour before. Abruptly she knew she was going to need her judo training.

The bathroom door swung open, and a man rushed toward her. She turned slightly aside from his trajectory and swung her foot left in a backward kick. In the *ura-mawashi-geri* kick, the heel is used as the impact surface and has the force of a horse's kick. The training words ran through her mind. The man was unprepared, and Irene's kick landed right in his solar plexus. He folded like a Swiss army knife. As his chin came down, Irene followed up with a *yoko-geri*, lifting her foot to knee height and kicking sideways. There was a hollow echo as the man's lower jaw clashed against his upper jaw. He fell headlong onto the floor and lay there without moving.

A burst of adrenaline gave Irene energy and cleared her head. She took a few deep breaths before she bent down to take a good look at the man. She carefully rolled him over so he lay on his side.

He was tall and athletic, with blond hair that had started to thin at the top. He had a deep tan, which looked real. His clothes were elegantly casual. He wore khaki chinos, a matching piqué sweater, a jacket of light brown corduroy, and hand-crafted shoes. A handsome man in his mid-forties with good health and appearance.

Just as Irene decided to search his pockets, he grunted and opened his eyes. Irene leaped backward. Obviously, this guy had a much harder chin than most people. He narrowed his eyes and peered up at her. His expression was grim as he reached inside his jacket. Irene immediately dashed for the door. Luckily, she hadn't locked it when she'd entered. She flung it open and leaped to the side as a bullet whizzed past her cheek. The plaster on the other side of the hallway flew apart as the bullet smashed into it. She hurtled down the stairs and heard doors opening and people yelling in French behind her.

Once on the street, she slowed her run and hugged the wall in case an apartment resident was looking out the window. Once she got to the seafood restaurant where a man in rubber overalls was still shucking oysters, she stepped into the crowd of pedestrians. Street traffic hadn't slowed at all, but she managed to cross the street at the crosswalk, and she entered the hotel looking cool and collected. She crossed the lobby, where Lucy was sitting behind her computer screen chatting in swift French. They smiled briefly at each other, and Irene went into the tiny elevator.

Once she reached her room, she kept the lights off. She hid behind the curtain to peer out the window toward the entrance to Rothstaahl's apartment building. The door opened, and she saw the man come out and head toward Montparnasse Boulevard. It was definitely the man who'd shot at her.

Who is he?

Although she didn't know his name, she felt there was something very familiar about him.

Chapter 12

INSPECTOR VERDIER PHONED at seven thirty that morning. Irene had set her cell phone alarm to the same time, so she was confused when she realized not only did she have to turn off the alarm but also answer the call.

Verdier didn't open with hello, but just said, "Did you sleep well, *Madame* Huss?"

"Yes, thank you. Your French medicines are extremely efficient," Irene said.

She tried to sound more energetic than she felt.

"There was an incident last night . . . perhaps you know something about it?"

"No, I don't. What happened?" Irene blessed the fact that they didn't have a videophone. Verdier would have been suspicious if he'd seen her slight smile.

There was a pause before he said, "I'm on my way to your hotel."

"All right. I'll be in the breakfast room in half an hour," Irene replied.

A LARGE COFFEE thermos, warm croissants, various French cheeses, and a soft-boiled egg put Irene into a good mood right away. She'd slept like a log the night before and had dreamed of neither cranky French policemen nor hired killers with guns. Her elbow still ached, but it felt much better than yesterday. She'd needed only one pain pill that morning.

Painkillers tended to dull her responses, and she'd have gone back to sleep if she'd taken two.

Inspector Verdier arrived as she was finishing her third cup of coffee. He looked the way he always did, even wearing the same clothes as yesterday. His expression was even more grim than before, however. He pulled out the chair on the other side of the table so he could sit directly across from Irene. As usual, he wanted direct eye contact so he could register every shift of emotion on her face, but Irene was also a master interrogator, and she'd already formed her strategy.

"*Bonjour, Monsieur* Verdier," she said, smiling.

"*Bonjour, Madame* Huss," he said brusquely. There was no effort to appear friendly.

"Have a cup of coffee, if you'd like," Irene offered, gesturing to the coffee thermos.

"No." His mouth formed a thin line as he pressed his narrow lips together. For someone in such control of his expressions, this was surprising. However, his eyes revealed nothing as he looked Irene up and down. "So, tell me what happened yesterday evening," he said.

"As I told you on the phone, I have no idea what you're talking about," she said firmly.

"Are you absolutely sure?"

"Yes, of course."

He glared harder at her, but Irene was used to his tactics and remained calm and collected. The loaded silence lay heavy on the table until Irene decided to break it by asking, "Isn't it time you fill me in on what's been going on here?"

The inspector's chilly façade began to crack. He wasn't an idiot, and he had the instincts of a good policeman. Of course, he would find it frustrating that this Swedish policewoman knew much more that she was willing to divulge. He certainly suspected that she'd been involved in yesterday's incident, but he didn't know how or why. It would be dangerous to underestimate him, though. Irene definitely would not make that mistake.

"I hope it had nothing to do with Kajsa," Irene added, trying to sound worried.

"Not at all."

Verdier took a cup of coffee, poured in a great deal of milk, and sipped.

"There were shots fired at the Rothstaahl apartment at quarter to ten yesterday evening. Neighbors called the police, but when our colleagues arrived, there was no one left in the apartment. The door was wide open, however, and there was a bullet hole in the hallway close to the stairs."

Irene widened her eyes and tried to appear distressed.

"A shot? But who. . . ." She intentionally left her sentence unfinished.

"We don't know who it was. On the other hand, we know that two men were in the apartment."

Two men? Irene hoped her expression didn't reveal her surprise. Verdier gave her a searching look before he continued.

"The neighbors heard the shot. No one opened their doors because they were afraid, but they put their ears to their doors to hear what was going on. First one man rushed down the stairs. A few minutes later, they heard another man go down the stairs more slowly. At that point, one resident dared open his door and caught a glimpse of a tall man with wide shoulders and blond hair."

"Did the neighbor see the man's face?" Irene asked.

"No, he just saw him from the back."

"And the first man—did anyone see him?"

She sent up a grateful prayer that she was wearing her boat shoes. No clacking of feminine heels there. She was certainly fast on her feet, thanks to all her years of jogging. Not to mention that being shot at tended to cause an extra burst of speed.

"No, no one saw him. Still, there are some witnesses whom we still have to question," Verdier said sharply.

The image of the oyster-shucking men in front of the seafood restaurant flickered through Irene's memory. She hoped that they'd been too busy to notice a tall woman slipping into the crowd at the time of the shooting. And Lucy! Irene had almost forgotten her. Things could get sticky if Verdier talked to her. Irene wanted to get the inspector out of the hotel as quickly as possible. But how? She had the feeling that he'd keep an eye on her until she and Kajsa headed home on the plane. She still hadn't had the chance to look for what she guessed was still in the apartment. She realized something: obviously the French police had gone over the apartment after the shooting.

"Has anything been stolen?" she asked.

Verdier shrugged. "No idea. We had no way of knowing. Do you know of anything of interest?"

"Perhaps. Did you find any computer discs?"

He paused, then pulled out his cell phone and hit a button. After a short conversation, he turned it off.

"No discs were found. Why did you think of this?"

"Both Bergman's and Rothstaahl's computers were stolen after the murders, and we didn't find any computer discs in Göteborg. We believe that either the computers or their discs could contain evidence of what these two men were up to. As it is now, we can only guess."

"We found no discs here in Paris, either. There might be many people interested in these two."

Irene had a quick internal debate. It would be better to go back and search the apartment in Verdier's company than not to be able to return at all. Plus she didn't want Verdier talking to Lucy, so she said in a light tone, "Maybe they hid the discs. We should go and look for them."

"So they might have hidden them in the apartment?"

"I think so."

Verdier stood up. "Let's go."

THEY METHODICALLY SEARCHED the entire apartment but didn't find a single disc. On the other hand, they found three bags of a white powder hidden in a shoebox in the closet. Verdier rubbed a speck against his gums and declared it to be cocaine. In a video case, they found a number of cards with pink pills, which they both believed were a form of ecstasy.

They sat down on the plush armchairs again and laid out the narcotics they'd found on the coffee table. Verdier contemplated their discovery.

"This is a lot of cocaine. Did you know they were involved in drugs?" he asked.

"No, but during Bergman's glory days at his dot-com, rumor had it that they were no stranger to drug abuse," Irene replied.

Verdier nodded. "These two men called themselves consultants and enticed Scandinavian businesses to invest capital in Euro Fund. According to my colleague and your own account, this Rothstaahl was part of a similar scheme in London. Now we know they were also involved in drugs. I wonder why they dared take such risks."

He looked at Irene, and she had nothing to say to that, so she answered his question with another question. "What risks?"

"First of all, getting caught. Rothstaahl must have known it was only a matter of time before someone connected the dots. This scheme is identical to the one he'd already pulled off. Also, he and his partner get involved selling drugs; this amount can't just be for personal use. That was stupid of them. Selling drugs is severely punished in this country. I believe that the two of them must have been desperate."

"Desperate?" Irene said.

"Yes, they must have been absolutely desperate for money."

Irene had to admit he was right. She glanced around the slightly depressing apartment, far below Philip Bergman's heyday standards.

Why were they so desperate to raise money quickly? A vain attempt to get back to the kind of life they'd had during the nineties? Or was this about something else entirely?

Irene couldn't come up with any answers. Most likely Roth-staahl and Bergman were simply unscrupulous criminals who did whatever they could for money. They truly had no conscience and had already demonstrated shocking greed. Now they were willing to deal drugs as well.

There was a feeling of pathos in Bergman's rise and fall in the business world—from a golden calf surrounded by adoring crowds to a shady dealer in drugs and pyramid schemes. The past few years, he'd been living in the shadows as a partner of another shady criminal. It hit Irene that there was something wrong with this picture. *What could it be?* She couldn't put a finger on it, but the gut feeling was there. If she could spot the puzzle piece that didn't fit, she'd get closer to solving this crime.

"Do you have any ideas about their backgrounds? Why they got mixed up in all this?" Verdier asked, echoing her own thoughts.

"No, I don't. Maybe they were just greedy."

"Maybe."

A wild idea hit her. "What if the man who attacked Kajsa and me was there to plant narcotics in the apartment as a frame? As well as the two men who were here last night?"

Verdier nodded. "There's also that possibility." He stood up as he looked at his watch. "It's time to pick up your colleague Kajsa Berger . . . Birger. . . ."

"Birgersdotter."

"As you said."

• • •

THE SMELL OF cleaning solutions and urine was over-whelming as they walked into the care unit. Kajsa was sitting in a hallway chair waiting for them. She was pale and looked exhausted. The large bandage around her head made her look battered.

A huge nurse waddled toward Irene and began to speak to her in French. Inspector Verdier came to Irene's rescue and took over the conversation. The nurse, still talking to Verdier, handed Irene a large brown envelope. Then she turned toward Kajsa and patted her on the cheek before she headed back down the hallway.

"She's been treating me like a child all morning," complained Kajsa in Swedish.

Verdier pointed at Kajsa and asked Irene, "Can she speak English?"

A stream of French came from Kajsa's lips before Irene was able to answer. Irene didn't understand a single word, but from Verdier's expression, he did. Once she'd finished, a corner of his mouth rose as he said drily, "Considering *Madame* Huss does not speak French, let's keep to English."

Kajsa mumbled something in Swedish that Irene couldn't make out.

"The nurse said that *Madame*—I mean, *Mademoiselle* Kajsa should rest for a few more days, since her concussion was severe," Verdier explained.

Irene held out her hand to help Kajsa up, but she waved away any assistance and stood up on her own. Her face blanched, and she swayed for a moment before she began slowly but determinedly to walk toward the exit.

"How are you feeling?" asked Irene.

"What do you think?" snapped Kajsa.

They didn't say another word until they reached the car. Irene sat beside Kajsa in the back seat. Verdier started the ignition and they soon found themselves in the middle of lunch-hour traffic.

"We're heading to Rothstaahl's apartment so we can talk in peace and quiet," Irene said.

Kajsa gave her a worried glance. "Why do we have to go back *there?*"

"The other alternative is Verdier's office. Trust me, you *don't* want to go there."

Although Irene and Kajsa were speaking in Swedish, the inspector heard his name, and he gave Irene a sharp look in the rearview mirror. Irene leaned forward and said, "I'm trying to find out how Kajsa is feeling. When we get to the apartment, we'll speak English."

She leaned back into her seat and gave his reflection a small smile. As she turned back to Kajsa, she saw that Kajsa had closed her eyes.

Irene sighed and concentrated on the distant view of the Eiffel Tower.

KAJSA REFUSED TO lie down on the sofa. She sat in one of the armchairs, and Verdier sat in the other one, so Irene had to take the sofa instead.

Verdier began in English without prelude. "Did you recognize the man who attacked you?"

"No," Kajsa said firmly.

"What did he look like?"

"Tall. Blond. Not fat, but well-built. Or rather, strong. He was extremely strong."

Kajsa seemed happy with her description, and Irene agreed. It fit her impression of the man.

"Age?"

"Anywhere from thirty to forty-five. Things happened really fast. I wasn't able to realize much before . . . he hit me in the head and I passed out. I've probably forgotten a lot."

"Probably. We want to help you remember as much as possible," Verdier said.

"What did he hit you with?" asked Irene.

"No idea. He had something . . . like an iron bar. He had it in his hand. It was long."

"Could it have been a crowbar? Or a flashlight?" Irene asked.

"More like a crowbar. Did you find one?" asked Kajsa.

"No. He took it away with him. He didn't break in: he had a key, and he still has the key," Irene told her.

"I will request that *Madame* Lauenstein change the lock," Verdier said quickly. He looked at Kajsa. "There was a shooting in this apartment last night. The technicians have dug out a .38 caliber bullet. But perhaps *Madame* Huss can give us some more information on that point."

He turned his steely gaze on Irene as he said the last sentence. Irene had to admire his stubbornness as well as his instincts. He was right, even though he was coming at it from the wrong direction. She didn't intend to help him figure it out. The last thing she wanted was more fuss from the Parisian police. It was bad enough that they'd been involved already to such an extent.

They were not able to jog Kajsa's memory much. Finally, she asked them to stop. She was tired, and her head was aching. Irene offered to go get pizza from Pizza Hut, but Kajsa threw a tantrum as if she were a three-year-old. As long as she was in Paris, she was going to have French food, for goodness sake! They decided to return to *La Rotonde*. It was close, and they knew the food was good. After a tasty lunch of trout and potatoes boiled with dill, Kajsa cheered up remarkably.

"I don't want to go back to that depressing apartment ever again," she declared over coffee and apple tart.

"We don't need to," said Verdier. He hadn't wanted dessert but had a large cup of café au lait.

"It'll soon be time for us to take the bus back to the airport," Irene said. She was struggling to crack the hard glaze on her tart without causing a piece to fly across the table. *What if it landed right in Verdier's lap? What a horrible thought!*

She looked over at the inspector and saw that he was studying Kajsa intently. Unexpectedly, he asked, "What did he say as he rushed toward you?"

"Who?" asked Kajsa, caught unaware.

"The man who attacked you. What did he say as he hit you?"

Kajsa looked at him in surprise. She opened her mouth as if to answer and shut it again so hard her teeth clicked. Then she whispered in Swedish, "Oh my God." She turned to Irene and said, "He was saying '*Helvete, helvete, helvete.*' He was swearing. In Swedish."

Chapter 13

"*Helvete, helvete, helvete,*" Andersson repeated meditatively.

He was settling back into his chair. He had just returned from a phone call in his office. Everyone in the conference room had taken advantage of the unexpected break to stretch their legs and get more coffee. Irene and Kajsa had spent most of the afternoon relating the events that had befallen them in Paris. Birgitta, Tommy, Fredrik, and Jonny had listened with great concentration. Irene thought Tommy was making too big a deal of Kajsa's bandaged head. He hardly noticed Irene's poor arm in its sling.

Jonny said, "So. Bergman and Rothstaahl were building a new pyramid scheme. They were living together. Busy with drugs. Both murdered here in Göteborg while on a visit. Kajsa and Irene are attacked by a man mumbling a Swedish swear word. Probably the same guy Irene runs into later that evening. He shoots at her with a .38. Neither Kajsa nor Irene recognizes him. Possibly he planted the drugs in the apartment. One question: Why? Why was he at that apartment? Did he shoot Bergman and Rothstaahl? Why? And how the hell does Kjell B:son Ceder's murder come into the picture?"

Andersson gave Jonny a sorrowful look. "It gets even more confusing. Svante Malm called. They're out on that island investigating the cairn of stones the drunk woman complained had been moved. She was right. They found remains beneath the stones."

A dismayed silence followed his words. Irene was more disturbed than the others, even though she'd expected this since hearing the stones had been moved.

"Irene and Tommy, you're going there. After three years, you'll find Thomas Bonetti at last," Andersson said drily.

"Let me go, too," Kajsa said. She looked at Andersson defiantly from below her bandage. A large bruise had formed around her eye.

"There's no chance I'm sending you out in public. The Paris doctor said that you were supposed to go on sick leave until Monday," Andersson said with finality.

Kajsa looked disappointed. She threw her boss a purple-tinged angry glare, but she said nothing. Andersson couldn't read French and had no idea what the French doctor had actually written down, so he probably had just made up the number of sick days on the spot. However, forcing Kajsa to take a few days off was a good idea. A severe concussion needed to be taken seriously. Irene knew that from experience.

Birgitta requested the floor next. "About this connection to money. One time or another each of the victims had a lot of money. Now we've found out they all lost it again. Within the past three years, Ceder, Bergman, Rothstaahl, and even Sanna Kaegler lost their fortunes. And no one knows where Thomas Bonetti's money went."

"It disappeared during the dot-com crash," said Jonny with absolute certainty.

Birgitta shook her head. "We know there were rumors that the money disappeared from ph.com to land in the pockets of its founders. Sanna and Philip blamed Bonetti—who conveniently disappeared."

"That Kaegler woman! Tommy, once that body under the

stones is identified, you go and grill that broad until she cracks!" Andersson commanded.

"Getting back to Sanna," Birgitta said, "neither Bergman nor Rothstaahl is the daddy of little Ludwig. The DNA analysis came this morning."

"I hardly expect either of those homos to be the father," Jonny growled. "And it wasn't Ceder either. So who's the father?"

"Right now, we are more concerned with solving a murder, not a paternity suit," Andersson said.

Irene felt that the two were connected, but wasn't sure why.

THE POLICE BOAT picked them up at Fiskebäck's small boat harbor. Both Tommy and Irene knew the captain, Torbjörn Melander, well. They'd worked with him in the third district for years, sharing patrol cars in central Göteborg, enforcing law and order. Torbjörn was a few years older than they were. He'd been born and raised on Brännö, near the water, so when the opportunity arose for a sea police position a few years ago, he'd jumped at the chance. For him it was like coming home.

They sat next to him in the wheelhouse. The water was rougher as they left the coast of Styrsö Island, and they could feel the entire boat smack when it hit the waves. It was quiet as misty rain wrapped the area in a gray shroud. Although Irene was not an expert on boating, she wasn't worried by the decreased visibility. She trusted Torbjörn, who knew every nook and cranny of these islands from Nordkoster to Anholt. He didn't need a compass or a sea chart to find Branteskär.

"My compass is here," he chortled, pointing to his stomach.

The contours of Branteskär began to jut up before them out of the thick fog. It had steep cliffs, just as its name indicated.

"You can't land on this side. There's a small inlet on the other side, which is the only place anyone can land at all," said Torbjörn.

It took some time for the boat to tie up, since the increasing wind kept blowing it away from the dock.

"I'm going to stay on the boat," said Torbjörn. "I have to tie up and make sure that we don't slam into anything."

Just as she was about to jump onto land, Irene almost lost her foothold on the slippery deck. *That's all I need, to fall into the water in front of my colleagues! They'd tease me until I retired!* It wasn't easy to climb up the slope with only one good hand. It was so steep in some parts that they had to move sideways like giant crabs. It was much easier when they made their way down the other side where the stone pile was. There were large round rocks that had been deposited by receding glaciers.

Svante Malm was sitting with other police officers drinking coffee from a thermos. The wind was cold on this side of the island, and the chilling rainwater crept through unexpected crevices in their raincoats. They'd pegged a tarp over the grave for protection.

"Have some coffee," Svante said. "That guy's waited under those stones so long already. Five more minutes won't make much difference."

Irene gratefully took the mug in her fingers, which were stiffening from the chill. *What kind of person would remember to bring gloves at the end of September?* Not her. The coffee warmed her hands through the thin plastic cup. Her right hand was, of course, already warm and dry, protected in its sling beneath her jacket. She didn't think she'd need the sling much longer. Her elbow was starting to feel more normal.

"So, do you think it's Thomas Bonetti?" Tommy asked Malm directly.

"Judging by the length of time the corpse has been here, it could very well be. There's some tissue, but not much. The insects have done their job. The clothing is still here, though, as well as the hair. Male clothes. The hair is thin and blond with a reddish tint."

"Sounds like Bonetti," Tommy nodded.

Svante Malm poured more coffee, lifted his cup to his lips, and peered at the detectives through the steam. "And there's one more thing. All the fingers on the left hand except the thumb are missing."

"IT DIDN'T TAKE long to locate Bonetti's dental charts, since his parents had the same dentist," Tommy said. "The medical examiner studied the corpse's teeth yesterday evening and compared them to the X-rays. They matched. So it is Thomas Bonetti we've found."

It was Friday morning, and they were all sitting around the conference table trying to analyze the latest developments in the case. Heavy fog hemmed them in through the windows, so they'd turned on the lights. *Autumn has come*, Irene thought morosely. *There's no turning back.* She comforted herself with the thought that she and Tommy's wife Agneta would be going mushroom hunting over the weekend. They knew of a secret mushroom patch in Härskogen Forest.

"Svante was also right about the four fingers missing from the left hand. The technicians searched the whole area around the heap of stones and couldn't find them in or around the grave," Tommy continued.

The superintendent was breathing roughly, and he coughed up some mucus. His asthma had gotten worse from the damp weather. "Torture. I suspect he'd been tortured," he said roughly.

"Why?" Fredrik asked.

"Money. Everything in this case has to do with money," Irene answered.

"But that can't be right. When Bonetti disappeared, ph.com had already lost all the money," Birgitta objected.

"That's right, and who got the blame for taking it?" Irene countered. "Thomas Bonetti."

Fredrik Stridh asked, "How much money was gone?"

"Several million kroner. Maybe even as much as fifteen to twenty million, according to Sanna Kaegler," Irene replied.

"Fifteen million," Birgitta said. "Many folks have lost fingers and lives for much less."

"But why would they torture him before they killed him? Or were the fingers cut off after he was murdered?" Fredrik wondered.

"We don't know. The autopsy won't be able to answer that question, either. It's been much too long since the death, and the body was pretty decomposed," Irene said.

An image forced itself to the forefront of Irene's memory: a grinning skull protruding from the remains of a Peak Performance jacket. The jacket had been tough nylon and well preserved. The shoes and suit trousers had also lasted. *Buying quality really does pay off*, thought Irene. She grimaced.

"There is, however, no question how he died. Two shots in the right temple. There was a bullet still in the cranium. The technicians haven't determined what type, but I'll put my money on a .25," Irene continued.

"So he was killed three years ago. But why were Ceder, Bergman, and Rothstaahl killed recently?" Birgitta asked.

"When we have answers to those questions, we've solved the case," Tommy said.

MADAME BONETTI APPEARED calm and in control as she opened her heavy oak door for the police officers. Her eyes behind her glasses, however, were swollen and red. The older woman was hefty but camouflaged in a finely tailored, dark blue dress suit. Beneath her jacket, she wore a cream silk blouse and large rose pearls. She'd dyed her thick hair black and wore it in an intricate knot at the top of her head, but the dark dye was garish against her over-powdered, flabby face. Irene had trouble breathing from her overpowering perfume.

Diamonds flashed on her hands as she gestured for them to come inside. She waddled as she led them to a large, airy room furnished with elegantly cool Nordic furniture. This woman did not fit the décor of her living room. She must have had an interior designer.

"Please sit down. My husband will be here shortly," she said.

Her voice was as high as a girl's and was startling coming from her large body. She gestured to two armchairs covered in beige- and white-striped linen.

Irene had called ahead a few hours before and had reached the mother. She'd requested that the Bonettis come to the police station for a conversation, but Marianne Bonetti had refused. She was too upset to drive after learning her son was really gone, so she requested that the meeting happen at her house in Långedrag instead.

Now, Marianne Bonnetti sank into one of the other armchairs. Irene saw that she was nervously fiddling with a handkerchief in one of her hands. Tommy used his most sympathetic voice, "We're sorry for your—"

"It's better this way. To know for sure," Marianne Bonetti interrupted him.

"I understand. The uncertainty must have been very difficult," Tommy said.

She nodded and swallowed. "How could anyone . . . Thomas . . . he was so kind." Her voice dwindled away. In the silence, they heard the front door open and shut and quick steps head toward them. Antonio Bonetti walked into the living room. Both Irene and Tommy stood up to shake hands. His grip was firm, but Irene noticed his palm was damp from sweat. The famous lawyer was half a foot shorter than his wife. He was almost completely bald, and he'd combed what few strands remained over his freckled scalp. He was wearing an elegant suit, but the expensive tailoring could not hide a growing belly. A bright, fat signet ring flashed from his ring finger. It fit the style of the Rolex watch on his wrist. Antonio Bonetti was more than sixty-years-old, but he was still one of the most sought-after lawyers for criminal cases in Sweden. These days, he took only cases that promised both maximum media coverage and a guaranteed win. Through the years, he'd been interviewed many times on television, where he'd proclaim his version of the case's facts—always to his client's advantage, of course.

"So, you've begun already?" he asked, shooting a quick glance at his wife. His eyes were colorless pools framed by white brows and lashes.

"They've just arrived. . . . We've only had time to sit down," Marianne Bonetti said hastily.

Irene understood the lawyer wanted to make sure they had not started to question his wife without his presence. Antonio Bonetti sat down on the sofa. He crossed one well-pressed trouser leg over the other, and Irene saw he wore extra high-heeled shoes.

"So, do you have any information?" the lawyer asked as he stared at Tommy.

"No. We know as much as we did three years ago, except for the fact that he's been found murdered. We have no idea why. Do you?" Tommy used a friendly tone.

"No. Thomas had no arguments with anyone. Many lies went around after he disappeared—but they were groundless rumors." The lawyer emphasized the last word.

"He was indicted for embezzlement. . . ."

"Lies!" Bonetti cut him off. His foot was jiggling with irritation in its elegant shoe. His feet were unusually small for a man. "It was those other two. Sanna Kaegler and Philip Bergman. They conspired against Thomas and blamed him for ph.com's bankruptcy. But you notice they certainly took care of themselves before the crash." Antonio became calmer as he spoke.

"Do you have any proof?" asked Tommy.

"No. Just what Thomas was saying that last summer. He accused Philip and Sanna of taking kickbacks. I never bothered to follow up any of this after Thomas disappeared and the indictment was dropped. There was so much we had to do. We had to deal with Thomas's disappearance at the same time I was involved in a rather large pharmaceutical lawsuit—the biggest one ever seen in Sweden. It was rough, but we won."

He seemed unaware of the contented smile that spread across his face. They had come to talk about his dead son, and he was smiling about a long-ago trial. Irene shuddered and wrote *kickbacks?* in her notebook.

"Do you remember if Thomas was ever threatened?" Tommy continued.

Both parents shook their heads.

"Never," said Antonio.

"Did he have any enemies?"

"Not a single one," said Marianne Bonetti.

Irene remembered Annika Hermansson saying: *He had no friends. No one ever wanted to play with him. Not even Billy.*

She asked, "Who were Thomas's friends?"

The parents turned their heads to look at her, but neither one answered the question. The silence was painful. Finally, Marianne Bonetti said, "Thomas had many acquaintances in business. He lived in London. . . . We didn't know all his friends."

"Did he have any acquaintances here in Sweden?" Irene asked.

"Maybe . . . but he wasn't home much," Marianne said doubtfully.

"Joachim Rothstaahl was murdered just a few kilometers away. He grew up here in Långedrag, too. Did they know each other when they were children?"

"No, the age difference was too great," said Masianne

Bonetti. "They were four or five years apart. That's a lot, especially in the teenage years. They first really got to know each other in London."

"Did he have any friends on Styrsö?"

"Not that I know of. Why do you ask?"

"Thomas went to Styrsö on the last evening of his life. Perhaps he planned to meet someone. Did he still see Billy Hermansson?"

"No, I don't—" Marianne Bonetti stopped abruptly as her husband suddenly stood up. She looked at him nervously as he held his hand to his chest. His signet ring shone against the dark cloth of his suit.

"My medicine. . . ." he mumbled. He hurried away from the room, and they could hear the clatter of his heels on the wooden floor.

"Antonio has heart trouble. He takes medicine for it," Marianne Bonetti explained. "As you can imagine, this has hit him fairly hard. He doesn't show his emotions. . . . He keeps his sorrows to himself."

"We understand that this must be extremely difficult for you both," Tommy said soothingly.

She nodded and dried her eyes with the handkerchief she'd been clutching during their entire conversation.

Styrsö. Why did Antonio react so strongly when the island was mentioned? Up to that moment, he seemed in complete control of the situation. Does he know something that he doesn't want to talk about? Irene decided this was something she wouldn't let go.

"I'll fetch us some mineral water," Marianne Bonetti said as she pushed herself with difficulty up out of the soft, cushioned armchair.

Before the police officers could decline, she marched off in the same direction as her husband.

Irene bent over as if she were going to adjust her sock.

"Don't let go of Styrsö," she whispered to Tommy. "There's something there."

"Mmm," he replied, barely audible.

They could hear the flushing of a toilet. After a while, the Bonetti couple returned to the room. Antonio Bonetti was carrying three bottles of mineral water, and his wife held a silver tray with four crystal glasses. A few ice cubes were in each glass. She set four golden coasters on the coffee table and placed a glass on each. The ice cubes clinked as her husband filled the glasses with the mineral water. The couple returned to their seats, and Antonio drank some water.

"I have angina," he explained. "I'm supposed to have an operation this winter."

Both Irene and Tommy nodded to show they understood his situation. Tommy also drank some water before he said, "Getting back to Styrsö. Was there anyone on the island that Thomas might have wanted to meet?"

"Absolutely not." Antonio Bonetti banged down his glass onto the golden coaster.

"So he and Billy Hermansson no longer. . . ?" Irene let the question hang in the air.

The lawyer's face had no expression when he looked at her. And yet—there was something there, but before she could put her finger on it, he'd looked away again.

"No. They only played together as children," he replied firmly.

"So neither one of you have any idea why he wanted to go to Styrsö that last evening?" Irene was too stubborn to let go yet.

"No. We already told you. He said that he wanted to think things over in peace and quiet."

Antonio Bonetti regathered his superior and collected manner. Irene saw that his hands shook slightly as he set his glass back down, but perhaps this was a side effect of the medicine he'd just taken.

"Do you still have his computer?" Irene asked.

"Computer? What kind of computer?" Antonio said with irritation.

"His personal computer. We think he had a laptop. Do you have it?" Irene asked.

Both Bonettis appeared to think about it. Finally, Antonio shook his head.

"I don't remember finding a computer among his things. Do you?" He turned to his wife.

"No, there wasn't one. Neither here nor in London," she said.

"Any computer discs?" asked Irene.

"No," they both said.

"When we were thinking of possible suspects in his death, we considered his part in Poundfix. He was with Joachim Rothstaahl on that project. You know that Rothstaahl was murdered just a—"

"That Norwegian, what was his name . . . Dahl! He was behind that scandal!" Antonio snapped. "Thomas was lured into it! Dahl was found guilty. Poundfix is an old story, one that shouldn't have been a big deal from the beginning."

"I've looked into Erik Dahl," Tommy continued calmly. "The Norwegian police got back to me this morning. A fellow prisoner stabbed Dahl to death in December of the same year your son was killed."

This was news to Irene, too. She sat, silent, as the Bonettis stared at Tommy.

"So there have been many people in this circle who have come to a violent end," Tommy said.

"Even if businesses go bankrupt, people aren't usually murdered for it!" Antonio Bonetti exclaimed.

Depends on what kind of business they're in, Irene thought.

"You must keep in mind that global financial crises are inevitable and occasional recessions will follow in their wake. It's part of business," the lawyer said.

And your son helped bring about one of the worst recessions we've seen lately, Irene thought. *Stock markets crumbled all over the world.*

"We have another question. Did Thomas have a girlfriend?" Tommy asked.

"Thomas had many girlfriends," Antonio Bonetti said imperiously, emphasizing *many*.

"Do you have any names? Especially in the last year of his life. Winter, spring 2000," Tommy clarified.

"He never brought any of them home to us," Marianne Bonetti said. "You must remember that he was living in London, and he traveled all over the world. He was seldom home. His business kept him occupied—I don't believe he had time for a steady girlfriend."

The rest of the conversation with the Bonettis revealed little more. It was clear that the couple knew very little about their son's private life.

As they got up to leave, the lawyer took some business cards from the breast pocket of his jacket and told them, "I want to be informed as soon as the autopsy has been completed. Just call any of the numbers on this card. As his father, I want to know . . . if he suffered much." His voice failed him. Irene nodded and looked directly into his eyes. It was difficult to do. And at this point, she could not bring up the missing fingers. It would come out soon enough after the autopsy was done.

"AGNETA TOLD ME that you and she were going mushroom hunting," Tommy said as they were driving back to the center of the city in the afternoon rush hour.

"We planned to go this Sunday. There was no time last weekend. She was busy with something," Irene said.

Tommy muttered, "She certainly was."

An odd kind of silence fell over the car. Irene didn't understand why. It lasted until they parked at the station. Tommy cut the motor and pulled out the key. He took a deep breath as if he wanted to say something, but then he didn't.

"No . . . she'll have to tell you herself," Tommy said out loud as he got out of the car and strode toward the building. Irene had a hard time keeping up as they headed into the building.

"So . . . you didn't find out much," the superintendent stated. He had his elbows on the table and was clenching his fingers together so hard that his knuckles cracked.

"No, we didn't," Irene said. "But he had a strong reaction when Styrsö Island was mentioned. Tomorrow morning I should go out there."

"It's a Saturday. Do you think you'll find anything?" Tommy asked.

"Krister is working, and I can take my dog Sammie with me," Irene thought out loud. "Or no . . . that won't work. Annika Hermansson has a cat."

"That wouldn't be a wise move," Andersson agreed. He'd heard the story of Sammie killing the neighbor's cat with one giant bite and all the repercussions afterward.

"Sammie will have to stay home," Irene said. "But, yes, I do think there's something there. I just have a feeling that we've overlooked something. I've forgotten something important. Or I haven't understood the weight of a detail I've heard. You know the feeling."

Both Tommy and Andersson nodded.

KRISTER WAS FREE Friday evening since he would have to work both Saturday and Sunday. They lit candles. The light reflected on the golden wine in their glasses. They were enjoying one of their favorite dishes, warm stuffed crabs, and the aromas of French mustard, sherry, dill, cheese, and the sea combined to tease their taste buds. Krister lifted his glass and looked into Irene's eyes.

"*Skål*, my darling, and thank you for your company this pleasant evening," he said.

They clinked their glasses together and sipped the chilled wine, letting it slide across their tongues.

"And I have some good news," Krister said, as he put his glass down.

"Tell me," said Irene.

"Sis called. Maggan, that is, not Ulla. Neither of them want Pappa's car. They both have much newer ones. In fact, Maggan's family has two."

Krister's father had passed away unexpectedly just before Midsummer. His mother was eighty-four now and suffered from rheumatism. She had found a two-bedroom ground floor apartment with a small patio, just a few minutes' walk from his sister Ulla's house. Both Ulla and Margareta, nicknamed Maggan, still lived in Säffle with their families. So Krister and Irene had been spared much during the past summer. Now his parents' home in Säffle would be sold. Krister's brother Stefan lived in Stockholm since his divorce. He was the oldest. He kept to himself, without much contact with the rest of the family. Whenever he did turn up, he always had a brand new sports car. In spite of all the recent crises in the banking and financial world, he, in upper management, still earned a pretty good salary. Now the sisters wanted to get rid of the Volvo in their parents' garage. They wanted the house ready to sell by December.

"It's a Volvo 7410. From '92. Hardly eight thousand kilometers on it. It's practically just off the lot," Krister said.

"But it's eleven-years-old," Irene said. "That's only two years newer than our Saab."

"My father took good care of it," Krister said. "And it has only a quarter of the mileage on the odometer. They'll give it to us for twenty-five thousand."

Irene smiled. "It sounds like a good deal. Let's take it. *Skål* for our new car!"

"*Skål!* I'll be off work on Monday. I'll take the train up to Säffle, and then I'll drive the car home. And I'll put an ad in the paper for the Saab. We've had it checked not that long ago. If we get five thousand, that'll be great."

"What's the Volvo like?"

"Not sure. But it's a station wagon, which would be great for Sammie. He'll be safer in the back. We'll get a dog gate and partition the baggage area. And it'll give us more room when we have to pack for our house in Sunne."

Irene looked at her husband in surprise. "What do you mean 'pack' for our summer house? The Saab has always had enough room."

The summer house on the outskirts of Sunne had been owned by Krister's parents, who had signed it over to their children years ago. In the beginning, the family had divided the weeks they spent there equally, but during the past few years it hadn't been necessary. Irene and Krister had been able to go there whenever they wanted. Stefan almost never came over from Stockholm. Maggan's family had bought a beach-front cabin on Lake Vänern, and Ulla's family had bought a large boat they sailed all over Sweden during the summer.

"Ulla and Maggan want us to buy them out," Krister said.

Irene almost choked on her wine. "We can't afford that!" she choked out.

"Yes, we can, if we sell our townhouse and buy a condo instead."

"Sell our townhouse!"

"Why not? The girls will leave home soon, and it'll be just you and me. And Sammie, of course," he added as he heard the dog's snoring from underneath the table.

"Condos in town are as expensive as houses out here," Irene protested.

"Not really. Especially when you consider how much upkeep a house needs. Neither of us like working in the garden. The outside window shutters will need to be painted soon, and in two years we'll have to paint the whole thing. Not to mention that the wood on the siding isn't that good since the house was built in the seventies when there was so much fraud in the construction industry. So that means we'll have to replace—"

"That's enough! We'll sell it! But I must say, this is a bit sudden. I have to get used to the idea," Irene said. They touched their glasses again and smiled at each other, although Irene felt a pang in her heart. Just the thought of selling the townhouse they'd lived in for fifteen years left her with a sad and heavy feeling.

Chapter 14

THE SEA'S FLINT-GRAY waves lashed against the stony beach. The whole morning, the rain clouds had hung heavy and given regular bursts of showers. Irene pushed ahead, bent over in the strong wind. She knew the way to Annika Hermansson's house fairly well by now. Having learned from her previous visits to Styrsö, she wore thick clothing, and she had even put on a pair of mittens.

It felt as if a neutron bomb had exploded over the island. Only the scattered houses gave any sign of habitation, and the only living thing she encountered was a lone seagull, which stared at her from a perch on a stone. It took off with a cry when she approached. She saw nothing else moving until she came to Annika Hermansson's front porch. The tuxedo cat sat on the stairs and watched her approach. Its eyes glittered with ill will.

"Hello, kitty cat. Do you remember me?" Irene asked and bent toward it.

In reply, the cat folded back its ears and hissed. Irene pulled back her hand immediately. *You can't win over everybody. Cats must know by instinct that they're meeting a dog person.*

Irene knocked loudly and then opened the door when she heard someone's voice. The same suffocating odor as last time hit her nose when she entered. She took a deep breath before she stepped into the still-cluttered hallway.

"Hello, Annika! It's Irene Huss. I called yesterday, and you told me I could come on over."

She headed toward the kitchen as she talked. She heard a muttering voice from that direction, as if someone were muzzled. She stopped in the doorway when she saw the sorry-looking shape on the floor. For a second, she thought that Annika was unconscious or even near death, but to her great relief, the muffled sounds still came from her. She was alive, just stone-cold drunk.

Irene knelt beside Annika and tried to determine her condition. Annika had vomited, and the stench was incredible. She was trying to say something, but an incoherent mumble mixed with bits of vomit and alcohol was all that came out. She was lying on her side, which probably saved her from choking on her vomit. Blood was on the floor around her head. As Irene looked more closely, she saw a large cut on Annika's left temple—not from a Parisian attacker, as Irene's memory immediately conjured up, but from the corner of the kitchen table. Annika's left arm jutted out at an odd angle from beneath her. When Irene tried to feel it, Annika screamed. *Probably broken.*

Irene stood up and got her cell phone out. She called 112 and requested an ambulance. She attempted to describe where Styrsö was.

"We'll send out an ambulance boat. Will you be there to meet it?" asked the female operator.

"Of course," Irene assured her. "The house is close to the water. I'll stand right outside the door."

"Great. I'll relay your cell phone number," she said. "They'll call as they get close, so you don't have to remain outside in this weather longer than necessary."

"Thanks." There wasn't much more she could do for Annika, who was already lying in a good position and she had enough alcohol to dull the pain. Irene found a dirty blanket in the mess on the kitchen bench and spread it over her.

She might as well use the time to look around before the

ambulance arrived. She slowly walked through the dilapidated house. She wasn't afraid of disturbing anything; she moved slowly to make sure she wouldn't step into anything smelly. She decided to start on the upper floor and headed up the creaky staircase.

The bedroom's large gable window opened to the southwest for a fantastic view of the ocean. Irene opened it so that she could endure being in the room at all. The wind rushed in, shaking the window, but the window hook held.

There were a few framed photographs on the green-lacquered dresser. Irene walked over to get a better look.

The first photograph she picked up showed a teenage girl with a baby on her lap. It took Irene a few seconds to realize she was looking at Annika and Billy. Irene saw that Annika had once had long, reddish-brown hair. She was smiling slightly, and she looked directly, defiantly, into the camera. The baby was only a few months old and was totally bald. Irene was surprised to see how cute Annika had been as a young woman. No one who saw her today would ever guess.

The next photograph showed a skinny boy of seven or eight. He was standing shirtless on the dock, holding a fishing pole in one hand and the small fish he'd caught in the other. He was smiling, and Irene could see the gap in his teeth. His towheaded hair blew in the wind. A fishing hut stood in the background.

The last photograph showed a young man wearing his graduation cap. His face was spotted with pimples, and he definitely did not look happy in his suit and the tight white cap with its black band.

In the hallway, the telescope was in its usual place. Irene didn't bother looking through it again. Instead, she crossed the hallway and entered the other bedroom.

The room had a stuffy-but-clean scent. Along one wall was a narrow twin bed with a dark blue terry-cloth cover washed so often over the years it was threadbare. By the window was an IKEA pine desk holding only a red desk lamp and a letterpress in multicolored glass. A faded plastic gardenia sat on the windowsill. The curtains were light blue with white squares, and they matched the worn rug on the floor. An empty bookshelf, fastened to the wall over a dresser, was the same model as in Annika's bedroom, although it had been lacquered in blue. Also on the wall was a poster titled "The Cycle of Citric Acid." As far as Irene could tell, it pictured a number of chemical formulae arranged in a ring. The dresser drawers were empty when Irene pulled them out. The two wardrobes were also empty. The room was clean and abandoned. No one had lived here for quite some time. *Was Annika just making up a story when she said that Billy helped her out?*

Irene had walked out of the room and was heading down the creaking stairs to the ground floor when she heard the front door open. She stopped mid-step and held her breath. The ambulance boat could hardly have gotten here yet, and no one had called her cell phone, either.

At that second, her phone rang.

She pulled it out and answered loudly to ensure her voice would carry all the way to the front door. "Detective Inspector Irene Huss."

She walked into the hallway as the voice on the other end said, "Tobbe Johansson here, from the ambulance boat. We're heading underneath the bridge to Dansö Island now. Can you go stand in front of the house?"

"Yes, I'll be there."

A confused young man stood staring at her. She remembered seeing him on the ferry as she'd crossed, since there had been very few passengers because of the rain. He was just inside the door and held a plastic sack of groceries in one hand and a black plastic bag in the other. He had on a khaki-green Fjällräven jacket and matching pants. Obviously, he knew how to dress for the islands. His hood was still over his head. He put the plastic bags on the floor with a thud and pulled back his hood. His reddish-blond hair had started to thin in two deep bays on each side of his hairline. The surprise changed to anger. "I couldn't help hearing you're from the police. What are you doing here?" he said.

Irene flipped her cell phone shut as she said, "I called Annika yesterday, and she asked me to come here today. I found her on the kitchen floor when I arrived a while ago. It looks like she fell and broke her arm. I called the ambulance boat, and they'll be here any moment now. They were the ones who just called. They wanted me to meet them outside. Why don't you go on in to your mother in the meantime?"

He moved out of her way as she stepped out of the house. The fresh air felt liberating, and she filled her lungs with deep, long breaths.

"Let's go talk in your room," Irene said.

The ambulance boat personnel had already taken Annika Hermansson away, and Billy was hanging around in the kitchen, looking lost. Irene saw the exhaustion and pain on his pale face. He nodded in agreement.

Irene sat down on the pine chair, and Billy sat abruptly on the bed. He looked troubled, and his large Adam's apple bobbed up and down beneath the skin of his skinny neck as he swallowed nervously.

"It's not like you think," he said defiantly.

"What am I supposed to think?" Irene asked.

"That I don't give a damn about my mother! That I don't care that she lives in this . . . shithole!" His face flushed red from his throat to his cheeks.

"So you do care," Irene stated.

"That's right."

Billy swallowed a few times more before he continued. "I

saw you on the ferry over. I went shopping. I always do her shopping for her. But she won't let me *clean* this place."

Both his voice and his glance pleaded for understanding. Irene wanted him to keep talking, so she asked in a neutral tone, "Why's that?"

He glanced away and stared at the worn-out rug. He said nothing for a while, and then he sighed. "My girlfriend . . . my mother doesn't like her. She—that is, Mamma—went ballistic when Emma and I decided to move in together. I'd always been the one here taking care of her. She's been drinking ever since I was little. But when Emma and I got together . . . this is part of her revenge. She lives in this squalor to get back at me."

"How long have you and Emma been living together?"

"Almost four years now."

"But I see you keep Annika supplied with alcohol," Irene stated.

"I have to." Billy shrugged. "She refuses to leave the house. If I don't get her liquor, she has *friends* who get it for her—and they take a big chunk of her cash for themselves. All of her money goes to liquor if they get it. I come once or twice a week to bring her booze and food. That way, there's more control over her money."

"I understand. And she doesn't want to go into treatment for her alcoholism, does she?"

"You know Mamma," Billy smiled a crooked smile.

"Not that well," Irene admitted. "But I did meet her a couple of weeks ago. We're working on the Thomas Bonetti case. Had you heard his previous partner in ph.com, Philip Bergman, was murdered almost three weeks ago? Annika had seen something through her telescope the last night Bonetti was alive, but she wasn't taken seriously—she was obviously intoxicated when she called. So no one had checked back. But I came recently for a chat, and because of her information, we located Thomas' body on Branteskär."

Irene watched Billy's Adam's apple bounce up and down as he tried to figure out what to say. At last, he said, "I read about—the discovery. But Mamma never said anything about you coming to talk to her. I had no idea that she'd seen anything important. She kept going on and on about hearing Thomas's boat that evening."

"Did she ever mention that Nisse's Cairn had been moved?"

"That's all she's talked about the past few years."

"Three years at least. It *had* been moved. Thomas's body was hidden beneath it. The killer had put his body next to the stones and then moved them, stone by stone, until it was covered. So the whole stack had been shifted about a meter. Annika was absolutely right."

Billy nodded. "She's actually pretty smart. She had good grades in school, but she was one of so many children, my grandparents wanted her to go to work. So she got pregnant after ninth grade. With me, of course. And after that she never had a full-time job. Sometimes she cleaned or subbed for other people. Once she met Hasse, everything went downhill fast."

"Who is Hasse?"

"Who *was* Hasse, you mean. He's dead. He drank himself to death about seven or eight years ago. Missed and mourned by no one. Not even by Mamma, but by then she was already pretty far gone herself."

"You seem to have had a fairly difficult childhood," Irene said, choosing her words carefully.

"It wasn't that bad. I had my grandparents. You could almost say they raised me. And I have a number of aunts and uncles here on the island. Not to mention all my cousins. My grandfather died ten years ago, and my grandmother was diagnosed with Parkinson's. She passed away not all that long ago."

"I'm sorry for your loss," Irene said. "What do you do these days?"

"I'm a chemical engineer. I work in Stenungsund, but live in Kungälv."

"It's quite a ways from Kungälv to here."

"Yes, but it's manageable."

Irene thought about how she could delicately phrase the next question, but in the end, she was forced to simply ask directly. "Annika mentioned that you and Thomas played together when you were kids. What kind of a person was he?"

Billy looked back down at the rug, and his Adam's apple moved up and down for a few moments. Finally, he said, "He was almost five years older than me. Nobody wanted to play with him. I didn't want to, either, but sometimes he'd come over and pick me up. He always wanted to be the one in control, and he always boasted about how rich his father was and about all the great stuff he got. Of course, he was rubbing in the fact that we were poor and I had no father. He was a bully, which was kind of strange since he was bullied himself, all the time, you know, because he was fat and wore glasses and always turned as red as a lobster in the sun. That's the only thing we had in common. They called him 'the flayed rat.'" He grinned.

Irene almost said, *You two share more than just turning red in the sun—you also share the same eye color and hair color,* but she managed to stop herself. She found herself staring at him so intently he was squirming under her gaze.

"Billy, Annika said to me that she'd never told you who your father was. Is that true?"

"Yes, it's true, and I don't really care anymore who he was. He hasn't come forward in twenty-eight years, so now he means nothing to me."

Irene noticed that there was still an undertone of disappointment in spite of the defiance in his voice.

"She also told me that he paid her a great deal of money to keep quiet about him," Irene said.

"She's gone on and on about that over the years. He's

supposed to be rich and married. She's just trying to make herself more interesting."

"You think? Have you seen her bank accounts?"

"Yes, I take care of all her money. There are no unexplained deposits. But—" He interrupted himself in mid-sentence and bit his lip before he said, almost choking, "What do Mamma's finances have to do with Thomas Bonetti's murder?"

"There might be an indirect connection," Irene said.

She was lying. She really wanted to find out if Thomas Bonetti had a half-brother named Billy Hermansson. Thomas had inherited his mother's weight issues and eye problems, but his coloring came from his father, the same coloring as Billy's.

Billy was studying her with a suspicious gaze from his blue eyes, but then he shrugged.

"There's one thing I've always wondered about. There's been a lot of letters coming over the years. Brown envelopes, no return address. Typewritten address. And she'd always react to the letters like—well, as if she'd won something."

"Well, it's always nice to receive a letter."

"You don't get it. Mamma never receives letters. No one ever writes to her, except for these brown envelopes."

"Have you asked her who sent them?"

"Yes, but she'd just laugh at me."

"And it looks like she's keeping a secret?"

"Right."

"Like she does whenever the conversation turns to your father?" Irene asked quietly.

Billy looked at her sharply. "Maybe." He said nothing for a moment as he frowned in thought. Irene realized he was getting ready to answer. "If, as she said, she was getting money from . . . my biological father . . . then the money probably came in those brown envelopes."

"Do you think you can find one of them? Maybe she's kept them."

"I'll look for them."

Irene felt relieved. Searching through all the garbage in this house was something she would prefer not to do.

"Good. Here's my card. It has my address and a phone number where you can reach me. If you find some envelopes, be careful. Don't handle them much, but put them in a larger envelope."

"You're going to be looking for fingerprints."

"That's right."

Chapter 15

By Sunday morning the foul weather had begun to dissipate, and the weather service forecasted beautiful sunshine for the last days of September. Irene did her jiujitsu training during the morning, although she didn't stretch herself too far. She wanted to protect her elbow, which was still sore.

After a quick lunch, she piled Sammie, her coffee thermos, her rubber boots, and a mushroom basket into her car and headed off to Härskogen. She and Agneta had a place where they'd picked mushrooms for quite a few years now. It was on the outskirts of a nature reserve, but not on private property, so the mushrooms were up for grabs.

However, there would be no mushroom picking that afternoon.

"There's something I have to tell you," Agneta said right away.

Irene nodded encouragingly. *What are friends for, after all, if you couldn't confide in them?*

"Tommy and I are getting a divorce."

Irene felt dizzy and had to look for a place to sit down. A wave of nausea hit her. *How can she stand there and just say something like that without even looking distraught?*

"I'll be moving out on October first."

"So . . . soon. . . ." Irene managed to stammer.

Why, oh why? Her best friend! And she hadn't even seen this coming! Or had she? The thoughts swirled in her head.

"Is it that serious . . . with Kajsa?" she managed to ask.

"Kajsa? Who's that?" Agneta said, wrinkling her brow.

Before Irene had a chance to reply, Agneta continued, "Well, if someone at work is interested in him, I certainly hope something will come of it. He needs someone. He is the father of my three children, and I still like him very much. . . platonically."

"But . . . if you still. . . ." Irene was grasping at straws.

"I can't help the fact that I don't love him any longer. I've met the love of my life. I know it sounds stupid, but I've been carried away by passion. It's a true . . . force of nature. You're just swept along with it and can't even fight it."

Her brown eyes began to fill with tears.

"What's his name?" Irene asked.

"Olof. He's a doctor at our hospital. We've known each other for years, and we've always had a strong attraction to each other, which we've resisted for a long time. We had our families to think about. His two children are grown. But now we can't wait any longer, so we're both getting divorced."

Irene felt as if she'd heard more than enough; she felt her temper rising. *How can Agneta do this to Tommy and the children?* Irene tried to keep her feelings under control. "How long has this been serious?"

"Since the spring."

"How long has Tommy known about it?"

In truth, Irene didn't really want to know any more. She felt like driving straight home and throwing herself on her bed for a good cry, but the investigator in her took over. She had to know what was truly going on.

Agneta blew her nose and dried her tears with a paper tissue. "Tommy . . . began to realize what was going on during the summer. And we talked—my God, how we talked and talked! But it is what it is. I can't deny my feelings any longer. Olof and I will be moving in together. We've found an apartment in Alingsås. It's large enough for the children. Tommy will be keeping the townhouse for now."

Irene was disheartened. Tommy and Agneta had never brought up the marriage crisis they were in. They were her two best friends, and they hadn't said a word.

"Why didn't either of you say something to me before?" she felt forced to ask.

"You were so busy this summer with your father-in-law's illness, and then of course he died, and there was the funeral. Then you were gone for two weeks to Crete. And we wanted to figure things out for ourselves and not burden other people." Agneta looked Irene straight in the eye. "Please don't let this hurt our friendship. Let's keep on meeting each other. Picking mushrooms like always." She smiled slightly at the last sentence.

"Sure," Irene mumbled. But she knew in her heart that nothing could be the way it was before.

ON THE WAY home, Irene felt a sense of shame when she remembered the conversation with Kajsa in Paris. She'd treated Kajsa badly. They hadn't even spoken to each other properly since the attack in the Rothstaahl apartment. Kajsa had slept the entire way back on the plane. Once they'd arrived home, they hadn't had a moment's peace, and then Andersson sent Kajsa home on sick leave. Tomorrow she'd be back at work. Irene knew that she owed Kajsa an apology, but first, she'd have to talk with Tommy.

TOMMY HAD REMAINED calm when Irene told him Monday morning that she knew he was getting a divorce, but when she asked him why they didn't try harder to save the marriage, he went into a rage.

"You have no idea what I'm feeling! This is between Agneta and me. Just letting you know that we're getting divorced is enough. The rest is none of your business!"

"But I just wanted to talk—" Irene tried to say, but Tommy interrupted her.

"As I said, it's none of your business! And stop giving people advice when they haven't asked for it!"

Tommy jumped up angrily and left the room. As the door slammed shut behind him, Irene was crestfallen. Tommy's last comment about giving unwanted advice made her think that Kajsa had already told Tommy about their conversation in Paris. Perhaps that's what let him dump his anger on her. Deep inside, however, she knew that she probably deserved it.

Could this Monday morning be any more of a Monday?

As if hearing her unspoken thought, there was a knock on the door. Jonny Blom stuck in his head before Irene even had a chance to speak.

"You seen Sven?" he asked.

"He's in a meeting."

"I see. What's wrong with you? Looks like you didn't get your daily dose of coffee."

If there was one person on the planet with whom she did not want to share her private concerns, that person was Jonny. Irene tried to look more energetic and forced herself to smile.

"I got my coffee all right. I was just thinking. Saturday, I went to talk to Annika Hermansson one more time. I couldn't question her because she was lying drunk and unconscious on the floor when I got there. She'd hit her head on the table when she fell, and she'd broken her arm. I made sure she got to the hospital. While I was there, her son came by. I've checked out his background, and his birth certificate says "father unknown." However, I suspect I know who his biological father is." Although Irene hadn't planned on telling Jonny all this, she spoke the truth.

Jonny came in and shut the door behind him. He plumped down on the sofa with a thud. "So who is he?" Jonny wanted to know.

"I didn't want to say anything until I'd researched . . . a few details."

She picked up a white envelope and waved it in the air. "This came with the morning mail. There's another envelope inside that, hopefully, has the mystery father's fingerprints. In a plastic folder in my desk drawer, I have the business card of man whom I think is the father. I suspect that his fingerprints are on it, because he wasn't wearing gloves when he handed it to me. The question is, should I pursue this or not? It might not have a bearing on the case, but you never know."

Jonny sat, thinking it over. "But you guess there's something fishy here."

"I have no idea. It's perhaps nothing more than my usual bad habit of sticking my nose where it doesn't belong." She wasn't able to hide the bitterness in her voice.

Jonny lifted an eyebrow. He'd caught her tone. He leaned across the desk and said with emphasis, "All good investigators are curious to a fault. You're famous because you stick your nose where it doesn't belong."

Jonny got up and gave her an encouraging smile before he went out the door.

Irene stared at the closed door. A miracle had occurred. Jonny had saved her day.

"STRIDNER SAYS THAT the cuts of the wounds show that Thomas Bonetti's fingers were severed from his hands by a pair of wire cutters. She even wrote *wire cutters*, though how she could determine the differences between the slice of wire cutters versus pliers is sure as hell a mystery to me," Andersson said with sarcasm.

"Well, if she wrote wire cutters, that's what I'd put my money on," said Birgitta.

"Me, too," Irene agreed.

The superintendent pretended not to hear their comments. Instead, he continued to skim through the autopsy report.

"Let's see . . . height, teeth, blood type . . . all match Bonetti. Clothes, too. Cause of death: pistol wound in the right temple. She wrote *os temporale* but put temple in parenthesis. We can be grateful for her thoughtfulness. Two shots. Twenty-eight. No big surprise there. More evidence linking this to the asshole who killed the other three a few weeks ago. Stridner's report confirms the body has been there for three years, like we suspected. I called the tech guys a few minutes ago and asked if they'd found Thomas Bonetti's glasses, but they haven't. Any questions? The floor is open."

Andersson leaned back into his chair and imperiously surveyed his detectives. He even glanced at Kajsa briefly, but looked away quickly, since she wasn't a pretty sight. He had to admire her bravery, though. Most women would refuse to show themselves in public looking like that.

"The first thing that comes to my mind," Tommy said, "is how did the killer manage to drag the body to the top of the island? It's hard just to walk there. Why not simply dump him in the water? That would have been much easier."

"Especially considering that Bonetti was not exactly a lightweight," Irene added.

"He was short, but he weighed more than a hundred kilos. There must have been two people involved," Birgitta said.

"Are there any injuries on the body or marks on the clothes to indicate that he'd been dragged up the side of the cliff? By using a rope or something like that?" asked Fredrik.

Andersson shook his head.

Irene thought about how difficult it had been for her to climb up the slope of the island, especially the first bit. The cliffs went straight down to the water. They'd have had to get a foothold via a crack in the side of the cliff and would have had to use their fingers to grab uneven sides of the rock.

"I've just been there," Irene said. "I believe there's only one way Bonetti made it. He went up under his own power."

"Why would he do that?" asked Jonny.

"Perhaps someone was pointing a gun at him. Or perhaps someone had tortured him or threatened to do so. Perhaps because he was scared to death if he didn't."

"Right about that," Birgitta muttered.

There was a moment of silence in the room as everyone pictured the scenario Irene had described: chubby Thomas, shaking with terror, scrambling to the top of the cliffs on the island, only to be executed in cold blood in the September darkness.

It was an unpleasant scene.

"How could they see in the dark to climb?" asked Fredrik. "A flashlight?"

"Probably, or a head lamp. You can climb with just one hand, though it isn't easy. I had to do that, but it was during the daytime," Irene said.

"Still, it *was* difficult, wasn't it?" Tommy said. "So I'd guess his fingers were cut off after he was shot." No one said anything, and Tommy continued. "So why cut off his fingers? Or at least four of them?"

"Trophies," Jonny said with conviction.

Irene and Jonny's eyes met over the conference table. They remembered a case they'd worked on before, and the trophies a serial killer had kept. These were memories they'd both tried to repress.

"Possibly," Tommy said. "You're thinking of that serial killer."

Jonny nodded. "Yes, this looks like another one to me."

"That killer certainly was, but the question now is whether or not this suspect is one. He has killed a number of people, but all the victims have connections to each other. None of the last three had amputations or desecration, just Thomas Bonetti. Why?"

"I still believe it was trophies. A souvenir of the killing. Power over the victim," Jonny insisted.

Well, he's read up on his serial killers, Irene thought. *Nothing like personally running into one to spur on the research. Although that's most likely the only one he'll ever meet in his entire career as a police officer, statistically speaking.*

"Well, if he were into trophies, wouldn't he have taken the fingers off his other victims as well?" Tommy asked.

"If we're talking about one killer. Bonetti could have fallen victim to one murderer while the others were killed by someone else," the superintendent pointed out.

"Hardly. Think about the unusual caliber of the bullets," Birgitta said.

Andersson looked at Birgitta with irritation, but didn't defend his theory. Just moments before, he himself had pointed out that there was only one killer. Instead, he cleared his throat and said, "So the question is why did someone go to all the trouble to shoot him at the top of that remote island?"

"The murderer did not want the body found. It was important. But then why not just dump him in the water?"

The word "dump" echoed in Irene's mind.

"He didn't dump him in the water because he had nothing to weigh him down!" she said excitedly.

"Oh no, here she goes again," sighed Jonny and rolled his eyes.

Irene ignored him, forming her words carefully. "You can't just dump a body in the water. You have to weigh it down, and what happens if you don't? The body pops back to the surface. Our murderer did not want the body to be found. Certainly not right away. And I think that's behind the trip to the stones up there on Branteskär. "

"Sounds plausible," said Andersson.

"What about the fingers?" Tommy said.

"Trophies," Jonny insisted stubbornly.

"If they were cut off before he was killed, then it was torture," said Birgitta.

Jonny sighed. "Why on earth would anyone want to torture that fat, rich puppy dog?"

"Because he was a fat, *rich* puppy dog," Kajsa said. Everyone turned to her in surprise at her first words of the meeting.

"What do you mean by that?" asked Andersson. With everyone in the room staring at her, Kajsa's garishly bruised face flushed red, an interesting color combination with the blue and purple around her eyes.

"That's exactly what he was. A *rich* puppy dog. He was involved in illegal business ventures in London and was suspected of financial finagling in the ph.com crash. Perhaps he was tortured so that he would give up his bank account numbers," she said with conviction.

Irene found herself nodding. "Kajsa's right. This is the one thing all our victims have in common. They were young and made themselves wealthy illegally. Perhaps Kjell B:sson Ceder was the exception there. But all four knew each other."

"Did Ceder really know Rothstaahl and Bergman? Did he know Bonetti?" asked Andersson.

"No. But Sanna did," Irene said.

Suddenly Andersson straightened in his chair and glared at Tommy. "So, have you questioned her again?"

Tommy shook his head. "Nope. She was too broken up after the murders of Ceder and Bergman. Especially Bergman, I believe."

"You go and lean on her, and lean hard!" bellowed Andersson. "Irene and Tommy! The two of you will go question our lady Ceder again. Continue probing for any trace of connection between her and the four victims. Birgitta and Kajsa, keep researching their finances in case there's something out of the ordinary we missed. In particular, track down the complaints that Bonetti made off with the ph.com money. And the

Ceders' finances, too. Have a little chat with Bosse in the financial crimes division, although I'm not sure how much he can do since they're short-handed over there because of the cutbacks. Jonny and Fredrik, find out why Bergman and Roth-staahl came back to Sweden. What were they up to? Why did they meet at Rothstaahl's house? There might be something there. Talk to their parents again. I have a feeling that they're trying to hide something that would put their sons in a bad light."

"Keep your eyes open for any computer discs or laptops," Birgitta added. "Those guys don't leave paper trails. Everything would be on their computers."

Something Andersson had said bugged Irene. *Why had Bergman and Rothstaahl come to Göteborg when they were already living together in Paris?* There was only one logical explanation.

"They didn't come to Göteborg to talk to each other," she said "They came to talk to someone else. Someone who couldn't or wouldn't come to Paris."

Elsy informed them over the phone that Sanna couldn't see them today. Her doctor had given her tranquil-izers, and she was fast asleep. Elsy also added, rather sharply, that Sanna was not to be upset again.

"Inform Sanna that she must appear at the police station at nine o'clock sharp tomorrow morning. She is to ask for me," Tommy said, sounding very stiff and official in response. He hung up the phone and looked at the clock. "It's almost four thirty. I'm going to take off early. I've got some stuff to do at home. Also, I feel like I'm getting a cold. I have a sore throat. See you tomorrow."

Before Irene had a chance to say anything, he hurried out of the room.

"Bye," she said to the door.

Tommy had avoided being alone with her the whole day

until late in the afternoon. Kajsa had been working with Birgitta in another room further down the hall.

Remembering what had happened made Irene want to go
home too, and climb in bed and pull the covers over her head.
But she stayed put.

The telephone rang.

"Hi, there. It's Svante. I tested your envelopes and the card
for you as soon as I could. It took no time at all to see the fingerprints matched. There are so many samples on both of them
that I'm one hundred percent sure of it."

Irene thanked the technician and slowly put down the
receiver. Was it worth it to pursue this? But then, finding out
more about the Bonetti couple would be worthwhile. Mrs.
Bonetti hadn't said much. Irene lifted the phone again.

"Good afternoon. This is Inspector Irene Huss speaking. I
would like to follow up on our conversation. Would it be possible to talk to you tomorrow afternoon?"

Chapter 16

SANNA KAEGLER-CEDER NO longer looked lovely. Exhaustion had carved deep lines around her mouth and smudged dark circles beneath her eyes. There was an aura of resignation, which hadn't been there before. Irene felt sorry for her. Many of her closest friends had been murdered. Although Thomas Bonetti couldn't be considered a friend, they still had worked together in the heyday of ph.com. She must have known him well.

Sanna was trying to keep up appearances with the help of a black leather suit and a white blouse with a low-cut neckline and wide lapels. Her expensive cross necklace was hanging in its usual spot, and her ring was still on the same finger. She walked effortlessly in black boots with high stiletto heels. Irene had never been able to do that balancing act. She told herself that at five-foot-ten barefoot, she would never need to do it.

"This is much too early for me," Sanna said, not beating around the bush. "I still need strong sleeping pills. And I'm extremely tired in the morning." As if to demonstrate the truth of her statement, she yawned widely as she sat down on a chair.

Tommy nodded and said with a friendly smile, "I can understand that, and so I requested nine o'clock and not seven thirty, when we usually begin."

Sanna gave him a suspicious look, but couldn't decide if he was telling the truth or not. Irene was not about to enlighten her.

Tommy shuffled some papers on his desk. He flipped through them as if he were looking for something. Finally, he stopped and looked Sanna right in the eye.

"Today we will talk about Philip Bergman," he said curtly.

Sanna stiffened.

"You and Philip were old friends from school. You were close friends. Some people say you were more than that. What was your relationship?"

Sanna took a few seconds to answer. "He was my best friend," she said, with a slight tremor in her voice.

Irene couldn't help casting a glance at Tommy, but he wasn't looking at her.

"You never had a sexual relationship?"

"Never. We shared everything except a bed." She didn't try to disguise the bitter tone in her voice.

"Did you know that he was homosexual?"

There was another long pause before she said, "Yes, I did, but not until two years ago. He made it clear then, when he told me that he and Joachim planned to move in together in Paris."

"How did you react when he told you?"

"I believe . . . I was shocked."

"Did you ever suspect?"

"No. Never! He was careful about his appearance, and he was often at the gym, but lots of guys do that. He was always surrounded by young women, even teenagers, which I thought was a little strange. Such an intelligent guy and all those ditzy girls. Once he told me that he never wanted to deal with any kind of nagging. I never really understood—until he told me he was gay."

"Were you ever in love with Philip Bergman?"

"Me? No . . . well . . . maybe in school. For a while. Actually, I had my hands full with all the guys running after *me*, but he never was one of them. The girls ran after him, too. He did date one girl for a little while, but after that, he wasn't in any kind of relationship with anyone . . . until Joachim. And it wasn't something they announced to the world. I believe I was the only one Philip told. I really don't think he even meant to tell me . . . he was very drunk."

"Did either of them tell their parents?"

"I doubt it," she said, shaking her head.

Irene thought Sanna was right. There was no proof of Bergman and Joachim's relationship before she and Kajsa had gone to their apartment in Paris.

"Did you know what kind of business Philip and Joachim were conducting in Paris?"

"We had little contact those two years, hardly any all after . . . after he told me . . . about all that with Joachim. Once he went to Paris, we only called each other a few times and sent a few emails. He sent me a fine wedding present when I got married and also a card when Ludwig was born."

"So you went from best friends to distant acquaintances in the blink of an eye, you could say," Tommy stated.

"Yes. As I said, after he told me about Joachim everything changed."

"Were you the one who didn't want to keep in touch, or was it him?"

She thought about this carefully. "Maybe it was both of us. Mostly him, though. Joachim took my place as his best friend and confidant." The bitterness in her voice was loud and clear.

"Was this why you married Kjell B:son Ceder?"

"No. I was getting older, and I wanted a child. Kjell was also getting along in years and wanted an heir. We liked each other and . . . we decided to get married."

Irene held her breath. This was Tommy's opening, and he took it.

"Who is Ludwig's father?"

Sanna's color drained so much her lips seemed to disappear

into the whiteness of her face. Irene got ready in case she fainted again.

"What . . . what are you talking about? Kjell, of course," she said lamely.

"Didn't you know that Kjell had undergone a vasectomy about five or six years ago? He was not able to father a child."

"He . . . he did what?" Sanna gaped at Tommy. Tommy looked back at her with absolute calm. Sanna broke; she covered her face with her hands and sobbed. Irene held out a packet of paper tissues, which Sanna took gratefully. It took her quite some time to recover, but finally she blew her nose and dried the tears from her red-rimmed eyes.

"He never told me that he couldn't have children. I had an on again, off again relationship with him the year before we got married. We got together whenever we felt like it; we were just having fun. I had other guys, too. I was partying in New York, and one day I met this guy, Mark. We holed up in a hotel room and had sex for two days straight. I'd forgotten to take my pill, but I thought it wouldn't matter. I probably got pregnant then. It was the best sex I ever had in my entire life. But the truth is that I don't know anything about Mark except his first name. He was married, and we'd decided from the start that we'd have just this one weekend in New York," she said, her voice hoarse from sobbing.

"He never got in touch with you later?"

"Of course not. I never gave him my address or my last name. We were just Sanna and Mark." She straightened up defiantly, triumphantly. Tommy just nodded. His expression held no judgment.

"And then Kjell proposed," he said.

"That's right. I told him that he was the father of the child. He was extremely happy and didn't say a word about having had a vasectomy—is it true he had one? This is not a lie just to get me to talk?" She looked up, suddenly suspicious.

"No. The vasectomy was discovered during the autopsy."

"Autopsy? Oh, God help me! He said he'd had an operation for a hernia once—that must have been what he was having. It was a few years before we got married. That could be right."

Tommy gave a sidelong glance at Irene. Irene remembered he'd told her once that he'd had an operation for a hernia. Was that when he'd gotten *his* vasectomy? It was certainly possible. And Kajsa had reacted strongly when he'd mentioned his little operation a few weeks before. *Perhaps she'd already been dreaming about how they would get together and make their own little family?* Kajsa had no children. She was in her thirties and maybe she felt she was getting older, too. How far had her relationship with Tommy gone?

Irene realized that she'd gotten lost in her own thoughts and hadn't heard what Sanna was saying to Tommy.

". . . both Philip and me, many times. But he wasn't doing his job. He was the one who had a degree in finance, and he was the one in charge of the company's accounting."

"How did he get money out of ph.com?"

"The audit showed fake invoices and then several transfers until the money reached his personal bank accounts. Then the money left for Luxemburg, and a few days later from Luxemburg to the Cayman Islands. Then it all disappeared. Classic embezzlement!"

"How much money was this?"

"Perhaps fifteen or sixteen million kroner. He had one account for the Poundfix money. He also had private capital he'd gotten from the company in loans and allowances. All in all, the police found almost five million kroner in that account, and if that is correct, he had about twenty-five million kroner when he disappeared."

Sanna's voice had gone ice-cold with rage. It was clear she was quite happy to share all she knew about Bonetti's shady dealings with the police.

Irene was amazed how the amount of money kept growing as the investigation went on. Now that they knew Thomas hadn't absconded with the money but was murdered, where had all the money gone?

"How could he get so much money in just one year? Almost five million—that's pretty good remuneration."

"Like I told you, there were allowances and subsidies in that amount. All three of us were paid to travel all around the world like crazy. It was damn hard work! And ph.com paid for his apartment in London, too."

"What about yours?"

Sanna gave him a quick look, shrugged, and mumbled something.

"I'm sorry. I didn't hear what you said," Tommy said, still friendly, but firm.

"I said we deserved it! We worked like crazy! Twenty-four-seven! You wouldn't understand. . . ."

Tommy gave her a long, studied look before he replied, "No, we wouldn't. Managing to scrape together a billion kroner in capital and then burning through it in a year's time is an incredible achievement."

"It wasn't our fault!"

"Whose fault was it?"

"I'm not an economist or a stock market analyst! My degree is in design and marketing!"

She gave Tommy a cool look. All of her willingness to talk had gone.

"What kind of education did Philip have?"

"Law." She lied again without hesitation. Both Irene and Tommy already knew that neither of them had any degree after high school. Why did she lie about something so easy to check up on? She underestimated them and their investigative competence. She was trying to impress them with fictitious college degrees.

Tommy just nodded and flipped through his papers again. Irene knew he was about to switch the line of questioning.

"How well did you know Joachim Rothstaahl?" he asked.

"Joachim? Not at all." Sanna's surprise was genuine.

"How did you meet him?"

"At a party in London. Thomas introduced him to Philip and me. It was the first time we'd met him. We knew his relatives. They'd bought a fashion chain that Philip and I had created."

"But you hadn't met Joachim before that day?"

"No."

"And you didn't meet him at any later event?"

"No. Not at all."

"But Philip and Joachim must have started to see each other after that first meeting in London, right?"

"Obviously."

"You didn't know about it?"

"No. Philip and I each had friends we didn't share." She held her hand to her forehead theatrically. "That's enough for now. I'm drained. And I'm actually on sick leave. This has been a horrible time for me. I can't talk to you any more."

"One last question. Where were you between seven and eight P.M. on the Monday Philip and Joachim were killed?"

Sanna stared at him. All the exhaustion disappeared. There was naked fear was in her eyes.

"At home. I was at home with Ludwig."

"At home in Askim?"

"Yes."

"Were you alone?"

"Yes."

Irene tried to picture Sanna jumping out of the closet to fire four well-aimed shots, murdering both Philip and Joachim. If they were able to break her alibi for the murder of Kjell B:son Ceder, it was conceivable that she'd held the gun. Still, it was hard to imagine her killing Thomas Bonetti. It would be too physically demanding for her.

Or was it? Sanna had just demonstrated her ability to lie during this interrogation. Of course she seemed small and fragile, but she was in good shape.

Irene broke the silence to ask, "Have you ever fired a gun?"

Sanna shook her head. "No! Never!"

For the first time during the questioning session, Irene was convinced Sanna was telling the truth.

"WHAT A LIAR!" Irene burst out with indignation once Sanna left the room.

"Right, but she's not as smart as she thinks. She's not good at lying because it was so easy to see when she did," Tommy said. He was drumming his pen on the desk as he looked thoughtfully at Irene. "Do you believe the story about Ludwig's conception?" he asked.

"Not one bit. A woman of the world who has unprotected sex with an American guy she just met? Not in a world with AIDS."

"So you don't buy it?"

"No, it would be too dangerous. But somewhere there *is* a grain of truth in her story."

"How so?"

"Ludwig was probably conceived in New York. Do you remember what he was wearing the day Kjell B:son Ceder was shot? We'd changed Ludwig and given him some food. He was wearing a light blue sweater had MADE IN NEW YORK printed on it."

"Now that you mention it . . . I remember that sweater," Tommy said with a nod.

"I wonder what she's trying to hide with her lies?" Irene said.

"Or who she's trying to protect."

"She has no alibi for the Monday night that Philip and Joachim were murdered. Still, I don't think she was the one who killed them. I believe she is still in love with Philip Bergman."

"Maybe that's why. Classic jealous love triangle," Tommy suggested.

"No. Maybe jealous of Joachim, but not of Philip. She took his death the hardest. I don't believe the other three meant that much to her."

"That's the truth. I don't believe she cared for Kjell one bit. Why did she marry him? Why did he agree to marry her?"

"Maybe he did want an heir after all, like she said?"

"Hardly. He definitely did not want any children. A man who undergoes a vasectomy has it drummed into him what it means. He knows that restoring fertility is extraordinarily difficult. Kjell knew that he wasn't going to be able to have children after this operation. I know from my own experience."

Irene decided this might be a good time to ask about a delicate subject.

"I'm really very sorry that I butted in about your relationship with Kajsa. My only defense is that I was trying to protect your marriage. And our friendship. That is, the friendship between Krister and me and you and Agneta. Not in my wildest dreams could I imagine what was really going on. Not until Agneta told me on Sunday. All I can say is that I am truly sorry about what I said to Kajsa in Paris."

Tommy sighed and gave Irene a weak smile. "You'll have to talk to her about that. And it was partially my fault as well. I should have brought it up sooner, but I didn't feel like talking about it then. I still don't feel like talking about it now."

"So . . . does it help to have Kajsa at this difficult time for you?" Irene asked gently.

"Well, there's nothing going on. She's a sweet girl who seems to have fallen for me a little bit. It's flattering, and I appreciate it. We've had lunch together. I gave her a peck and a hug afterward. That's all. Satisfied?"

Irene heard the sarcasm in his voice. She felt her ears starting to burn. "I really wasn't meaning to pry. . . ."

"You weren't? That would be so unlike you," he said caustically.

Irene was truly hurt. It was incredible how she had gotten the reputation of always putting her nose in other people's business. Jonny's words came to mind: *A good investigator always sticks his nose in where it doesn't belong.* Again the words brought her comfort and reassurance. She was a good investigator. Her instincts had told her that something wasn't right between Tommy and Agneta, but Irene had drawn the wrong conclusion due to lack of facts—just like the beginning of any investigation.

THE AFTERNOON RUSH hour had just started as Irene drove toward Långedrag. Irene let her thoughts wander as she matched the speed of her car to the rhythm of the traffic. Marianne Bonetti had requested that Irene come out to her home again. Apparently, she was not able to leave her house easily. Irene was hoping that the husband would not be at home. She could not have said that when she set up the meeting, but if he knew, the lawyer would make sure he was sitting by his wife's side the minute Irene entered. *As sure as saying Amen in church*, Irene thought.

A pang of guilt hit her. She'd not talked to her own mother, Gerd, in a while. There'd been so much to do in this investigation. The trip to Paris had taken an extra day. And her mother had been gone the previous week, too; she and her companion, Sture, had taken a trip to Lübeck. *When you're happily retired, you're always busy*, Irene reflected. Sture had convinced her mother to get a "green card" for frequent golfers last summer. There was even a little article about it in the Göteborg newspaper: GERD TAKES GREEN CARD AT 75! It had been a slow news week. They'd even published a picture of her mother leaning on a borrowed golf bag and showing a jaunty smile. Irene had clipped the article from the paper and stuck it on the fridge. A few days later, they'd had to go to Säffle for her father-in-law's funeral.

Ah yes, Säffle. Krister had gone to get the Volvo on his Monday off. It looked surprisingly good and was now at the mechanic's to be checked. One of Krister's friends owned the mechanic shop. After some routine service and a brake check, the car should be running like new, according to Krister's buddy. Irene's heart hurt as she thought about selling the old Saab. It had been a faithful servant. But even faithful servants can't go on forever—

At the last second, Irene hit the brakes to avoid plowing into the trunk of the car in front of her. A small boy had come running across the street a few cars ahead. It was a miracle that nobody crashed into each other and that the boy made it across safely. They'd all barely escaped injury. Irene felt her pulse race, and she forced herself to pay attention to traffic. It was no good to let her thoughts wander while driving. The problem was that she seldom had any other time to think things through.

IRENE WAS THRILLED to find Marianne Bonetti alone at home. She was clearly still crying a great deal, since her eyes were red-rimmed. Irene realized that she was truly mourning her son even though she hadn't heard from him for three years—for obvious reasons. It was just as she'd said during their last visit: their worst fears had been confirmed. At least now they could truly begin to process their grief, although the knowledge of how he died was probably not much help. So far, the parents did not know about the four missing fingers. Irene felt it was high time they were informed. Such a macabre detail would certainly leak out to the press soon. The tipster would get some cash, and the newspaper would make some money from the sensational headline. Irene had no illusions that this piece of information would stay hidden. The parents were due some advance warning, but Irene really did not want to bring it up when the mother was alone. It would have to wait until she had a chance to talk to both of them together.

Marianne had changed her dark blue dress to one of nougat brown, but otherwise looked exactly the same.

Irene was escorted to the living room, just as before. On the coffee table, tea for two was set out. The cups were made of thin Chinese porcelain, while the teapot and the sugar bowl were silver. The dark chocolate cake on the crystal tray had been cut in thick slices and smelled as if it had just come out of the oven.

"I've forgotten the milk!" Marianne Bonetti exclaimed and clapped her hands, which caused her diamonds to glitter in all the room's reflective surfaces.

"Don't worry on my account," Irene said.

"That's good. I don't drink milk myself, because I'm lactose intolerant."

She placed slices of cake on plates and leaned forward, breathing heavily, to pour tea into Irene's cup. They chatted for a few minutes about this and that, and Irene let herself enjoy her cake. Irene realized that Marianne needed to feel as if this were a normal conversation around a couple cups of tea. Irene had run into this before in her work as an investigator, often with older women. The police were treated as an invited guest. Marianne, lawyer's wife with sorrowful eyes, was a very lonely person.

Once Irene had washed down the second slice of cake with her second cup of tea, she decided it was time to get to the matter at hand. Choosing her words carefully, she began, "As I mentioned on the phone, there are still a few things we need to talk about."

Marianne nodded seriously, and it was clear she understood.

"We are trying to confirm the timeline of events and make sure we know as much as possible about the last day of Thomas's life. I've read through all the witness reports written three years ago. There are some things that are still not clear and others that aren't in any of the reports. Try to think back to the day Thomas disappeared. He was going to Styrsö. Did you meet him yourself that day?"

"Yes. He came home around five thirty and picked up some food and a few bottles of wine. He also wanted to borrow my boots. Antonio's were too small."

"Did he tell you then that he was going to Styrsö?"

"Yes. I asked him why, and he said he needed to think about things in peace and quiet. I could understand that. Those awful people, Sanna Kaegler and Philip Bergman, were trying to put all the blame on Thomas. The truth is that he tried to warn them, over and over, that the company was going bankrupt. They didn't want to listen. He'd already told Antonio and me about this the previous fall. He was truly worried about it."

Irene spoke to keep the conversation moving in the right direction. "Did he say anything else that day as far as you can recall?"

Mrs. Bonetti began to shake her head, then stopped. "He said he was going to the state liquor store on Jaegerdorffsplatsen because he didn't have any whiskey at home. I remember that clearly," she said, eagerly, clearly just remembering.

"How did Thomas act that last day?"

Mrs. Bonetti's eyes welled up. She removed her glasses and dried them with her handkerchief. "He . . . he was stressed. He was always stressed. He always had business plans in the works. He was in demand. People were always calling him on his cell phone."

"Did anyone call while he was packing to leave?"

"Yes . . . I believe so. People were always calling, as I said. Yes! Now I remember something. A man called our home telephone asking for Thomas."

"While he was still packing?"

"No, after he left. About fifteen minutes to a half an hour later."

"Do you remember who it was?"

"Not really. It was so long ago . . . but it was someone from a bank in England. I remember that!" Marianne was clearly glad her memory was still working after such a long time.

"Do you remember which bank?"

"No, just that it was English."

"I realize it wouldn't be easy to remember the name of a bank, especially if you had to concentrate on speaking English."

"I didn't have to speak English. He spoke Swedish."

"I see. But then he must have had a Swedish name?"

"No, I don't think he introduced himself. In fact, I'm sure he didn't. He just said he was calling on behalf of the bank and he needed to talk to Thomas. He was wondering where he could find him."

"What did you say to him?"

"I said that Thomas needed a few days' vacation and that he'd gone to the summer cabin. I gave the bank man Thomas's cell phone number."

"Did you tell him where the cabin was?"

"Of course not. Thomas had told me not to tell anyone where he was."

Irene felt a shiver run down the back of her neck. Her instincts told her that something was wrong here.

"Did you ever wonder how the bank man found your telephone number here?"

Marianne looked aghast. "I never thought of that. But Thomas must have given it to him."

Why would he have given an important bank person his parents'
number but not the number of his cell phone? Something is definitely
not adding up.

Irene decided not to press Marianne Bonetti further. She
was a friendly person who really was doing her best to help
them solve the case, which was more than Irene could say for
other people involved in this investigation.

Irene changed the subject.

"Why weren't you and your husband more concerned when
Thomas disappeared? It took you almost two months to file a
missing person report."

Marianne started sobbing. Irene handed her napkin since
her handkerchief was soaked.

"We thought . . . we thought . . . he was still alive," she
managed to say between sobs. She blew her nose and took a
few deep breaths to calm down. Her hands shook as she
replaced her glasses on her nose. She looked directly at Irene
through the thick lenses, which made her eyes look huge.

"A package . . . we received a package," she said.

She stood up with difficulty and went out into the hallway.
The floor creaked under her heavy footsteps as she moved from
room to room. After a while, she returned to the living room
with a small brown box. She handed it to Irene.

"Go ahead and open it," she said.

Irene lifted the lid. There was a sheet of crumpled paper.
Irene placed the box on the coffee table, carefully lifted the
paper by one corner, and shook the box so the contents would
come out. It was a simple piece of paper ripped from a notebook. In blue ink, a note had been written.

All is well. Will be in touch.
Thomas

The note was in capital letters right on the center of the

sheet. At the bottom of the box was a pair of round glasses. Irene didn't touch them.

"Are those Thomas's glasses?" she asked.

Marianne Bonetti nodded. She seemed much calmer now that she'd shown the box to Irene.

"When did this come?"

"A week after he left. We were starting to become nervous that we hadn't heard from him. Then these came. . . . Antonio speculated that Thomas needed to . . . disappear for a while. In order to put things right. He needed to find proof that he wasn't guilty."

As she said the last words, she glanced away. Irene realized that Marianne Bonetti had just lied to her for the first time, and intentionally. Of course Thomas's parents feared he might be guilty and have good reason to lie low for a while. They knew it wasn't the first time he'd been involved in financial crimes. In London, Thomas had known which way the wind was blowing for Poundfix, and he'd managed to get out in time. Perhaps they thought he'd managed to escape the ph.com fallout just as easily.

"Did this box come in the regular mail?" asked Irene.

"Yes. It was in a padded envelope."

"Do you still have the envelope?"

"No, I'm sorry, I don't."

"Do you remember where it was sent from?"

"Yes. Göteborg."

Perhaps that meant the murderer was from Göteborg, but Irene couldn't be sure yet. "Could Thomas get along without his glasses?"

"No. He had bad eyesight."

"He sends you the glasses he needs to see. Didn't you think that was strange?"

Marianne's gaze wavered. It was clear she was debating what to say and how to say it. After a few seconds, she pressed her lips together until they formed a narrow line. She said with finality, "Antonio said it was a sign. A secret signal. Thomas was trying to tell us he'd changed his appearance. It was not something he could say directly, but we were supposed to figure it out."

"Of course we would! We're his parents!" roared a voice.

Both Irene and Marianne jumped. Neither of them had heard Antonio Bonetti come in.

"I—I was trying to explain why we thought—Thomas was still alive," Marianne said in a tiny voice.

Her husband strode angrily into the living room in his extra-high shoes. He ignored his wife completely and aimed his glare at Irene. If he'd hoped to intimidate her by his stare, it didn't work. Irene stood up calmly and looked straight back at him. In order to keep eye contact, he had to crane his neck. "How nice that you've come," Irene said. "I have something which I have to tell both of you together. We have received the final autopsy report. I'm afraid that there is a strange and rather unpleasant detail I must tell you."

Chapter 17

THE FIRST OF October dawned beautiful and clear. When the sun appeared over the horizon, the temperature was just above freezing, but it was supposed to rise with the sun's journey across the sky. If luck held, there would be a few days of Indian summer. *Or is an Indian summer when it falls in October? Which one is Saint Birgitta's summer and which one is an Indian summer?* Irene decided it wasn't important. She would just enjoy the day as it came.

She parked her car in the lot next to the police station and got her backpack with the plastic bag holding the brown box of Thomas Bonetti's eyeglasses and his short letter. Both parents were convinced that Thomas had written the letter, but they'd had trouble finding another sample of handwriting to compare it with. Thomas was not much of a letter writer, according to his parents; he'd mostly sent emails and called on the phone. After a thorough search, they finally found a post card, a birthday greeting to Marianne. The card showed the Statue of Liberty and was dated *NY 1999-03-04.* Thomas had used capital letters on this as well. Irene thought they appeared similar to the writing on the letter that had come with the glasses, but she wasn't much of an expert. On the back, written in black ink from a ballpoint pen, were the words:

Happy birthday, Mamma!
Hope this card arrives in time for your birthday. Things are just

fine here. Many meetings but business is going in the right direction for us. Hugs, Thomas

Irene had found room for this postcard in the plastic bag, too. There was no room for it in the box, but there was enough for one of Antonio Bonetti's business cards. Both parents had put their fingerprints on that to help the technicians, who could then eliminate them right away. In her own mind, Irene wondered what the lawyer would say if he knew that his fingerprints had already been lifted, a few days earlier, from another one of his business cards.

Antonio Bonetti's rage had deflated as soon as Irene had told them about the missing fingers. The parents were deeply shaken. They also had asked why anyone would do such a thing. Irene had had a vague hope that they might know something more about the reasons why, or suggest a theory, but they didn't. The mystery remained.

Irene swung by the lab and gave the plastic bag with its contents to Svante Malm. She decided to leap up the stairs two at a time as a way to get her blood moving; she was feeling energetic and happy because of the sunny day. As she leaped over the top stair, she almost crashed into Fredrik Stridh, who was striding down the hallway at top speed.

"Whoops!" cried Irene.

"Whoops, yourself. I'm in a hurry. Rothstaahl's dad just called, absolutely hysterical. They had been defrosting a freezer in the basement in preparation for that girl and her boyfriend to rent the place, in spite of what had happened. They were going to move in today. Yesterday evening, as they checked the freezer, they saw that there was something left behind—a tube of vitamin C tablets—at the very bottom. Rothstaahl's mother picked it up and thought it was empty, but it rattled, so she opened it. Guess what she found?"

"No idea. Cocaine?"

"Nope. A finger."

THE SUPERINTENDENT HAD changed the normal time of their morning prayer from eight A.M. to eleven A.M. Fredrik Stridh had returned from fetching the vitamin C tube and its macabre contents from the Rothstaahl's summer house. The tube had been forwarded to the pathology lab. Even Professor Stridner had raised an eyebrow when it came in, he reported. That was small comfort for Andersson. He glared grimly at his team.

"Some devil is having fun at our expense," he growled.

No one contradicted him.

"We can be reasonably certain that this is Thomas Bonetti's finger. Or one of them," Birgitta said.

"So where are the other three?" Jonny wanted to know.

"It shouldn't be impossible to guess. Perhaps Rothstaahl had all four in his possession, but that is doubtful. The other three would have turned up," Birgitta thought out loud.

"What if it was planted?" asked Jonny.

"That's a possibility. After shooting Joachim and Philip, the killer could well have gone to the basement and put the tube with the finger into the freezer," Birgitta agreed.

"According to Rothstaahl's parents, the tube had been embedded in a thick layer of snow. It looked like Joachim hadn't defrosted the freezer in years. This explains why they didn't see the tube when they first started to remove things. They only found the tube once the snow was gone," Fredrik said.

"It's not called snow when it's in a freezer," Jonny said.

"I don't care what it's called," Andersson said. "Keep going."

Even Jonny thought it best not to cross their boss in his present state of mind. Jonny folded his arms and muttered something to himself. Andersson looked at Birgitta and commanded, "Go on."

"If we surmise that Joachim had only one of the fingers, we could assume that three other people had the others. If the finger was a warning, we ought to suspect that Kjell B:son Ceder and Philip Bergman had also received one finger before they were killed. The question is, who got the fourth one, and who is likely to be the next victim?"

The investigators sat quietly and digested this information. Finally, Jonny asked to speak. "It could be that the killer kept the other three fingers for himself. As trophies. Or to keep for the future."

Obviously, Jonny hadn't let go of the serial killer theory, but there could be some truth to what he said.

"We have to look for the remaining fingers. We should start with the houses of the other victims," Tommy suggested.

"If that Rothstaahl guy kept Bonetti's finger in the freezer, maybe he was Bonetti's killer. Or at least one of his killers," Jonny said.

Silence fell again as everyone thought this through. This was a new idea, and it wasn't all that far-fetched. Irene agreed Jonny had a good point.

"We should keep that in mind," she said. "It could give us a clearer picture of how Thomas Bonetti was killed. But it would have been hard for one person to carry out this complicated murder. Two or more killers might've been needed, one to maneuver the boat and handle the flashlight while the other kept Thomas under control. Two people could have forced him to the stone heap by holding a gun on him, and then he was shot when they got there."

"What the—?" Andersson exclaimed. "Two killers? So we're supposed to be looking for two killers now? And who would the other one be?"

"Why not Philip Bergman?" suggested Irene.

"Philip Bergman! Why would he be involved?"

"We don't know if Rothstaahl had an axe to grind with

Bonetti—it's possible. Yet we don't even know if they knew each other. On the other hand, we do know that there was animosity between Bonetti and Philip Bergman when ph.com was going under."

"And the motive?" asked Andersson. He didn't look as grim and was listening carefully to Irene.

"Money. Of course it has to be money. We know that Thomas Bonetti got out of Poundfix by the skin of his teeth but with a lot of money. We also know that he was being blamed for swindling between five and twenty-five million kroner from ph.com. Joachim and Philip would certainly believe that this was their money, too. Perhaps they wanted revenge."

Andersson brightened even more. He liked Irene's reasoning.

"Two suspected killers, but neither is alive to be questioned," Fredrik complained.

"And there's this—who killed *those* two?" asked Tommy.

"Not to mention Kjell B:son Ceder. Fewer than twenty-four hours later he was dead, too," added Birgitta.

"THERE'S A GAP in the timeline," Tommy said.

He was leaning back in his desk chair and tapping a pen on his front teeth. Irene felt that the personal tension between them had lessened, but she would be careful not to mention his upcoming divorce. She was not about to reopen a recently healed wound. If he wanted to talk about it, he'd have to speak first. *The difference between a wise person and a foolish person is that the wise one does not repeat his mistakes,* as Mamma Gerd used to say.

"Where's the gap?" asked Irene.

"You said that Thomas picked up some belongings at his parents' house at about five thirty. Then he went to Jaegerdorffsplatsen to buy whiskey. However, he didn't turn up at the boat until eight P.M. Two hours. What was he doing? Was he meeting someone?"

"He was going to the state liquor store. Maybe there was a long line," said Irene. She was irritated at herself for not noticing the time gap.

"They close at six. It only takes fifteen to twenty minutes to go from Jaegerdorffsplatsen to the small boat harbor. What was he doing before then?"

"No idea," Irene admitted.

Tommy sighed and stuck his pen back into the clay pencil holder his daughter had made at her daycare center. It had been painted bright yellow and decorated with red hearts. In the middle, Tommy's daughter had written *Pappa* in large, sprawling letters.

"Let's get something to eat before we go out looking for those fingers," Tommy said. "It's probably the best thing to do, so we don't lose our appetite later on. Do you think that Bonetti's parents have a finger?"

"Why would they?"

"Perhaps the killer was trying to blackmail them? If you don't pay *x* amount of money, we'll send his head next time. Something like that."

"No. His mother would have told me. She couldn't have kept quiet about such a thing. You have no idea what it cost her to show me the box where Bonetti's glasses were. That lawyer husband of hers really keeps her on a tight leash. Though he softened up when I told him about the missing fingers. He was truly shaken up about it."

"So you don't think that the Bonettis received one?"

"No."

"So who, then?"

Just as Irene was about to say she had no idea, she realized who might have had one. Or two.

• • •

ELSY KAEGLER SLOWLY opened the door to the Askim house. Irene had pushed Tommy in front of her on a hunch, and she was right. Sanna's mother beamed when she saw Tommy.

"How nice to . . . I mean . . . please come in. Sanna is not . . . I mean, she'll be here a little later. Ludde has just gone to sleep," Elsy said, sounding as scatter-brained as usual.

Irene wondered how Elsy Kaegler could be Sanna Kaegler's mother. Sanna was so cold and calculating. And didn't she hold down a job? Or maybe she was retired? Elsy didn't appear to be older than sixty, but maybe she was.

"I've just made a pot of coffee," Elsy said. "I don't have any buns or cookies, though. Is that all right?"

"It's fine," the two detectives said in unison.

"On a day like this, it would be wonderful to sit in the outdoor room, but it feels so . . . horrid. It's where poor Kjell. . . . Let's sit in the living room instead," Elsy said with a shudder.

"That's fine. I'll help you bring out the coffee," said Tommy.

Tommy and Irene followed Elsy into the kitchen. Elsy found some special tall glasses meant for coffee.

"It's going to be café latte," explained Elsy.

She warmed milk in the microwave; then the milk and coffee from the percolator were blended in just the right amounts and poured into the tall glasses. Elsy, chatting with Tommy the entire time, set the glasses on a tray that Tommy picked up. They headed to the living room while Irene hung back.

"I'm just going to get a drink of water and find a tissue to blow my nose. I know my way to the living room," Irene explained.

"OK," Tommy said, almost without interruption in his conversation with Elsy, who seemed oblivious of anything Irene said or did.

Irene quickly crossed the tile floor to the freezer and opened its steel door to peer inside—with butterflies in her stomach.

It was empty.

There was nothing in the freezer, not even a thin layer of frost on the shelves or at the back. On the top shelf was an ice cube tray, and just to be sure, Irene looked into it, but there weren't even ice cubes there. Disappointed, she closed the door, got a glass of water, and headed back to the others in the living room.

Tommy hadn't wasted any time. As Irene sat down in one of the pale armchairs, she heard him say, "Perhaps we can just get the key from you so that we don't have to bother Sanna at all. We'll be back with it before she even gets home."

He gave Elsy a trusting smile.

"Well, maybe . . . she's so stressed and unhappy, my poor child. All of this . . . it's been too much for her. First Kjell, then Philip . . . it can't hurt to let you have the keys. You're police officers, after all."

At her last sentence, Elsy gave him a beatific smile.

They finished their coffee as quickly as they could, and when they went to the door to leave, Tommy reminded Elsy about the key. Elsy dug around in a huge flowery cloth bag for a long time before she fished out a key ring with three keys. There was a metal tag etched with the words *Hotel Göteborg*. "Here they are!"

They thanked her once more for the coffee and hurried to the car.

"THE HOUSE WAS searched pretty thoroughly after Ceder was shot," Irene said. "But perhaps we missed something in the freezer. Maybe a finger was hidden in a package of fish sticks or something like that, and there was time to get rid of it."

"Well, there was nothing there at any rate," Tommy said. "Maybe we'll have better luck here in the apartment."

He parked in an empty space close to Kjell Ceder's entrance. They took the swift and quiet elevator up to the sixth floor and got out. Just as Tommy was about to insert the key in the lock, Irene said, "Wait! What if Sanna is here?"

Tommy sighed and said, with conviction, "If there's one place where Sanna is not, it's this apartment. She hates it."

He turned the key in the lock and opened the door. Bowing as if to a lady, he gestured for Irene to enter first.

It seemed as if a sheet of unseen sound hit her, and Irene reeled from the shock. She stood absolutely still, and it took her a second or two to realize that the noise was a high-pitched scream. It took her another few seconds to locate the dark figure pressed against the wall at the other end of the hallway.

Tommy fumbled at the inside wall and found the switch to the ceiling lamp. The light blinded her. Sanna stopped screaming just as quickly as she'd begun. Her eyes were wide-open from fear as she stared at the two police officers. Apparently, she didn't recognize them. She pressed against the wall as if trying to disappear into the wallpaper.

"Sanna, it's me, Tommy, and Irene, from the police. We're so sorry we frightened you," Tommy said in his deep, calming voice.

The whites of Sanna's eyes were shining just like those of a frightened deer. Irene remembered a runaway horse she and Tommy were called to control when they still shared a patrol car. The animal was skittering and hysterical in the middle of traffic on a highway, creating total chaos. As they'd approached the horse, the detail that had struck her was the shining whites of the horse's terrified eyes.

Why was Sanna so terrified?

"We didn't know you were here," Tommy apologized. "We were checking on the apartment and found the door open, so we decided to come inside and see if there'd been a break-in."

Good Lord! Irene thought. She had no idea that Tommy was as good as she was at lying on the fly. Hopefully Sanna wouldn't start to wonder how the police had walked into her apartment.

They didn't have a search warrant. Of course, they could have arranged one, but it would have taken at least a day. Tommy had been improvising when he'd asked innocent Elsy whether he could borrow the apartment keys. Now Irene strode across the threshold to within a few meters of Sanna.

"Don't be afraid," she said. "It's just us."

The fear in Sanna's eyes faded to tears, which started to slide silently down her cheeks.

"Come, Sanna," Tommy urged. "Let's go talk in the library." He carefully took hold of her arm.

Without any resistance, Sanna allowed herself to be led into the large room with its floor-to-ceiling bookcases and leather armchairs; the aroma of leather and dust created a sense of security. Tommy let her sink down into one of the armchairs.

Meanwhile, Irene took a quick look at the surprisingly modern kitchen with dark stone counters and cupboards in light oak. Not a bit of brushed steel here. It was attractive and functional, not surprising considering Kjell B:son Ceder had been a cuisine professional. It also spoke to the great differences between the Ceders. Why had Kjell married Sanna?

Irene pulled a sheet from the roll of paper towels on a dispenser near the stove. She decided to take a quick look into the upright freezer before she left the kitchen. It was next to the refrigerator and was just as tall as Irene.

She had never before seen such a tightly packed and well-organized freezer. It would take hours to go through its contents, so all she could do was shut the door and leave the kitchen.

Sanna had calmed somewhat, and Tommy was making small talk with her. As Irene came in, Tommy smiled and said, "Here's Irene with a paper towel. We thought you'd gotten lost in the hallway," he told Irene.

"Good thing I learned orienteering when I was a kid," Irene

joked in reply and gave Sanna a small smile as she handed over the paper towel.

Sanna took it without looking at Irene, dried her tears, blew her nose, and then tossed the crumpled paper into the fireplace.

"What are you doing here?" she asked sharply.

"That's just what we were going to ask you," Tommy replied.

"It's my apartment!"

"Not quite yet," Tommy said.

"I'm well within my rights to be here!" she said defiantly. Sanna seemed to have recovered from the shock and was turning back into her former controlled self. *If we're going to get a sensible answer from her*, Irene thought, *we're going to have to throw her off balance*. She decided to be blunt.

"We're looking for the finger," she said.

It was a wild guess, but it hit the mark. Sanna stiffened. "You can't—know anything," she whispered.

"We have found the finger Joachim had, and he'd written that other people had received fingers. . . . " Irene said, purposefully not finishing her sentence. Sanna interpreted it as a truthful statement.

"Then . . . we're marked for death." Her terrified eyes flitted between Tommy and Irene.

"Who is threatening to kill you?" Irene asked.

Sanna shook her head and her pale lips moved, but no sound came out. She was truly scared to death.

"Who is threatening you?" Irene repeated.

"I don't know. I have to find the finger. I don't know if Kjell hid it or if he'd gotten rid of it." Sanna covered her face with her hands and began to sway back and forth.

Tommy got up and sat on the chair arm next to Sanna to protectively drape one arm around her. Irene was surprised, not so much at Tommy but at the fact that Sanna let him do it. Tommy spoke softly as if he were speaking to a child.

"Now, now, Sanna. You don't have to be afraid any longer. We know about this business with those chopped-off fingers. We know that they've been sent to a few people. Is someone trying to extort money from you?"

"Yes . . . now, Ludwig. . . . " she whispered.

"So they've threatened both you and Ludwig," Tommy stated.

Sanna nodded but didn't take her hands away from her face.

"Why now? Is it still about money?" Irene asked.

Sanna said nothing and it took a long time before she took her hands down. She looked simultaneously desperate and hopeless.

"I have to find Kjell's finger or else . . . something bad will happen to me and Ludwig!"

"So you received it three years ago."

"Yes, though it was just about money then. Blackmail. Now . . . that Thomas's body has been found. . . they want the fingers back."

This was quite a macabre story. Sanna had been living under the threat of blackmail for three years. Irene realized why Sanna had reacted the way she did in the hallway. She naturally believed that the murderer had come to kill her.

"What did you do with yours?"

"My—? I threw it out! Right away! Directly into the apartment's garbage can."

Her answer was so rapid it had to be the truth.

"It came when you returned to Sweden?"

"Yes. I moved home in August. The finger came at the end of September."

"What was in the message you received with it?"

Sanna's knuckles were chalk white. After a while, she relaxed her grip and began to wring her hands exactly like her mother did.

"You received one just like everyone else," Irene said firmly.

She was improvising, but based her statement on the knowledge that a criminal tends to use the same method over and over.

"Yes . . . I was supposed to pay money. It was extortion. The note said it was Thomas's finger. If I didn't pay up, the same thing would happen to me. I've been paying and paying . . . and soon I'll have no money left at all."

Tears welled in Sanna's eyes again, and Irene refrained from asking how Sanna had financed the house in Askim. That wouldn't be wise. Sanna would just shut back up like an oyster. Right now she was actually talking to them, and most of what she was saying sounded like the truth.

"Who have you been paying?" Irene asked.

"Edward. He passed the money along to another account. He doesn't know who owns it."

"How much have you paid so far?"

Sanna swallowed a few times before she could answer. "Twenty thousand American dollars a month."

Irene converted the amount quickly in her head and understood immediately why Sanna was running out of money. She'd been paying a hundred and fifty thousand Swedish kroner a month for three years. Even a fortune would disappear at that rate.

"So your brother-in-law's brother, Edward Fenton, took care of this?" Tommy asked. "The man in charge of HP Morgan's European head office?"

"Yes. He'd also gotten rid of the finger sent to him. But now they're demanding all four back. So Edward asked me to look for Kjell's. I've looked for hours, and I haven't found one!"

Irene and Tommy exchanged glances. No surprise that Kjell B:son Ceder had received a finger, but why Edward Fenton? Since only four fingers were cut from Thomas Bonetti's body, this meant that Edward Fenton, Sanna Kaegler, Kjell Ceder, and Joachim Rothstaahl had each gotten one.

Something didn't add up here, and Irene's police instincts kicked in.

"When did you get the demand for Kjell's finger?" she asked carefully.

"Yesterday morning. It must have been after Thomas's body was found."

"Did the note tell you that Thomas had been killed?"

"No, just that it was Thomas's finger. It was so horrible. He was . . . gone. Though I have to say, Thomas is clever. He could have bought some fingers off another corpse and then sent them himself to extort money. Even if he'd gotten all ph.com's money, it still must cost something to stay in hiding."

"But he wasn't the one who sent them," Irene said, drily. "He was already dead."

Sanna jumped as if she were a scolded schoolchild. Obviously she preferred her theory about Thomas's cleverness to the stark reality.

"Did Philip say he'd received a finger?"

Sanna appeared sincerely surprised. "No, not that I know. But I wouldn't be surprised based on . . . what happened to him later." Her eyes filled with tears again, and she couldn't hold back a sniffle. Irene crossed off any lingering suspicion that Sanna had been involved in Philip's death. She was truly hit hard by his death. Perhaps she'd have been able to shoot Joachim or Thomas, but not Philip.

If Philip, too, had received one, that would add up to five fingers sent. Obviously not the case. Irene felt more sure that something wasn't adding up—not just fingers.

"Why Edward?" asked Tommy.

Sanna sighed and seemed to huddle into herself. "He'd gotten some money for ph.com from a man who absolutely did not want to lose anything. But that happens with risky capital. It's part of the game. Anyway, Edward also received a finger and had to pay up or he'd meet the same fate as Thomas. It was the same threat as in my note."

"So Edward knows the name of this man who is demanding his money back," Irene said.

"He says he doesn't." Sanna looked totally uninterested. Obviously she had no idea how important this question was. Or maybe she did. Irene felt something did not fit in Sanna's tale, but she couldn't put her finger on it. Instead, she asked, "How was the finger packed when it arrived?"

"In a plastic tube. One of those for vitamin C tablets that fizz."

"How was the plastic tube packed?"

"A padded envelope."

"Do you remember the post mark?"

Sanna wrinkled her forehead and seemed to concentrate before she shook her head. "No, I don't remember."

"Did the package come to your mother's address?"

"Why would it? I'd just moved to my own apartment. That's where it came."

This meant that the sender kept tabs on Sanna. He knew that Sanna had moved back home to Göteborg and even knew her new address. So the murderer probably had ties to Göteborg.

"Did you know then that Kjell had also received a finger?"

"No, not until yesterday."

"Why did he get one?"

Sanna raised an eyebrow and looked directly at Irene. "I really have no idea." Her surprise was genuine.

"Was Kjell involved in ph.com?"

"No, absolutely not! He was busy with the hotel and the two restaurants."

"Did he put money in Poundfix when Thomas Bonetti and Joachim Rothstaahl were in London?"

"No. Kjell put all his money into the hotel. It was a money

pit, according to him." Suddenly Sanna leapt to her feet. "Oh my God! If you take the finger then I can't send it back! Then it's all over for me and Ludwig!"

Tommy just looked calmly at her. "Who were you supposed to send it to?"

Sanna took a huge breath, and fear shone in her eyes again. "I have no idea. They're going to contact me."

"*How?*"

"Through Edward. He is going to call tonight or tomorrow. If I find it, I'm supposed to get further instructions."

Irene and Tommy stood up at the same time. Tommy placed a hand on Sanna's arm. "We're going to help you look for it. Then you can tell Edward in good conscience that you've searched but didn't find it. Kjell could have gotten rid of it, just like you and Edward. And remember, the press hasn't found out anything yet about Thomas's missing fingers. They also don't know we found one of those fingers at Joachim's place. Your blackmailers have no idea that the police already know about them."

A bit of what he said managed to reach Sanna and she visibly relaxed, but only a little, as if she wasn't entirely convinced.

To Irene's great relief, Tommy took it upon himself to go through the freezer. Sanna disappeared into a room that was probably her late husband's bedroom. This cluttered apartment seemed to present a monumental task to search. Irene walked into the hallway and tried to think logically.

Where would someone hide part of a dead body? In a box, a chest. Irene looked around and her eyes fell on an old-fashioned wooden chest with iron hinges set next to one of the walls. The key was in the iron lock, and Irene lifted the heavy lid. The only things inside this chest were a pair of rubber boots, a flashlight, and a set of blue Helly Hansen rain clothes.

She searched carefully until she was convinced that the finger wasn't there.

Where's another likely place? If not a chest, what would one use? A picture rose into her mind from her subconscious. *The urn. Quite possible.* She strode purposefully back to the library. The black stone urn was still in its place on the mantelpiece. The elegant handles still swirled up its sides, and its surface was polished until it reflected everything like a mirror. The stone had beautiful green veining with slight glistenings of gold. She lifted it and put it down on the lace cloth of the coffee table. She had to use both hands; the urn was deceptively heavy. The lid was difficult to remove. After a bit of twisting back and forth, it finally gave way.

One glance into the dark was enough to see that a vitamin C tube was the only object inside.

In a friendly but firm way, Tommy convinced Sanna that she was in no state to drive. They decided that Tommy would drive her back to the house in Askim, but Irene suspected that Tommy was more interested in getting to drive a Mercedes Cabriolet. She wouldn't mind acting the chauffeur in that car herself. As Tommy handed her the keys to their much more anonymous unmarked car, he also slid the key ring to Kjell B:son Ceder's apartment into her palm. It was a smart strategy. While he kept Sanna occupied, Irene would have a chance to return the keys to Elsy without drawing much attention to them. They hoped Elsy would forget about it as soon as possible and not mention it to Sanna.

Tommy followed traffic to Vasterleden. Irene had no trouble keeping up with him since she'd driven this route for fifteen years.

So much new information had come to her just in the past few hours. She had much to think through. *Could someone extort money simply by sending a severed finger in the mail?*

Probably not. The person might go to the police. *If that person had nothing to hide, that is.* So the finger must be a threat to reveal something.

What did all these people have in common that they would want to hide? Money. Large amounts of money. Cheating to get large amounts of money. Certainly lots of people felt cheated by the Bonetti-Bergman-Kaegler trio in the ph.com crash. Scandinavian businesses had been scammed by Bonetti and Rothstaahl in the Poundfix swindle. Now Rothstaahl and Bergman had started up a similar scam in Paris. How many people had they already managed to cheat? Bonetti was suspected of moving many millions out of ph.com before it went bust, but what about Sanna and Philip? They'd gotten through the dot-com crash relatively unscathed. They'd both had a lot of money three years ago. Then the plastic tubes with the fingers arrived, and four people were forced to pay up.

Why didn't Philip Bergman get a finger? Everything indicated that he'd been blackmailed, too; his fortune had also gone down rapidly. Same thing with Joachim Rothstaahl.

And how did a finger suddenly show up in Edward Fenton's mailbox? His investment bank dealt in risky capital. It was part of the game that some investments would go bust, according to Sanna. Why would he be of interest to an extortionist? Only if he, like the others, had something to hide.

That's where it went wrong. Five victims of extortion would mean five fingers, and there were only four.

Irene decided it was high time to contact Edward Fenton.

THEY WERE LUCKY. Elsy appeared at the door anxious and wringing her hands.

"Ludwig has a tummy ache. He's screaming and . . . has diarrhea," she said breathlessly.

Loud screaming in the background confirmed her story. Sanna rushed into the house to take care of her son.

Irene smiled as she turned to Elsy and handed her the key chain.

"Sanna was in the apartment, so we didn't need these," she said.

"I see. Never mind. I mean . . . that's good," Elsy said.

She opened her flowery bag and dropped them inside.

"Has the boy been in pain since he woke up?" asked Tommy.

"Yes. He often wakes up with a tummy ache. Maybe it's colic. Poor little thing . . . he didn't want anything to drink, either. And I've been changing diapers every fifteen minutes."

They stood in the hall and let Elsy chat on and on about her grandson with his stomach pains. When they finally thanked her for her time, it appeared she'd completely forgotten about the key chain.

"How do we find Edward Fenton?" asked Tommy when they got back to the car.

"I think I'll give Glen a call," Irene said.

"Good idea."

Irene had met Glen Thompson in London when she was investigating a triple murder in Kullahult. It had been a complicated and high-profile case, written up in both the British and Scandinavian presses. Irene and Glen had become good friends. His mother was Brazilian and his father was Scottish, which made Glen one of the most exotic people at Scotland Yard. The Thompson family had visited Irene on their way to Nordkap. They'd driven up in an RV with lively six-year-old twin boys. Having twins was another thing Irene and Glen had in common, although Glen's boys were identical.

Irene knew she could count on Glen for help finding Edward Fenton.

Chapter 18

THE FIRST THING Irene did the next morning was to give Glen Thompson a call. She was in luck and reached him on her first attempt. They had a good long chat before they got down to business. When she finally began to tell him about the ins and outs of the difficult investigation, it took much longer than she thought, even though she didn't include everything. Glen did not interrupt her once, even when, at times, her English was problematic.

"A hell of a lot of problems you have there!" he said, laughing, once she'd finished her long-winded tale.

She could only agree.

"I'll go ahead and contact this Edward Fenton and tell him to call you in Göteborg. Are you reachable this afternoon?"

"You have my cell phone number," she said.

"All right, I'll call back later."

"SO, WHAT THE hell is going on here?" demanded Andersson.

Irene and Tommy had just reported the latest twist in the case, which seemed to make the superintendent feel that things were just too complicated.

"A talk with Edward Fenton might clear things up," Tommy soothed.

Irene had explained her theory of blackmail to the rest of the team, and both Birgitta and Kajsa agreed with it.

"Extortion seems entirely consistent with what we know," Birgitta said. "We've gone through all their finances again, and everyone involved seems to have spent their fortunes remarkably fast. Thomas Bonetti's money went missing right after he did."

"Bonetti was the first victim," Andersson said.

"And he had the most money," Kajsa pointed out.

Kajsa's shudder-inducing bruises had begun to fade to green in certain spots, although light purple still dominated. Her stitches had been taken out the day before, and she no longer had a bandage around her head—just a small one over the actual wound. She didn't appear to worry too much about how the colorful display affected her appearance. Irene had to admire her stubbornness and her endurance. She also noted that Tommy was sitting next to her. *Had they gotten together over the weekend?* She didn't dare ask.

"But why a sudden rush to kill Ceder, Bergman, and Roth-staahl?" asked Andersson.

"If we knew the answer to that, maybe we could wrap this up." Irene sighed.

"Someone panicked for some reason. Or perhaps they just decided to get rid of all the leads back to them," Tommy said, thinking out loud.

Irene nodded. She had also been struck by a thought. "Everything in this investigation is tied to money. Even the extortion, which led to murder. Oh, and some narcotics in Paris, so many that it suggests dealing. Enough to be a felony."

"Oh, Paris," Andersson said. "I almost forgot. Where did I put it. . . ." Andersson was huffing as he searched through his stacks of papers on the table. "Here it is!" He put on his reading glasses and looked down at the sheet of paper. "We've gotten the results on the hair samples you found in the Roth-staahl apartment."

Andersson paused for effect and looked at Irene over the

top of his glasses. Irene was surprised to see the hint of a smile at the corners of his mouth. "As we expected, most belonged to Rothstaahl and Bergman. We put those aside right away. That left samples from four people; two of whom we know, of course, Irene and Kajsa. We put those aside as well. So there are two left and"—he broke out into a real smile as he let the bomb fall—"one of them, with a high degree of probability, is Ludwig's father!"

Andersson had really created dramatic scene with his information, and he couldn't complain about the effect it had on his team. Irene realized she was sitting there with her mouth open. She'd known instinctively that it would be important to identify Ludwig's father, but it was a twist that he would be a person of interest in the case. It took a few seconds for the wheels in her mind to begin turning again. One thing was clear: the unknown man in New York was a fake. Now they must really locate Ludwig's father. They had good reason to go back to Sanna and lean on her for the truth, and she couldn't weasel out—Ludwig's father was tied up in the murders!

"So, Ludwig's father was probably in the apartment. There is one more hair sample, and it seems to come from an older person, since it's gray," Andersson continued.

"The man who shot at me was blonde! Is he Ludwig's father?" Irene asked. She thought a moment. "We have to press Sanna hard. Who is the father of her son? What kind of hold did the extortionist have on her? I know that she's reluctant to talk to us, but how much pressure can she take? She was beside herself with fear yesterday. She's afraid for her life."

With a shudder, she remembered how the whites of Sanna's eyes had glittered in terror when she'd been caught in the hallway. She feared being killed, and with good reason, considering how many people had been murdered that she knew.

Fredrik Stridh asked to speak. "Jonny and I have tried to find out why Bergman and Rothstaahl had to go to Göteborg at the same time. It's now clear they went to meet a third party, but we haven't found out who that is. I tested the theory that it might have been Kjell B:son Ceder, but no. An interesting sidelight is that Ceder was having an affair with his secretary, Malin Eriksson. She finally confessed everything to me when I asked her one more time what Ceder had been doing that Monday evening before he was killed. Eriksson finally decided to tell us the truth. They were supposed to meet at Ceder's apartment. Malin Eriksson had a key, and she waited there all evening until midnight. She'd made dinner for him, but he never came. For obvious reasons."

"So, Ceder knew that Sanna and Ludwig would be away at her sister's apartment that evening. In his own apartment, his mistress was waiting for him with a candlelit dinner. So he decided to meet the killer in the empty house. That's why he was shot in Askim! And unfortunately, he never told Malin Eriksson who he was meeting," said Irene.

At last they knew why Ceder had been killed at Askim instead of in his apartment. Everyone, even Sanna, had been mystified why he'd been killed in a house he seldom visited.

"Goddamn woman, this Malin! Why didn't she tell us sooner?" growled the superintendent.

"She's a married woman—and to a policeman!"

Andersson looked crestfallen. "She is? I see. . . . Anyone we know?"

"Not really. It's a new guy in PO 1," Fredrik explained. "He'd been working in Stockholm and came here last spring with his wife. They're both originally from Göteborg. She wanted to move back home, and she'd gotten a job with Ceder."

So Kjell B:son Ceder had wasted no time in starting another affair with his new secretary. Sanna and Ludwig meant nothing to him—just as he meant nothing to Sanna. So why on earth did they ever get married? Another question for Sanna.

Jonny cleared his throat so that everyone would pay attention to him. "I've found a lead on Thomas Bonetti's missing boat. Remember, after he was declared missing, there was a huge search for it but it was gone without a trace? Do you also remember that last summer our colleagues in Malmö told us about the gang which dealt in stolen pleasure boats? They would falsify the numbers on the motors and the boat's registration to sell them abroad. I had a hunch and called our friends in Malmö and asked if they'd come across a Storebro Royal Cruiser 420. They sent me a fax yesterday. One of those boats was sold to a guy in Karlskrona about two years back. The motor number had been forged, so they're going to get back to me with the secret number they've retrieved from inside it."

"Wonderful!" exclaimed Andersson. "Now we finally know what happened to that luxury boat."

Irene was surprised that Jonny had taken some initiative, although she knew he could be quick on the uptake when he made an effort. Perhaps that was what had been wrong with him the past few years—he hadn't really wanted to make an effort. Irene asked for the floor.

"This still indicates that at least two people must have been involved in killing Thomas. A boat that big requires two people to handle it—one to steer and the other to moor it and cast off again. Plus Thomas had to be kept under guard. After they killed him, they had to get the boat to where the gang of boat thieves could pick it up. Perhaps they used two boats, one following the other, to make the delivery. Or, alternatively, the murderers had a car near that location, or perhaps they even used public transportation to get home afterward."

"Hardly," said Birgitta. "That would be too big a risk. After something like that, you'd want to keep low. So he took a boat or a car."

"Maybe he jogged," said Tommy.

"Jogged?" repeated Andersson as his brow furrowed even

farther. He looked surprisingly like a bulldog whenever he did that. Irene recognized the other similarities he had with bull-dogs—once he got hold of an idea, he had trouble letting go of it again. His stubbornness had helped them get to the bottom of many an investigation over the years.

"Yes, jogged. A jogger was seen out in Askim at the time of the murder. We've had no replies to our many calls to come forward, even after we've put it in the newspaper. We also found a jogging reflector inside the house," Tommy reminded them.

Irene had almost forgotten about the man running in the pouring rain, who'd been seen by the dog walker. Of course talking to the jogger would be important; if nothing else, he might have seen something vital so near the house at the time of the murder. Tommy was right; the jogger was a person of interest.

"I'm also concerned about Sanna," Tommy said. "According to her, someone has threatened both hers and Ludwig's lives. Of all the people who received a finger, she's the only one still alive."

"Edward Fenton has one," Irene said.

"Or so he told Sanna. We won't know the truth until we've talked to him."

Irene had to agree. Besides, she thought it was odd that the head of HP Johnson's European office would be the victim of blackmail.

"The killer is still active. He's threatened Sanna via that Fenton guy," Tommy said. "The next question should be: What can we do to insure her safety?"

"If an officer is posted at her door, the killer will know that she's squealed," Fredrik said.

Andersson sucked air into his cheeks like a chipmunk and then let the air out again, lips sputtering. All of his subordi-nates knew this meant their boss was deep in thought. Finally, he clapped his hands. "Surveillance! Twenty-four-hour surveillance on Sanna and the boy. We have two reasons: to protect their lives and the chance to grab the killers when they try."

"What if she's lying?" Jonny complained. "Then we'll have a meaningless surveillance team that will cost a huge amount of—"

Tommy interrupted. "If you'd seen her yesterday, you'd know she's telling the truth. Believe me. I've heard a lot of lies out of her mouth the past few days—and she's not even a good liar."

Jonny glared around the table, but he said nothing more. Everyone knew he hated to be on surveillance. You had to be awake and alert for hours at a time.

"So when do we start?" asked Irene.

"After lunch," said Andersson. "Kajsa and Birgitta, you two take the first watch."

"Should we let Sanna know?" asked Birgitta.

This question caused a repeat of the chipmunk-cheek performance. After another round of lip-sputtering, Andersson made up his mind. "No. We don't know who the killer or killers may be, nor does she. If she knows that she's being watched, she might inadvertently tip off whoever it is."

Irene was relieved that Andersson took the threat to Sanna and her son so seriously. There were certainly good reasons to act on it.

They worked out a schedule for the surveillance teams. Tommy and Irene would take the evening shift from six P.M. to midnight. On Saturday morning, Irene would be paired with Jonny. Tommy had asked for that morning off for "private reasons," and Irene had a lump in her throat when she heard. The "private reasons" had to do with Agneta moving out of the house. Tommy and the children would be at his parents' home over the weekend. *He certainly must be going through hell right now.* Irene glanced sideways at him and saw the dark circles under his eyes. Obviously he hadn't been getting much sleep. His face had grown thinner. He'd lost a lot of weight around the middle. Of course, he'd joked about needing to lose the pounds, but he certainly would not have wanted to look so tired and hollowed out. So far, only Irene knew that he was going through a divorce, and the others didn't seem to notice the physical changes. Tommy was trying hard to hide his pain, but how long could a person hold it in before they burst? Sooner or later, everyone reaches a breaking point. Tommy had been hiding his difficulties so well that even Irene hadn't noticed them.

The last time Irene and Krister had gotten together with Tommy and Agneta had been Midsummer weekend. It was their tradition to meet at the Persson's summer cottage on Orust to celebrate the holiday. There'd always been a crowd of relatives and neighbors. Tommy's eldest son, Martin, was Irene's godson, and usually the two of them would laugh and joke around. But last Midsummer there hadn't been much of that; the fifteen-year-old had kept to himself and hadn't been particularly friendly. Martin and his friends had gone away on bikes, and they hadn't returned until two A.M. Agneta had mentioned that Martin's girlfriend was in London taking a language class that summer, which had made him depressed.

Maybe the girlfriend story was a cover for why Martin was so unhappy. Maybe he'd actually been dealing with the true emotional state of the entire family. He certainly was old enough to understand what was going on. Maybe he'd overheard something. Other than Martin's behavior, there had been no other hints about what was really going on in the Persson household. Tommy and Agneta had done a good job hiding everything.

Irrationally, deep in her heart, Irene felt that somehow they'd betrayed her.

• • •

JUST AS IRENE was finishing her lunch of Falun sausage with macaroni in cream sauce, her cell phone rang. It was Glen Thompson, and before she could even say hello, he started to speak.

"It's amazing how you manage to stick your nose into the most unusual cases, but this time I think you've really kicked the hornet's nest!" He laughed, and Irene wasn't sure whether she should, too, but before she could decide, he went on in a more serious tone.

"When I started checking around this morning, no one knew where Edward Fenton was. Everyone I talked to sounded nervous when I brought him up. Finally I was connected to a guy who told me he was an information manager. He finally let it slip that Edward Fenton has been missing for the past few days."

"For the past few days?" Irene repeated. Not good news to hear.

"That's right. The management team for HP Johnson had an emergency meeting this morning. This is the story I was told. Edward Fenton had been in the United States to visit his family during the first two weeks of September. His wife and sons stayed behind for another two weeks when he returned to London. What was strange is that he didn't show up for work on Monday. He also didn't show up on Tuesday. It wasn't unusual for him to work from home, but he usually checked in. On the seventeenth of September, Wednesday, he returned to the office. According to the secretaries, he had a wound on his face. He said that he'd tripped on the stone path of his garden, but he said nothing about where he'd been on Monday and Tuesday. Then he worked as usual for the rest of the week. On Friday afternoon, he told his secretary that he was going to Berlin on Monday morning, and the whole week following he checked in with his secretary every day. His last telephone call was on Friday the twenty-seventh. Since then, no one has heard a word from him."

"What was he supposed to be doing in Berlin?"

"Nothing."

"Nothing?" Irene repeated.

"He never went to Berlin. He booked a flight, but he never boarded."

"So where did he go?"

"No one knows. And now he's gone."

Irene felt her mouth go dry. Something was terribly wrong.

"Glen, remember what I already told you? Four people have been killed. Because of death threats we have two people in Göteborg—a woman and her baby—under surveillance. And these threats were passed on two days ago through Edward Fenton. He told this woman that he, too, was being threatened."

Glen was silent a moment and then asked, "So you think he might have been murdered, too?" All cheer had disappeared from his voice.

"There's always a risk that that might have happened."

"What do you know about this Fenton fellow?"

Irene told him everything she knew. Glen listened and said nothing for a while after she'd finished. Then he asked, "Did you say he was married to Janice Santini? The daughter of Sergio Santini?"

"That's right."

"You really did stir the hornet's nest, Irene. I have a colleague who specializes in this kind of thing," he said thoughtfully.

"What kind of thing?" Irene asked. She had trouble hiding her impatience.

"He worked for the FBI. A few years ago, he met an English-woman and moved to London. Since then, he's been working for us."

Irene felt as if things were whirling around in her brain like the hornets whose nest she'd supposedly kicked.

"I'll call you back as soon as I've found out anything more," Glen said.

"Thanks—thanks so much," Irene said.

As she ended the call, she felt exhausted, as if she'd just undergone an extra long bout of jiujitsu.

Chapter 19

IRENE CHOSE TO park in the lot above the pedestrian and bicycle path. It was surrounded by high trees and dense bushes that could hide their unmarked car. On the other side of all the greenery was an open field all the way to Sanna Kaegler-Ceder's house. Irene parked by a gap in the greenery. They could easily see the house with the help of the abundant outdoor lighting.

"From here we can overlook the front and west side, but not the back or the east, so one of us will have to relocate to cover the whole house," said Tommy.

Tommy had an average set of binoculars, even though they were especially light-sensitive. Irene had lifted a set from the guys in the narcotics department, despite their protests. "Now, now, you have to learn to share, just like the children at day care," she had chirped, smiling broadly as she headed out the door, her plunder in a tight fist.

Since the Askim house did not have trees or bushes close by, they would have to set up their lookout farther away. If the weather turned bad, a normal set of binoculars wouldn't do, so the set of night goggles that Irene had snagged would be put to good use. Night goggles strengthen light by 10,000 percent; Irene had learned that when she'd used them on earlier investigations.

Now she used them to make a quick survey of the surroundings. She saw what she was looking for.

"I'll stroll the bike path and duck in near the back of the house. I'll be in the grove of trees over there on the other side of the field; you can see the treetops behind the house," she said, pointing.

"Good."

They synchronized their watches and put their cell phones on vibrate. Irene hung the night goggles from her neck underneath her coat. She also had her holstered Sig Sauer. There were heavy clouds in the sky, and the wind had picked up, so she'd chosen a winter overcoat. The forecast called for cooling temperatures.

"Give me a call when you want to change places," Tommy said.

Irene got out of the car and started to walk down to the bike path. She'd go about one hundred and fifty meters and then leave the bike path for the grove of trees. A strong wind blew in from the sea, carrying the smell of salt into her nostrils while droplets from the ocean hit her face like gnats. Black clouds scurried across the sky. Between the sparse streetlights, the twilight had already turned to darkness. The wind was chilling, so she pulled up her hood. In the distance, she saw a man walking a German shepherd. Maybe this was the same witness who'd seen the jogger that night when Kjell B:son Ceder was murdered? The man and the dog were going the same direction as she was, and they seemed to take no notice of her. To keep oriented, Irene counted her steps. When she reached one hundred and fifty, she turned off the bike path and headed up the slope for the trees. It was grass-covered and steep, and she had trouble making her way up. She saw the tall trees about fifty meters to her right. *Not bad, not bad*, she thought. *At least I still know how to count.* The tall, dry grass and a tangle of raspberry stalks impeded her steps. She finally got to a good spot in the grove of trees, ideal for a stakeout. She could look out from behind a tree trunk while still being concealed by a thicket of young birches, and there was no risk that someone from the house could see her dark figure beneath the branches.

She lifted the night goggles to her eyes and studied the back of the house. The night goggles didn't show color—every object was different shades of green. Through the glass of the outdoor room she could see directly into the living room. It looked empty. There was light in Ludwig's room. Irene could see Elsy Kaegler moving around in it. She was moving her lips and bending over often. Sanna had closed the curtains to her room although a sliver of light shone through a tiny gap. Perhaps Sanna was lying in bed and watching the wide-screen TV.

Irene and Tommy had made sure to eat dinner before their shift, but by nine o'clock, Irene was starting to feel thirsty. She would have loved something hot. Even though the wind from the ocean was not very strong on the lee side of the island, especially within the grove of trees, cold fingers of air had found gaps at Irene's ankles and wrists, and she was starting to feel the chill in her bones. It was surprisingly strenuous to stand still and keep watch as long as she had done, even with periodic stretching to keep her blood flowing. Perhaps it was time to call Tommy and change places?

Just as she was about to press his number, the door at the back of the house opened. Irene froze with her finger over the button. Through the goggles, she saw how Sanna Kaegler stuck her head out and peered around. When Sanna saw that the coast was clear, she slipped out and shut the door behind her. Irene hit the button.

"Tommy," he answered.

"Sanna is leaving the house by the back door. She's wearing outdoor clothes: a long coat to her knees and long pants. Hair in a ponytail. She is heading in your direction," Irene said quietly.

"I see her. She's coming around the corner of the house now, heading to a point between me and the bike path. Perhaps she's aiming for it. Oops, she just stumbled."

"Doesn't she have a flashlight?"

"I don't see one."

Irene could also see how Sanna wobbled. It must be difficult to walk across the damp field in the darkness of night. *I hope she's wearing a good pair of boots!* Irene couldn't help thinking, but she had her doubts. She had never seen Sanna in any footwear with spike heels less than ten centimeters high.

"I'm going to move along the edge of the grove," Irene said. "I'll try to follow her."

"OK, I'll go down to the bike path. Don't turn off your cell phone."

"Got it."

It was difficult to step without sound through the thickets and undergrowth. Sanna was also having difficulty moving. She kept stumbling and catching herself. Irene suspected that her conjecture was right—Sanna was wearing heels that would sink into the mud. Irene realized she was catching up to her.

Tommy also seemed to be correct in his assumption that Sanna was heading to the bike path. She had just about crossed the field and was nearing the fringe of bushes lining the bike path, Irene barely more than fifty meters behind her. Then Irene caught a sudden movement in the bushes ahead. She stopped and put the night goggles to her eyes.

A figure in a stocking cap and wind jacket was crouching among the branches. Sanna was only about ten meters away when Irene saw him lift an arm and leap toward the unsuspecting Sanna. Without thinking, Irene ran forward, fumbling under her jacket to pull her gun from her holster while yelling as loud as she could:

"Police! Stop or I'll shoot!"

At the same time, Tommy came running from the other side of the bike path. He was also yelling, "Police! Stop right there! We're the police!"

Irene saw how Sanna stumbled and fell just as a flash came from a gun muzzle. There was no sound. *Silencer*, Irene thought.

Irene paused to locate the man again with her binoculars. All she saw was his back as he disappeared into the trees and bushes.

"I'll take care of Sanna!" Tommy yelled.

"Keep your cell phone on!" Irene yelled back.

"Got it!"

Irene ran in the same direction as the gunman. Once on the bike path, she raised the goggles again to spot the man running toward Billdal. He was fast, and he had a good head start. Although she was a good runner, too, Irene realized she'd never be able to catch up to him. And, since he was armed, she realized it wouldn't be a good idea to try to stop him on her own. Perhaps if she got close enough to wound him in the leg, it might be worth it, but, truth to tell, Irene was not the best shot. She always managed to pass the yearly test, but often by the skin of her teeth.

She still had her cell phone, but she had to redial Tommy since he'd had to break contact to call for an ambulance. As she ran, Irene told him to send patrol cars toward Hovås to intercept the gunman.

The wind had gotten stronger now, and hard drops of rain hit her in the face. It became even more difficult to run against the headwind. The distance between Irene and the gunman was increasing. Irene doubled her efforts to at least keep him in sight. The man ran easily, to Irene's great irritation. He seemed young, tall, and athletic in his stocking cap and black jogging suit. She tried to remember every detail. Not much of a description, but better than nothing.

From the corner of her eye, Irene saw that they were passing a small boat harbor. The gunman seemed to know exactly where to go. He went straight through the harbor parking lot and kept on, never seeming to tire in the least. Irene was sweating and panting. Her warm clothes were not meant for running. To make matters worse, her bad left knee was starting to ache again.

Finally she could no longer spot him through the goggles; the bike path was completely empty. Irene stopped and tried to listen. Between the pounding of her blood in her ears and the howling wind, it was impossible. Even if a steam locomotive were headed right at her, she wouldn't have been able to hear it. She struggled her way up a steep grassy slope and surveyed as much as she could through the night goggles. She peered inland and finally caught sight of him at the edge of a golf course. His pace hadn't faltered at all. Although the trees were sparsely planted, he hadn't tried to veer off course or to hide. He probably did not realize that Irene could still see him with her night goggles.

Irene called Tommy again.

"He's heading toward the club house parking lot on the golf course," she panted into the phone.

"Do you still see him?"

"Yes, but the parking lot is surrounded by bushes. . . . Now he's gone. Can one of our cars get him when he reaches the road?"

"I don't know. There's no patrol in the vicinity. They said they'd send out what they could. I can—"

"A car is exiting the lot!" Irene exclaimed. She tried to see its make and license plate number, but it went out of sight too quickly. Its rear lights flickered between the trees, and then it was gone.

"Damn it all!" Irene said with feeling.

"The ambulance is coming," Tommy said.

"How's Sanna doing?"

"The bullet grazed her head. She's conscious but in shock," he said.

That was easy to understand. It's very unpleasant to have someone shoot at you. Irene's memory of the gunman in Paris was fresh—and that man was probably the same man who'd just shot at Sanna.

"Let's hope the patrol car can intercept him," she said in an attempt to cheer herself up.

But by then, Tommy had already hung up.

Chapter 20

SANNA'S STILETTO HEELS had saved her life. The second before the gunman fired, one of her heels had stuck in the mud and made her lurch sideways. The bullet had plowed a deep groove along her scalp and taken a surface layer of bone, but hadn't shattered her skull and penetrated her brain. She would have a scar on the side of her head right above her right ear for the rest of her life: a permanent reminder that she'd almost been killed.

The doctors determined that Sanna didn't have a serious skull fracture. On the other hand, she did have a serious concussion and was in shock. Instead of showing gratitude to the police for intervening to save her life, Sanna kept up her lies and wriggled out of answering any of their questions. She finally said, "I have to go home and take care of my baby boy."

She turned her tear-filled eyes toward Tommy and let her lips tremble. *Great performance*, thought Irene, and snorted out loud. Sanna tried to ignore her, something not easy to do in the small, single-bed room.

The police had kept a watch on the Askim house all during the night. In the morning, Elsy Kaegler and baby Ludwig had been brought to Elsy's apartment.

"Why do you have to go home now? What if the killer returns?" asked Tommy.

Sanna looked away and then turned her moist eyes back to Tommy.

"He wouldn't dare now the house alarm is armed, and he knows that you're keeping me under surveillance," she said with a weak smile.

She's not at all afraid of the man who shot her, Irene marveled. *Something is off about her reaction. Sanna ought to be petrified and howling for protection, begging to stay at the hospital for as long as possible.*

"Who tried to kill you?" asked Tommy.

"No idea," Sanna insisted.

Tommy leaned toward her bandaged head, which was almost the same color as the pillowcase on which it rested. He caught her eye and said in a low voice, "Sanna, listen to me now. This man has killed four people. We have proof. These people were all close to you: Thomas Bonetti, Joachim Rothstaahl, your husband Kjell, and Philip Bergman."

He had saved Philip's name for last on purpose, as she had the softest spot in her heart for Philip. Before she could mobilize new strength to retort, he continued in his hypnotizing voice, "Yesterday, he tried to kill you, too. If Irene and I had not distracted him with our yells, if you hadn't stumbled, you'd be dead."

Tommy leaned even closer to her pale face. He emphasized each word. "Why are you protecting this killer?"

She stared back defiantly, but finally she had to look away. "I'm not protecting anyone. I don't know who he is," she whined.

Irene and Tommy exchanged looks. Time for the bad cop to take over. Irene cleared her throat and prepared to play her part.

She asked, "Why did you sneak out the back door?"

Sanna wet her dry lips with her tongue. "My coat was hanging in the laundry room because it was wet. I'd used it earlier. So I'd hung it there—"

Irene interrupted her. "I'll ask you again. Why did you sneak out the back door?"

Sanna looked at Irene angrily. It wouldn't help things if Sanna could mobilize her tough attitude. Irene told herself: *scare her into telling the truth.*

"It was easier. My coat—"

"Why did you go out at all?"

"I needed some fresh air. An evening walk—"

"Through a muddy field. In high heels," Irene said. She had no trace of sympathy in her voice, and she made sure Sanna understood that Irene knew she was lying.

"I usually just walk around the house," Sanna said lamely.

"I watched you through binoculars. You headed straight for where that man was hiding. There is also no doubt that he intended to kill you. I saw him aim. If we hadn't been there, you would now be dead. Killed by the same person who killed your four friends. For some reason, you feel you must protect him. You know who he is. Tell us."

Sanna looked frightened for a few seconds, but then she put her hand to her head theatrically as she declared, "My head hurts!"

"Fine, then let's get this interview over with quickly. Let me make this absolutely clear. As soon as you're released from the hospital, we will escort you to the police station and hold you there until you tell us what you know. It is a serious crime to protect a murderer. If I were you, I'd be much more afraid for my life."

What Irene said about holding Sanna at the station wasn't exactly true, but Sanna wouldn't know that. It looked like the words hit home, but Sanna still refused to speak. She pressed her lips tightly together, turned her face away from Irene, and shut her eyes.

"We'll be back in a few hours," Irene said.

The two police officers stood up and got ready to leave. Irene already had her hand on the door handle when she turned and said, "I hope this killer is as much of a friend as you seem to believe. People have been killed in their hospital beds."

They could see Sanna stiffen, but she did not turn to look at them as they walked out.

"That was harsh," Tommy said as they headed to the elevator.

"It won't hurt her to have a little more fear for her life," Irene replied. Inwardly, she had to admit that she'd been enjoying her role of bad cop just a bit too much. There was a uniformed officer at Sanna's door. Irene had instructed him to keep an eye on the door but not to bother looking through the glass window.

"THE HARD RAIN last night washed out most traces, but we managed to secure a footprint under the bushes where the gunman hid. It's a good print—really clear," Svante Malm said.

Irene and Tommy had gone straight to his lab to get a first-hand report.

"Is it the same kind of footprint we have from the laundry room of the Ceder house?" asked Tommy.

"We're still analyzing it. But at first glance, I'd say they're pretty similar," Malm said with satisfaction. "Won't you stay for a cup of coffee to celebrate?" he asked excitedly.

Both Irene and Tommy accepted gratefully, but regretted it when they tasted the coffee in the plastic mugs he handed them. Irene understood why Svante had the uncanny ability to appear at the Violent Crime Division right around their coffee break. The fourth floor coffee was definitely better.

"THE PATROL CARS couldn't catch our man, but at least they stopped two drunk drivers and retrieved a stolen motorized lawn mower," Jonny summarized that afternoon. "They were too late for ours."

"Some guy was really driving a stolen lawn mower in the middle of an October storm?" asked Birgitta incredulously.

Jonny glared at her. "No, it was on a flatbed truck. The guys on patrol became suspicious when the driver was too nervous. When they checked things out, they found that the lawn mower was reported stolen two weeks ago. The thief had written a classified ad to sell it and was about to deliver it to the buyer. He probably thought the storm would prevent him from being caught."

"Did the guy have a record?" asked Fredrik.

"No. Thirty-year-old immigrant with just small stuff in his background. Shoplifting as a juvie. They found two stolen TVs, two brand-new bicycles, and a computer in his garage. Obviously fronting for someone. Our colleagues think they've stumbled onto a ring of petty thieves. Not our problem, though."

"Our problem is this stupid Kaegler woman!" growled Andersson. "Why does she believe she can't talk to us?"

Tommy shrugged. "I have no idea. It seems odd to me."

"So you two believe she knows who the murderer is," Andersson said.

Tommy and Irene nodded in unison.

"What's your theory?" Andersson leaned back in his chair, which began to creak ominously. Andersson had gained quite a few kilos during the summer. *Not good for his asthma or his blood pressure*, Irene thought with worry. She couldn't do anything about it even if she wanted to. She knew Andersson wouldn't listen.

Irene doubted her own intuition, even as she started to speak. "I've been thinking hard about this. One, she's not afraid of the man who shot at her. Two, she refuses to believe that he actually tried to kill her yesterday. Why is she behaving so strangely? The only explanation I have is that she doesn't believe us. She thinks we're lying and trying to set a trap for an innocent man."

"Who would that be?" asked Andersson.

"Ludwig's father," Irene said.

"The boy's dad? Why would he want to kill her?" exclaimed Jonny.

"If I knew that, we'd know it all," Irene said wryly. She reached over the table for the pot of coffee and poured herself a cup. *Much better than that cat piss down at the lab*, she thought with contentment. She sipped carefully in case it was hot. Fortified by her elixir of life, she continued to explain her theory.

"Rothstaahl's apartment in Paris. We found hair from a man who might be Ludwig's father. Blond hair. The man who shot at me there was also blond. I assume he was Ludwig's father."

"Not far-fetched," conceded Tommy.

"The boy's father. . . . That would explain why she couldn't believe he might really be the murderer," Birgitta said.

"What a dumb bitch!" exclaimed Andersson. "Irene saw him try to kill her!"

"We women are like that," Birgitta said with a smile. "Loyal to the man we love until death."

Andersson glowered but decided not to comment further on the general lack of logic among women. Irene had arranged a gift certificate for Andersson's sixtieth birthday, a flight to London. He'd met Glen Thompson's Brazilian mother, and it appeared that the two of them had hit it off. Three nights at Glen's sister's hotel in London with lunches and dinners at Donna's restaurant had left Andersson quite pleased about his trip when he'd returned. He'd been so pleased, in fact, that he returned to London for a week at the end of July. No one in the department knew about it except for Irene. Glen had tattled to her.

Irene's thoughts were interrupted by her cell phone. She excused herself and went into the hallway to take the call. Coincidently, it was Glen.

"Hope you're sitting down. Things are moving like crazy around here. We found out that Edward Fenton went to Paris, confirmed by our Parisian colleagues. They'd found Fenton, all right. He was listening to a bit of trunk music."

"Trunk music? What's that?"

"An old mob expression," Glen said. "It's when a victim is shot and put in the trunk of a car."

"What's that you're saying? Fenton is dead?" Irene exclaimed. She headed for her office and sat down at her desk. Glen was right. She really had needed to sit down.

"Yes, he's been dead for a few days at least. They found him the day before yesterday. The rental car had been abandoned in an unused industrial park. A security guard on patrol was alerted by the smell, so he called in the police. Fenton had rented the car, but he'd used a false name. They couldn't find anyone by the name of Morgan Chesterton, and they had no way to identify him until we called. We sent along a photograph, and they could tell it was him."

Irene's head was spinning. If Edward Fenton had been dead for days, he could not have been on the telephone with Sanna. Strange that she'd lied about that. She'd convinced them when she'd told her story about the telephone threat. Obviously he wasn't the one who tried to shoot her, either. Irene's thoughts were interrupted as Glen said, "Hello? Are you there?"

"Yes, but I'm a little . . . shaken up. A lot has happened on this end, too," she replied.

She swiftly filled him in on the attempt on Sanna's life and about the supposed telephone threat from Edward Fenton where he warned they had to find all the cut-off fingers from Thomas Bonetti. But that conversation had taken place while Edward Fenton was lying dead in the trunk of a rented car.

"He'd definitely been dead for days," Glen said. "He was giving off . . . a smell."

"I know. It doesn't make things any clearer. Can you send me as much information you have?"

"There's not much, but I'll send you what I have. And as for you. . . . " He paused for effect. "You Göteborg people have a much more interesting case than you know. More interesting than the one here in London, at any rate!" He chuckled.

Irene didn't smile.

WHEN IRENE HAD returned to the conference room and given everyone the latest news, a flurry of speculation burst out among the assembled police officers. Andersson rapped his knuckles on the table and roared, "One at a time! One at a time!"

When the commotion died down, he said, "Irene, where do we stand now?"

"We're standing up to our knees in shit," Jonny couldn't help interrupting.

Irene had to agree with him for once, though she didn't say that out loud. "My conclusion is that Edward Fenton did receive a finger, just like the others. So Philip Bergman must not have, since only four are missing from Thomas's body. Still, Philip was also murdered. Something's not adding up," she said.

"Perhaps because he was with Rothstaahl? Maybe the killer didn't want to leave a witness?" Fredrik suggested.

"Philip's money dwindled just like Joachim's and Sanna's during the past three years. They've all lost a lot," Birgitta said. "That indicates that Philip was also the victim of extortion."

"I'll call Glen Thompson back," Irene said. "Fenton lived mostly in London. There must be financial records for him there."

"Sounds good," said Andersson, nodding.

It was always a good thing if other departments took on part of the expenses of an investigation. An investigation in London would be prohibitively expensive for the Swedish police force, not to mention all the entangling red tape.

"Who is going to inform Edward Fenton's Swedish relatives about his death?" asked Birgitta.

Andersson furrowed his brow. Finally he replied, "We'll wait until we have positive identification. Irene, you coordinate with London and Paris. When everything is settled, you'll be the one to contact the family."

Irene said, "Then I'll have to have Kajsa as a partner. She's the only one among us who can speak French. That would make talking to Paris easier."

"All right. But this afternoon I want you and Tommy to go back to the hospital and force some truth from Sanna. I've told you over and over! A thousand times already at least! You have to lean on her as hard as you can."

Tommy sighed. "Easier said than done."

Andersson gave him a sharp look. "Stop coddling her! Scare her with Fenton's murder! She's the only person who is still alive after getting one of those fingers. Our little Miss Ceder. If she doesn't wake up and smell the coffee, there'll be no one left. And goddamn, but I'm getting tired of all these corpses piling up!"

IRENE COULDN'T REACH Glen Thompson when she called. She left a message that he should get in touch with her again as soon as he could.

She realized she'd also have to get in touch with Inspector Verdier in Paris. He was the only one she knew there who spoke English. If she couldn't reach him, she'd have to bring in Kajsa. She sighed. Tommy glanced up at her from his place behind a stack of papers, but he let his glance fall back to his work when she didn't say anything. Irene dug around her desk drawer until she found the business card with Verdier's name. His direct number was on it. She sighed again as she dialed the number.

IRENE WAS PLEASANTLY surprised by how well everything went. Inspector Verdier was in his office. When she explained that the discovery of Edward Fenton's body was part of their earlier Paris investigation, he sounded genuinely interested.

"I'm not a part of the team investigating his death, but I will go to my boss and tell him about this connection. Then I'll probably be put on the case, too. It's very complicated. An American living in London is killed in Paris and the case is being investigated by the Swedish police," Verdier said.

"You understand our involvement," Irene said. "We're dealing with the murders of Bergman and Rothstaahl, who were living in Paris, as well as the restaurant owner Kjell Ceder. We now have the body of a fourth victim killed three years ago. His name is Thomas Bonetti. Then, yesterday evening, there was an attempt on the life of Sanna Kaegler, who knew all four victims well."

"She must have been their lover."

Verdier wasn't asking; he was making a statement. Irene managed to stop herself from sighing right into his ear.

"No. She was the childhood friend of Bergman, the business partner of Bonetti, knew Rothstaahl in passing, and was married to Ceder. We all agree that Bergman and Rothstaahl were a couple."

Verdier replied, "Yes, yes. And her relationship with this Edward Fenton?"

"Her sister is married to Fenton's older brother. The mother of the two brothers is Swedish. The father is English. They probably had dual citizenship, though I haven't tracked that down yet. We also know that she and Fenton were close during the ph.com years."

"This is worse than a soap opera. Everyone is connected to her. But it also makes our job easier. The killer is in the same circle."

True enough. Irene had had the same thought a few times, but no light had dawned. Who gained from the deaths of these people?

Irene gave Inspector Verdier Glen Thompson's number at

New Scotland Yard. Police in all three countries needed to work together on this case.

Irene's mouth was dry after all her talking, and she felt a headache forming at her temples. To top it off, her period was due. She closed her eyes to shut out the daylight. Friday afternoon. One entire workweek from hell, and there was still a long way to go before these crimes were solved. Now five murders hung around their necks. Four fingers cut from a corpse. Five murders were more than four fingers. . . .

"Hey, Irene. Are you falling asleep?"

Irene jumped at the sound of Tommy's voice.

"No, I have a headache. I was just shutting my eyes for a minute. I need some coffee," she mumbled as she got up and stumbled toward the machine. She got two cups, just to be on the safe side. She offered one to Tommy.

"No, thanks," he said. "You're the one with the headache. Drink them both," he said in his friendly way.

Irene searched through her desk drawer until she found some pain pills. She had no idea how long they'd been there, but the bubble was unbroken and the foil was intact. She opened it and swallowed the pills with a sip of coffee.

"I'm not sure you're in shape to come with me to Östra Hospital and 'lean on that Kaegler-Ceder woman,'" Tommy said in a perfect imitation of their boss.

The only mistake he made was that Andersson had just appeared at the door. He gave Tommy a sour look. "I thought you two had already left. What are you waiting for?"

Andersson turned on his heel and headed back to his office, happy he'd gotten in the last word. He had actually wanted to know what Irene had found out from Paris and if there were developments about Edward Fenton. Still, that could wait. Paris would need at least a weekend to come up with anything, like the caliber of the bullet that had killed Fenton.

Chapter 21

"SHE'S SLEEPING," THE gray-haired nurse warned them, coming out of Sanna's room just as Tommy was about to open the door. The nurse closed the door firmly behind her, adding, "She must not be disturbed."

The officers on watch in front of Sanna's room had changed shifts. A young female officer now sat by the door. She informed them that Sanna's sister and mother had been by to visit around eleven A.M., but otherwise the situation was the same.

"Let's go have something to eat," Tommy suggested.

They took the elevator down to the hospital cafeteria. It was crowded, but they managed to find a seat by the large glass windows facing the inner courtyard. They each ordered the same thing: ham quiche, salad, milk, and coffee. Not a culinary adventure, but it filled the stomach. As they sat and started to drink the lukewarm coffee, Irene worked up her courage and asked, "Will you and the children be with your parents all weekend?"

"No. Martin wants to be home by Saturday night. His girl-friend is having a party. But Agneta should have her things out by then. She's already packed everything up."

His last words sounded a bit peevish as he stared hard into his coffee cup. Irene couldn't take it any longer.

"Good Lord! You seem so restrained and . . . self-disciplined! No tears, no accusations—nothing at all!"

He glared straight at Irene. "What the hell do you know?"

Irene tried to calm herself, glancing around the cafeteria to see if anyone had noticed them.

"I know nothing at all, of course, because you've told me nothing! I really don't understand how you could hide all of this . . . keep up a strong front . . . and suddenly, I'm confronted with a done deal that you're getting divorced!"

Tommy took a deep breath. "It's actually my fault."

He seemed to mean what he said, but Irene objected immediately. "*You* shouldn't take all the blame! Agneta was the one who started the affair with that doctor and wanted a div—"

Tommy interrupted her. "That's not the whole story."

Irene was confused and didn't know what to say, so she kept her mouth shut. Tommy looked through the windows to the courtyard, where the greenery had taken on the shades of autumn. As he spoke, he kept his face turned away from Irene. She had to lean closer over the table to hear what he was saying. "*I* had an affair with another woman a few years back. We were neighbors. She was extremely attractive and had a certain . . . reputation. We hit it off at an August crayfish party. Things between us just went on until her husband and Agneta both found out. A few months later, they moved, and Agneta and I went to marriage counseling."

He sighed heavily and drank the last dregs of coffee. Irene found herself staring at her oldest friend. Neither she nor Krister had ever imagined their friends had been through such troubles.

"We managed to fix things for a while. But . . . it happened again. You remember when I went to that course in Stockholm two years ago. I met a colleague from Gävle. She was also married, and we just thought we'd have a little fun. Or so *I* thought, at least. As things turned out, she and her old man were in the process of divorcing, and she had set out to find someone new. She'd decided that was going to be me. When she realized that I wasn't interested, she got angry and called

Agneta. Things went ballistic, to say the least. Only the thought of the children made us decide to stay together and try again, but it wasn't ever the same. Last summer we gave up. Agneta decided that she and her doctor friend were truly in love, and she wanted a divorce. They had trouble finding a place to live that would have enough room. But now they have, and she's moving out. That's all, folks!" He waved his hands in a gesture from the cartoon, which appeared carefree, but his eyes told another story.

Irene finally was able to stammer out, "But you—why—why were you unfaithful in the first place?"

Tommy looked at her defiantly. Irene could hardly believe what he'd told her, and at the same time, she felt an irrational yet very natural emotion: anger.

"We've known each other for twenty years," she continued. "I have always said that you are an honest and sensible person. Now you've acted just like all the other men! Brains go out the window whenever things stir in the pants!"

"I am a man, after all," Tommy said. "And if you're saying that all men are alike, may I remind you that your Krister is one, too?"

Tommy was angry enough for a fight.

Irene felt all her anger dissipate as quickly as it had come on. She gestured dismissively. "Let's stop all this. Here we are, almost fighting, but we have nothing to argue about. I have no right to judge you or your behavior. You are right that this is between you and Agneta. However, I still have to say that what's happening to you affects other people who are fond of you—of both of you."

The air went out of him, and his shoulders slumped. He stared at his empty coffee cup, then straightened and stood up. "I need another cup, and I know I don't have to ask *you* twice."

He smiled at her, but his smile looked more like a grimace. Irene tried to smile back encouragingly, but felt her smile was just as false as his. With a spark of tenderness in her heart, she watched his back as he headed over to the coffee pots on the hot plates.

So many strong emotions had left her feeling drained. On the other hand, she felt grateful that Tommy had finally told her what was really going on.

But why had Tommy risked his family just to have a bit of fun on the side? Excitement? To scratch the itch for validation? Check if he still was attractive to other women? Or is it really true that when lust comes in, all rational thought goes out the window?

Tommy returned to put the cups of coffee on the table. He'd also bought some truffles filled with arrack.

"Thought we'd need something strong with our coffee," he said.

SANNA WAS AWAKE when they finally got back to her room. When she saw who had come in, she ostentatiously turned her head away and looked out the window. Irene didn't let Sanna ruffle her feathers. She picked up a chair and set it between the bed and the window. With a police officer on each side of the bed, Sanna was forced to look at the ceiling to escape their eyes. She still couldn't escape their questions.

Tommy began. "Hope that you've had a good sleep and can now answer our questions."

Sanna, staring at the ceiling lamp of opal glass, only snorted in reply.

"While you were asleep, several things happened in the outside world," Tommy said, then fell silent to observe Sanna for a long time. Sanna closed her eyes to keep the police and their uncomfortable questions away. She tried to pretend she was falling asleep. Tommy's next question made her open her eyes again.

"You told us that you were on the phone with Edward Fenton two days ago. Is this true?"

She nodded weakly. A trace of worry flickered through her eyes.

"What did he say exactly?"

She croaked out, "I don't really remember."

"Try," Tommy said shortly.

She shut her eyes again, but Irene saw that they were moving frantically under her eyelids, which were so white that the blue veins were clearly visible.

Unexpectedly, they popped back open. "Someone demanded the fingers back. But he'd gotten rid of his, just like I had. The person told Edward to pass the same demand on to me. I was told to find Kjell's as well. Edward said that the same person threatened Ludde if I didn't obey."

A tortured grimace settled on her face. Of course, getting a letter with a cut-off finger would be bad enough, but she seemed mostly worried about the threat to her son.

"Did he say anything else?"

"No."

"Did you already know that Kjell had gotten a finger before this talk with Edward the day before yesterday?"

"No."

Irene leaned forward and said calmly, "Do you remember what was written in the blackmail letter that came with the finger?"

Sanna stiffened and began to breathe swiftly. "Do I remember what was in the letter? No, I don't! It's too long ago . . . ." was her best attempt.

"What had you done that you needed to hide? What leverage did the extortionist have?"

Sanna pressed her lips together as if to keep any more words inside. Irene and Tommy exchanged glances across the light yellow terry-cloth bedcover, and Tommy nodded for Irene to continue.

Irene debated her next question for a moment. Finally, she decided to go right to the heart of the matter.

"What was . . . is . . . your actual relationship to Edward Fenton?"

Irene hoped that Sanna hadn't noticed her slip on the tense of the verb.

Sanna replied evenly, "Edward? He's the brother of my brother-in-law. We don't see each other very often. Hardly at all the past few years. He was the head of the bank that provided financial advice at ph.com. We had a few business dealings then, but that was all."

"Why do you think Edward received a cut-off finger?"

Sanna didn't pause as she replied, "I really don't know. Of course, it was a threat to make us pay up."

"What did they have on him?"

"I've already told you. He works for an investment bank and specializes in risky capital. Somebody was upset with how he'd invested their money. But everybody lost money when the stock market crashed. That's just the way it was!"

Irene wondered if Sanna realized how she sounded—childish and whiny. *It's nobody's fault the money is gone—least of all little Sanna's.*

"So the person who threatened Edward demanded his money back, is that right?"

"Yes, I believe that's right." Sanna sighed.

"When did Edward tell you this?"

There was a noticeable pause as Sanna decided how to reply. "When we talked two days ago," she finally said.

"You didn't know before that he also was being blackmailed?"

"No."

"When did you find out that both Kjell and Edward had received fingers?"

"I told you! The day before yesterday."

Irene returned to the softer approach. "How did Edward sound two days ago?"

"Sound . . . ? Like usual."

Good Lord, guess the woman can add psychic abilities to her long resume! Irene did not say this out loud, but continued, "Can you remember anything else that Edward said to you during that conversation?"

Sanna looked at Irene with irritation. "I've told you everything! Why do you guys keep harping on and on about Edward?"

Now Tommy laid a hand on Sanna's arm. "I'm afraid there's some bad news we have to share with you."

She turned her head to look at him. Her irritation began to give way to vague worry. "Bad news? How so?"

"Edward Fenton has been found . . . dead. He—"

Sanna screamed so terribly that both Tommy and Irene felt paralyzed. The fearful screaming seemed endless. Neither one of them had expected such an extreme reaction. According to Sanna herself, she and Edward didn't know each other well. He was just a relative of a relative. Edward Fenton was not supposed to be as close to her as the other four victims—with the possible exception of Joachim Rothstaahl.

So they had believed—but her reaction proved them wrong. Helplessly, they stood there and watched her scream and thrash around until the gray-haired nurse rushed in and yelled, "What have you been doing to her? Get out! Out!"

The nurse grabbed their arms and forced them out of the room. Before Irene and Tommy could catch their breath, they found themselves on the other side of the door. The nurse had set off an alarm, and the red light by the door started blinking and beeping. It made for an uncanny cacophony mixed with Sanna's screaming.

"What just happened?" asked Irene.

Tommy lifted an eyebrow and replied, "I think we just hit the bull's-eye."

• • •

IRENE AND TOMMY drove back to the police station to confer with Andersson, but he was in a meeting that wouldn't get out until five P.M.

"I'll wait here," Irene said. "You go on home and get your kids ready to go to your parent's place."

Tommy made a half-hearted protest, but Irene could tell he was grateful for her offer.

Irene continued, "Why don't you come over on Sunday with the kids? You don't have to worry about the food. Krister will be home. It's his day off."

"In that case, I'll certainly come," Tommy said with a mischievous grin.

Cooking was not Irene's strong suit, but why should it be, when she'd married a professional chef?

"And say hi to Sonya and Ragnar from me!" she called after him as he strode down the hallway. After so many years of friendship, Irene knew his parents well.

It would be at least another hour before the superintendent was out of his meeting. Irene decided to turn on her computer to check what email had arrived during the afternoon. She was glad to see a message from Glen Thompson. It was short but to the point:

Irene,

My colleague has checked with the FBI. E. Fenton's murder seems to be of interest to the United States, so this is an even bigger deal than you've realized. The FBI is sending a special agent, Lee Hazel, to Paris tomorrow. On Monday, Lee will be here in London, and then in Göteborg either on Tuesday or Wednesday.

Have a great weekend and say hi to Krister and the girls!
Glen

Ties to the United States? Perhaps not so unexpected, since Edward Fenton worked for an American bank and was married

to an American woman whose father was a well-known businessman. Tommy had found that all out. Still, it felt odd to be
part of an investigation involving the FBI. Was Rikskrim,
Sweden's National Bureau of Investigation, going to be called
in, too? It was high time to talk to her boss.

Absent-mindedly, she clicked on the attachments Glen had
added. It was a good thing that she was already sitting down
when the photos began to appear on the screen. Her fingers
were trembling when she clicked *print*.

"I DON'T WANT those idiots running around and ruining
my investigation!" yelled Andersson. "Things are already too
complicated as it is!"

Rikskrim always made him see red. He would usually snort
"bunch of bureaucrats" whenever they were mentioned. Irene
had long ago given up on trying to correct his view. He would
only get angry.

"So you don't believe we should inform Bodil Göransson?"
Irene asked carefully.

Andersson muttered a few more opinions. Bodil Göransson
had just been appointed as the head of the provincial police
department, and she always wanted to be kept up-to-date on
each development. This case had been truly spectacular, and
the media was feverishly trying to sniff out new details. These
victims were unusual, too, and Göransson kept repeating,
"Hard to believe that Antonio Bonetti is involved in this."

Andersson weighed his options. Finally, he said, "Yes, we
should inform her, but let's wait until Monday." He leaned
back in his chair and looked at Irene. "I just got a call from
some head doctor with a Polish name that sounds like a
sneeze," he said. "He complained about you two. He started
talking about Gestapo methods and other foolishness. I told
him that you were following my orders. 'We believe Sanna is
protecting a murderer,' I told him. 'During the time she's kept

silent, another man has been killed. If she doesn't talk soon, other people may be killed, which is why I told my detectives to use the thumbscrews,' I said. Doctor Sneeze finally shut up."

A smile spread across his plump face as he remembered how he'd put the doctor in his place. The superintendent entwined his fingers over his fat stomach, looking deceptively like an old pious priest—the exact opposite of his true self. But, nonetheless, he was undoubtedly as round as a wheel of cheese.

"So, what do you think of our little miss Ceder's breakdown after you told her Fenton was dead?" Andersson asked.

"Her reaction was unbelievable," Irene said. "Perhaps even an overreaction—if her relationship was as superficial as she made it out to be. So I believe they had to be much closer than she'd said, not superficial at all."

Irene handed her boss a plastic folder with the printouts of the photographs Glen Thompson had sent. Andersson spread them out on his desk.

Written below the first photograph was: *Edward Fenton with wife Janice and sons Victor (nine) and Albert (seven)*. Edward was standing with his arm around his wife, a woman much shorter than he. He was smiling directly at the camera. The two boys were standing in front of the couple. Both had black hair, like their mother. The family was on a deck or a balcony of some kind, with the ocean and palm trees in the background. Janice Fenton was a Mediterranean beauty, and she had black hair to her waist. Her face was beautiful, with strong, shapely eyebrows and full lips. Although she was short and thin, she had curves right where curves belonged. Her diamond necklace and glittering diamond earrings made her look very American.

Andersson couldn't help whistling. "That's what a woman should look like!" he exclaimed. "A full-blooded—"

He stopped himself and looked over his reading glasses at Irene. Irene had no idea how he'd wanted to finish his comment, but from the red flush on his cheeks she assumed that the comment was not intended for female ears. She pretended she'd noticed nothing and simply met her boss's look patiently. He looked down quickly and turned his attention to the next photograph.

"And here's another of Fenton," he said in a suspiciously happy tone.

He glanced at the third sheet of paper in his right hand. "And here we have Fenton as a corpse. Shot in the head, just like everybody else." He quickly put that photograph aside.

Edward Fenton had been an elegant man. Tall, in good shape, attractive features, blond hair, and an extremely charming smile.

"Yes, he's the one who shot at me in Paris," Irene said. She tapped the portrait.

"Are you absolutely sure?" asked her boss.

"One hundred percent."

"But wasn't he in London?"

Irene shook her head. "No, he'd flown back from the United States, leaving his family behind to continue their vacation. He was supposed to come to work on Monday the fifteenth and Tuesday the sixteenth, but he never showed up, according to his secretary. On Wednesday, he came to work as usual with no reason for his absence. I think we can assume he wouldn't want to mention going to Paris and shooting at Swedish police officers—not to mention beating one up so she had to go to the hospital. According to his secretary, he had a wound on his face that he said came from falling on a stone path. The truth was, I gave that to him when I hit him and he fell to the floor."

Andersson looked at Irene respectfully. He no longer looked like a pleasant priest; he was back to being the stubborn bulldog on the other side of the desk.

"So why was Fenton in Paris? Why did he beat up Kajsa and try to shoot you? He could have killed you!"

Irene was grateful that Andersson actually cared. "Well, he was willing to take that risk to find something very valuable to him."

"What? Drugs? The fingers?"

"Maybe. But I've come to believe he was after Philip's and Joachim's computers and discs."

"Why?"

"I think he needed to eliminate evidence."

"What evidence?" Andersson could not hide his impatience.

"I don't know. Evidence of some crime, perhaps." Irene sighed. "But there's one thing I can say with certainty. Take another look at Edward's picture."

Andersson stared hard at the photograph.

"He was blond. We know that he was in the apartment, since he shot at me there. I'd found blond hair, which our tech guys say in all probability came from Ludwig's father."

Andersson fixed the photo with his glare and started to nod to himself. "So you think. . . ." He tapped the photograph with his index finger.

"Oh, yes," Irene said. "Edward Fenton is the father of Sanna Kaegler's son."

Chapter 22

THE NEXT MORNING, Irene called Sanna's hospital unit. According to the nurse, they could not talk to Sanna that day, or for the rest of the weekend.

"She's heavily sedated right now," the nurse said. "But perhaps on Monday you could talk to her."

The nurse had introduced herself on the phone as Nurse Ann-Britt. Irene suspected that the nurse was the same gray-haired one who'd chased them out of Sanna's room yesterday. Irene wondered how the nurse would react to everything else she needed to say, but she decided to continue anyway.

"As you know, we are worried about her safety," she said. "Sanna was the victim of an attempted murder. Even though we have a guard there twenty-four-seven, I hope that all the hospital employees will also be vigilant."

"What should we look out for?" asked the nurse.

"Odd telephone calls. People trying to reach Sanna or trying to find out her room number. They might introduce themselves as journalists or the police—"

"I recognized your name and voice right away," the nurse interrupted. "We met yesterday afternoon."

"I remember you as well," Irene replied.

"Otherwise I would not have whispered a word about her condition," the nurse continued.

"I understand," Irene said. "But getting back to things to watch for. . . . Be on your guard for someone showing up where they have no reason to be, especially if the same person keeps appearing. In that case, raise the alarm."

"But what if it's a false alarm? Someone who's just in the wrong place at the wrong time?" asked the nurse.

"That might happen. But better a false alarm than missing a real threat. Remember, Sanna's life is in danger."

"I understand. I'll inform the staff."

Irene gave the nurse her home telephone number as well as her cell phone number. Even with a police officer outside the door to Sanna's room, Irene would not rest easy. This killer was audacious and ruthless—a dangerous combination. If the hospital employees also kept their eyes on the lookout, it made Sanna safer.

BOTH JENNY AND Katarina were still sleeping. Krister had already left for the day shift at Glady's. He was supposed to get off work at around five in the evening, and Irene looked forward to a pleasant evening in her husband's company.

Tomorrow Tommy and his kids will be over for dinner, she thought. She had mixed feelings about it. Of course she was happy that Tommy had decided to share the truth of the situation with them—they were best friends—but what would happen to her relationship with Agneta? They'd been good friends for quite a few years. Could that continue once the divorce was final?

Irene decided that was something only the future would reveal. If she had to choose, she'd choose Tommy, of course. They went back a long way. Both of them were aware it was unusual for a man and a woman to be friends while having a spouse and a family. It was a unique friendship and well worth protecting. They'd gotten along well ever since the police academy. They'd worked in the same patrol district of Göteborg and often in the same patrol car. They'd moved to the violent crime unit at about the same time, Tommy one year before Irene. His tales of investigation had made Irene think of joining the same unit, and she'd undergone the required detective education. Even though it was hard work that yielded little reward in and of itself, she never wanted to go anywhere else. *I must have been born to be a cop*, she thought. *My dad was in the customs office—maybe I have a love of uniforms?* She grimaced at herself. It had been fifteen years since she'd left behind routine police work and the uniform.

Since only one living creature demanded her attention that morning, Irene went out into the hallway, put on her coat, and took the leash from its hook on the hat rack.

"Come on, Sammie! Time to go for a walk!"

The scraping of claws against the hardwood floors announced Sammie's arrival from his spot on the rug beneath the kitchen table. He charged into the hallway at full speed, which made the hallway rug crumble like an accordion and slide halfway across the floor until it landed in the living room.

This was the normal routine in the Huss household when it was time to take the dog for his walk.

THE SUN WAS hidden behind the clouds, but it didn't look like rain. Wind was blowing off the ocean, but Irene headed toward the beach anyway. She needed to smell the salt water and seaweed and listen to the waves hitting the rocks. Nothing else ever gave her the same sense of peace and the calm for thought.

Sammie strained at his leash beside her. He was sniffing up important information in other dogs' markings. They neared Fiskebäck's small boat harbor. There weren't many people there. The season for sailing was over, although she could see one or two sails out on the blue-gray surface of the water. A few motorboats also plowed the waves. Did any of those boats resemble Thomas Bonetti's? Irene had no idea what a Storebro Royal Cruiser 400-whatever-it-was looked like, but she thought it wouldn't be one of these small crafts. Certainly it would be something with a built-in shower and more than one level, not to mention flushing toilets.

It happened in a flash. She had no idea where it had come from, as she'd been lost in her own thoughts, but a growling German shepherd attacked Sammie, who seemed as surprised as his master. He'd been minding his business, and all of a sudden there was this huge dog attacking him! Sammie never said no to a fight. Luckily, his leash was a roll-up, and Sammie had room to maneuver around for several meters. The German shepherd was twice his size, but Sammie still thought he had the advantage. Irene saw that the German shepherd's ruff was up and his teeth were bared. She tried to break off the attack by waving her arms and yelling at the top of her voice, often a successful strategy. As Irene did her scarecrow performance, the German shepherd hesitated for half a second, and that was all Sammie needed.

He leaped diagonally over the German shepherd's back and dug his teeth into its rump. The German shepherd was startled when his teeth snapped shut into empty air where he had expected terrier fur. Then he undoubtedly felt the sharp pain in his backside. He whined, and all fight left him. Even though his enemy was demoralized, Sammie was having much too much fun to stop. Just to be on the safe side, he dug his teeth deeper into the flesh of the bigger dog so he couldn't be shaken off. The German shepherd howled from pain. Irene was beginning to feel sorry for him. She looked around for help, but she couldn't see anyone, especially not anyone who looked like the German shepherd's owner.

"Sammie, please! Let go!" she pleaded.

Sammie heard her and gave her a look from under his shaggy bangs. Let go? Just when things were getting fun? He had the best grip. His master must have lost her mind.

"Come on, Sammie, please! Let go!" she said. Tears were in her throat.

To her surprise and relief, Sammie obeyed and let go of the bigger dog. The German shepherd slunk away with his tail between his legs toward a parked Passat Combi and scrambled in through the open passenger seat door.

"So that's where you came from!"

Sammie was still looking at her in confusion. Ending a fight in the middle when he had the upper paw? His master was definitely crazy.

"Good boy, Sammie. Good boy! What a good dog!" she cooed. "You're not hurt, are you?" she babbled nervously as she kept the Passat in sight from the corner of her eye.

Sammie shook himself and looked quite all right. Irene decided to continue home with him. She kept an uneasy watch on the Passat, as long as it was in her view, in case the German shepherd came bounding back out, but it seemed the dog had had enough. He did not reappear.

Sammie kept looking up at Irene in disbelief, but she was his master, after all. He would have to be patient with her odd ideas.

Shortly before they got to the townhouse, Irene noticed that Sammie was limping. She hardly noticed at first, but it became more and more pronounced the closer they got to home. When they reached the garage, Sammie stopped entirely and held up his front paw. When Irene felt his leg, he growled. Irene couldn't see a bite mark, but something was wrong.

"Old men like you shouldn't get into fights," Irene scolded. "Now we have to call the vet."

Sammie didn't care. He was not going one step farther, so, sighing, Irene had to hoist up her forty-five pound dog and carry him in.

"I HAD TO call the vet," Irene said. "The vet said it sounded like Sammie's leg had been punctured. He's got a prescription for pain and swelling. If he isn't better in two days, we'll have to bring him in."

The entire Huss family was sitting around the dinner table. Krister had made pasta with two different sauces: a tomato sauce for Jenny and gorgonzola sauce for the rest of them. They had just finished dessert: fresh pineapple with vanilla ice cream.

"Sammie's ten-years-old," Krister said. "Not bad to get the better of a German shepherd." There was an unmistakable trace of pride in Krister's voice.

And we wonder why dog fighting is popular in other countries, thought Irene.

"He fights badgers in Värmland," Katarina said. "He used to do that a lot."

"Yes, but not in the past few years. He's actually getting too old for this. We should be grateful that he got out of it with just a punctured leg."

Sammie was snoring under the table. The medicine had made him sleepy. It hadn't been hard to give him the pills. Jenny had hidden them in fish balls, on top of his dry food. As usual, Sammie gobbled up the treats first and was happily unaware that his food had been drugged.

"So, when Sammie dies, are you two going to get a new dog?" asked Jenny unexpectedly.

Irene swallowed hard. She had barely managed to suppress that very thought. Of course she knew that Sammie had passed the average age for a dog of his breed, but she didn't want to admit he was that old.

Krister replied before Irene could get her thoughts together. "I don't think so," he said. "You girls are moving away from home, and we're getting to that time of life where we want to travel and not be tied down any more. We're thinking of selling the house and buying a condo in town. That won't be a good place to have a dog. It would be too hard to find someone to take care of him when we're away. Your grandmother is not getting any younger."

"Even Majlis is getting older," Irene added.

Majlis was Sammie's dog walker. She was over seventy and walked four dogs every afternoon when their owners were at work. Payment under the table, of course. It helped her stretch her pension. Irene and Krister had no other way to solve the dog problem; they couldn't leave Sammie alone at home for eight to ten hours.

"Well, then, I'll get my own dog," said Jenny firmly.

"Wouldn't it be hard to take a dog when you're on the road with your band Polo? Especially when you start your world tours?" Krister joked.

Jenny pursed her lips and said defiantly, "So what if it is?"

ON SUNDAY MORNING, Irene was woken by her cell phone. She was tired and far from being refreshed. The display on the clock radio said 6:57. A call on Sunday morning! Still half asleep, she fumbled for the phone, held it to her ear, and said her name.

"Sorry to wake you. It's Nurse Ann-Britt here. You said we should keep our eyes open for odd behavior. I've seen something . . . not quite right. And you did tell me to call if there was anything suspicious. . . . " The voice was apologetic.

Irene started to wake up. "Go ahead. I'm listening."

"Yesterday, I saw a man outside of our unit by the elevators. He had dark hair. We have glass doors, so I got a good look at him. It was not visiting hours. He went up to the doors and read the posted hours for that. At three in the afternoon, he came back at the same time other visitors were coming in. I kept him in sight at all times, because I remembered what you said. When he saw a police officer in front of Sanna Kaegler's room, he turned on his heel and left. It looked very strange. Then he turned up again this morning."

"Can you describe him more fully?"

"He looks Mediterranean. Dark hair, dark, bushy eyebrows, dark brown eyes. He's good looking, about thirty or thirty-five, and he wore a suit and an overcoat."

Irene did not recognize anyone from this description. Was this a false alarm? In order to hurry Nurse Ann-Britt along, she said encouragingly, "You said he came back this morning?"

"Yes. Actually, I was supposed to be on the afternoon shift, but I'd changed shifts with a colleague. She had to go to a birthday celebration for someone who turned forty—doesn't matter. This morning I saw that man again when I got off the bus. He was smoking outside the emergency entrance. Today he was wearing dark pants and a dark blue jacket, but I'm absolutely sure it was him."

"What time was this?"

"Five after seven. When I came into the nurses' office, I found a note from Lasse, the night nurse. I'd told him about the suspicious man the night before when I went off shift. In his note, Lasse said that the man had come back at visiting hours around seven P.M. He wore the same clothes and matched my description. He went around the unit as he had in the afternoon. However, Lasse wasn't sure it was the same man, and since the man left the unit and wasn't on the hospital grounds any more, he decided not to call."

"Did he stop near Sanna's room again?" Irene felt her pulse start to race. Adrenaline was pumping through her system; she had caught scent of her prey. This could be the man they were looking for. Irene swung her legs over the edge of the bed and was now paying full attention.

"Lasse didn't say anything in the note. But the man must have passed the room, although Sanna's mother and sister were there. They'd arrived at three in the afternoon and stayed all evening. And, of course, there's the policeman at the door."

Irene's heart pounded. A plan came to her. "We'll be there

within the hour. In the meantime, here's what you should do. . . . "

IRENE WAS ABLE to reach Kajsa and Fredrik, but neither Birgitta nor Jonny picked up. Irene didn't bother to call Tommy at his parents' on Hönö Island. She contacted Andersson from her Volvo on the way to Östra Hospital.

Exactly one hour after the phone call Irene had received, the four police officers were gathered outside the closed cafeteria on the ground floor of the hospital building. There were hardly any other people around at that hour.

"Did you two get your guns from the station?" asked Andersson.

Kajsa nodded and Fredrik opened the side of his jacket to reveal his holster.

"Good. Two should be enough."

They split up and took different elevators to the floor of Sanna's unit. If the suspect spotted all four of them together, he'd know the police were after him. *It's like we give off a special scent that the bad guys can smell*, Irene thought.

Irene and Andersson were the first to arrive, and they strolled slowly to the reception desk. The gray-haired nurse was inside the glass walls of the nurses' office on the phone. She waved to Irene to indicate that she'd seen her and ended her call. Just as Irene had guessed, Nurse Ann-Britt was the same nurse she'd met the day before. She was in her sixties and had energetic brown eyes.

"He hasn't come," she said in a low voice. "At least, not yet."

"Good. This is Superintendent Sven Andersson," Irene said.

"You must mean 'Head Doctor Nils Dürsell,' don't you?" the nurse said, conspiratorially.

She looked over the superintendent's shoulder and a

surprised expression crossed her face. *Oh God! The killer's right behind us!* Irene thought, but one glance at the reflection in the glass wall of the office made her relax. It was just Kajsa and Fredrik joining them. Irene realized that the Nurse was reacting to Kajsa's face, still a remarkable sight, although the colors were fading.

"Wounded in the line of duty," Kajsa said with a broad smile.

Although Nurse Ann-Britt now understood the reason behind Kajsa's appearance, she didn't seem to relax.

"So, where are the uniforms?" Irene asked. She felt that their standing like this, all in a group, would call more attention to them than they wanted.

"Follow me," said Nurse Ann-Britt.

In the employee dressing room, there were scrubs, pants, and doctor's coats in different sizes laid out neatly in a row on a bench.

"This is the best I could do," the nurse said apologetically. "We are always short on clean scrubs."

"These are fine," Irene said. "Could you show us how to dress so we look authentic?"

There were no pants big enough to go around Andersson's stomach bulk, but they solved the problem with a stretchy band, and the top was long enough to conceal the makeshift closure. They added a doctor's coat, a stethoscope, a few pens in the breast pocket, and a nametag that read NILS DÜRSELL, HEAD DOCTOR.

Irene got a set of scrubs and an oval nametag decorated with a wreath of flowers around it. It said BRITT, ASSISTANT NURSE. Fredrik was dressed in a similar way to Andersson, but his nametag just said: ATTENDING DOCTOR.

"These tags were left in a box here on the unit. All the employees know that you'll be mixing with them. They'll pretend nothing out of the ordinary is going on. Just don't forget your names," said Nurse Ann-Britt.

"Nils Dürsell, Nils Dürsell," Andersson mumbled to himself.

Nurse Ann-Britt had found a disguise for Kajsa as a cleaning lady with the typical blue uniform and a cart she could push around. Her simple nametag just said DANOUTA. Kajsa took a pair of gray-tinted glasses from her shoulder bag. Sunglasses would have been too obvious, especially in October, but a bit of tint would draw less attention to the multi-colored area around her eyes.

The most pressing problem was what to do with Fredrik's Sig Sauer. The holster was far too apparent underneath his scrubs top, even if he put a doctor's coat over it. They solved this by borrowing Kajsa's shoulder bag.

"Let's stuff some folders and paper into it, so that it looks like you have a lot of paperwork," suggested Nurse Ann-Britt. "Then you can put your, um, gun, right into the open bag." Nurse Ann-Britt gave the weapon a nervous glance. Fredrik practiced drawing his gun out quickly a few times, and then they were ready to go.

"If a patient or a relative stops you, just say that you don't work in this unit," Nurse Ann-Britt suggested. "You can also say things like, 'This is not my patient, I'll go get Nurse Ann-Britt for you.' Then just come and get me. We're going to put Head Doctor Dürsell in the nurses' office. You'll be able to look out through the glass wall and see everyone coming and going. Pretend you're reading a medical journal or something."

Andersson nodded nervously. He hadn't expected to deal with questions from patients or relatives.

"On Sundays, we don't have normal rounds," explained Nurse Ann-Britt. "We usually just check on specific patients. For instance, it wouldn't be unusual for the head doctor to take a peek into Sanna's room. . . . " Nurse Ann-Britt said, smiling meaningfully.

Andersson nodded again.

"You can clean near the elevators and then at the doors to the entrance of the unit," Nurse Ann-Britt told Kajsa.

Kajsa nodded. "Just let me know when he comes into the building. I'll have my cell phone on vibrate."

"Oh, so sexy," said Fredrik.

"You're sounding more like Jonny every day," said Irene. "You've been working with him too much."

"Stop chatting and let's get down to business," growled Andersson.

Irene spoke up. "We have to leave one by one. Try to leave a minute or two between the person before you."

Irene and Nurse Ann-Britt kept each other company as they left the changing room.

Once on the floor, they saw that the breakfast trays were being delivered. Irene got in line with the other nurses and was handed a tray. A young man behind her cleared his throat and then whispered into her ear, "Take another one. That patient needs to be fed by hand."

The young man was wearing a scrubs shirt with a piece of tape fastened on which the name MAGNUS was printed in blue marker. He had an astounding tattoo of a colorful dragon whirling up his neck. Irene shuddered in spite of herself, because the tattoo reminded her of an unpleasant case she'd had a few years back. His black hair was shaved on the sides and back, leaving only a tuft at the top of his head.

Irene smiled gratefully and handed him the tray. She had never tried to feed a grown person, and if she did try, it would take too long. Instead, she took the next tray, which the card said was for "3:2 J. Fredriksson DK."

"Room three, bed two," Magnus whispered from the corner of his mouth.

Irene nodded slightly. Carrying the tray, she decided to reconnoiter a bit around the floor. She peered at each door; it was no trouble to look like someone new to the unit.

The door to Sanna's room was closed. The same police-woman was sitting at her place beside it. She looked up at Irene but didn't appear to recognize her. *Did Ann-Britt forget to inform her about their plans?* Irene wondered.

Irene hesitated, but then her colleague gave her an almost unnoticeable wink. Not much, but enough for Irene to feel calm again.

Just to complete her tour, she also went down the hallway parallel to Sanna's. She didn't see anything unusual there, either. On her way back to Room 3, she spied Kajsa cleaning near the elevators. Kajsa was mopping the floor so profession-ally it looked like she'd been a cleaning lady all her life.

Room 3 had two beds, each occupied by an elderly gentleman.

J. Fredriksson was angry. "Finally! Here you are with my food! And it's cold! Why am I always last? And I bet they forgot I need special food for diabetics!" He was tall and emaci-ated. His gold-tinged parchment skin looked like it was molded to his cranium. His hand, with visible blue veins, shook as he pointed an accusing finger at Irene.

"Come now, Jocke, don't complain so much. The girls are running as fast as they can," his roommate said in a friendly tone.

The roommate was already sitting up in bed and eating. He seemed to be a few years younger than Jocke Fredricksson. He was short and muscular. At the end of his bed was a wheel-chair. Irene realized both his legs had been amputated above the knee.

Irene smiled at both men as she placed the tray on the opened flap of Fredriksson's nightstand.

"I'm sorry," Irene said. "I'm really new here."

"You don't look all that new and fresh to me," muttered Jocke Fredriksson.

Jerk, Irene couldn't help thinking. She kept her smile, how-ever, even if it wasn't as bright as usual.

"So you're a nursing assistant?" asked the amputee, who'd seen her nametag.

"That's right."

"So are you the one who will be turning me over today?"

Irene hoped that the sudden anxiety she felt did not show on her face. "No, no, I believe that's Nurse Ann-Britt. I'll make sure to ask her," she replied.

The man nodded and seemed content with her answer. Irene slunk out of the room again.

As she came back into the hallway, she saw Fredrik walking hurriedly toward her with his coattails flying behind him. Folders stuck up from his shoulder bag, and he held a thick book. He'd found some glasses to perch on his nose, and he peered over them as he strode along. From a distance, he even appeared fairly intelligent.

Head Doctor Nils Dürsell was inside the glass wall of the nurses' office with a thick compendium in front of him that he was pretending to read. One eye was trained on the entrance to the unit, which made him look somewhat cross-eyed.

Irene jumped when she felt someone tugging on the back of her scrubs. She whirled around and saw nothing until she looked down at a tiny woman whose face was frozen in fear.

"Excuse me, nurse, could you tell me when my husband's test results are in?" she said timidly.

Irene fell back into her role quickly. "What's your husband's name?"

"Jakob Fredriksson," the tiny woman whispered.

So, here we have the jerk's unlucky wife, Irene thought. Aloud, she said, in a friendly manner, "Unfortunately, I'm not assigned to his room. I can ask Nurse Ann-Britt for you."

"Thank you . . . thank you so much. You want to know everything when you're dealing with . . . cancer." The tiny woman whispered the last word and headed into Room 3.

Cancer. Irene's father had died of cancer more than ten years ago. She remembered how hard it had been for everyone before he died. Certainly modern medicine had made great strides since then, and people who once would have been doomed to die were now being saved. Still, just the word "cancer" was enough to strike fear in anyone. Irene felt a rush of sympathy for old Jocke. He was going through a tough fight. Perhaps he'd already lost the battle; no surprise that he was gruff. But better that than passively accepting his fate. Then it'd be all over. You have to keep fighting to the bitter end, as her mother Gerd always said, using one of the few English idioms she knew.

Magnus stuck his head, with its black topknot, through the doorway.

"Britt, it's soon time for coffee break. Can you start collecting the trays?"

It took a second for Irene to realize he was talking to her.

"Sure, I'll get them," she said.

"I'll stick around and help you," said a small, blonde woman about Irene's age. She introduced herself as Anette, and she was a real assistant nurse. She smiled at Irene.

"We can wait a few more minutes, though. Let them have a chance to eat up. Then we can start at each end of the hallway, you on that side, and I'll start on this one."

The assistant nurse pointed to the rooms at the end of the hallway by the entrance. Irene nodded and walked that way, passing the nurses' office.

The superintendent was really into his role as the head doctor. His eyeglasses had slid down his nose as he pored over the thick compendium, all the while keeping a good eye on the entrance. When he saw Irene, he raised the compendium as a discreet greeting. Irene read the title of the compendium: *Hygienic Routines for Cleaning Infected Rooms in Both Open- and Closed-Care Units*. It didn't look like anything a head doctor would read on a Sunday morning, so Irene was relieved when he put the thick compendium back on the table.

Fredrik was standing by the nurses' office and appeared to be in deep discussion with Nurse Ann-Britt. *He's the perfect picture of an engaged and hard-working attending doctor*, Irene thought, pleased.

A glance at the clock told her that it was time to pick up the breakfast trays. They were supposed to be collected into a large cart, which would be wheeled back to the main kitchen.

Four women were in the room at the very end of the hallway. One elderly woman had an IV and had not been given a breakfast tray, but the other three had eaten with good appetite. Irene exchanged a few words with everyone and explained that she was just an extra for the weekend. She said she was from hospice and not used to the routines of a surgical ward. The three women said they thought there must be a great difference in routine between hospice and surgical and that she was extremely brave to try something different. *If you only knew just how different*, Irene thought as she collected the trays.

Just as she was leaving the room, she felt her cell phone vibrate in her pants pocket. Adrenaline shot through her, and she hurried as much as she could without calling attention to herself.

Once in the hallway, she saw a doctor go into Sanna's room. Otherwise, the hall was empty, except for Kajsa, who was running toward her. She gestured wildly toward the door where the doctor had just gone in.

Irene ran into the room. The police officer was lying on the floor just inside the room. She wasn't moving. Irene saw the back of the doctor, who was lifting his arm. In his hand was a gun.

Her training kicked in. Irene instantly judged the distance, grabbed a sandwich plate, and hurled it like a Frisbee. With a dull thud, the plate hit the back of the doctor's neck and broke in half. He fell forward without a word, but a dry bang indicated he'd still managed to fire the gun.

And, of course, Sanna was screaming. Irene was used to her by now, but Kajsa, who had followed Irene through the doorway, was thrown by the noise.

"Don't worry. It just means she's alive," Irene said to Kajsa.

Irene felt the man's pulse. He was alive, too, but unconscious. His gun had a silencer. Irene pulled it from his grasp and held it carefully between her thumb and forefinger.

Sanna was screaming like a banshee from the bed. There was a pool of red forming near her right shoulder.

"Calm down, Sanna," said Irene. "It's just a surface wound."

Her words were in vain. Sanna's screams filled the whole floor.

A REAL DOCTOR, a surgeon by the name of Westerlund, came hurrying in. He ordered the officer and the wounded man to intensive care. The policewoman was beginning to wake up as she was placed on the stretcher. A deep red mark on the side of her neck showed that she'd been brought down by a single blow.

Doctor Westerlund gave Sanna a tranquilizer and then put a pressure bandage on her shoulder. "I'm having her brought straight to surgery," he explained. He smiled at Irene as he added, "That guy should be happy he's alive. You really got in a good hit!"

"I'm a handball player and a Frisbee thrower from way back," Irene explained. "I love to play Frisbee with my dog."

"I'm not surprised," the doctor said.

Sanna had calmed enough to stop screaming. She looked at Irene from underneath a wrinkled brow as she stammered, "That . . . police officer. The clothes . . . Mike also had white clothes on."

"Mike? Was the man who shot you named Mike?" asked Irene.

"Yes, he was dressed . . . like a doctor, too," she said. She closed her eyes. At the same time, two men in green scrubs and paper caps came into the room.

It's getting pretty crowded in here, thought Irene.

"I'll go with you," the doctor said to the two assistants.

He nodded at Irene, and they all left the room, pushing Sanna in her wheeled bed.

The room felt empty at once. Only Kajsa and Irene were left.

"Mike. . . ." Kajsa said. "I thought I recognized him, but I don't know from where. . . ."

"When did you realize he was our suspect?" asked Irene.

Kajsa sighed and took off her gray-tinted glasses.

"He was damned smart about it. The elevator stopped, and three doctors got out at the same time. Two of them went to the unit on the other side, and he—Mike—waved at them before he came in here. If he'd been alone all along, I would have been suspicious at once, but since there were three of them and they all seemed to know each other, I didn't react right away. He came down the hallway and then suddenly I thought—he might be our man. The description matched, but not the clothes, of course. He opened the door to Sanna's room without a pause and I called you on your cell phone immediately. Good thing you got there in time!"

It was easy to hear the relief in Kajsa's voice.

"What did Andersson do?" asked Irene.

"He didn't see him. He didn't move until Sanna started screaming. Like me, he probably thought that the man was a real doctor. He looked absolutely believable. He had a stethoscope and everything. He moved as if he belonged here. He was totally self-confident," Kajsa explained.

Irene nodded. "He'd checked out the scene a few times before. We know he—"

"I got it!" yelled Kajsa. "I know who he is!"

"Who?"

"Mike! He's the head of security for Hotel Göteborg! Birgitta and I watched the security camera video of the parking lot when Ceder drove away the night he was shot. Mike showed us the video! Mike—Michael Fuller, the American!" Kajsa's voice was filled with triumph.

Michael Fuller. The name rang a bell for Irene, too.

"Sanna said that the head of security helped them install the security system in the house just before her husband was murdered. I'll bet that Fuller had a key to the house. I can picture him standing beneath the spiral staircase waiting to shoot Kjell B:son Ceder right between the eyes."

"Absolutely, but why would he want to kill his boss? Why did he shoot Bergman and Rothstaahl? Why did he have to shoot Sanna? How does this fit with the murders of Thomas Bonetti and Edward Fenton?" Kajsa said.

"That'll be your homework for tomorrow," Irene said. Her voice revealed her exhaustion. She smiled to let Kajsa know she was kidding and put her arm around Kajsa's shoulders.

Chapter 23

A GUARD WAS assigned to Michael Fuller even though the doctors felt he wasn't capable of fleeing. The blow from the edge of the plate on the base of the skull had left him in great pain, and he had trouble with his balance.

The female officer remembered only sitting on her chair when a doctor walked up, but before she even had a chance to raise her eyes, everything went black. She'd suffered a karate chop to the neck, dealt by an expert. If it had carried just slightly more force, she might have died.

Sanna underwent surgery to remove the .25-caliber unjacketed bullet lodged in the bone of her left shoulder blade. The technicians already had it at the lab. The gun and all the bullets collected from the murder sites were being shipped to the National Crime Laboratory for comparison. The detectives would have to cool their heels waiting for that result. It was really backlogged over there.

On Monday morning, a doctor reported that his locker had been broken into. He was still angry when he showed up at the technician's lab and identified the stolen items. Fuller had taken his outfit. Other police officers had searched for Michael Fuller's civilian clothes on the grounds of Östra Hospital, and by Sunday evening, they'd found a rental car left in the lot. The dark blue jacket and dark pants were inside. Nurse Ann-Britt identified them as those she had seen on the suspect the morning of the attack.

When questioned, the two doctors who had ridden in the elevator with Fuller told them that he'd fooled them completely. He had spoken to them in English with an American accent and told them that he was not sure where he was supposed to go. All he knew was the floor number and that it was a surgical unit. Both of the Swedish doctors offered help and gave him directions, explaining that the one across the hall was a pharmaceutical unit. Neither of them had suspected a thing. They had been glad to help a visiting colleague.

Andersson updated the team on all the drama that Sunday morning. Irene had already called Tommy on Sunday and filled him in, but she hadn't informed anyone else. The rest of the team thought the plan had been sophisticated and smart.

"Just like a bad TV cop show," muttered Jonny. Luckily, Andersson didn't hear him. The superintendent was thrilled with their work, and was even happier with capturing the suspect. The plan had put an elegant feather in his cap.

"The American embassy sent us what they have on Michael Fuller," Fredrik said. "According to them, he was born in New Jersey and moved to New York. He is thirty-five-years-old and an American citizen. He arrived in Sweden in May of 2000."

"He came around the same time Sanna returned," Irene interrupted. "Maybe it's not connected, but it's worth noting."

"Bonetti was executed that same year," Fredrik reminded them.

"When did Fuller start work as head of security at the Hotel Göteborg?" asked Andersson.

Fredrik looked down at his sheet of notes. "He started upon arrival. He lives with a girl who works at the hotel's reception desk. They've just moved into a new apartment on Norra Älvstranden."

"Nice address. Must have earned a good salary as head of security," Jonny said.

"Maybe I should switch jobs," joked Fredrik.

Andersson snorted in disgust but otherwise ignored Fredrik. Instead, he said, "As soon as Fuller is stable, he's going to be moved from the hospital to jail, where we can question him."

He touched his fingertips together and looked at his team thoughtfully.

"Since neither Sanna nor Fuller can be questioned today, I want you to interview every single employee of the Hotel Göteborg and find out what that Yank was really up to. Check when he had time off and see if it correlates to the murders. Fredrik, you question that unfaithful secretary, Malin What's-Her-Name. . . ." Andersson wrinkled his brow trying to remember.

"Malin Eriksson," said Fredrik.

"Right. Malin Eriksson, who had an affair with Kjell Ceder. That a woman like that could even be married to a police officer! She might know something shady about Fuller." He turned to Irene. "Have you heard anything from London or Paris?"

"Yes, I have. Special Agent Lee Hazel from the FBI is on the way here. He's supposed to have gone to Paris first, and then on to London this afternoon. Tomorrow or the day after, he should arrive here."

"A special agent from the FBI?" Andersson said.

Now the shit had hit the fan. Having other foreign police departments involved in the investigation was fine as long as they stayed put. Having them come here and rummage around in Andersson's department was another story. The news infuriated him.

"Glen Thompson says this case is much more complicated than it first appeared. Special Agent Hazel can provide us with his specific knowledge. It should help us," Irene said, although her voice sounded doubtful.

She really had no idea what this "specific knowledge" was supposed to be. Glen had been somewhat vague about it, too.

Perhaps he was also unsure what the special agent actually specialized in.

IRENE WAS AT her desk writing up her report on Sunday's events when the telephone rang. A carefully modulated voice, speaking Swedish with an American accent, introduced himself as Jack Curtis from the American embassy. He asked that Irene send Michael Fuller's fingerprints to the embassy as soon as possible. His tone was polite and measured, but Irene understood that "as soon as possible" actually meant "right away," with no time for delay.

She felt surprise as she hung up the phone. Fingerprints? Jack Curtis had rattled off his title quickly: "Director of Security Something-or-Another."

So what was this about?

LATE MONDAY AFTERNOON, the detectives were called to the conference room for a quick run-through, but only Irene, Tommy, Fredrik, and Andersson were in the building. The others were still interviewing people at the Hotel Göteborg and at Östra Hospital.

Fredrik reported first.

"Malin Eriksson was willing to work with us. She found vacation lists, reports of employee absence, and similar records. It was odd that the normal rules did not apply to Mr. Fuller. He could come and go as he pleased. According to these records, he was given ten to sixteen weeks per year in addition to the normal five weeks off. He'd attended a number of 'security conferences' in the United States; all of it, bear in mind, paid by his employer. For some large hotel chain, it might be almost believable, but that's certainly not the case here. Obviously way out of line."

"Strange, indeed," Andersson agreed.

"Another thing—he doesn't actually manage other

employees. The company used a security firm, which did all the actual work, even setting up and recording things on the security cameras. For his 'hard work,' he was paid a salary of fifty thousand Swedish kroner a month."

"Fifty thousand!" Irene and Andersson exclaimed at the same time.

Fredrik nodded. "That's right. Fifty thousand."

"No security guard, even the head of security, would earn anywhere near that amount. Did other employees receive such an exorbitant salary?"

Fredrik shook his head. "No, theirs looked normal. Only Kjell B:son Ceder had one similar. In other words, his so-called 'Head of Security' earned as much as he did."

"Doubly strange. Still, it explains how the American was able to keep tabs on Ceder. He watched the camera when Ceder went into the garage and got in his car. All Fuller had to do was follow and park a little way away. Then he changed into jogging clothes and was unremarkable as he approached the house. By the way, the lab got back to me, and the half-fingerprint on the jogging reflector does come from Fuller," Andersson added, happy about the positive identification.

"But how did he get into the house without Ceder knowing about it?" Fredrik wondered.

"Fuller had a key. Remember, Sanna told us that Fuller was helping them install a security system around the time of the murder," Irene said. She turned to her boss and said, "I believe that Mike Fuller was already inside when Ceder got there. He came in through the back door and waited for him in the laundry room. He came out when Ceder went upstairs to get his whiskey. I believe Ceder planned to meet Fuller there, in a house Ceder believed was empty. His lover, Malin Eriksson, was parked at his apartment waiting for him. She'd have recognized Fuller and wondered why Fuller would need to come so far to meet his own boss."

"Don't forget that Fuller, too, would have been surprised to see her there," added Tommy.

"Of course. But why the meeting in the first place? Was it something that they couldn't talk about at work? If it were a security issue, all Fuller had to do was knock on Ceder's office door."

No one could come up with any ideas why the two of them needed to meet at the Askim house.

It was Irene's turn to speak. "Just an hour ago, I received an email from Glen Thompson letting us know that Special Agent Lee Hazel will be landing at Landvetter Airport at two P.M. tomorrow afternoon. Glen also wrote. . . ." Irene picked up the sheet of paper and translated into Swedish on the fly: ". . . Agent Hazel is a marvel of efficiency and has incredible knowledge about these kinds of cases. Special Agent Hazel is special in many ways."

Tommy lifted an eyebrow but refrained from commenting.

Andersson drummed the table with his fingers, then slammed down his palm with a loud bang. "Fuller is in a bad spot since physical evidence ties him to the murder at Askim. Also, he was captured in the act of committing a felony with several police officers as witnesses. Not to mention assaulting an officer, rendering her unconscious. He'll have a rough time getting out of this. I've been informed he'll be moved to jail this evening. Tommy and Irene, you'll interrogate him tomorrow. After you talk to him, go back again to that damned Kaegler woman and force her to open up! Now that Edward Fulton is dead, there's nothing left for her to hide. And, just for a change of pace, can you get her to tell the truth?"

Then he turned to Fredrik. "You'll go to Landvetter Airport and pick up Agent Hassel, or whatever his name is. We'll meet here again tomorrow afternoon and bring Mr. Totally Special Special Agent up to speed about what's been going on here."

• • •

ON TUESDAY MORNING, Michael Fuller was led into one of the interrogation rooms at Headquarters. He was in handcuffs with two huge guards on each side. Since he was judged extremely dangerous, he was fastened to the interrogation room table with both hand and foot chains. By the nasty glares he gave Tommy and Irene, this was a wise precaution indeed.

Michael Fuller had light-olive skin, thick black hair, and dark brown eyes. His face was both attractive and powerful. There was a slight tendency toward plumpness beneath his chin. He was muscular and in good shape, but, again, there was a bit of a spare tire around his middle.

Fuller sat there without speaking for half an hour. He didn't even blink or nod when they asked if he was Michael Fuller. He just eyed them quietly with glowering hatred. Eventually they gave up.

THE POLICE HAD decided to continue a watch over Sanna for the time being, since no one was sure if Michael Fuller had been acting alone. So, yet again, a police officer sat by Sanna's hospital room door. This officer was a strong young man with swollen biceps stretching his sleeves. He didn't know Tommy or Irene, so he demanded their identification when they arrived.

Sanna Kaegler now looked extremely vulnerable. Dark shadows dipped into her thin face. The nurse had told them that she'd been given a large dose of tranquilizers and pain medication.

They asked Sanna how she was doing and chatted a bit before they got down to business. Just as before, Tommy was the one who started the real questioning.

"Were you surprised when you recognized Michael Fuller as the one was trying to kill you?"

"Was I ever! It was *Mike* . . . . I just don't get it."

"Let's go back to Askim, to the time he tried to shoot you. How did he get you to come where he was hiding?"

When Sanna looked unwilling to answer, Tommy said bluntly, "We know that Edward Fenton is Ludwig's father."

Sanna closed her eyes, the same response she had whenever she wanted to keep the world at bay. Finally, she opened her eyes and said, "How did you know? Oh, well, it doesn't really . . . matter . . . anymore. Edward and I never used a regular telephone. We always texted or used special cell phones. Only at certain times, too. We didn't want anyone to find our messages or overhear us. We'd used the same meeting place once before when he was in Göteborg. I got a text message. I was supposed to go there and meet him. I was so happy—I didn't even know he was in town! And, as it turned out, he wasn't. . . ."

She began to cry. Since Sanna couldn't use her left arm, Irene helped her with a paper tissue to dry her tears and blow her nose. She quieted a bit and looked at them with eyes that seemed enormous in her thin face.

"How did Mike know about our meeting place? And how did he use Edward's cell phone? Mike even knew our code: 'Meet me at the bushes?' with a question mark as a signature. This meant we were supposed to meet at the other side of the field from my house by the bushes near the bike trail. I just don't get it!"

Irene and Tommy were not able to answer her. It was another important question. How did Michael Fuller end up with Edward Fenton's cell phone? Since Tommy had no follow-up question just then, Irene decided to ask the one that had been burning in her mind for a long time. Maybe Sanna would prefer not to answer, but she just might. . . .

"I've been wondering, through this investigation, why did you and Kjell B:son Ceder get married in the first place?"

Sanna sighed and closed her eyes, but she still answered. "It was Edward's idea. He was frightened when I told him I was expecting a baby, and I had no intention of having an abortion. His wife—she's wealthy and her father owns the bank Edward works for. They, that is, her family, are all Catholics. If they found out that Edward and I were expecting a baby together, there'd be hell to pay. He'd already told me that the family had threatened him because of . . . the money."

She paused to blot at the tears that trickled down her face as she told the story. Irene helped her with the paper tissues again, while Tommy asked quietly, "What money?"

Sanna's blue, water-washed eyes flashed. "The money that disappeared, of course!" she snapped.

Tommy continued in the same calm manner. "Which money?"

"The ph.com money!" She was angry. The money that had puffed into smoke when the tech bubble burst—the money lurking in the background all along.

"Was Edward's family angry about money lost in the crash that took down ph.com?" Tommy made his question perfectly clear.

Sanna nodded and sobbed slightly. She blew her nose again with Irene's help and then tried to pull herself together.

"Edward told me he had to pay it all back. All the money that was lost. That was *sick! Everybody* lost money in the crash!" She toned down her rant. "He said it would take years, but once it was paid, he'd be free. Free to leave her and join Ludde and me. But during that time, no one must suspect that Ludde was his son. So it was for our safety—that is, for Ludde's safety and my safety—that he arranged my marriage to Kjell B:son Ceder."

She lifted her chin defiantly, but her trembling lower lip undermined the effect she wanted to make. She didn't look proud, but like a little lost girl abandoned by all.

Irene didn't mention her own thoughts on the matter. She

asked quietly, "What did Kjell think about this arranged marriage?"

"He was doubtful at first, but then he agreed to it. We'd actually slept together a few times in earlier years. . . . We had fun, nothing more. I mean, he had nothing against me per se. . . . So, for friendship's sake—friendship to both Edward and to me—he decided to help us. We got married pretty quickly after that."

Irene speculated that maybe Edward Fenton had some sort of blackmail on Kjell B:son Ceder, too. After all, Edward was the only witness to the disappearance of Marie Lagerfeld-Ceder from the deck of the sailboat that night. With all three now dead, no one would ever know for sure what had really happened to the first Mrs. Ceder.

"Did you agree on your living arrangements once you were married? Your different residences and the like?" asked Tommy.

"Yes, we were in complete agreement. Neither one of us wanted to live in the same place as the other. But the most important thing you have to keep in mind is that we were not enemies. Far from it! We had lots of fun together. For example, we went to Portugal last August. Though when we were there, I stayed with Edward, and he took a French lover. Her name was Birgitte. We rented a large house for all of us."

Without knowing it, Sanna smiled at the memory. Tommy and Irene exchanged glances. The pieces were falling into place. Still, a lot didn't make sense. Parts of the puzzle were still missing, and other parts did not fit properly. Perhaps even Sanna didn't know the whole truth. Perhaps she only knew what Edward had told her. However, her attitude now showed she'd given up lying.

"How long did you stay in Portugal?" asked Irene.

"For two weeks."

"Was Edward with you the whole time?"

Sanna appeared horrified. "No, of course not! He stayed for

only four days. His wife and children had already gone to the States, and he'd told them he had to wrap up a thing or two before he could join them. Then he came down to Portugal to see me and Ludde."

The tone of her voice hinted at a sense of triumph over her competitor. *Good old Fenton*, Irene thought. *You really made a mess of things, didn't you? No wonder you ended up in the trunk of a car.* When he'd shot at Irene in Paris, he must have felt desperate. Had his thumbscrews been tightening? Apparently so.

Irene decided to ask another question about Edward. "One more thing. If I understood you correctly, Edward was the go-between for the money between you and the blackmailer."

"That's right."

"So how did that work? Transferring the money, I mean."

Sanna was surprised at the question. "Why, I just put the money into his account at HP Johnson, of course."

"And then Edward would take care of sending the money on."

"Yes, I told you that."

The question obviously irritated Sanna, and Irene suspected why. The arrangement was odd no matter how you looked at it. If nothing else, Edward Fenton must have known the identity of the extortionist.

Tommy cleared his throat and took over the questioning. "Can you talk about those fingers?"

Sanna nodded bravely and looked at him with trust.

How does Tommy do it? wondered Irene. *What is his special way with women that he can turn on like a switch? And why does he never use this gift on me?* The answer was obvious. She wouldn't be taken in. Maybe that's why they had a good friendship—neither played those kinds of games on each other.

"You told us that Edward had also received a finger. Is that right?"

Sanna nodded.

"Did he tell you that through a text message or did he tell you directly on the phone?"

"A text."

"Do you remember the exact words?"

Sanna closed her eyes to think and then said, "He wrote that the extortionist wanted the fingers back. I answered that I'd thrown mine away. He texted that he'd thrown his away, too. Still, if I found the finger sent to Kjell, the threat against me and Ludde would be lifted."

"So you and Ludde were in danger?"

"Well, I didn't know about any new threats . . . before the text from Edward. More than—" She stopped. "I'm saying too much. It must be all the medication." She looked at Tommy in terror.

"We know that everyone at ph.com was being blackmailed. You know that we know. But we still don't understand what the extortionist threatened to reveal. Without that, why would anyone pay up?"

"They threatened to kill me! Just like they had the person whose fingers they'd cut off. . . ." Sanna's voice dropped to a whisper. She'd realized she'd revealed too much—something she couldn't take back.

"So, you always knew that it was Thomas's finger."

Sanna nodded. She'd given up. "Yes. They sent me his ring finger with his signet ring still on it. His fingers were fat. I don't think they could get the ring off, actually. . . ."

Sanna began to tremble and then to heave. Irene grabbed a round bowl from the nightstand and held it below Sanna's chin. She vomited, but the only thing that came out was yellow slime, which she spat into the bowl until, finally, she sobbed, "I need an injection!"

Tommy said, "I'll call the nurse. You've been very brave answering all our questions. "

"Just get the bastards!" whispered Sanna.

"What?" Tommy asked.

"Get the bastards—the guys who murdered Philip and Edward! Punish them for me!" She was talking so low and fast it was hard to understand her words.

"So you think other people are involved? Not just Mike Fuller?" Tommy asked.

"There's no way Mike did this on his own! He's too full of himself. He's an idiot. We didn't deal with each other much . . . and he had no beef with me. He was following orders when he came to shoot me. And I'm sure he asked for a lot of money for his trouble!" Sanna's voice deepened with hatred.

Irene was surprised that Sanna had come to the same conclusion that she had and hurried to ask one last question.

"Which language did you use to text Edward?"

"Swedish or English. But mostly English."

"Do you remember the language of the last text you received?"

"English," she replied without hesitation.

Must have made it easy for Mike Fuller, Irene thought.

Chapter 24

TOMMY AND IRENE returned to Headquarters shortly after three P.M. Fredrik had not yet brought in Special Agent Lee Hazel. While they were waiting for their guest, Tommy and Irene informed Andersson about the results of their questioning. Going through the interview with Michael Fuller took no time at all, as he hadn't said a word, but Sanna had given them a great deal of information.

Irene had been considering Sanna's responses to their questioning.

"I believe that we can now assume that everyone being blackmailed was paying into that HP Johnson account. Supposedly, Edward Fenton then forwarded the money to the extortionist. That part is very odd. He'd told Sanna he, too, was being blackmailed. He was even supposed to have received a finger. If it *is* true that each murder victim—including Sanna, who barely escaped death—received a finger, it would mean that five were sent, but *we* know that was not the case. Thomas Bonetti still had his thumb. So four fingers were sent to four victims." Irene paused for effect. "Edward was lying about the finger."

"Why would he lie about that?" asked the Andersson.

"Maybe to fool her, so Sanna would find him more believable. 'We're in the same boat.' Something like that."

"Or he had something to hide himself," Tommy was thinking out loud.

"Humph! Nothing but theories and wild guesswork!" said Andersson. "I certainly hope this special agent is as special as they made him out to be!"

A few moments later, a deep, rich voice said in American English, "Hello. I'm Special Agent Lee Hazel."

All three of them turned to the door to see where the voice came from. Their mouths dropped open, and they couldn't help staring.

By height, Special Agent Lee Hazel could have been a basketball player. The smile directed at the Swedish police was dazzling white in a mahogany face. Not to mention that she had the largest breasts Irene had ever seen.

Lee Hazel glided into the room with Fredrik following in her wake. Fredrik was grinning like an idiot. Irene was amazed at how easily the special agent moved. She realized why at once: Lee Hazel must be at least as highly ranked in a martial art as Irene—if not higher.

Special Agent Lee Hazel was wearing a nougat-colored dress suit so tailored to her form it was easy to see that her shoulders were broad and muscular. Under the jacket, she wore a white blouse which was somewhat strained over her extensive bust line.

Irene remembered her manners. She stood up to shake hands. She smiled as she introduced her boss, Superintendent Andersson, and her colleague, Tommy Persson. Irene hoped that her boss was grateful she'd taken the initiative since Andersson's English was truly terrible. What Irene couldn't know was that Andersson had purchased a CD course in English and was practicing at home. He hadn't mentioned it at work, but he was hoping to be able to converse with Glen's mother Donna a bit better the next time they met.

It was seven in the evening before the team had finished discussing the facts of the case with Special Agent Lee Hazel.

The agent took few notes, and Irene was almost irritated when she saw that, during the past four hours while she had struggled with English, Agent Hazel had barely filled one page. Irene had to admire the American's attentiveness, however, since Agent Hazel had immediately asked for clarification whenever she needed more information.

Once they had finished, the superintendent looked at his watch. "Let's have dinner. It's on me."

Irene did not know what had surprised her the most: that the superintendent had invited them all for dinner or that he had used idiomatic English to do so.

"How about going to Glady's?" Andersson continued with a glance at Irene.

It was a good thing Irene was already sitting down; Glady's was one of the finest restaurants in Göteborg. She heard her own voice sound feeble as she replied, "Good idea. I'll call and see if they have a table."

As she headed for her office to place the call, a suspicion arose in her mind: Andersson must have wrangled special funds to impress this visitor from the United States.

THEY HAD THE good luck to reserve a table for eight P.M. Lee Hazel had praised the delicious succession of dishes: moose carpaccio as an appetizer, followed by a main dish of grilled cod. The food disappeared rapidly behind Agent Hazel's sparkling white teeth. By the time dessert arrived, Irene was overcome with exhaustion. She could barely keep herself from letting her head fall into her bowl of chocolate mousse. Neither she nor Tommy had drunk any wine, since they were both driving. Andersson, on the other hand, had enjoyed both food and drink.

"I'm going to leave my car at the station and take a taxi home," he informed them happily. "It's not every day we have a visitor from the States! *Skål!*"

Lee Hazel lifted her glass of wine and smiled at Andersson. The candles reflected in her dark brown eyes, and the silver polish on her long nails glittered. Agent Hazel was an uncommonly beautiful woman. Irene heard some of the other guests at other tables whispering among themselves. A woman at the neighboring table whispered, "That's supermodel Naomi Campbell, I'm sure of it!"

Irene and Tommy thanked Andersson for their dinner and left the restaurant together. They detoured through the kitchen to say hello to Krister. He only had time to lift his knife from the lobster tail he was slicing to wave at them.

ANDERSSON LOOKED SURPRISINGLY alert at morning prayer. Fredrik, on the other hand, looked worn out and exhausted, completely different from his usual demeanor. Irene often thought he could be a spokesperson in an advertising campaign for energy pills—a trait of his she usually found to be colossally irritating. She was remarkably happy to see that his stylish hair was not as carefully gelled as usual, but looked like he had rolled straight out of bed into the station. He hadn't even changed his sweater from yesterday.

This case is really starting to wear us out, Irene thought. As for her, she'd fallen asleep before her head hit the pillow and had slept without dreams until the alarm clock buzzed.

Andersson spoke. "I believe our special agent has been sufficiently briefed about the case. She told me that she was going to correlate everything she'd learned here, in Paris and in London. As I think about it, I realize that yesterday she hadn't said a word about what she'd already found out. But I believe all will be made clear to us today. Fredrik, you drove her home last night. Did she mention when she'd come in this morning?"

"Agent Hazel is going to make a few phone calls back to the FBI and will be here around lunchtime," Fredrik said.

"I see. But New York is six time zones behind ours. It'll be difficult to reach anyone on the other side of the Atlantic," Tommy pointed out.

"That city never sleeps," said Fredrik.

"Nothing to worry about," Andersson said knowledgeably. "The FBI and CIA are open all day and all night because of all the bad guys running around over there. Or so I've seen on TV."

His worldview is so limited, Irene thought. *At least he's been to London recently.*

"Well, then," Andersson said. "Let's get to work, and we'll meet here at one P.M." He clapped his hands together energetically.

Fredrik yawned and headed directly for the coffee machine. For the first time in five years, Irene found it easy to endure him before she had her first cup of the day.

AFTER LUNCH, THEY all came back into the conference room. Lee Hazel was already seated. She looked remarkably chipper. *Looks like she doesn't have any problems with jet lag,* Irene thought. She also noticed that Fredrik had gone home over lunch and had showered and changed clothes. He smelled as fresh as usual.

"I'm going to hand the floor to our American colleague," Andersson said.

Yet again, Irene was surprised at his use of English. His pronunciation was not bad at all. Hazel flashed a dazzling smile as she stood up. Her enormous bosom heaved as she took a deep breath before she started to speak. This seemed to cause breathlessness and bodily discomfort among the men. Meanwhile, Birgitta, Kajsa, and Irene all wondered if silicone had something to do with this effect.

Hazel began her report in her deep, husky voice. A few moments later, no one was focused on her physique. They all wanted to catch every single word she was saying. "I work for a special division in the FBI that concentrates on organized crime. In particular, I focus on the mafia and how they carry out money laundering. My degree is in economics, by the way. I follow every financial twist and turn whenever criminals try to hide the sources of their illegal gains. Right now, money laundering is the mafia's biggest concern. Drugs, prostitution, theft, and extortion make up a good part of their income, but they want to appear respectable. They want to integrate their operations into the regular community. With 'clean' money, they can invest in legitimate business as well as get involved in politics, support the political projects they favor. In this way, the mafia gains legal power."

"Excuse me for interrupting," said Andersson. "May we record your report?" He was nervous. He was shocked to realize that his listening comprehension was not as good as he'd imagined after completing his language course.

"Fine by me," said Hazel.

She waited patiently as Andersson got out the tape recorder and set it up. As soon as she saw the record button light up red, she continued her report.

"As you already know, Edward Fenton was the head of HP Johnson's European office. This bank is a respectable investment bank, established before World War I by a ketchup magnate. However, in the early seventies, the institution ran into financial problems and began to let investors buy into the bank. One investor, Sergio Santini, bought out the others a few years later. As you know, Santini is the father of Janice Santini, and therefore the father-in-law of Edward Fenton. Mr. Santini also has a son named Sergio Junior. Today the Santini family is one of the most powerful mafia families in New York. Sergio Santini's parents were immigrants from Sicily in the twenties, and the family still has connections to Cosa Nostra.

"The organization is also known as the Octopus, and for good reason. Its tentacles reach into places where you'd least expect. Italy even had a president supported by the mafia. Cosa Nostra has infiltrated a number of provincial governments within Italy as well as in other European countries, and their representatives are on the boards of numerous banks and businesses, not just in Europe but also in the United States. The question is, which activities hurt democratic countries the most: their illegal or their legal ones? As far as the illegal operations go, we can actually break them up by putting as many Mafiosi behind bars as we can catch. Usually we get them on tax evasion."

She took a sip from the glass of water. None of her Swedish colleagues said a word. They hardly dared move, as if they didn't want to break a spell.

"Pappa Sergio Santini had a gift for making money. Unfortunately, the son did not, at least in the eyes of Pappa. Sergio Junior is more like the stereotype of a Mafioso—smart, tough, and excitable. He's dyslexic, though, and can barely read, much less handle complex financial matters. He's forty-three-years-old and married. He has no children, at least not with his wife, Amelia, born Bonetti."

Hazel paused for effect.

"Did she . . . really say Bonetti?" asked Andersson. He spoke Swedish, but Hazel seemed to understand what he wanted even before he asked the question.

"Yes, that's right. Amelia Bonetti. She is the daughter of a cousin of Antonio Bonetti, Thomas's father. You told me that Antonio Bonetti is a famous lawyer here in Sweden. I ran a check on him and discovered he was Leonardo Bonetti's cousin. Leonardo Bonetti is the head of a Mafia clan in Massachusetts. Antonio and Leonardo are first cousins. Their sons grew up in the United States. From what I understand, Antonio Bonetti says he is from Italy, but he's not. He was born and raised in Boston. He studied law there as well. When he came to Sweden after he married Thomas's mother . . . I seem to have forgotten her name. . . . He quickly learned Swedish and studied for a Swedish law degree."

Irene raised her hand to ask a question. "Does this mean that Antonio Bonetti is a contact person here in Sweden for the American Mafia?"

"No, we have no indication of that. He has never been directly involved in Cosa Nostra's organizations. On the other hand, his three older brothers are. Perhaps this is why the baby brother was allowed to get out. It's not easy to leave the family."

Irene raised her hand again. "How was Janice Santini allowed to marry Edward Fenton, then? He's not Italian."

"Love. Edward Fenton was an investment manager at the HP Johnson European office since the early nineties. He was good at his job, and Sergio Santini took notice of him. Remember that the Mafia is always on the lookout for ways to launder money. Investments make the money clean as snow, and no one can get at it. Edward doubled, tripled, and even quadrupled Mafia money, so Santini brought the promising young man to the United States. He found a place for him at Headquarters in New York.

"Janice met him there. She fell head over heels in love and decided that he was the man for her. At first her father was furious and threatened to cut her off from her inheritance, but he eventually he came around. Janice can wrap her father around her little finger. She's obviously the one who inherited her father's acumen and intelligence. She should be the one to take over the reins from him, but in Cosa Nostra, no woman is ever allowed into a hierarchial position of power. In the end, Janice had the prince of her dreams, but it took some time before they could celebrate her wedding. Tradition does not allow the daughter of a high-ranking Mafioso to marry outside Cosa Nostra. But tradition can be waived if the man is strategically important and can expand the organization's influence. The biggest hurdles were that Edward was not Italian and not Catholic. Fenton couldn't help not being Italian, but he did convert to Catholicism. Finally, Santini Senior gave in, and Janice married Edward ten years ago. Two years later, he became the head of the European office, and the family moved to an estate outside of London."

"So Edward Fenton knew he was working for the Mafia," Fredrik said, without raising his hand first.

Lee Hazel smiled slightly. "More than that. Edward Fenton had become part of a powerful clan. Of course, his influence lay in investments, but this is an extremely important part of the organization. It made him powerful in turn. He was absolutely sure of who was pulling the strings."

Irene asked, "If he had risen so high in the family, he'd lose all his influence if he ever divorced Janice, right?"

Hazel gave Irene a meaningful look from beneath her black eyelashes.

"Of course. He'd lose it all—his power and influence, his wife, his sons, his house, his money, and, even more likely, his life, which is, in fact, what happened."

She looked around at her enraptured audience. "You can't just join Cosa Nostra willy-nilly. But once in, you absolutely can't get *out*. Death is the only release from the family—and that brings us back to the murder of Edward Fenton." Agent Hazel bent to retrieve a red plastic folder, from which she drew out a newspaper clipping.

By now, Irene felt some slight sympathy for Sanna Kaegler. Edward Fenton had deceived her. He was never going to ask for a divorce from Janice Santini. He *couldn't* leave his wife even if he wanted to—which he'd known all along, even before getting mixed up with her.

Her thoughts were interrupted when Hazel started to pass copies of the newspaper article around the table. Irene was startled when she saw it.

The photo was taken from above—probably from over the top of a wall—and showed a couple kissing by a swimming pool. The man was holding a fair-skinned baby. There was caption beneath the picture:

Our reporter had a tip that the princess of ph.com, Sanna Kaegler, twenty-nine, vacationed in Albufiera with her baby son and an unknown man. Since we know she married the Swedish restaurant mogul, Kjell B:son Ceder, fifty-three, less than a year ago, we expected to find her with her husband. But when her husband showed up at a nightclub with French actress Birgitte Defoe, thirty, our reporter realized there was more to the story. And it's true. Sanna Kaegler has a new man in her life—though we haven't yet identified him. Still, it's obvious that a divorce is in the works, and we'll soon find out the name of this new lover. They seem to be made for each other. He's holding Sanna's new baby boy as if it were his own—what a charming family!

The picture was in perfect focus, and it was easy to see that the man Sanna was kissing was Edward Fenton.

"The vacation in Portugal. Sanna told us about it yesterday," Tommy said.

"This photo appeared in a big US tabloid just over three weeks ago," Hazel said. "Janice Santini got wind of it, I'm sure."

"This was right after Edward left his family behind in the States to come back to England," Tommy said.

"Exactly. A week later, this appeared, and Edward Fenton was identified."

Lee Hazel took another clipping from her red folder. The headline was LOVE AFFAIR BETWEEN HIGH TECH PRINCESS AND BANK KING! The article stated that neither person in the article could be reached for comment. Sanna had refused all contact with the media after Kjell B:son Ceder had been murdered, so she might not have known she'd shown up in the tabloids. But Edward must have.

"He was hiding in Paris. Irene and I found him when we were searching the Bergman-Rothstaahl apartment there," Kajsa said, gesturing at her multicolored eye socket.

Hazel raised an eyebrow. "So that's how you got that black eye. Yes, right, Irene told me about that yesterday. Edward was being chased by both the paparazzi and the Mafia. Janice had certainly set her father on him. And the Mafia found him first."

"So this explains why Edward Fenton was murdered, but what about the others? Ceder, Bergman, and Rothstaahl couldn't have been killed for the same reason," Fredrick pointed out.

Hazel nodded and smiled at Fredrik. He blushed instantly.

"The affair with Sanna Kaegler was not why Edward Fenton was killed. It was only the reason he lost immunity in the family; Janice had lifted her protecting hand from him. He'd felt pressure from the Mafia for years, and that's where the murders of the three men come in, as well as the attempted murder of Sanna Kaegler."

"The band is *slut!*" Andersson said, not realizing he'd used a Swedish word with an entirely different meaning in English. He'd meant to say that the tape recorder had come to the end of its band. Andersson hadn't understood much of what Agent Hazel was saying, but, to his great consternation, it appeared that his subordinates did. His newfound confidence in his English ability was shaken to the core. Once everyone else was gone, he'd have to ask Irene to repeat everything for him in Swedish. Naturally, he'd use the excuse that they needed to recap to make sure nothing was missed.

Lee Hazel waited patiently for Andersson to flip the tape over. Once the red light of the record button had come on again, she resumed her report.

"All of this began with the murder of Thomas Bonetti. In November 2000, the FBI received information that a cousin of

Leonardo Bonetti had disappeared in Sweden. Thomas Bonetti's family had turned to Leonardo to see if he could help them find their missing son. His parents already feared that their son had been killed. We connected the name pretty quickly with the same Thomas Bonetti who'd been featured in financial magazines during the heyday of ph.com and then its later crash. "

Agent Hazel stopped for a second and found a disc in her red folder. She held it up in front of her audience and tapped it with a silver fingernail.

"Let me change the subject for a moment. As you know, I was in London. This was retrieved from among Edward Fenton's belongings. He had a smaller house on the estate, which he used as an office, with a safe behind a bookcase. There, in the safe, were a number of computer discs neatly sorted into boxes by the letters *Bo*, *Be*, *C*, and *R*. That is, Bonetti, Bergman, Ceder, and Rothstaahl. I've gone through them and have gotten a good idea of what went on. It makes you wonder why he didn't destroy them, but he probably didn't have the time. Or perhaps he thought he could use them to protect himself from the Mafia."

She set the disc on the table, and then she took another folder from the pile of documents. She said, thoughtfully, "Perhaps Poundfix is where everything started. As you know, Thomas Bonetti, Joachim Rothstaahl, and Erik Dahl, the Norwegian, had created a company where they could invest capital, mostly from Scandinavian companies, in an investment fund. Unfortunately it was just a huge pyramid scheme where they paid wonderful returns to initial investors from money they got from the later ones. Finally, the bubble burst. Thomas Bonetti and Joachim Rothstaahl escaped the net because they were Swedish citizens, while Erik Dahl went to jail." Lee Hazel paused again. "But not only Scandinavian companies invested in Poundfix. Edward Fenton had put in one million dollars on behalf of an anonymous investor—illegal funds from the Santini family. Bonetti and Rothstaahl managed to steal most of this before the scheme was exposed. They used it to form ph.com."

Hazel let this information sink in for a minute before she continued. "It is obvious by Rothstaahl's financial records that he was being blackmailed right from the start. You can say he got away with his life but not his money. They weren't leaning on Thomas Bonetti, though. Perhaps because he was a Bonetti. The fact remains that Thomas Bonetti invested his entire share into ph.com. Those days it actually seemed smart to get into the rapidly expanding high-tech sector. Everybody was jumping onto the bandwagon. Even Edward Fenton realized that HP Johnson, and, indirectly, the Mafia, was ready to hop on board before the money train reached the end of the station. Edward saw to it that the Mafia invested over fifteen million dollars into ph.com."

"The last round—the anonymous investor! That's where the 'unknown person' came into the picture!" Kajsa exclaimed.

"Exactly." Lee Hazel nodded. "We know what happened to ph.com. Every penny was lost; Sergio Santini was one of the biggest losers. Fenton was dealt two blows: his bank lost a great deal of money and prestige, and his Mafia family lost fifteen million dollars. Fairly quickly everyone suspected that the three founders had squirreled away a good amount. Thomas Bonetti had gotten the most because he'd already begun shifting money into his own accounts long before the crash. It was also thought that Bonetti, Sanna Kaegler, Philip Bergman, and Joachim Rothstaahl were involved in kickback schemes—for instance, Joachim Rothstaahl 'consulted' for the company while also being on the payroll. Of course, his salary was already astronomical as vice president and comptroller for the company. He also made sure, through his 'consulting' firm, that the three partners raked in a lot for their fictitious services."

Hazel fell silent to give her Swedish colleagues a chance to catch up. Everyone seemed to follow her words except for the heavy-set superintendent, who had a brooding look on his round face.

"You can't cheat the Mafia out of anything," Hazel said. "Money from prostitution, drugs, and extortion—they bought it with sweat, blood, and lives long before it wound up in a banker's hands. Sergio Santini decided it was time for payback."

Even Superintendent Andersson seemed to understand her last three words.

Chapter 25

At this point, Special Agent Hazel requested a coffee break. She needed to catch her breath and give her Swedish colleagues time to digest all the information and maybe come up with a few questions. Once they all regrouped in the conference room, Irene raised her hand first.

"It's obvious from what you said that all the murders are related. It's also clear that the attempt on Sanna Kaegler-Ceder was part of this, too. They'd all swindled the Mafia out of a great deal of money. But how about Kjell B:son Ceder? He was not involved in ph.com. His marriage to Sanna Kaegler was arranged by Edward Fenton—so why was he killed?"

Special Agent Lee Hazel tapped the disc again. "Thanks to this, we know the answer. When Mr. Ceder started to build his enormous hotel, the cost was estimated to be five hundred million Swedish kroner. In the end, it cost much more than that. No Swedish bank wanted to loan him more money or invest in the project except for his old friend Edward Fenton. Fenton invested ten million dollars. From an anonymous investor, of course. Six years ago, the FBI was already tracking some of this money. Two hundred million dollars was invested in various European hotels. We noticed this one immediately since, despite how lovely it is, Göteborg can't be seen as one of the world's most impressive cities. We may never know why Edward decided to send Mr. Ceder money, but he probably did it out of friendship. Edward Fenton learned to regret letting old loyalties determine his investment. The Hotel Göteborg lost money right from the start. Mr. Ceder was sometimes behind on paying back his creditors, but once you're caught in the tentacles of the Octopus, it never lets go. So his good friend, Edward Fenton, was able to request a few favors in return. For instance, the marriage to Sanna Kaegler. Employing Michael Fuller. And speaking of Michael Fuller, I received confirmation from my colleague, Jack Curtis, that Michael Fuller was really Michael Falcone, a relative of Sergio Santini—his cousin's son. Falcone was the Mafia contact man on behalf of the Santini family. Now we know who placed him here and why."

Irene was beginning to feel rather dizzy from all the names and new information, but she knew she had to concentrate on Hazel's report. She saw all the remaining puzzle pieces sliding into place.

"Edward Fenton made sure Michael Falcone got a job at the Hotel Göteborg. The Santini family was leaning hard on Edward. They could handle the loss of the money from the Poundfix blunder, but ten million in the Hotel Göteborg project and fifteen million in ph.com was just too much. Twenty-five million is not small change. They'd invested money so it could grow, but instead, it all went up in smoke."

At the time, the American dollar was around nine kroner to one, which meant that more than 220 million Swedish kroner had disappeared. *No wonder the Mafia was mad!* Irene thought.

"Cosa Nostra does not like to lose even a single dollar. The Mafia ordered Edward to get the money back. Edward was desperate for fast cash. He took off the gloves. Thomas Bonetti had taken the largest amount of cash, so Fenton went after him first. Edward and Mike Falcone did the job. As you know, he was tortured before he was killed. All the money had vanished from his bank accounts, so they tortured the account numbers from him. These discs show us that the total amount from him was two and a half million dollars. Selling Bonetti's boat gave them a few more bucks. His father-in-law was happy, so Edward kept it up. Mike Falcone probably suggested that they send the fingers to the others. It certainly has the whiff of Mafia tactics. The fingers, in the end, had two purposes, first to torture information out of Bonetti and then to threaten the other four. The message was clear: if you don't pay up, your fingers are next."

Again, she paused for a sip of water.

No one asked a question, so she continued, "The death threat was enough for Bergman, Rothstaahl, and Kaegler to start paying at once. They continued to pay up right until their deaths. Their estates are now worth nothing. Easy come, easy go." She waved elegant hands.

"But why were they killed? They'd actually paid back everything they had," Kajsa said.

"The murder of Thomas Bonetti was beginning to catch up to them. The Bonetti family had gotten a whiff of the fact that the Santinis were involved in Bonetti's death. Any proof of that would be catastrophic. Suddenly, the fingers seemed like a bad idea. Edward wanted to get all the fingers and all the threatening letters back. He knew who'd gotten them. They would be physical evidence of blackmail, and if the Bonetti family got wind of blackmail, they'd know that Thomas had also been extorted. They knew his accounts had been stripped after his disappearance. Where did all his money go? To the Santini family, of course. A Mafia war might break out. Edward knew he'd never survive being caught in the middle, so he and Michael Falcone decided to eliminate all four people who knew anything about the letters and the fingers."

Irene decided to speak up. "This explains why Rothstaahl and Bergman came to Göteborg from Paris. Edward got them there by demanding they attend an important meeting. Perhaps he enticed them with an offer to invest in their new EuroFund. Falcone was waiting for them at Rothstaahl's summer house. The same thing happened to Kjell B:son Ceder. He never suspected that Edward would lure him to that meeting in Askim just so Michael Falcone could kill him. Edward had an alibi—he was still in the United States. He pretended to be a go-between and conned all four of them out of their money, which then went directly to his father-in-law Sergio Santini."

Hazel nodded. "Exactly. Falcone sent Rothstaahl's key to Edward. So Edward didn't need to break in. The apartment key was found in his rental car, where he was found, too. Falcone, after killing his victims, sent all the discs and computers he found to Edward. Edward had gone to Paris to look for more, which was when Irene and Kajsa stumbled upon him." Hazel pointed at her own eye while looking at Kajsa, and they both grinned. "My theory behind the attempted murder of Sanna Kaegler is this," she continued. "Edward sent his cell phone to Michael Falcone and told him how to lure Sanna out of the house. Only Edward knew the proper code. If you hadn't been there, Sanna would have been killed, and Michael Falcone would have gotten away. We might never have cracked the case. Now, at least, you have Falcone in custody."

"Is he going to talk?" asked Fredrik.

"He might confess to the attempted murder of Sanna Kaegler, but probably nothing else. Perhaps you can *convict* him for the other murders on the evidence you've gathered, but he will never confess to them. Attempted murder, yes. Premeditated murder, no."

"Why anything at all?" Kajsa wondered.

"Because he needs to chill for a while. A short stint in a Swedish prison doesn't look half bad to him. In fact, being in an American prison would be life-threatening. The Bonetti family would be waiting. And I'd guess that the Santini family hasn't much use for him, either. He was a hit man working for

Edward Fenton, outside the family, and that's not something they appreciate."

Hazel looked down at her paperwork thoughtfully. She tapped the top folder with her glittering fingernail.

"Edward Fenton did his best to survive the Bonetti murder in one piece. He might have done it, too, if he hadn't had the affair with Sanna Kaegler. In hindsight, that was probably the last nail in his coffin."

FREDRIK WAS GIVEN the task of driving Hazel to the airport. She would be able to catch the last plane to London with plenty of time to spare. Irene was by her office window on the fourth floor and saw Fredrik and Hazel walking to his car. They were exactly the same height. Her long black hair flowed down her back, contrasting with Fredrik's blond tufts. They made a beautiful couple. She watched them until they'd gotten into the car and Fredrik began to back the car out of its spot in the lot.

Sighing, Irene returned to her desk and sat down in front of the computer. She hadn't had the chance to check her email for two days. The last message in her inbox was from Glen. It had been sent earlier that day. At the end, he wrote:

Isn't Lee Hazel something else? You should have seen her at work here when she was going through all those discs at superhuman speed. She must have a computer between her ears. Maybe she's a Terminator? At any rate, she's much better looking than Arnold Schwarzenegger. Still, it's easy to see why she doesn't work in the field. She is much too noticeable!

Say hi to the family,

Glen

Epilogue

ON THE FIRST Monday morning of November, Irene's desk phone rang. After she answered, there was only silence on the other end. She was about to hang up when she heard someone clearing his throat.

"Hello. Good morning. It's Billy—Billy Hermansson. I just wanted to talk to you and let you know that my mother passed away on Saturday. I was thinking about . . . your investigation. That is, she can't be your witness any longer about what she saw through her telescope. And . . . I thought of calling you because I couldn't think of anyone else who would even care."

"I'm very sorry for your loss," Irene said. She was touched that Billy had thought to contact her. He was probably right, too. No one else cared whether or not Annika Hermansson had died. Irene thought a long few moments about what she knew. She decided to go right to the point.

"Billy . . . I know who your father is. Do you think you'd ever want to come down to the station and talk about it?"

There was silence on the other end of the line for a long time.

"No," he said slowly. "I don't think I want to know. At least, not yet. Maybe later. It's too much to deal with now, with Mamma's death and all. . . ."

"I understand. I'll get back to you," Irene said.

Once they'd hung up, Irene sat silently at her desk for a long time, until she decided what to do. She took out the business card from the pile of things in her desk drawer, where it had lain for weeks. She stuffed it into a small white envelope. She carefully sealed the envelope with a piece of wide tape. Then she wrote a message on her computer:

Dear Billy,

In this sealed envelope is a business card, which belongs to your father. If you don't care to deal with it now, I suggest you put this envelope in a safety deposit box. You can get it when you feel ready to know. Otherwise, you could always burn it unopened.

If you decide to contact your father, do not tell him how you got this. Instead, tell him that Annika told you when she was delirious during her final illness.

I wish you the very best for the future.

Yours,

Irene Huss

My thanks to:

Gunnar Lindstedt, author and journalist. His books *Trustorhäven* and *boo.com* inspired me to find out more about how great sums of money can vanish. Gunnar has also been kind enough to review sections of this book. His grasp of economics is much greater than mine.

Morgan Johansson, ornithologist and my neighbor. He has been extremely helpful sharing his knowledge of binoculars, which play a major role in this book.

Eva Odd, my hairdresser, who not only helps me figure out how to deal with my hair but is also knowledgeable about motor boats.

Inger Brunbäck, my childhood best friend, who has lived for many years on Styrsö. I have visited many times, and now I can comfortably rearrange the geography of the island and the surrounding rocks and smaller islands to suit the needs of this book. The houses described here do not exist in reality (at any rate, not where I've placed them) and my description of the southern archipelago does not correspond to the sea charts.

The author wants to make it absolutely clear that because of the geographic changes, this book cannot serve as a guide, for either Göteborg or Paris. The reader is discouraged from attempting to navigate the southern archipelago of Götheborg using the geographic descriptions found in this book.

All resemblances to any persons living or dead is coincidental and not the intention of the author. The single exception is the dog Sammie, who has no objection. Since he is my dog, he's managed to remain aloof from all literary fame and takes life as it comes.

About the author

Helene Tursten was born in Göteborg on the Swedish west coast, where she lives today. As you have probably read on the back cover, she is in fact trained as a nurse and a dentist. After working as a nurse for three years, she decided to go to dental school. It was when she returned to school for her dental degree that Helene met her husband, who had been a policeman. They are still married more than thirty years later, with a daughter who is now an adult. The dog in the Irene Huss books, Sammie, is based on their real-life dog, who lived to the ripe old age of fifteen.

Helene spent ten years practicing dentistry before her career was curtailed due to rheumatic illness. That was when she turned to writing. Today she has written ten novels about Irene Huss and her colleagues at the police headquarters in Göteborg. The books have been translated into eighteen languages.

There are also twelve TV films that have been made featuring Detective Inspector Irene Huss. The films have been shown in many European countries. Helene wrote the story synopses and edited all the film scripts in collaboration with professional script writers. Working on the films has been a real kick for her, and she thinks, has also been good for her books. "There's a big difference between writing a book and writing a script for a film," Helene says. "When I am working with a film plot I have to think in pictures and within the limitations of a budget. It is very inspiring for me as a writer to think and work in a different way."

Turn the page for a sneak preview of the next
Inspector Irene Huss investigation

THE FIRE DANCE

Prologue

THE NOISE AND heat from the crowd rose toward the ceiling and mixed with cigarette smoke in a thick smog around the chandeliers. People crowded at the enormous bar and tried to catch the bartender's attention. The atmosphere was frenzied and excited, as it usually was in the Park Aveny Hotel bar during the annual meeting of the Göteborg Book Fair. Some guests were already showing signs of incipient intoxication. Famous cultural personalities, as well as some not-so-famous ones, were hanging around the bar, though a few of them had wandered to the pub's armchairs and were starting to doze.

People kept coming and going through the revolving door, mingling as they headed toward the bar or to join the groups sitting at tables. Many still kept one eye on the entrance—a high-level celebrity could walk in at any moment since most of the important authors were booked at the hotel. Unfortunately, most of the people who appeared were publishers and their employees, a goodly number of librarians and one or two poets, drunk from the attention given to their readings.

So many eyes were on the door that people remembered the moment she stepped into the lobby and paused just inside the revolving door. Even if their other memories were diffuse—or totally absent, in some cases—many people reacted to her entrance, and not just because of her extraordinary appearance. Many witnesses recalled a certain "vibe" or "aura" about her.

She was tall and thin. She wore a black miniskirt that ended just below her rump, shiny bright pink tights and black knit leg warmers that were pushed down around her ankles above her ballet flats. Even without high heels, her legs appeared to be sensationally long. She wore a short black leather jacket over her thin pink T-shirt, which revealed more of her small, perky breasts than it covered. Metal studs decorated her jacket. But despite her conspicuous outfit, her pale face drew most of the attention. It was heart-shaped with high cheekbones, and her full lips seemed made for kissing. The way she pursed them, however, made it clear that any attempt to kiss her would be met with failure. Her eyes only magnified that message. They were slightly almond-shaped and had thick, long lashes, which she accentuated with heavy black eyeliner. But her brown eyes themselves showed no emotion. As a hungover poet would say later during questioning, "Her eyes were bottomless wells that led to the permafrost of her soul."

She turned her head to search the crowd. When she found the face she was looking for, she began to walk straight toward a table in the middle of the pub. All her movements were graceful and smooth.

One man, his back to the entrance, had not seen her when she came in. As she passed him, he lost his grip on his frosted beer glass. He blew on his hands and shook his fingers as if they'd been frozen with cold.

A children's book author, who was already hammered, began to pull on his suit jacket clumsily, complaining about the draft from the door.

The truth was that the woman could move through the compact crowd with ease, and yet every person drew away from her, either intentionally or unconsciously.

She reached the table she wanted and quietly regarded the boisterous people gathered there. One by one, the young people, dressed in black, fell quiet and looked at her with astonishment. There was only one man who didn't seem to have noticed her. He kept singing: *"Poeira, poeira, poeira, Levantou poeira."*

His voice was deep and pleasant, and his entire appearance differed from his companions in their black uniformity. A skin-tight red T-shirt emphasized his buff upper body, and his jeans clung to his narrow hips. Around his neck, a wide gold chain glittered against his café au lait skin, and a few tiny gold rings in his ear lobe shone with an intensity to match his gleaming white teeth.

When he finished singing, he calmly turned to face the silent young woman. His entire face broke into a smile.

"Hola!" he exclaimed with great happiness.

He gestured for her to join them at the table.

A slightly worse-for-wear blonde, her eyelids soot-colored and her lips painted black, gave the newcomer a disgruntled look. She left her seat beside the man and headed to the rest-room on unsteady feet.

The silent woman sat on the chair and stared at the man without blinking. Totally unaware of the icy chill she was spreading all around her, he draped his arm over her shoulders. Begrudgingly, she allowed him to draw her close. The tension in her face and body began to soften somewhat. One of the young men began to recite a poem at a volume more suited for a poetry slam. The brown-eyed woman kept watching him. Though it appeared that she didn't understand the poem, she applauded politely when he was finished. She even smiled a little at a joke the black-clad poet made.

A BOUNCER IN a dark suit walked between the tables to warn the pub's customers that it was closing time. A few older people had come to join the group at the table. At the center was a tall man with scraggly white hair who was twice as old as most of the others, but he was a famous author and seemed to know one of the young people in the group. The sulky blonde had returned after an extremely long visit to the restroom.

"Let's go up to my room and keep the party going," the white-haired author offered, his words slurring. "I have a suite on the top floor."

They all got up and headed toward the elevators. As the doors opened, everyone jostled inside, pushing and shoving a bit, but laughing all the while. Everyone except the woman in the miniskirt and pink tights.

"I'm leaving," she said.

These were the only words she said all evening. The others called to her and tried to convince her to join them in the packed elevator. She didn't turn back, but walked steadily past the security guard toward the wide stairs. The last they saw of her, before the elevator doors shut, was the reflection of the chandeliers shining down on her pageboy haircut.

SHE HAD TO pee but tried not to think about it. She had to bike as fast as she could in order to get to the convenience store. Tessan's mother would not wait for her. She was that kind of mother. If you weren't where you were supposed to be on time, there'd be no ride for you. She had to get that ride or her dance class would be over before she even got there since the bus took twice as long. Her bicycle was almost new, and she pedaled as hard as she could. The narrow gravel road spread out before her. There were no streetlights, and it was getting dark. She didn't mind that, as she knew the way by heart, but she felt uneasy thinking about what could be hiding behind the shrubbery along the side of the road. What if there was a flasher behind one of the bushes?

Stupid flashers, stupid flashers, stupid flashers, stupid flashers. The words tumbled in her brain while her feet mechanically drove the pedals.

She began to feel relief as she caught a glimpse of the streetlights on the main road. Once she got to the turnoff, she had to wait to let some cars pass. She got off her bike and glanced at the convenience store on the other side of the street. Her heart skipped a beat as she saw Tessan's mother's red car parked in front of the building. She leaped back onto her bike and darted across the street, almost getting hit by a truck but missing it by a hair. The truck braked with a loud squeal, and the driver laid on the horn. She skidded in beside the Audi, and, breathless, jumped off the bike and threw it into the bushes beside the store. She grabbed the back door handle and scooted into the backseat. Tessan was sitting in the front seat, as usual, beside her mother.

"Really, Sophie! You were almost run over! That could have been a terrible accident. And you didn't lock your bike."

Her pulse was pounding so hard in her ears that she didn't hear what Tessan's mother was saying. She panted, trying to get her breathing under control.

"Didn't you hear me? You have to lock your bike," Tessan's mother repeated. She was very strict. She often sounded irritated, though she routinely tried to hide it with pleasant words.

Sophie got out, dragged her bike out of the bushes and led it to the bike stand. She locked it and hurried back to the car.

Drive now, drive now, drive now, drive now . . . the words ricocheted through her head with the same rhythm as before.

Finally the car was moving and leaving the parking lot. Sophie leaned back in her seat and relaxed with a great sigh.

Made it, made it, made it, made it . . .

AN ICE-COLD WIND was blowing in from the sea. The chill bit Sophie's ears and fingers as she biked back home a few hours later. In her hurry, she'd forgotten her mittens and knit cap, of course.

In the distance, she saw swirling blue lights pulsing through the darkness. Farther away she could just make out people moving in front of a red glow.

Her legs did not want to keep moving. She couldn't make it the last few hundred yards. She didn't want to make it . . . *don't want to . . . don't want to . . . don't want to . . .*

"WE FOUND THE girl at the side of the road over there. It looked like she'd fallen over, and the bike was in the ditch below her. We were leaving the fire scene because we'd finished there, and our headlights caught her just sitting there. We thought it was strange, because the ambulance should have spotted her when it passed by just a few minutes earlier."

"Did she say anything?"

"No, she just looked at us."

"Was she in shock?"

"Absolutely. We drove her to Östra Hospital. Her little brother and her mother had already gone."

"Did you talk to her in the car?"

"No. I wrapped her in a blanket and sat with her in the backseat. I tried to say something comforting, but she didn't say a single word. It was odd."

"What was odd about it?"

"Hard to put my finger on it . . . just the fact that she didn't say anything. She wasn't calling for her mother or brother. She didn't even ask about them. She wasn't crying, either."

"She just sat and stared?"

"That's right."

Superintendent Sven Andersson looked at his newest inspector thoughtfully. She'd joined the department just a month earlier. He had a hard time hiding his irritation that he'd gotten a female inspector, and one with two small kids to boot. He didn't like it one bit. The superintendent sighed and got a questioning look from his fresh-baked detective inspector.

Irene Huss had a great deal of respect for her new boss. He had a good reputation as a policeman, even if he had some rough personality quirks and was known to have a short fuse. She'd been nervous her first few days on the job, but she was beginning to get used to him. As long as she did her job, he would come to change his mind about her. And besides, women officers were no longer so unusual on the force.

"It's been three months since the day you and your partner found the girl on the side of the road. Let me tell you, she still just sits and stares, saying nothing at all!"

The superintendent's voice rose; his anger was apparent. Or perhaps he was just frustrated, not angry. Irene knew that the superintendent had no children of his own.

Irene raised her eyebrows but remained quiet. She didn't really know what she should be saying. She was not part of the Björlanda District house fire investigation. She and her colleague, Håkan Lund, had been the first patrol car on the scene, but that was all. The only thing she knew about the investigation was what she'd read in the newspapers.

"Both Hasse and I tried to get her to talk, but it was impossible! She just sat and glared at us with those big brown eyes of hers."

"Is she able to speak? I mean, are you sure she's not mute?"

"No, she can talk. She's apparently the silent type, even before the fire, I mean. Do you know how old she is?"

Andersson gave her a look before he replied, "Read it for yourself. It's all in the paperwork. You and Sophie Malmborg are going to take over the questioning."

"But why should I . . . ? I mean, if she won't talk to you or Hans . . . "

"You've just answered your own question. She does not want to talk to us. Why? Maybe because we're men. So the shrinks say. We're going to test that by putting you in. You're a woman. You have kids yourself."

Irene was floored. This was a big case to be just dumped in her lap. A man had died in the fire, and there were still lots of unanswered questions. There were even indications that Sophie might know something important, or maybe more than that . . .

"Or do you think you can't handle it?" Andersson challenged.

There was a threat beneath his sarcasm. *If you can't figure this out, you won't stay long in this department.*

Irene felt her stomach turn into a lump of ice. Then a warm

wave swept through her body and she forced herself to look her boss in the eye and steady her voice before she replied.

"I'll talk to her."

"Good. She'll be here tomorrow."

IRENE SAT AT her desk in the office she shared with Tommy Persson. He'd started working as a detective inspector the previous year, and he was also the one who'd convinced her to apply for the job in the department. They'd met at the police academy in Stockholm and they'd become good friends—perhaps, in the beginning, because they were the only ones from Göteborg at the academy. Irene's then-boyfriend, Krister, had been wary of Tommy at first, but now they were all close, and Tommy had even been Krister's best man in their wedding five years ago. Irene was seven months pregnant with the twins when she married, and she thought she looked like the *Potemkin* in her wedding pictures.

She was twenty-four at the time. Her own parents had been older when she'd been born. Her mother, Gerd, was thirty-six and her father, Börje, forty-five. Irene found it funny that her parents had the same age difference she and Krister had.

"So here you are—daydreaming!"

Tommy's happy greeting jerked Irene out of her thoughts. She hadn't heard him open the door. He was grinning from ear to ear as he headed for his desk.

"Martin can say 'Pappa!' Well, he says 'pa—pa—pa—pa.' It's almost his first birthday. He's obviously advanced for his age, just like his old man."

Tommy was filled with pride. Martin was his first son with his wife, Agneta. Irene was the boy's godmother.

She couldn't help but smile. "Great! Or should I say congratulations? Just be happy that pa—pa—pa is all he can say. Once he's started talking, you'll wish you were back in the good old days. I was almost late this morning because

Jenny threw a fit the minute we walked in the door at pre-school."

"Did she want to go?"

"Oh, yes, she loves preschool. But she wanted me to promise to buy her a pet tiger before I left."

"The tiger she wants to keep in the yard?"

"That's the one. She's not letting go of the idea."

Krister and Irene had brought the twins to Borås Zoo one fine Sunday afternoon in August. Jenny and Katarina had run around from animal to animal and jumped with joy whenever they caught sight of a new one. Katarina liked the monkeys the best, but Jenny had fallen head over heels for the tigers. She wanted one for herself. She said they could put a high fence around the backyard they shared with the other people in their townhouse row. Jenny was not dis-suaded by the argument that tigers were dangerous and might like to make a meal of the residents. She insisted it would be the nicest tiger in the world. She'd raise the tiger from a cub and teach it not to eat meat, so the neighbors would be safe. She started to save all her allowance toward the tiger, putting her money into her red plastic piggy bank. Jenny called it her tiger bank. Every bit of money that came her way would go toward the tiger.

Last weekend, Jenny demanded that Irene open the piggy bank so she could count the money. Irene struggled with the lid on the piggy's stomach, but finally got it open. She counted to thirty-two Swedish kronor and fifty öre. Jenny looked at Irene with her big eyes and asked breathlessly, "Is that enough?"

"No, a tiger is pretty expensive. Keep saving and maybe you'll have enough money in . . . oh . . . two or three years. Or maybe you could buy something else that you'd like."

"A Barbie house!" Katarina suggested.

"No, I want a tiger!" Jenny said with determination.

Katarina loved to play with her Barbie doll. She could occupy herself for hours combing the doll's long hair and changing her clothes.

Jenny, on the other hand, was completely uninterested in Barbies. She would rather stand in front of the mirror and sing, imitating her idol, Carola.

"She's old enough now that she's beginning to understand she will hardly be able to come up with enough money for a tiger, so this morning she decided to see if throwing a fit would work. It was awful. All the preschool teachers came running. They probably thought I was abusing that child," Irene said with a sigh.

"If I know Jenny, I believe she'll settle with this tiger issue one way or another." Tommy was laughing.

"I'm sure she will. Speaking of children, I just got the word from Andersson that I'm supposed to take over the questioning of that girl, Sophie Malmborg."

The smile disappeared from Tommy's face and his voice had no more laughter in it as he said, "That's a tough case. Why'd you get it?"

"Well . . . for one, she refuses to talk to Andersson or Borg. And two, I've met her once before, right after it happened. An additional reason seems to be that I have children."

"But the twins are only four! Sophie is eleven," Tommy objected.

"Right. But kids are kids, according to the boss."

"Of course. Kids are *not* his thing," Tommy said, his smile returning.

IRENE SPENT THE rest of the workday going through the thick folder from Superintendent Andersson and stayed a few hours after her shift had ended. She had no reason to hurry home, as her mother had picked up the twins from preschool already. They'd enjoy themselves with their grandmother until

Krister came home at five. He had just gotten a part-time job as a cook at a new gourmet restaurant on Avenyn. He was thrilled to death that he'd gotten the job, despite the fact that he could only work thirty hours a week. The owner had been surprised and had tried to convince him to go full-time, but Krister told him that his wife was a policewoman in the criminal unit. "There are no part-time jobs there, so I'm the one who has to take part-time work for the sake of my girls."

When the owner realized that Krister was not about to change his position, he reconsidered and hired his first-ever part-time cook.

On Monday afternoon on the sixth of November, 1989, Sophie Malmborg had taken the school bus home as usual. She was in a rush, as she had a ballet lesson at 5:15 P.M., and a classmate's mother was going to drive them to The House of Dance. The friend's name was Terese Olsén, and the mother's name was Maria Olsén.

The school bus had stopped by the convenience store at around 3:35 P.M. The bus driver had seen Sophie go to the bike rack and unlock her bike. She had to ride about one kilometer down a narrow gravel road to get home, which would have taken, at most, ten minutes. Probably less. According to her mother, Angelika Malmborg-Eriksson, Sophie would gobble down a few sandwiches and a glass of milk and grab her ballet bag, which would have already been packed the night before. She'd then bike back to the convenience store, where Maria Olsén would pick her up. She had been driving her every Monday for the past year.

According to Maria Olsén, Sophie Malmborg had come biking up at top speed a little after the predetermined time, which was unusual, as she was always prompt and often early.

If the time given by the bus driver was accurate, Sophie

would have arrived home at 3:35 P.M. at the latest. In order to make it back to the convenience store, she would have had to have left her home at about 4:20, or 4:25 at the latest, especially since she'd been running late. What had happened while Sophie was at home? No one knew except Sophie herself.

After ballet class ended at 8:00 P.M., Sophie's mother, Angelika Malmborg-Eriksson, had taken her turn to drive the two girls. They shared the same classical ballet class. First they dropped off Terese Olsén, then they drove toward their own home but stopped by the convenience store so Sophie could get her bike. It was too large to fit in the Golf. Angelika Malmborg-Eriksson had been alone when she drove up to the house—or what was left of it.

Irene took a break from reading and leaned back in her chair. She remembered how the beat-up Golf had slammed to a halt right next to the patrol car and Angelika Malmborg-Eriksson had leaped out almost before the car stopped.

"Frej! Where's Frej?" she'd screamed, her voice filled with fear.

An old Saab Combi had driven up just then, and a young boy got out, holding the hand of the large woman who had driven the Saab. It seemed as if he were unsteady on his feet and needed the woman's support. It was likely that he'd been scared by the commotion and the devastation of the fire and wanted to be anywhere but there. The heavy, pungent smell was suffocating enough to make anyone want to get away.

The boy and the woman had walked toward Angelika, who had become quite hysterical. When Angelika caught sight of the boy, she ran to him, laughing and crying in turns, holding the boy to her tightly as tears streamed down her cheeks. The woman who had come with the boy went to the fire chief and asked him a question. The chief shook his head and, judging by his gestures, delivered some bad news. With a grim expression on her face, the woman walked back to the mother and son. Irene Huss and Håkan Lund were standing close by.

The woman said, "They weren't able to enter the house. It was completely engulfed when the fire trucks arrived. So they don't know if he . . ."

She stopped and cast a glance at the boy.

Håkan took her by the arm and gently but firmly pulled her away from the other two.

"Can someone have been in the house?" he'd asked.

She'd bitten her lower lip hard before she replied, "My brother, Magnus Eriksson. Frej's father."

Irene had heard the woman's statement and turned back to the glowing inferno. If a person had been in that building, there would not be much left of him.

Two days later, the fire investigators found some remains of a skeleton, including the lower jaw, which the forensic dentist had used to determine that the remains had indeed belonged to Magnus Eriksson.

OTHER TITLES IN THE SOHO CRIME SERIES

Quentin Bates
(Iceland)
Frozen Assets
Cold Comfort

James R. Benn
(World War II Europe)
Billy Boyle
The First Wave
Blood Alone
Evil for Evil
Rag & Bone
A Mortal Terror
Death's Door

Cara Black
(Paris, France)
Murder in the Marais
Murder in Belleville
Murder in the Sentier
Murder in the Bastille
Murder in Clichy
Murder in Montmartre
Murder on the Ile Saint-Louis
Murder in the Rue de Paradis
Murder in the Latin Quarter
Murder in the Palais Royal
Murder in Passy
Murder at the Lanterne Rouge
Murder Below Montparnasse

Henry Chang
(Chinatown)
Chinatown Beat
Year of the Dog
Red Jade

Colin Cotterill
(Laos)
The Coroner's Lunch
Thirty-Three Teeth
Disco for the Departed
Anarchy and Old Dogs
Curse of the Pogo Stick
The Merry Misogynist
Love Songs from a Shallow Grave
Slash and Burn
The Woman Who Wouldn't Die

Garry Disher
(Australia)
The Dragon Man
Kittyhawk Down
Snapshot
Chain of Evidence
Blood Moon
Wyatt
Whispering Death
Port Vila Blues

David Downing
(World War II Germany)
Zoo Station
Silesian Station
Stettin Station
Potsdam Station
Lehrter Station
Masaryk Station

Leighton Gage
(Brazil)
Blood of the Wicked
Buried Strangers
Dying Gasp
Every Bitter Thing
A Vine in the Blood
Perfect Hatred

Michael Genelin
(Slovakia)
Siren of the Waters
Dark Dreams
The Magician's Accomplice
Requiem for a Gypsy

Lene Kaaberbøl & Agnete Friis
(Denmark)
The Boy in the Suitcase
Invisible Murder

Graeme Kent
(Solomon Islands)
Devil-Devil
One Blood

Martin Limón
(South Korea)
Jade Lady Burning
Slicky Boys
Buddha's Money
The Door to Bitterness
The Wandering Ghost
G.I. Bones
Mr. Kill
The Joy Brigade

Peter Lovesey
(Bath, England)
The Last Detective
The Vault
On the Edge
The Reaper
Rough Cider
The False Inspector Dew
Diamond Dust
Diamond Solitaire
The House Sitter
The Summons
Bloodhounds
Upon a Dark Night
The Circle
The Secret Hangman
The Headhunters
Skeleton Hill
Stagestruck
Cop to Corpse
The Tooth Tattoo

Jassy Mackenzie
(South Africa)
Random Violence
Stolen Lives
The Fallen
Pale Horses

Seichō Matsumoto
(Japan)
Inspector Imanishi Investigates

James McClure
(South Africa)
The Steam Pig
The Caterpillar Cop
The Gooseberry Fool
Snake
The Sunday Hangman
The Blood of an Englishman
The Artful Egg
The Song Dog

Magdalen Nabb
(Italy)
Death of an Englishman
Death of a Dutchman
Death in Springtime
Death in Autumn
The Marshal and the Madwoman
The Marshal and the Murderer
The Marshal's Own Case
The Marshal Makes His Report
The Marshal at the Villa Torrini
Property of Blood
Some Bitter Taste
The Innocent
Vita Nuova

Stuart Neville
(Northern Ireland)
The Ghosts of Belfast
Collusion
Stolen Souls
Ratlines

Qiu Xiaolong
(China)
Death of a Red Heroine
A Loyal Character Dancer
When Red is Black

Akimitsu Takagi
(Japan)
The Tattoo Murder Case
Honeymoon to Nowhere
The Informer

Helene Tursten
(Sweden)
Detective Inspector Huss
The Torso
The Glass Devil
Night Rounds
The Golden Calf

Janwillem van de Wetering
(Holland)
Outsider in Amsterdam
Tumbleweed
The Corpse on the Dike
Death of a Hawker
The Japanese Corpse
The Blond Baboon
The Maine Massacre
The Mind-Murders
The Streetbird
The Rattle-Rat
Hard Rain
Just a Corpse at Twilight
The Hollow-Eyed Angel
The Perfidious Parrot
Amsterdam Cops: Collected Stories

7-3-14
4-25-22
33
4